She lowered her window. The car was filthy, coated with salt and grime that no amount of squeegeeing could wash away. Now, with the barrier gone, she saw with twenty-twenty clarity the man approaching her.

She swallowed.

Wow, that was a lot of muscle. A lot of seriously honed muscle if the way his jeans hugged his long thighs was any indication. His belt buckle was at eye level, a big oval thing just right for gripping. Dismissing this errant thought, she forced her gaze up, past his flat stomach and broad shoulders to the strong column of his neck. As her gaze reached the flat line of his mouth, it stalled, and she felt her own smile slip.

"Uh, hi." For some reason her voice was breathless. It carried no further than a whisper. Nerves, she told herself. This place, the prospect of working here, even this man, they all unsettled her.

BY LAURA MOORE

Once Tempted
Trouble Me
Believe in Me
Remember Me
In Your Eyes
Night Swimming
Chance Meeting
Ride a Dark Horse

Once Tempted

A Silver Creek Novel

Laura Moore

BALLANTINE BOOKS • NEW YORK

Once Tempted is a work of fiction. Names, characters, places, and incidents are the products of the author's imagination or are used fictitiously. Any resemblance to actual events, locales, or persons, living or dead, is entirely coincidental.

A Ballantine Books Mass Market Original

Published in the United States by Ballantine Books, an imprint of The Random House Publishing Group, a division of Random House, Inc., New York.

ISBN: 978-0-345-53698-3
eBook ISBN: 978-0-345-53699-0

Cover design: Lynn Andreozzi
Cover photograph: © George Kerrigan

Printed in the United States of America

www.ballantinebooks.com

9 8 7 6 5 4 3 2 1

Ballantine mass market edition: March 2013

To my father

Once Tempted

Chapter ONE

HER HUSBAND WAS dead and she couldn't cry.

Tess Casari clutched the phone. "Anna, it's me. It's over. David died two days ago."

"Oh, Tess! I'm sorry. Where are you?"

"At my parents'. I needed to break the news and there was stuff I had to arrange—"

"Do you want me to come over? Or would you like to get away for a while? Giorgio is covering tonight's event so I have the night off." Giorgio Bissi was the manager of La Dolce Vita, the events planning company where both Anna and Tess worked—rather, where Tess had worked until two months ago.

"I'll come to your place. It's been rough going. But I don't want to talk about it in front of Mom and Dad. You understand."

"Of course." Anna's voice was a well of sympathy. "Come as quickly as you can. There haven't been too many delays on the lines lately."

Having grown up in the same neighborhood in Astoria as Tess, Anna knew to the minute how long the subway ride to Manhattan from Queens would be, coupled with a quick walk to the brownstone apartment on Sixty-Second between Second and First Avenues. That's where Anna lived with her boyfriend, Lucas, an associate at a law firm who logged insanely long hours.

Forty-five minutes later, Tess was outside Anna's building and shivering despite the unseasonably mild December evening. Distracted as she was, she'd left her parents' house without thinking to put a coat on over her long sweater and leggings. She pressed the button for apartment number three and Anna's voice came over the intercom.

"I'm here," Tess said and was buzzed inside. She stepped into a small entry hall illuminated by a shiny brass chandelier and matching wall sconces. In the corner by the staircase, a Christmas tree was decorated with bright lights, red and gold balls, and a cascade of tinsel. The star perched on its highest branch listed a little to the left. A menorah stood in the center of a long side table. Two of its candles glowed.

The holiday season was upon them, Tess realized with detached surprise. Normally this was her favorite time of year, the hustle and bustle of the streets, the laughter of people gathering together, the delicious food, and, above all, the sense of hope and promise.

Her steps rang out as she climbed the winding marble staircase. Reaching the third floor, she found Anna standing in the door of her apartment. She rushed forward, enfolding Tess in a fierce hug.

"God, I've missed you. I'm really sorry about David. Here." Anna took her hand as though Tess were a child. "Come into the living room. I've opened a bottle of wine and made us something to nibble on."

Anna and Tess had been friends since junior high when they played, or rather made feeble attempts to play, on the same school basketball team. They'd become bosom buddies for the simple fact that neither of them could dribble or pass, let alone shoot an orange ball through a silly net suspended ridiculously high in the air. Why the other girls wanted to race up and down the court in those hideous uniforms was beyond their comprehension. Sister Louisa called them off the bench only when the team was losing so miserably it no longer mattered.

Anna's family was huge, but the Vecchios always made room at the dinner table for Tess when her mom was either at church or visiting Christopher at the institution, and when her Dad was out drinking at Rosso's until he was sufficiently anesthetized to come home.

Tess let Anna lead her into the living room with its vintage Kilim rug, burnt gold velvet sofa, and, the pièce de résistance, an ornate Murano chandelier that Anna had inherited from her grandmother. Its crystal teardrops twinkled above them, sharp-edged and fragile. Tess wondered whether the tears trapped inside her looked like that.

Releasing her hand, Anna said, "Sit. Eat. I'll get the glasses and wine."

A platter, artfully arranged with paper-thin slices of salami, prosciutto-wrapped asparagus, and mushroom caps filled with goat cheese, was centered on the mirrored coffee table. Tess knew each bite would be delicious. Like her mother and grandmother, Anna lived and breathed for the making and enjoying of food. She worked as the menu planner for La Dolce Vita but was already planning the next step in her career, fulfilling her dream to open a little trattoria where she could serve exactly what she wanted. She and Lucas had begun scouting real estate in Brooklyn.

For Anna's peace of mind, Tess hoped she'd be able to swallow a mouthful of the appetizers in front of her.

She sank down on the sofa in the room she knew so well and felt a wave of disorientation wash over her. Everything, here and in the city, was familiar, yet she still felt oddly disconnected. Since receiving the phone call from her estranged husband, David Bradford, two months earlier—the first she'd heard from him in twice that long—telling her that he was in a hospital in Boston, and that the doctors needed to operate on his brain, Tess's world had flown to pieces, as if swept up in a vicious twister. But rather than landing in a Technicolor Land of Oz, she'd been transplanted to the sterile confines of Mass General Hospital.

From Logan Airport she'd jumped into a taxi, arriving just as the nurses were preparing to take David down to pre-op. Her wild glance took in the older couple standing rigidly by the narrow bed—his parents, she realized—before settling on David, thinner and paler since the day he'd walked out on her but still looking very much like the man she'd fallen head over heels in love with. He'd raised his gaze to hers and offered a single word. "Sorry."

Then he'd closed his eyes.

She'd barely registered the bitter truth that once again David was going to shut her out and leave her with no answers when the nurse and the aide, with practiced efficiency, transferred David from bed to gurney. Shooting her a quick look of sympathy, they wheeled him away.

And he was gone. That one "Sorry" was the last word he would ever say to her. When she next saw him, David lay in a coma, unresponsive to any stimuli.

The sound of Anna's heels clicking on the parquet floor drew Tess away from her sad recollections. How grateful she was to her best friend for always being there when she needed someone. Especially now. She straightened and relaxed her knotted hands.

Carrying two wineglasses and an open bottle of Sangiovese, Anna sat down next to Tess on the sofa, poured the deep red wine into the glasses, and passed her one. "Here."

Tess accepted the wine gratefully. At least now she had something to fill her hands; she wouldn't be able to glance down at the pale indentation encircling the second finger of her left hand. Unwilling to add yet another line of sadness to her mother's face, Tess had continued to wear her wedding ring even after David, without a backward glance, had walked away from their marriage six months ago. She'd removed the ring only yesterday.

How soon would it be until the mark, too, was gone?

"Do you want to talk about it?" Mixed with Anna's concern was a hint of eagerness.

Tess didn't blame Anna for her curiosity. It was natural. Were they to switch places, she'd have had just as much trouble resisting the urge to know all the horrific but no less juicy details. And as Tess's coworker, Anna had been given a front-row seat from the very beginning of Tess and David's dazzlingly swift romance, the setting a swank cocktail party at a Fifth Avenue duplex with windows on Central Park, which La Dolce Vita had been hired to cater.

"It's hard to know what to say," Tess murmured. "Sometimes I wonder how different my life would have been if we'd never worked that event."

The cocktail party was intended to launch the political career of some mucky-muck, and the first floor of the duplex had been crammed with lavishly dressed socialites dripping in gold and diamonds, and Armani-suited power brokers who lunched at their midtown clubs. Tess had been passing hors d'ouevres among the guests when David stepped in front of her silver tray. Though the other men were just as impeccably attired as he was, David, with his curly blond hair and laughing eyes, was far better looking than many of them. Tess, however, would never have gone beyond acknowledging that he was an extremely attractive man.

It was David who'd appeared smitten, struck by the proverbial lightning bolt. After Tess had offered him a lobster puff, he'd ignored the other assembled guests, stationing himself at strategic points throughout the vast apartment to intercept her as she passed. Later he'd teased that it was her bow tie that had made him fall in love with her on the spot. Looking at it, he'd imagined himself in ten years' time regaling their children with the tale of how he'd fallen in love with their mother because of her pink and purple polka-dotted bow tie.

That was David through and through: outrageous and totally unpredictable. Heartbreakingly so.

Tess had done her best to politely brush him off and concentrate on serving the other guests, but David had persisted in his attempt to talk to her with such a strangely endearing combination of humor and determination that she'd been charmed in spite of herself. By the end of the evening he'd convinced Tess to have dinner with him.

They'd eaten at a candlelit bistro that served a perfectly seasoned bouillabaisse and talked until the restaurant closed. She learned that he was a journalist and had been invited to the party because he was writing a profile of the political wannabe. David told her it was lucky he'd already gathered more than enough material for the article. Once he'd spotted Tess and her bow tie, he would have ignored Gandhi himself.

David had regaled her with amusing stories about his far-flung travels and the articles he'd written, but he'd also seemed interested in her, asking questions when she spoke about her background and where she'd grown up. He even got her to open up about a topic she rarely shared: the challenge her parents faced in trying to care for her severely autistic older brother, Christopher, and how devastating it had been for them when they could no longer keep him safe and were forced to place him in a private facility.

By now, of course, she wondered how much of David's interest had been feigned or simply well-honed professional skill. But at the time she'd believed he truly cared. So when he asked her about La Dolce Vita, she'd revealed another aspect of herself, that she loved working at events planning because it gave her the opportunity to create a special, happy moment for people to remember. She needed to know she could make people smile and take away their cares—if only for a short while.

David had reached across the linen-covered table and laid his hand over hers and said that she'd given him a wonderful evening. He hoped it was the beginning of many such moments with her.

Maybe it was the lighting, the timbre of his voice, or the slow sweep of his thumb across the inside of her wrist, or maybe it was the earnestness of his expression when he'd spoken those words. She didn't know. But she fell. And fell hard.

Because of David's flexible schedule, they'd seen each other every day. Within a month he'd asked her to move into his SoHo loft. Six weeks after that he'd surprised her by coming to La Dolce Vita one afternoon when Anna and Tess and nine other employees were madly dashing about preparing for yet another high-octane party, this one a book launch for a celebrity's tell-all memoir. In the middle of the kitchen, where Tess had been helping Anna top tiny Asian crab cakes with paper-thin slices of ginger, David had dropped onto bended knee and presented her with an emerald-cut diamond engagement ring. The rock had impressed even Anna. And Giorgio, who in the hours before big events made Mussolini look like a lackadaisical cream puff, decided the moment called for his best prosecco.

In hindsight, Tess recognized she should have resisted David's entreaties or at least tried to slow down the supersonic speed of their relationship, but there'd been a magic to the courtship and she'd been enchanted. Clever and dashing, he'd been her very own Prince Charming, and Tess had believed herself the luckiest woman in the world.

But now he was gone and Tess remained bewildered, unable to sort truth from fiction, unable to comprehend why he'd bothered to pursue her in the first place. Why he'd bothered to tell her he loved her. Why the need for so much deceit . . .

She drew a breath. Next to her, Anna was looking at her sadly, helplessly, as if she, too, was remembering the string of events that brought David into Tess's life. Okay, it was time to block out the endless loop of questions.

"The most important thing is that the doctors assured us that David didn't suffer," she said quietly.

"I know you told me that he'd had an aneurysm when they were trying to remove the tumor and then he slipped into a coma. So did he just . . . die?" Her friend's voice was tentative. She didn't know how to talk about what David and Tess had gone through. Anna wasn't alone. There was so much Tess couldn't talk about, not even with Anna.

"No. He contracted pneumonia."

"Pneumonia? Gosh. That sounds so . . ." Anna trailed off awkwardly.

"Boring," Tess supplied. "I know." She nodded wearily. Boring was the antithesis of David's character. "The doctors did everything they could, but the pneumonia took hold quickly. While he was in the coma, I sat beside him day after day, watching as the doctors and nurses came in and checked his vitals and performed their tests to measure any sign of responsiveness. During all that time I didn't truly understand that the coma hadn't simply robbed him of consciousness. It stole his strength, his ability to fight."

"Well, he was better at fighting with words, wasn't he?"

The comment was uncharitable, but Anna had seen

how brutal David could be, how he used words the way some men used their fists. Once the marriage had started to deteriorate with the same dizzying speed with which it had been born, Tess would come over to Anna's—she couldn't burden her parents with the news that her very short marriage was already on the rocks, not when they'd suffered so much—to fall onto this very sofa, sobbing from the pain of David's viciousness. Incensed, Anna would pace the room, cursing him with an eloquence that would have made a marine sergeant blush.

Doubtless regretting her previous remark, Anna said, "Still, I'm sorry. What a terrible way to go."

"Yes." Raising her glass, Tess drank deeply to banish the vision of the tubes inserted into David's body and the wires attached elsewhere that had served to keep him in that terrible state for far too long. Although now painfully aware of how little she'd understood her husband, she was certain of one thing: David would have hated being dependent on those machines to keep his heart beating and his organs functioning . . . no matter what his parents wished to believe.

She had no sooner managed to push aside the image of David unmoving and unresponsive in his hospital bed when it was replaced by another one almost as distressing: of Edward Bradford turning to her minutes after the doctor had confirmed David's death.

Grief had leached the color from Mr. Bradford's patrician face but his blue eyes blazed, lit with pain and with rage. Removing an envelope from the inside pocket of his suit, he'd shoved it at her.

"Here."

Uncomprehending, she'd stared at it and then up at the unforgiving lines of his face. "What's this?"

She'd been on the receiving end of Edward Bradford's disdain from the first day she met him and his wife, Hope, at the hospital, minutes after David had been transferred to pre-op. He never looked at her without making his contempt clear. Now his thin lips tightened as he sneered. "Don't pretend you've forgotten. It's the money I promised you. You've fulfilled the bargain. You stayed by my son's side. Take it and go."

The money. The absurd offer David's father had made to pay her a million dollars if she stayed at the hospital until David was able to be discharged—an offer so preposterous she hadn't taken it seriously.

Anna's voice rescued her from the memory that filled her with biting shame. "It's terrible to speak ill of the dead, but I'm not sure I can forgive David. How could he have married you without saying a word about the fact that he'd *already* suffered a brain tumor?"

If that had been the only secret David had kept from her. It now seemed as if everything about their marriage had been based on a lie. The biggest one being David's saying he loved her.

That was what she got for believing in fairy tales, for believing for even a minute that a dashing, cosmopolitan journalist would fall in love at first sight with a working girl from Queens, sweep her off her feet, and propose marriage within the space of weeks. How could she have thought that she and David would make it, that they would enjoy a happy ever after?

Most likely it was because the David Bradford she'd known during those first weeks had been the most charming man she'd ever encountered. The most determinedly persuasive, too. It was only later, after she'd agreed to elope with him and they'd made their trip down to city hall, that, with the suddenness of a light being switched off, his charm had been replaced by a poison-tipped cruelty. Both extremes, his charm and his hostility, had been equally devastating.

She took another sip of wine to wash away the bitterness but then reminded herself not to drink too much.

She would need a clear head tomorrow when she talked to her parents and told them of her plans.

"I've decided it's better to stop asking why David did the things he did and said—or, in his case, left unsaid. I might go crazy otherwise. But at the hospital, I learned from the doctors that David's first brain tumor had been benign and that the treatment had been successful. He was only eighteen at the time, Anna. A kid."

"Oh God. That must have sucked."

"Yeah. I don't know whether he didn't recognize the symptoms or if he simply dismissed the possibility that after ten years in remission the growth had returned. As I was completely in the dark about his medical history, it didn't occur to me that his headaches signaled something deadly serious."

"Especially since he blamed them on you."

"Yes." Whenever she raised the topic of seeing a doctor, he flat out refused, turning what had begun as a conversation into a full-scale blowup. Living with her was enough to give anyone a migraine, he would rage, since all she did was nag and interrupt him when he was trying to write. He would never meet his deadlines because his wife was too much of a stupid bitch to leave him bloody well alone.

This would be his cue to storm out of the apartment, sometimes not returning until the next day, reeking of alcohol, other women's perfume, and sex.

And when tears filled her eyes, he'd smirk and tell her the hookers he'd bought were better lays than she'd ever be. Once they'd used their mouths, they knew to shut them.

Anna glanced at her pityingly, as though she could read her thoughts, and moved the tray of appetizers closer to her. "Are you hungry? The salami's from Balducci's."

She shook her head. "I can't, Anna. I'm sorry."

"It's okay. I don't know what I was thinking, making all this. The good news is that Lucas will have a nice midnight snack when he comes home from the office."

Tess seized the chance to talk about something else. "Is Lucas taking any vacation time?"

"Mmm-hmm. Starting tomorrow. We're driving to New Haven on Christmas Eve to spend it with his parents. We'll celebrate Christmas Day with mine. Mama's over the moon. She's been baking for weeks. What were David's parents like?"

Tess shrugged uncomfortably. "Okay, I guess, considering that I was the interloper. I thought his mother was beginning to soften toward me near the end." But not enough to persuade her husband that Tess should be allowed to attend David's funeral, she added silently. The hurt was still raw. It made her want to curl protectively into herself. How she wished she could forget every last one of the Bradfords' insults.

"So he really never told them he'd married you?" Anna asked. "Incredible."

"He hadn't talked to them in years," she said wearily. "It was the principal reason he used to convince me to elope. That, and how we would be sparing my own parents a whole lot of expense if we skipped a church ceremony and reception." She'd been so touched by his sensitivity.

Love had made her blind as well as foolish. It would have made her mother happy to see her walk down the aisle. But since the marriage had ended nearly as soon as it began, Tess couldn't help but be glad that her parents hadn't wasted a penny on it. Cold comfort, but she'd take it.

"Bastard. He knew that the cost of Christopher's care hangs over your parents' heads so he used it to get his own way. I'm not a good friend, Tess. I should have stopped you from marrying that *stronzo*."

"No, you've been great. The best. I'm not sure anything or anyone could have persuaded me that David wasn't exactly what he seemed at first."

"Yeah, I know." Anna nodded glumly. "He played us all so well. Even I was fooled."

Tess gave a little smile. "And that's saying something."

"It sure is. So when did you finally meet Mr. and Mrs. Bradford?"

"At the hospital. They were there when I arrived. David's doctors must have convinced him to let them inform his parents of his condition."

"Great place to meet the in-laws. How did they act when they met you?"

That was an easy one. "Like I was a walking, talking slap in the face. After meeting them I understood why David didn't want them at a wedding ceremony or even standing with us before the justice of the peace. If they'd had even an inkling that David planned to marry me, they'd have done everything in their power to stop us."

"Simply because you weren't what they'd envisioned as wife material for their son?"

Tess laughed bitterly. What could she say to her big-hearted friend? "I doubt I'd have even made the cut as one of David's hookers."

Anna shifted on the sofa to hug her again. "Stop. You were too good for him—were too good for the entire snooty family. And I'm just talking about your character. Surely the Bradfords weren't blind?"

"I'm afraid my looks hardly appealed to them," she answered drily.

"Oh, right." Anna made a face. "You're gorgeous. Mama's right when she says you look like a young Gina Lollobrigida—though maybe not when you've spent the last two months watching your good-for-nothing husband slowly die—but the Bradfords were probably hoping David would get hitched to some emaciated blonde in a tennis skirt. Prissy puritans."

Tess smiled tiredly. It would have been great to have Anna beside her when Mr. Bradford had demanded she take his money. Anna would have told him where to go.

Tess had been tempted to. Tempted to rip up the check under his nose and then spit in his eye for good measure. But she hadn't. So now Edward Bradford had incontrovertible proof that Tess Casari was no better than the money-grubbing fortune huntress he'd believed her to be.

"They sound like real stuck-ups," Anna continued, drawing her own conclusions.

"Pretty much. At some point over the last two months I decided that if the *Mayflower* had been equipped with first-class cabins, they'd have been reserved for the Bradfords' forefathers. Boston bluebloods elevate the snobbery thing to a whole new level. But you know what, Anna?"

"What?"

"All their wealth and perfect bloodlines meant nothing when the surgeon came and broke the news that David had suffered an aneurysm during the operation and was in a coma. Edward and Hope Bradford could have been my parents when they're with Chris at the facility." Powerless. And desperately sad.

"So that's why you stayed in the hospital?"

Tess shrugged. "When David was wheeled away, I was ready to leave and come back home to New York. Seeing him made me realize that nothing had or would ever change between us. The marriage was over." Her voice lowered. "The truth is, Anna, it hurt too much to stay."

"I can understand that."

"David's father didn't. When I tried to tell him and his wife I had to go back to New York—that I'd lose my job if I didn't return and that I wasn't in a position where I could be unemployed and still expect to eat and pay the rent—my explanation didn't matter. He was determined I stay."

And that was when Mr. Bradford had made his proposal, saying he'd pay her a million dollars if she stayed until David left Mass General. He was a father maddened with fear for his son. How could she have taken him seriously?

Once more, she shoved the memory away. "But then the doctor came to us with the news about the aneurysm, and in those three minutes everything changed. No matter how I felt about David, I couldn't leave him while his life hung in the balance." A balance she'd understood from the doctor's tone was tipped toward death.

"But why did the Bradfords want you there when they didn't even like you?"

"Crazy, huh?" Tess sighed. "When I entered his hospital room, David said 'Sorry' to me."

"Saying 'Sorry' hardly absolved the sins he'd racked up."

"His parents thought it meant something—that he actually cared for me. Apparently he'd refused to speak to them at all."

"Wow." Anna shook her head in amazement. Even though she wore a fuzzy angora sweater, she rubbed her hands over her arms as if to ward off a chill. Tess knew how she felt. "You weren't kidding about them being on lousy terms. That probably made them resent you even more. So they became fixated on the idea that your sticking around would somehow make a difference?"

"They were clutching at straws. I explained that they were placing way too much significance on David's 'Sorry.' I told them he and I were as over as a couple could get—how before he'd walked out following our last fight he'd announced he was contacting his lawyer to begin divorce proceedings."

That she'd never received the divorce papers didn't change the ugly truth that David had regretted "becoming shackled to a tedious bitch like her" the second the ink was dry on their marriage certificate.

"Let me guess what happened. The Bradfords insisted."

"They arranged for me to stay in one of those rooms at the hospital reserved for family."

"And not at their house?" At Tess's look, Anna grimaced. "Right. Silly me."

Silence descended as Anna digested this last piece of news. Tess couldn't bear to divulge more of how the Bradfords' hatred for her had manifested itself. Over the long weeks she'd spent at Mass General, she'd forgotten Edward Bradford's offer of money. To her it had been a surreal episode in a world gone horribly wrong, one in which the man she thought she'd loved and with whom she'd pledged to spend a lifetime was lost in an unearthly sleep, slipping further away with each passing day.

But when David finally succumbed to the pneumonia laying waste to his body, Edward Bradford hadn't chosen to grieve with his wife and Tess. Instead he'd withdrawn the envelope from inside his jacket and thrust it at her as if it were a weapon, a weapon he'd been carrying next to his breast for God only knew how long. The painful vigil she'd shared with him and his wife hadn't eased his disdain at all. Right after shoving the check at her, he'd ordered her to leave. As a parting shot, he'd icily informed her that she would not be welcome at the funeral service.

Stupid with shock, she'd put the envelope in her bag. Numb, she nonetheless recognized that refusing the money would have accomplished nothing. The man had judged and condemned her the second he'd learned that his son had married her, a nobody from Astoria who worked at an events company.

She'd left the hospital feeling dirtied and ashamed. But upon arriving in New York, she'd gone directly to her parents' neighborhood bank and made arrangements to open a special account to pay for her brother Christopher's care at the private facility. The million dollars as such meant nothing to Christopher, yet he needed what that money would buy more than anyone she knew.

Edward and Hope Bradford would never know what she'd done with their money. Tess was glad. Their knowing wouldn't change their belief that somehow she'd tricked David into marrying her.

"Hey, Tess. It'll be okay, really." Anna's arms were wrapped protectively around her. With a shock, Tess realized her shoulders were shaking, racked by the memories assailing her. Yet still her tears remained locked inside. Her shame, too.

She couldn't tell Anna about the Bradfords' money. The details were so sordid. Of course Anna would defend her actions. Tess could even predict her response. She'd give one of her inimitable shrugs and then say something along the lines of, "Really, Tess, what's one million when you've got, what, five hundred of them? Chump change. No biggie, *cara*, let it go."

But it was a biggie in Tess's mind, and she couldn't let it go, or confess aloud how dirtied that final episode with the Bradfords had left her feeling. So much during this past year had hurt her, but for some reason being treated with such withering animosity, as someone who was nothing more than a gold digger, was the cut that sliced deepest. She didn't want to show the wound to anyone.

Though Anna was as close as a sister, she couldn't share this with her. She simply wanted to forget it all.

Perhaps after David's funeral Hope and Edward Bradford would find peace, too. And if their hatred of her provided some release from the grief of losing their only child, well, so be it. She would never see them again. Tonight she'd be taking the next step in her plan to get as far away as she could from everything that had happened in the last year.

With a sniff she straightened her shoulders and tried to smile. "I'm sorry I'm such a mess."

"Don't apologize, silly. I'm just glad you're back home. The guy Giorgio hired to replace you is like Martha Stewart on steroids. I think even Giorgio's getting a little weirded out. He's probably forgotten half the things he said when you told him you had to stay in Boston—"

"I felt so bad leaving you guys in the lurch. It must have been crazy at La Dolce Vita."

"Everyone understood, even Giorgio in his heart of hearts." Anna leaned forward with sudden energy. "Why don't I call him for you, Tess? Tonight's event was a birthday party for a ninety-year-old stockbroker who still plays ice hockey with his great-grandchildren and takes them out on his yacht every summer in Newport. It's a small gathering, only forty people. It'll be over by now."

This was it. Slowly Tess shook her head. "I can't come back to La Dolce Vita, Anna. I'm leaving New York after Christmas."

"Leaving? For where?"

"California." It was as far away from Boston and the Bradfords as she could get without leaving the continent.

"California." From the way Anna pronounced it, Tess could have announced she was moving to Mars. She fell silent, her expression solemn. "It's so far. But I guess I understand why you're doing it. If I'd been through what you have, I'd want a fresh start, too. So, where in California?"

Tess reached over and picked up her handbag from where it leaned against the edge of the sofa. Opening it, she pulled out a folded map. "I picked this up. It shows the entire state." Moving the untouched platter aside, she laid the map on the coffee table and smoothed out its folds. "I thought you could help me choose my destination. What do you think of L.A.? Or maybe—"

"Wait! Wait! I know!" Anna interrupted, her eyes bright with excitement. "Let me get my nonna's favorite scarf. We can use it as a blindfold. I'll tape the map to the wall, spin you around a few times, point you in the right direction, and give you a little good-luck shove. You'll walk toward the wall with your index finger extended. Wherever your finger touches on the map, that's where you'll go. Fate will decide."

Chapter TWO

As far as Tess was concerned, fate was a nasty witch.

She was pretty sure she'd have felt this way even if she hadn't been exhausted from driving solo cross-country, roughly a couple thousand miles farther than she'd ever driven before, and in a car she now had serious doubts about.

It had been sold to her by a distant cousin of one of the retired employees from her dad's construction company. The price had been right and the mechanic had assured her it should make the trip to Northern California with no problem. But maybe she should have had the car looked at by someone more interested in inspecting the engine than in checking her out, and one who wasn't related by marriage to the car's owner. That was Astoria for you: on every corner a cousin or an in-law.

And she'd been in a hurry to get a set of wheels and go, convinced that the only way to escape the ghosts of the past year was to get the hell out of New York and put the pedal to the metal. That was how messed up her life had become.

Now she could add yet another life lesson to her personal list. It wasn't just marry in haste, repent at leisure—but also buy a car in haste, repent as your palms grew slick when the steering wheel failed to respond at even the easy stuff, like switching lanes. The less said about the blinding snow in Kansas and the car's iffy brakes, the better. Then there were the vehicle's ominous coughs and rattles. With each, her stomach had tightened.

But somehow she'd made it to the Golden State, which on a cold, gray January day didn't look very golden to her and didn't make her feel like shouting "Eureka!" at the top of her lungs while she launched into a quick jitterbug, or whatever the state dance was. As a going-away present, Anna had given her a guidebook to California that contained all sorts of trivia and factoids about the state. Before Tess reached her current level of exhaustion (somewhere around Colorado), she had studied the guidebook every night after she'd checked in to yet another motel.

The town of Acacia, California, where fate had decided she should go, hadn't made it into Tess's guidebook.

Hardly a surprise. Acacia's downtown had a grand total of four streets. A booming metropolis it was not. She'd never been in a place so small that "one-stop shopping" could be taken literally: Its post office was housed inside the same low-slung wooden building as the bank and a general store with a lunch counter.

To give it due credit, the town possessed an offbeat charm. Who could quibble with a place that had among its businesses an organic wool store that offered knitting and weaving classes; a boutique that sold candles and handmade jewelry, smelled of lavender and beeswax, and had crystals hanging in the window, making rainbows that danced upon the rough-planked wooden floors; a coffee and tea shop that stocked free-trade beans and brews and had the mellowest people behind the counter (they must be drinking the decaf); a clothing store that sold only natural fibers; a salon that offered all-natural products; and a liquor store that specialized in wines from the nearby vineyards?

The merchants she encountered seemed as wholesome as their merchandise. Tess had never heard "Right on" and "All good" used so often without a hint of irony.

Acacia was just the sort of place she might like to visit for lunch and a quick stroll before heading back to a real town, one with bright lights, buildings taller than three stories, and public transportation.

Its tiny size did have one advantage. It took Tess less than an hour to go door-to-door inquiring about a job. To be told in the nicest way possible that she was flat out of luck.

Determined to leave no stone unturned, Tess entered the beauty salon on the corner of Main and Laurel. At the front desk a woman smiled and said, "Hello, welcome to A Brand New Day. I'm Ava. Can I help you?"

Tess introduced herself and then said, "I'm looking for a job. I was wondering whether you needed a receptionist?"

"'Fraid not. I own this salon and, as you can see, we're pretty slow here right now." She gestured behind her to the three empty stylist chairs. "Can you come back in April?"

This was the same response she'd received from every other storekeeper she'd approached. They'd all told her that January was a slow period, with very little traffic until the spring tourist season started.

"I kind of need to find something now." Or yesterday, Tess added silently. Traveling across the country wasn't cheap. That dratted car drank gas like it was going out of style, and she had a terrible suspicion she was going to have to take it to a garage and get those weird noises checked out.

"What kind of experience do you have?"

"I worked for an events planning company in New York City for five years. So I've done a bit of everything."

"New York, huh? A lifetime ago I lived there. I was nineteen when I came out to San Fran with a guy. He went back. I stayed but eventually struck north. For a while I hung out in Sonoma, but that got kind of crowded so then I found my way here. It's been thirty-one years since I left New York. Is it still noisy and dirty?"

"You're fifty? Honestly, I wouldn't have put you above thirty." She looked at the skin-care products lining the wall. "Those products must be awfully good."

The woman smiled. "They are. We use local honey and beeswax, olive oil, and other all-organic ingredients for the skin-care line. You should come in sometime. I give a fantastic facial, if I do say so myself. It would make you feel brand-new."

Tess was excruciatingly aware of how she must look after almost a week on the road. "I'd love to, but I think I need a paycheck first."

"Like I said, Acacia's pretty quiet now. Tell you what, why don't you drive out to Silver Creek Ranch and see whether they have any jobs? It's a big spread. They're busy year-round."

"A ranch? Um, I'm not really all that familiar with ranching." Even working at the hardware store on Main Street—Wright's, established 1949, she recalled—would have been a stretch.

"It's a guest ranch." Her lips pursed in amusement when Tess looked at her blankly. "It's a working ranch. They raise horses, cattle, and sheep, but they also have accommodations—you know, cabins and a restaurant—for folks who want to come and stay. Like I said, it's a big spread, probably the largest ranch in the area, and beautiful. With the vineyards close by, the Knowleses—they're the owners—do a good business. They employ a lot of the townsfolk. In fact, they pretty much keep Acacia alive. Guests from the ranch wander into town and pick up mementos or come in for services like the ones I provide here."

Tess placed her handbag on the counter and drew out the folded map of California and opened it. "Would you mind showing me where this ranch is?"

Ava looked at the map and then up at Tess, her black brows arched in surprise. "It's here, pretty much where you've X'd the spot." She tapped a buffed nail on the blob of green where Tess's own finger had landed and which Anna had immediately marked with a ballpoint pen. "You'll want to follow Main Street out of town. It joins 128. Go for about four miles. On the left you'll see a road, Bartlett Road. Take that for another mile. Next you'll see a sign for Silver Creek Road on your right. The entrance to the guest ranch and main lodge is about a half a mile farther on your right."

Her finger had landed on a ranch. Okay. Things couldn't get much weirder. Pasting a smile on her face, Tess refolded the map and slipped it into her bag. "So I basically just head out that road and then make a left and then a couple of rights?"

"That's about it. You'll want to speak to Adele Knowles. She and her husband, Daniel, and their three children run the ranch. Tell her Ava Day sent you."

"Thanks for your help."

"Hope you find something. And remember to come back for that facial."

Tess walked back to the post office where she'd parked, a walk that took approximately three minutes and during which perhaps five cars passed her. It was chilly enough so that only a few pedestrians were about, but through the windows of the post office–general store–luncheonette–bank, she could see a number of people clustered about small wooden tables. It was obviously the happening place in Acacia.

Reaching her car, she opened the driver's side door. "Here goes nothing," she muttered, eyeing the bucket seat with distaste. After two thousand–plus miles, she was thoroughly sick of driving. But even though she couldn't believe there'd be a job for her at a ranch, it seemed like this was her last shot at finding employment in this one-horse town. And she'd promised Anna she'd do everything she could to find a place to live and work as close to where her finger had landed. Her conscience would never give her a moment's peace if she didn't at least try every available option. She hoped Ava Day hadn't been exaggerating about Silver Creek Ranch, and that it might actually need someone with her abilities.

She turned the key in the ignition. An unearthly noise greeted her—a gnashing and grinding of metal parts—and then nothing. The silence was even more nerve-racking.

"Oh, come on! Please, please start." She turned the key again and pumped the gas pedal for good measure, since the car loved gas the way a vampire loved blood. This time a high-pitched whine was added to the cacophony. Then, miraculously, the engine turned over.

Okay, the car sounded as if it had contracted whooping cough, but at least it was running.

"Thank you, thank you, I love you, really. I didn't mean any of those things I said in Utah," she whispered, knowing she was stretching the truth like taffy but too pathetically grateful to stop.

Shifting into gear, she pulled out onto Main Street and drove slowly toward the corner, partly out of respect for the speed limit, partly because she didn't want to do anything to further annoy the car.

The miles crawled by. Houses began to be spaced farther and farther apart and sit farther back from the road. Tess followed the winding two-lane blacktop past fields and woods. The road dipped and climbed, and the houses disappeared from sight altogether. She was wondering whether she'd misunderstood Ava Day's instructions when she saw the sign for Bartlett Road on her left. She turned onto it and then there was nothing around her but fenced meadows and trees and mountains, their peaks taking ragged bites out of the gray sky.

"Thank God," she breathed when she spied a small black-and-white sign saying "Silver Creek Road." It couldn't be too much farther now.

The gates to the ranch were on her right, "Silver Creek Ranch" painted on a carved wooden sign that was nailed to the gate. The road became gravel, and the pings of stones flying up and hitting the undercarriage made it seem like her car was under attack. It was certainly acting that way, coughing and wheezing and rattling ominously.

A plume of smoky dust drifted past her and she frowned, her tension ratcheting up. The road didn't seem that dusty.

She was definitely going to have to find a garage as well as a job. When she'd stopped at the last service station, they'd had some info placards posted by the gas tanks about stretches for drivers to ease their tight muscles and sore backs and a chart to help identify different bug-splattered carcasses on a windshield—California humor at its finest—but no mechanic on duty to take a look at her engine.

She kept her eyes fixed straight ahead, ignoring the long uninterrupted line of wood-and-wire fence running parallel to the private road, ignoring the disturbing noises erupting from under the car's hood. Ignoring everything but the fact that ahead of her a large timber and stone building was beginning to take shape. Her destination was in sight. She just had to get there.

The wheels of her car rumbled over a small wooden bridge, bringing her within a hundred yards of a big circular courtyard with trees and shrubs planted in its center. That's when she saw the man.

He was walking up another road that, like the spoke of a wheel, joined the courtyard. He wore blue jeans, cowboy boots, and a denim shirt. A dark beige cowboy hat, pulled down low, shaded his face. She'd noticed a number of men wearing cowboy hats in town, but this guy didn't look like he wore the jeans and a hat as a fashion statement. He must be one of the ranch hands. Even if the guests at the ranch liked to dress up like cowboys, she doubted they'd have so much dirt on their jeans.

She eased off the accelerator, slowing to a crawl and then braking. Unfortunately, the car didn't seem to appreciate idling any more than it did moving. If anything, the racket it made worsened. And those wispy clouds she'd noticed earlier? They seemed to be snaking out from beneath her hood. The sooner she found a place to park, the better.

She lowered her window. The car was filthy, coated with salt and grime that no amount of squeegeeing could wash away. Now, with the barrier gone, she saw with twenty-twenty clarity the man approaching her.

She swallowed.

Wow, that was a lot of muscle. A lot of seriously honed muscle if the way his jeans hugged his long thighs was any indication. His belt buckle was at eye level, a big oval thing just right for gripping. Dismissing this errant thought, she forced her gaze up, past his flat stomach and broad shoulders to the strong column of his neck. As her gaze reached the flat line of his mouth, it stalled, and she felt her own smile slip.

"Uh, hi." For some reason her voice was breathless. It carried no further than a whisper. Nerves, she told herself. This place, the prospect of working here, even this man, they all unsettled her.

It didn't help that the car was whining even louder.

She tried again, repeating more loudly, "Hi. Could you help me? I was wondering where I should park."

It happened so quickly she didn't have time to react. The stranger thrust his arm into the open window, reached across her, and, with a flick of his wrist, killed the engine.

Aghast, she felt her mouth fall open. His arm was still inside the car, in her space, a space that had shrunk to the size of a mouse hole. With the same arrogant deliberateness he'd just displayed, he withdrew his arm, but this time it grazed her breasts. And it seemed he moved twice as slowly while her heartbeat trebled.

The shock of feeling his arm brushing against her, of breathing in the scent of this man's sweat and whatever deodorant he wore, was like being caught in a lightning storm. No wonder her heart was palpitating. Everything was going haywire inside her. Stunned, she stared at him as she gasped for breath.

Blue-green eyes flecked with gold stared back at her dispassionately. He had dark hair. Thick and curly. How had he managed to remove his hat while he invaded her car, she wondered, infuriated that he was all smooth control while she was close to hyperventilating.

Recovering enough to shoot him her dirtiest look, she wrenched the key to restart the car. Nothing, not even a sick metallic groan. Just an awful silence.

"Oh my God! What have you done to my car?" Turning the key she jerked it one more time. "You've broken it."

"If anything, I saved it. You been driving like that for

long?" His voice was as dispassionate as his gaze. They could have been talking about Post-it notes or Brussels sprouts rather than the fact that her car had just croaked on her. And that he'd had a hand in its demise. Literally.

"Hey, what are you doing?" Now he'd opened her door without so much as a by-your-leave. Did he have no manners?

"Trying to get you out of this thing you charitably call a car. It's still smoking."

A pretty effective reply. She unbuckled her seat belt and scooted out of the driver's seat. She stood beside him then quickly stepped away. She was five foot ten in her high heels; he couldn't have been more than six-one, yet he made her feel tiny. All that solid muscle and a hundred percent disagreeableness were to blame.

Unsure whether he'd spoken the truth, she looked at the front of her car. To her chagrin, there was stuff coming out from under the hood. It sort of resembled the wisps of toxic vapors seeping out of a witch's cauldron in a cartoon. Whether these wisps were steam or smoke she couldn't tell. That this high-handed hulk could distinguish one from the other aggravated her even more. Maybe he had a lot of experience with tractors.

"May I ask whether you have a reservation?"

"No, I don't. I'm here about a job."

"A job?" His gaze flicked over her. Then she saw him glance at her car, not at its crud-encrusted exterior, but at the bulging garbage bags piled up in the backseat. The nicer suitcases were stowed in the trunk and, as she had only two, she hadn't been able to pack everything she thought she might need. Thus the presence of the depressingly ugly Hefty bags. During his visual sweep, his expression didn't change—in fact, he was expressionless—but she could tell that in those few seconds he had formed an opinion.

She'd spent eight weeks with the Bradfords' relentless

disdain and that, she decided, was quite enough. She let her own gaze pass over his worn cowboy boots and dirty jeans and smiled coolly.

"Yes. I'm here to see . . ." Her mind went blank for an awful moment before she found the name. "I'm here to see Adele Knowles, and I was trying to figure out where I should park when I made the mistake of thinking you might help me."

Dismissing the obnoxious man, she glanced at what must be the guest ranch's main building. It was large and constructed of pale creamy stone and wood. Windows dominated the façade and gave the building an open, expansive air. To combat the shadows of the afternoon, the lights were on, casting a golden welcoming glow. It looked nice. Really nice. But now, in addition to asking Adele Knowles whether she might have a job for her, Tess would also have to ask for a tow truck. Why the thought of having that detestable car towed caused tears to well in her eyes, she couldn't say. She'd succeeded in keeping them at bay for so long, beating them back even when she'd hugged her parents goodbye and her dad had whispered for her to stay safe. Her shoulders sagged. She should never have agreed to Anna's harebrained scheme.

From behind her came the sound of crunching gravel. She turned and made a choking sound.

"What are you doing to my car?"

The man had one arm and shoulder inside the open driver's side door and was pushing it slowly as he steered.

She refused to ogle his butt as it bunched and relaxed with every slow step. But, boy, it was tempting.

The hysterical note in her voice must have penetrated for he paused and looked at her. Of course, he'd put his cowboy hat back on and pulled the brim down low.

"Well, now, it can't stay here in the middle of the

drive, can it? I was just going to move it to a more appropriate spot. Our manure pile is a bit far but that would be the best place for this piece of—"

"My car is not! It brought me all the way from New York."

"A miracle. I guess I'll just have to push it to the parking lot then. Adele's in her office. I'll leave your keys at the front desk. If Adele says she has a meeting, tell her Ward can't make it. He's doing his good deed of the day."

"And so that would make you Ward?"

"Yes, ma'am."

Ooh, she thought, her eyes narrowing to angry slits. How had he guessed she would hate being addressed as "ma'am" as if she had blue-rinsed hair? She'd noticed the crow's-feet fanning out from the corners of his eyes. He was easily thirty. Older than she.

"I'd say it's a pleasure but then I'd be lying. Oh, and don't touch any of my stuff."

The interview was going better than Tess would have expected for someone who was jinxed, plagued by handsome men who wandered into her life and caused total chaos. That she'd managed to push the specter of Ward Whatshisname and her smoking car to the far recesses of her mind as she shook Adele Knowles's hand was quite an accomplishment.

Much of the credit had to go to Adele Knowles. The older woman was like a breath of fresh air. Chic in a pair of light beige trousers and a belted cardigan of a deep evergreen that made her blue eyes that much brighter, she'd greeted Tess politely, asking how she might help her. When Tess told her that she'd come to inquire about any open positions and dutifully relayed Ward's message about his not being able to meet with her, those eyes widened with surprise. Unwilling to trust her fate to a rude cowboy, Tess had hurriedly added that Ava Day had suggested she try her luck at Silver Creek.

Adele had brought Tess to an airy office and invited her to sit on a pretty indigo-and-cream-patterned upholstered chair. Before settling on the matching one, she asked if Tess might like a cup of tea.

Tess thanked her and declined. "I've been driving for the past six days and have consumed more caffeine than I ever thought physically possible."

"Six days? Quite a journey."

And so the interview began. Adele listened without interruption to the explanation she'd asked for of how Tess, who'd lived all her life in New York City, had come to be job hunting in Acacia, even though it must have been obvious to her that the story Tess told—of needing a change after her husband's death—had been carefully edited.

"I'm sorry for your loss," Adele offered when she'd finished.

"Thank you. My husband and I were estranged when I learned of his illness."

"Nonetheless, he'd been someone you loved."

"Yes." That was the simple truth. But though she had the strong impression that Mrs. Knowles was a deeply sympathetic person, Tess couldn't bring herself to say any more than that.

Tess felt a wave of gratitude wash over her when Adele Knowles nodded and moved on to a new topic.

"Why Acacia, may I ask? Our town is somewhat off the beaten track."

The understatement of the century.

With a trace of embarrassment Tess told her about Anna and her grandmother's scarf. "And so that's how I got to Acacia. Anna was convinced I had to go as close to where my finger landed as I could. She had complete faith in the luck the choice would bring. I did look for jobs in Acacia first, though, because honestly it didn't occur to me that the blob of green on the map contained anything other than trees. Unfortunately nobody's hiring in town."

For a second Adele studied her. "What an extraordinary story. And you actually went through with your friend Anna's plan?"

Tess attempted a smile. "I may not have been thinking too clearly, and Anna can be very persuasive. And she is my best and oldest friend."

"And you say you've worked at an events planning company called La Dolce Vita? What job did you hold there?"

"Jobs, really. Giorgio Bissi, the owner, was willing to let me try my hand at everything, from waitressing to basic line cook duties, to organizing parties and events. Giorgio hired me knowing that my hope was someday to open my own events planning company. His favorite joke was that I should forgo raises since he was giving me such great on-the-job training."

Adele smiled but remained silent.

To avoid appearing too nervous or desperate, Tess fixed her gaze on a large painting that hung behind Adele's desk. Rolling meadows tinted a summer green and spotted with round woolly clumps of sheep grazing contentedly led to a dark green slope of a forest-covered mountain. A brilliant azure blue sky met the mountain's jagged range. Though the color scheme was different, as January now marked the world with grays and browns, Tess knew she'd seen this same landscape while her car had rattled its way up the long private road. Then, as now, its vast openness intimidated.

Adele's voice drew her attention away from the painting. "Unfortunately at the moment we don't have any full-time openings, either. Unless you also happen to know how to rope steer or have experience in animal husbandry."

She couldn't manage even a sickly smile as her hopes plummeted like lead.

Great, she thought. She was stuck in Nowheresville, California, and the only place to work that seemed remotely viable wanted applicants who knew about animal husbandry. What a joke. She hadn't even been able to make her human husband happy.

When she got back to Acacia, she'd return to the organic grocery store on West Street or perhaps Spillin' the Beans, the coffee shop located a couple doors down from Ava Day's salon, and throw herself on the owners' mercy.

But the truth was, she'd gotten her hopes up as soon as the ranch's main lodge with its stone and timber façade had come into view. Her spirits had risen even higher once she'd stepped into the lobby and seen the wood and reddish tan upholstered chairs and sofas scattered around the lounge to the right of the main entry, and noticed the enormous urn filled with a combination of fresh flowers and twisted dried branches. She'd begun to think the unthinkable had happened—that she'd lucked out. But no.

And now she was going to have to ask for a tow truck. Mortified, she started to rise from the chair when Adele spoke again. "If, however, your references check out, and you pass a background check, I'll take you on as my assistant."

Surprise had her sinking back onto the cushion to babble her thanks.

Adele brushed them aside with a smile. "I'll be honest with you. I hadn't planned on hiring a new assistant until June or even the fall. But I'm impressed that you're willing to honor your friend's rules to the letter and make an effort to live and work as close to the point on the map where your finger landed. That kind of resolve is special. It is," she insisted when Tess protested. "And we appreciate that sort of attitude here. Who knows, maybe your arrival at Silver Creek Ranch is a sign for us as well. I wouldn't want to contemplate the bad karma I might invite by turning you away. So let's see where this fateful decision leads us."

This time Tess managed to offer her thanks. "I can't tell you how grateful I am or how lucky I feel right now."

"You're welcome. Though you may come to question your luck after a few days with me. I put in long hours."

"I like working hard." That was true. And, besides, what else was there to do in a place like this?

"So, have you found a place to stay?"

"No, not yet."

"We have a cabin you can use if you'd like. It's one of the original ones my husband, Daniel, and I built when we opened the ranch to guests. A few years back, we remodeled and expanded the number of guest quarters, but we decided to keep a few of the older cabins for the staff's use. It's pretty basic, with just a bedroom, a small sitting area, a kitchenette, and a bath. Perhaps you'd prefer to live in town—"

"It sounds about the size of my New York apartment, so I should feel right at home. If I may, I'd love to stay here, especially as my car seems to have met an untimely end at the hand of a cowboy."

Adele's eyes widened. "Really? What happened?"

"That guy Ward? He may be excellent at cowboy stuff, but I wouldn't let him anywhere near your car. Mine was running until he came along." Recalling his high-handed manner, she frowned and added in a low mutter, "His people skills could use a little work, too."

The amused smile on Adele's face told Tess she'd heard this last bit, too. She was going to have to break the habit of talking to herself, which she'd gotten into while driving across the country. At least it didn't seem as if she had offended Adele, she thought with relief.

"Well, Ward can be difficult at times. He was always a very opinionated little boy."

"So you've known him a long time?"

Adele's blue eyes twinkled. "Since birth. He's my son."

Oh, crap.

Chapter THREE

IT WAS FEBRUARY 14, and Ward Knowles didn't do Valentine's Day. Been there, done that, got the broken engagement to prove it. But it seemed he was pretty much a lone fish swimming against the tide. Everyone else was busy celebrating with all the heart-shaped gooey-centered sentiment the holiday invoked. It certainly was all around him at Silver Creek Ranch. As the holiday fell on a Saturday this year, the guest ranch was booked solid.

Since Friday, the corks had been popping from the bottles of a Mendocino sparkling wine that his younger brother, Reid, had selected for the weekend's wine list, and the bubbly was flowing freely. In the main lodge's gleaming stainless steel kitchen, Roo Rodgers, their pastry chef, had been creating chocolate fantasies to delight their guests' taste buds. Not to be outdone, Jeff Sullivan, the chef, was offering specials to appeal to every palate: duck à l'orange; pepper-encrusted filet mignon; seared scallops with roasted Meyer lemons and capers on a bed of Israeli couscous; and, for the vegetarians and vegans, a warm orzo salad with roasted beets and greens and a mung bean and butternut squash stew.

His mother, romantic to the core, had worked with

her new assistant to create the large floral arrangements in the lounge area as well as the centerpieces for the tables in the bar and dining room. The hushed oohs and aahs of appreciation when the guests entered the public rooms and beheld the gorgeous compositions was music to a hotelier's ears.

"Luv" was good for business so Ward supposed he shouldn't grouse. Nor should he be irritated by the fact that his mother's new assistant continued to treat him with polite hostility. New York brunettes with attitudes sorely tried his generally charming demeanor.

He and his kid sister, Quinn, were doing their part to make the holiday weekend special for their guests by guiding them on a trail ride that would take them over the ranch's sprawling acreage and into the neighboring state forest preserve's miles of trails. The two-hour ride would allow the guests to work off the indulgences of the night before and whet their appetites for the delicacies ahead. Ward would make sure he set a pace just challenging enough so that the guests who'd booked the hour-long full-body massage would be groaning in bliss when their muscles were kneaded and stretched.

The February weather made it too cold for the guests to enjoy the swimming pool, but his mother and Tess Casari, the snippy beauty with eyes as dark as espresso, had made up for any lack of physical recreation by arranging for extra yoga classes throughout the weekend so that guests could stretch their muscles and find calm equilibrium in the light-filled exercise studio. This way, everyone—horseback riders and those less actively inclined—would be in a proper frame of mind and body to enjoy the afternoon's high tea.

The Valentine's weekend special and all the accompanying pampering required extra work on everyone's part, both staff and family members, but the payoff—the glowing reviews posted on Internet travel sites and the bookings from new and returning guests—would be sweet. The businessman in Ward couldn't ignore the financial boon the holiday presented to his family's ranch.

So he tamped down on his desire to saddle his gelding Rio and head out for a soul-cleansing solitary gallop.

Like everyone in his family, Ward was fully committed to making Silver Creek Ranch the best guest ranch in Northern California. Today that meant spending several hours acting the genial trail guide to couples celebrating romance. He'd stifle his cynicism and ignore thoughts of irritating New Yorkers. After all, he'd been doing a pretty good job of it for five long weeks, ever since the afternoon she'd rolled up to Silver Creek looking lost and lonely and out of her depths.

The dawn air nipped the band of skin at the back of Ward's neck where he'd gotten a trim at Joe's barbershop in town. He shrugged his shoulders and with one hand raised the collar of his jacket while he currycombed Santiago's liver-colored flank. He'd selected Santiago and twenty other horses for the trail ride later in the morning.

He paused in the midst of grooming to take a sip of black coffee. He'd placed the thick ceramic mug next to one of the corral's posts, out of harm's way from hooves or booted feet. The coffee was sorely needed. He'd been up for hours, roused by Pete Williams, the ranch's foreman, who'd called to tell him that they had a situation down at the barn. Two of their ewes were having trouble lambing. One was carrying twins, who appeared to be trying to come into the world neck and neck. Definitely not a good situation.

Pete had hands a surgeon would envy. Nimble and delicate. Unfortunately, he had only two of them, so Ward had rolled out of bed to lend his own pair to the other ewe in distress.

The second ewe's problem was far more straightforward than the first's. Her lamb had been a breech presentation. As malpresentations went, rear legs exiting the uterus first weren't the trickiest, but Pete had made the right call: The ewe couldn't have birthed it on her own. The lamb was big—Ward could tell just by the size of its protruding hoof—and the ewe was exhausted. Luckily the ewe had been brought inside. The barn was warm and the straw was clean and dry.

After washing with an antiseptic and applying a lubricant, he'd dropped to his knees by the ewe's posterior and carefully inserted his fingers into the ewe and gently begun drawing the lamb forward. The ewe appeared quite relieved at the help she was receiving and renewed her own efforts. A couple of muffled, tired bleats and heaving strains later, she delivered a mucus-covered bruiser of a lamb onto the straw. He had wiped the lamb down with a towel and cleaned himself off as well, then waited to make sure the mother would be able to handle the rest.

Once she'd expelled the afterbirth, the ewe clambered to her hooves to nuzzle and lick her newborn. Ward had carried over a bucket to offer her water in case she was thirsty, but it seemed birthing had made her hungry more than anything else. She'd alternated between munching on wisps of hay and casually nudging her lamb.

The newborn hadn't seemed the worse for wear for entering the world ass-backward. Within a half hour he had gained enough strength to lurch to a stand. Encouraged by a sniff and a push from his mother, he had tottered over to her distended udder. After poking about and a few fumbled attempts to latch on to a teat, the lamb got the hang of it and began to nurse. At the other end, its woolly tail had begun to wiggle and wag, a sight that never failed to bring a smile to Ward's lips and a chuckle from Pete.

"So, three new healthy lambs and it's not even five A.M.," Pete had remarked.

"Yeah, all things considered, not a bad way to start the day," Ward said.

Since he was already down at the barns, Ward had decided he might as well stick around and help Carlos, Frank, and Holly, three of their ranch hands, water and feed the horses and get a jump on readying the ones needed for the trail ride.

Santiago was the last of Ward's lot. Like the rest of the horses, he was still sporting a winter coat, so even after Ward had gone over him with a bristle brush he remained somewhat unkempt and shaggy, what Reid called the Jerry Garcia look. By the end of March, when the temperatures had climbed, grooming would involve clouds of black, gray, chestnut, white, and palomino hair floating to the ground, each session revealing more of the horses' solid musculature.

Ward dropped the brush back into the carryall. Intuiting the grooming session was over, Santiago gave a full-body shake and then returned to his breakfast, feasting with equine delicacy.

A tabby, one of his sister's rescues, ambled past. His previous owner had allowed a scratch to his eye go untreated. The wound had festered until the whole area was infected and oozing. The owner had solved the problem by sticking the cat in a crate and leaving it in the middle of the private gravel road that led to the ranch, Quinn's reputation for rescuing animals known all through Acacia and beyond. She'd taken in the cat and footed the vet bill to have the eye, which by that point was beyond saving, enucleated.

Pirate had repaid Quinn's loving care by becoming one of their best mousers. This morning was no exception. The cat paused in his path and turned his head casually toward Ward, offering a clear view of the gray bulge in his maw.

"Must be off to give Quinn her Valentine's Day present," Frank said.

"Yet another clueless male." Holly's tone was as dry as kindling.

"What? I thought you said you wanted that set of saucepans," Frank said.

Ward remained silent, unwilling to wade into the treacherous waters. Holly and Frank seemed happily married, but Frank was at times a shade too literal, which worked fine when it came to dealing with cattle and sheep but also explained why he might consider cooking pans a viable Valentine's present for his wife of ten years. Ward would have to remember to find a moment to suggest Frank drive into Acacia after work and buy something a little less utilitarian for Holly. A necklace from Dazzled, the jewelry store, or a gift certificate from A Brand New Day might do the trick.

Christ, escaping this love business wasn't easy. He'd even found himself wondering what a certain dark-eyed beauty with great taste in clothes and lousy car sense might like. Luckily he'd caught himself before doing anything foolish, like buying her a bouquet of flowers. He somehow knew that if she smiled at him—a real smile—he'd be in trouble.

And it wasn't as if he didn't get a kick out of her New York cheek.

He picked up the carryall and his mug. "I've got to go hit the shower. I'll be back down after the meeting, guys." He ducked through the bars of the corral.

"Jim should be here soon, so we'll tack the horses for you and Quinn," Holly said.

Ward smiled. "Thanks. Hopefully the meeting will be over in time for us to lend a hand. You guys checking the fence later?" Maintaining the miles of fence that enclosed the ranch was a vitally important job, involving frequent inspections.

"Me and Mitchell are riding the line. Pete's staying here to keep an eye on the sorrel maiden mare. Her udder was real warm and full and she's been acting restless. Holly's on lamb duty," Frank told him.

"Let's hope any other lambs born today know which way to come out of their mommas," Ward said.

"I'll second that," Holly replied.

After a quick shower and shave, Ward changed into a clean pair of jeans and a shirt, grabbed his barn jacket, and left his house to walk up to the main lodge. It was only a quarter of a mile, and the morning air was fresh and invigorating. In the distance the mountains were still robed in a violet gray mist, but over to the east, the rising sun shot threads of gold into the weave. If the sun managed to burn off the mist, the blackish green of the fir-covered slopes would be revealed.

He loved both views equally.

His booted steps rang on the gravel road and his breath came out in short puffs. He hadn't eaten breakfast and so was looking forward to the staff meeting. This morning his family and the available staff were serving as taste testers for Roo Rodgers's late spring menu. And though he was resisting the mass gooey excess of emotion that accompanied Valentine's Day, he had to admit he was looking forward to seeing one woman in particular. He wondered what he could do to get Tess's back up this morning. He'd developed a real talent for it. A man shouldn't waste his talents.

In the pocket of his jacket his cellphone buzzed. Pulling it out, he pressed the talk button. "Ward here," he answered, and lengthened his stride. The main lodge had come into view.

"Ward, can you believe it? Carrie said 'Yes'!"

Romantic cynic though he might be, Ward wasn't so jaded he'd begrudge his best friend's happiness. The joy in Brian's voice was so outsized it could have reached Ward without the aid of all the cell towers or satellites positioned between California and Massachusetts.

His own face split into a grin. "So you finally mustered the courage to ask her. Took you long enough."

"Yeah, well, now that she's finished writing the paper she's giving at Harvard next week and has stopped looking like a zombie—Ow!" Brian's grunt of pain was mixed with laughter. "My fiancée's finding me objectionable already. Listen, Carrie wants to get on the line, too, so that we can ask you something. Make sure you congratulate her at having landed such a prize among men."

Ward shook his head in amusement as Brian's second grunt was followed by the unmistakable sound of lips meeting and clinging moistly, separating, then joining again. Clearing his throat loudly, he said, "Ahem, kids, don't forget you're not alone. I can hear you."

"Sorry." Brian's voice held a telling huskiness. "Can't help it. She's so cute. And she's going to marry me—hold on for one more sec."

Rolling his eyes, Ward pulled open the door to the main lodge's lobby. All was quiet. The breakfast for the guests wasn't scheduled to begin for another forty-five minutes. He waved to Estelle, who was on duty at the front desk and also on the phone—likely talking to someone back east as well, or perhaps booking a reservation from an interested party in Europe—and opened a door to Estelle's left that led to the back offices. The carpeted hall absorbed his footsteps.

The second round of smooching ended, and then Carrie's breathless voice sounded in his ear as he settled into the chair behind his desk. "Hi, Ward!"

"Congratulations, beautiful. Mom's going to be over the moon when she hears your and Brian's news. You know how she is. Oh, and do me a favor and scoot away from that man before he gets any happier."

"Hey!" Brian interjected, laughing. "I thought you were my friend! Maybe I shouldn't ask you to be my best man at the wedding."

Ward went still. Then he swallowed. "Brian, thank you—thank you for this honor."

"Come on, as if there were ever any question whom I'd want by my side on the most important day of my life. You're not just my best and oldest friend. If it weren't for you, it's doubtful I'd even be around to kiss Carrie, let alone marry her."

A familiar wave of self-consciousness washed over Ward. He wished Brian would stop thinking of him as his personal savior. All that had happened more than two decades ago and the events had escalated so quickly—the gang of hoods forming a menacing circle around Brian, Ward's decision to run over and help the new kid at school—what remained was pretty much a blur of heart-pounding, fear-blurred images.

While he might shake off the mantle of hero, one thing he would never reject was the bond of friendship forged between Brian and him that long-ago afternoon.

Determined to steer the conversation away from any further mention of his supposed heroism, he said, "Tell me more, guys. Have you set a date? I need to know when to line up the dancing girls for the bachelor party."

"You can think again about that idea," Carrie said as Brian exclaimed simultaneously, "Dancing girls, sweet! You're right, Ward, I should have popped the question long ago."

Ward grinned. "I foresee a lifetime of marital bliss, kids. It's all right, Carrie. I'm sure I can line up some old, wrinkled dancers who dress in purple kaftans for Brian's bachelor party."

"Thank you. That would be most acceptable." Carrie's voice was appropriately prim, but then she ruined it by giggling.

"I serve to please. So when and where's the wedding of the year to take place?"

In the quiet of Ward's office, Brian's voice was as clear as if he were three feet rather than three thousand miles away. "Well, bud, that's why we wanted to call you before anyone else. We don't want a huge wedding—"

"Just a beautiful one in a place we both love," Carrie chimed in. "Obviously the first place that came to mind was Silver Creek. We were wondering whether we might be able to have the wedding at the ranch."

"Sure. Mom and Dad will be thrilled. You know they consider Brian a third son. When do you want to tie the knot?"

"We were thinking of the first weekend in June. Carrie's teaching a summer school course, but it doesn't start until the week after."

Damn, early June? Memorial Day marked the beginning of the guest ranch's high season, when the gardens were bright with color, and the weather was perfect for all sorts of activities—hiking, biking, riding, fishing, swimming, and kayaking, not to mention the touring of vineyards near and far. Brian had worked a number of summers at the ranch alongside Ward and Reid, with Quinn tagging along after them. He knew how crazy the summer season got.

The excitement of Carrie's accepting his proposal must have caused a memory lapse.

For a moment "Uh-hmm," was all he could manage. Finally he pulled himself together. "I'll have to check with the front desk about reservations." Even as he said the words he knew he'd do his utmost to arrange things according to their wishes. "Okay, you've got the wedding date. How many people are you thinking of inviting?"

"Well, we've done a quick tally and think about sixty, though we might have to go higher once the parents get involved. A hundred max."

Ward coughed. A hundred? In case he'd needed proof, here it was. Love really did do a number on the brain cells. "I know you guys haven't been here in a while, what with your job, Brian, and Carrie's slog through the galaxies, but that would be all the rooms on the ranch plus spillover. We'll have to choose a couple of hotels and B&Bs nearby and book blocks of rooms quickly."

"We know it's a huge favor to ask. But Carrie and I have such wonderful memories of our summer stays there with you—"

"Of course. Listen, I'll have to run this by the supreme powers, but lucky for you I remembered to get Mom a Valentine's present."

"As if you'd ever neglect to," Carrie scoffed.

"Give Adele a big hug from both of us," Brian said.

"Will do. So let me go scout out the situation and I'll get back to you later today."

"Thanks a million, bud. We wanted to be able to tell Carrie's folks that we've got the wedding location fixed before they began pressuring us to hold it in Greenwich."

"Greenwich is just not our style. At Silver Creek we'll have a wedding to remember," Carrie added.

"I'll do my best for you, beautiful," Ward promised.

"You're so wonderful, Ward." At Brian's immediate objection, she giggled again. "Sorry, I guess today I have to hide my devotion to you."

"Say hi to everyone for us."

"And give your dad a big kiss."

"That's something he'd rather you deliver personally, Carrie," Ward said with a laugh.

His laughter died as he slid the cell back into his jacket pocket. As focused as he'd been on the more immediate problem—the organizational headache of hosting a wedding for Brian and Carrie—he'd been able to ignore another, bigger and far more personal, headache, one guaranteed to plague him throughout the entire wedding weekend. Probably for even longer than that. A wedding at Silver Creek meant he'd have to deal with Carrie's stepsister, Erica.

Having his mercenary ex-fiancée anywhere near Silver Creek was not high on Ward's wish list.

Chapter FOUR

"GOOD MORNING, TESS. Happy Valentine's Day!" Adele Knowles said as she breezed into the meeting room.

Tess paused in the middle of setting out on the long oak table a selection of delicacies that Roo had baked. She'd learned to skip breakfast on these special mornings when a taste testing was involved.

"Hi, Adele. Happy Valentine's Day to you, too." She'd sent her mother, father, and brother Valentine's cards—Christopher's a big goofy one with an enormous sparkly heart—but other than that she was trying to ignore the holiday. Her heart just wasn't in it.

"Don't you look pretty. I love that necklace."

Tess smiled. "Thanks, it was a present from Anna." The necklace was made of oversized purple resin beads. Tess had paired it with a charcoal gray wool tailored sheath and a wide black patent leather belt. Her stiletto-heeled pumps—also black patent—were arguably better suited to strolling down Fifth Avenue and giving hot dog–eating construction workers a lunchtime thrill than to her new job as Adele Knowles's assistant, which basically called for shadowing the older woman and helping out in the main lodge wherever and whenever she was needed, but for some reason Tess couldn't seem to dress in any other fashion. Since her arrival in Acacia, her outfits had become increasingly citified.

"This would be Anna of the 'Let's blindfold you, spin you around like a top, and let your finger decide your fate' fame?"

A vestige of embarrassment remained at having succumbed to Anna's crazy plan, yet Tess managed to smile happily and reply, "The one and only."

Five weeks later and Tess was still coming to grips with the fact that her finger had landed pretty much smack-dab in the middle of one of Silver Creek Ranch's pastures. Most likely on a cowpat.

How could she not feel out of place? Acacia, with its bustling downtown of—count 'em—four streets, had a population of 1,147. Just a bit different than New York City, where, depending on the time of day, it could feel like 1,147 people were crammed into a single subway car.

Thanks to Anna's game of "Pin your Future on the Map," she was now in the land of the redwoods and Bigfoot. Okay, the wildly huge trees were located farther to the north, as were the reported Sasquatch sightings, but still, she'd never seen so much *nature* in her life. Hence the stiletto heels. If worse came to worst and she was attacked by a wild animal, she could use them as a weapon.

"Anna's fashion taste matches her bold schemes," Adele said. "I like your friend more every time you mention her. Do you think she could get me one of those necklaces in blue to go with my scarf?"

Adele was undoubtedly the best thing about Tess's new life. She was smart, a savvy businesswoman, and as generous as the day was long. Tess couldn't believe she'd gotten so lucky as to land a job as her assistant.

And she was eager to repay Adele's generosity toward her however she could. "Sure," she said with a nod. "I'll call Anna and ask where she found the necklace—I think a deep sapphire would go really well with that scarf. It's beautiful, by the way."

Another thing to admire about Adele was her taste. Her style of dressing was what Tess would term "relaxed California," with lots of unstructured knits and natural fibers, but she always knew how to jazz it up with accessories to enhance her outfit. Adele might be the owner of a three-thousand-acre ranch surrounded by mountains and timber and where there were more animals—wait, she corrected herself, the term was "livestock"—than people, a place where the nearest high-rise was miles away and decent public transportation even farther, and where the only taxi was a rusted-out Dodge driven by one Ralph Cummins, a ponytailed grandfather who had a real casual attitude toward steering, but Adele could rival any New York doyenne when it came to looking great.

Her employer fingered the magenta-and-cerulean-blue-patterned silk scarf draped about her shoulders. "Isn't it lovely? Ward gave it to me. He left the package propped against our front door, wrapped with a bow. So sweet of him," she said with a proud maternal smile.

Tess's gaze shifted to a framed photograph resting upon the wide window ledge. Taken by a travel magazine that had run an article on the ranch, the photo showed the Knowles family standing in front of the main lodge. Her focus zeroed in on the tall, rugged, dark-haired man standing to the right in the picture, and her smile faded.

The photo had been taken in the summer. Ward's face was deeply tanned, and the curling ends of his hair were burnished with glints of gold. He was staring directly into the camera. The photographer had captured his steady gaze and his rock-solid confidence, too. It was there in the tilt of his square chin. Now that Tess knew what to look for, she saw the pride that was such a part of him, that he wore as easily as his business suits.

That she'd mistaken him for a ranch hand, a lowly employee—someone on her level—still had the power to cause a flush of hot embarrassment to crawl over her cheeks. Though Ward might choose to dress 85 percent of the time in faded jeans, scuffed cowboy boots, and a creased cowboy hat—the basic wardrobe of so many here at Silver Creek Ranch—he was every inch the powerful modern prince, heir to this Northern California kingdom.

And she'd had it with princes, whether they hailed from the East or West Coast, whether they dressed up or down. It was just too damned bad that Ward Knowles happened to look like the finest dark prince ever to come out of central casting.

As usual, she did her best to hide her antipathy. "Yes, that was very sweet of him." Of course Ward had bought his mother a Valentine's present. He was proud and arrogant but absolutely devoted to his family. She'd give him credit for that.

Adele glanced at her. Tess often had the uncomfortable impression that Adele guessed precisely how much Ward rubbed her the wrong way. But if the amused twinkle in Adele's eyes was any indication, Tess's refusal to sign up as Ward's number one fan didn't bother her much.

"I realize you and Ward got off to a somewhat shaky start, Tess. But you know, he didn't really kill your car."

"No, of course not," she agreed in a dry tone. She didn't say—and wild horses would not have been able to drag the truth out of her—that what had disturbed her almost as much as her car dying in front of the main lodge was how Ward had thrust his arm into the car, and her reaction when his arm had grazed her breasts.

How could a fleeting touch have generated so much electricity that her body still remembered the sizzle? The gnawing want?

So yes, she felt more than uneasy about Ward; she begrudged him the way he had aroused her. And how, in the weeks since her arrival, when she'd done her utmost to steer clear of him and forget the effect he'd had on her, she couldn't. It didn't help her peace of mind that whenever she was around him she found her initial impression of him reinforced. He remained irritatingly high-handed and eminently able to ignore her. He was as unconcerned about the plight of her car as he was about the fact that a simple brush of his arm had left her gasping like a sex-starved ninny.

Why should he be concerned about her? an inner voice asked. How she felt was her problem. So was her car. And she knew she'd better solve both problems. She couldn't take many more taxi rides into Acacia with Ralph Cummins. From the amount of time he spent on the wrong side of the road, it was possible Ralph believed he was in Australia. A few more weeks and the money she was putting aside from her paycheck might be enough to afford a new used car.

She'd figure out, too, how to quash the unwanted and strange fascination that filled her whenever she stole a glance at Ward's profile or heard the low timbre of his voice. It just might take a while.

"Something in your expression tells me you still believe he's responsible for your car's unfortunate demise."

Tess jumped guiltily. She wondered how long she'd been scowling at Ward's image. "It's just that in New York when a guy comes up and sticks his arm into your car, it's to steal your purse. I guess in California they do things differently. But, frankly, I'd rather he'd snatched my pursed than played Terminator with my car."

Adele laughed lightly. "And that's what's interesting about stories—there are at least two sides to them. The way Ward tells it, he was alarmed by the amount of black smoke pouring out your hood."

A handy excuse. But Tess refused to spoil the morning by thinking about Ward. Turning back to the conference table, she adjusted a plate of lemon macaroons a hair to the right, aligning the plate with the others she'd placed on the polished conference table.

Her gesture drew Adele's attention. "Mmm, this looks lovely. What's Roo baked for us?"

Tess relaxed. Here was a safer topic than Adele's handsome and imperious son, and one where she could prove her professional chops. She pointed to the different delicacies she'd arranged on china plates as she rattled them off. "These are lemon macaroons, and she also wants us to try an orange-scented olive oil cake, chocolate oatmeal drop cookies, hazelnut apricot bar cookies, and a rum apple cake. The plate at the end of the table has goat's milk cheesecake bites—they're made from Silver Creek's own goats, of course." She picked up the last plate. "And these are pistachio and fig cookies—"

"Oh, Lord have mercy!" Adele held her hands up as if warding off an attack. "I need to be able to zip the dress I've chosen for tonight. Daniel's taking me to our favorite restaurant in Healdsburg."

"Have no fear, Mom. For you I'll sacrifice myself on the altar of Roo's culinary experiments."

Both Tess and Adele turned. "Reid!" his mother exclaimed happily. "Oh! Are those for me?"

In Reid's hand was a bouquet of deep red tea roses.

"Of course, since you're my first and best Valentine." He kissed her cheek.

Beaming, she took the flowers. "Thank you, darling. They're lovely."

"Glad you like them. And these"—with a flourish, he produced another, smaller bouquet of deep purple tulips and white freesia that he'd been hiding behind his back—"are for you, Tess." He extended them with his customary devil-may-care grin.

If Ward Knowles embodied cool reserve and dark brooding good looks, his younger brother, Reid, was dazzling California sunshine—and as effortlessly appealing.

His dark blond tousled hair and ocean blue eyes alone were enough to turn a number of women's heads. But there was more to Reid's appeal than his handsome features and rangy athletic build; his bright blue eyes smiled as readily as his mouth. He was a man who enjoyed life and really enjoyed women.

His easy geniality set Reid apart from typical Casanovas. He was so good-natured that no one seemed to mind that practically every woman, age twenty to eighty, who entered his orbit became smitten.

Tess didn't hold it against him, either. Because in addition to being a charming rogue, Reid was nobody's fool. He clearly possessed an internal radar that signaled when a woman was interested . . . and when she wasn't. And he'd read her perfectly. He might tease and compliment her, but he never went further in his pursuit.

Easy in the knowledge that Reid had no ulterior motives in presenting her with a lovely Valentine's bouquet, she accepted the cluster of flowers with a smile. While her marriage with David had cured her of any susceptibility to golden-tongued, good-looking womanizers, that didn't mean she wasn't touched by Reid's gesture.

"They're beautiful, Reid. Thank you."

"I thought they suited you. Happy Valentine's Day."

A sudden movement caught her eye. Turning her head in the direction of the open doorway, she stiffened.

Ahh, the high and mighty Ward had arrived. From the scowl on his face, she could only surmise that he didn't approve of his younger brother giving her, a staff member, a Valentine's bouquet.

Come to think of it, he didn't seem to approve of her, period. She'd felt the weight of his gaze a number of times whenever he came to his mother's office to discuss a new marketing plan or advertising campaign for the guest ranch. His silent appraisal always seemed to find her wanting.

And wasn't that funny? She *was* wanting—a new car.

"Good morning, Ward!" Approaching her oldest son, Adele hugged him. "Happy Valentine's Day, darling. I just love my scarf." Stepping back, she looked up at him with an approving smile. "I'm so glad you finally got a haircut. You were looking shaggier than the sheep."

Reid laughed. His older brother shot him a look that probably would have sent most people slinking out the door. Reid was unfazed—if anything, he seemed even more amused.

Ward turned his attention back to his mother. "I'm glad you like the scarf. It looks beautiful on you." He kissed her cheek. "Hi, Reid." He paused infinitesimally and then nodded. "Tess."

She replied with an equally impassive, "Good morning." Determined to avoid a lengthier exchange, she raised the bouquet Reid had given her to sniff the freesias' peppery perfume, lowering it only when she heard the sound of the other staff members filing into the meeting room.

Phil Onofrie, who handled reservations and marketing for the guest ranch, and Macie Paulsen, the events planner, called out cheerful greetings before taking their seats around the table.

"Where are Dad and the brat?" Reid asked, walking over to the side table where Tess had placed a carafe of coffee and white porcelain mugs. He poured himself a cup.

"Your dad's calling Aunt Lucy to wish her a happy Valentine's. And your sister is—"

"Here." Quinn strode into the room. Striking and carelessly beautiful, Quinn had her mother's blue eyes and wide, slashing cheekbones, and her brother Reid's lanky build. Tess had yet to see her dressed in anything but faded jeans, T-shirts, and cowboy boots. Today's pick was a faded long-sleeve T with COWBOY JUNKIES emblazoned across her chest. She wore her thick blond hair in a ponytail. Tess wasn't sure she'd bothered to brush it before pulling it back.

"Alberta was hiding," she explained as she made a beeline for the laden table. "It took Carlos and me half an hour to find her. Clever she-devil." She plucked a slice of the orange-scented olive oil cake off the plate and popped it into her mouth. "Yum. This one has my vote."

"That's what you always say," Reid noted.

"Which one is Alberta again?" Ward asked.

"My Toggenburg kid. That's a young goat to you, city girl," she informed Tess with a teasing grin.

Tess inclined her head. "Thanks for enriching my vocabulary."

"You're welcome. Just so you know, it has not escaped my attention that you have yet to set foot in any of the barns or make the acquaintance of any of our animals."

On his way to the coffee station, Ward passed close

enough for Tess to catch his dry murmur of, "Might be difficult in those heels."

She pretended she hadn't heard him. Even if the closet in the one-room cabin where she now lived was stocked exclusively with cowboy boots, she had no desire to say hi to any of Silver Creek's horses, cattle, goats, or any other creatures in Quinn's extensive menagerie.

She had even less desire to win Ward's good opinion.

Maintaining her resentment made it easier to ignore the discomfiting realization that she now recognized his scent, an annoyingly pleasing combination of citrus, leather, and man. It didn't help that the curling ends of his hair were damp. She could smell the shampoo he'd used. And no, she was not going to imagine Ward Knowles naked in the shower, suds sliding down his muscled body.

"Speaking of animals, Happy Valentine's Day, brat." Reaching into the back pocket of his jeans, Ward drew out an envelope and handed it to Quinn.

Quinn began tearing it open but then paused. "Nothing mushy in here, right? No cupids or hearts?" she asked suspiciously.

"It was Reid's turn to prank you this year."

"Aww, now you've spoiled it," Reid complained. "Besides, Quinn might enjoy a lacy sequined push-up bra and matching—"

Quinn raised a hand to halt his flow of words. "Stop right there."

"—panties. The line's called 'Hello Bombshell.' I thought they were right up your alley," he finished.

"You wretch." Quinn was fighting back a smile and losing. "How do you dupe all those women into thinking you're anything but pure evil? No, I really don't want to hear your answer. Let me open my sober and responsible brother's present."

"Damned with faint praise, huh, Ward?" Reid observed. "Nothing worse than being labeled sober and responsible in the same sentence."

Ward didn't seem particularly perturbed. He was busy watching Quinn's reaction as she pulled the card from the envelope and opened it.

Quinn's delighted squeal confirmed the present's success. She launched herself at her oldest brother, flinging her arms around his neck. "Thank you, thank you." She planted a loud smooch on his lean cheek. "You're the best." She turned to address the others. "Ward's adopted another horse for me," she told them happily.

Quinn not only helped raise the animals at Silver Creek; she adopted them, too. Horses seemed to be her animal of choice, but there'd been mention of various cats, dogs, rabbits, and birds that Quinn had either rescued or fostered. And a potbellied pig. Tess wasn't sure what made a potbellied pig different from any other kind, and she wasn't about to inquire.

"You can pick the horse up next week," Ward told his sister.

"Very thoughtful, Ward." The deep voice of Daniel Knowles carried easily.

"Hey, Dad, how's Aunt Lucy?"

"Frantic. Apparently there's still a lot to be done before the inn's grand opening."

Tess had heard Adele and Daniel talk about Lucy and Peter Whittaker. Lucy Whittaker was Daniel's sister and also involved in the hotel business. She and her husband had bought an old farm outside of Aiken, South Carolina, and were transforming it into an inn for lovers of all things equestrian.

Daniel Knowles's gaze swept the room. With Daniel present, Tess could see where Ward got his tall, muscular build—as well as his air of command. "So now that we're all here, let's sit down and get started on the important business of the day." He grinned and Tess saw the source of Reid's endless charm—charm that Ward had obviously missed out on at birth. "I, for one, want to see if that cake tastes as good as it looks."

Chapter FIVE

A CASUALLY CHOREOGRAPHED dance had begun, a stretch and retreat of arms and torsos as the baked treats were plucked from the center of the table and placed onto the small dessert plates Tess had distributed.

Staff tastings, while far from arduous, were nonetheless taken seriously. Roo Rodgers and Jeff Sullivan, the chef de cuisine, were dedicated to their art. They expected the judgments passed on their culinary creations to be precise and considered. Adele had told Tess that she'd actually had to bar them from attending the staff meetings when food was being sampled. The sessions had begun to feel too much like a *Top Chef* episode in reverse, with the cooks grilling the judges. Often their interrogations took so long no other business got done.

Busy putting her and Adele's bouquets into vases, Tess had been the last to take her place at the table. When she lowered herself onto the leather and metal chair, she caught Ward's speculative gaze.

She suspected he reserved this special scrutiny just for her, solely to unnerve her. It wasn't that he looked at her often. Most of the time his focus was elsewhere. But when his gaze did settle on her, it never failed to distract.

And he was far too perceptive a man not to notice his effect on her.

Even worse was the constant temptation to sneak glances his way. She might not like Ward much, but it was difficult not to admire the boldly carved lines of his face, from his aquiline nose to the sensual fullness of his lips to his squared jaw. There was nothing weak or soft about that face. His chiseled profile could have graced an ancient Roman coin.

Sometimes she grew careless and her eyes lingered a fraction too long. Suddenly she would find herself caught in the magnetic pull of his gold-chipped gaze. A seeming eternity would pass, and then just as suddenly he'd release her and she'd be left feeling as ruffled and bothered as he'd made her feel that January afternoon when they'd first met, when their breaths had mingled and her pulse had raced as if she were on her first date. Infuriating man.

She'd gotten smarter. This morning she had her pen and notebook at the ready. Best, the tactic was completely justified. As Adele's assistant, taking notes on the meetings fell into her job description. Since their banishment from the tastings, Roo and Jeff received a full record of everyone's reactions.

The comments had already started. The orange-scented olive oil cake was a universal success; everyone mentioned its moistness and color and felt it could be served as a dessert for lunch as well as during high tea. The goat's milk cheesecake also received a thumbs-up. That the goat's milk came from Quinn's beloved goats would be a huge selling point for the foodies who visited the guest ranch. More and more of them were finding their way to Silver Creek.

This group wasn't a pushover, however. Adele, as generous as she was, made the first cut.

"The rum apple cake strikes me as a tad too heavy for a spring menu," she said.

"You're right, sweetheart," Daniel said. "Let's suggest to Roo that she incorporate it into the fall menu. And I'm not impressed by the lemon macaroons. They—"

"Just don't compare to her ganache ones," Adele finished his sentence. "I agree."

"Yeah, the ganache ones were amazing," Quinn said. "Can we ask Roo to start baking them again? Though I like these apricot-hazelnut bars, too." With the enthusiasm she typically displayed during the tasting sessions, she plucked a chocolate oatmeal drop cookie from the plate, took a bite, and chewed. Atypically she frowned. "But this one—nope. Too ho-hum." She fell silent, chewing, considering.

"The cookies need a little kick. A dash of cayenne, maybe," Ward said.

Tess frowned at her notebook as she wrote down his observation. Darn him for having figured out what she hadn't. He was entirely too good at zeroing in on a missing ingredient.

"So how are we doing for the day's schedule? Any glitches?" Daniel asked, his air of authority tempered by his obvious love and respect for Adele.

"As of five A.M. we have three new healthy, tail-wiggling lambs. The horses Quinn and I are using on the morning trail ride are brushed. Holly, Frank, and Jim are tacking them as we speak. Twenty-one guests signed up," Ward told him.

Tess had already come to understand the long hours Ward logged tending to the ranch and running the business end of the guest accommodations. As impressive as they were, they didn't outnumber his character defects. In her opinion, he still had a long way to go in the personality department.

Reid spoke. "I called down to the barn on my way here. No one's canceled for the morning trail ride or for the afternoon ride Mitch and I are leading."

Daniel nodded. "Good."

"How are we doing with rebookings, Phil?" Adele asked.

Phil's grin was happy. "Very promising so far. We've already got requests for next year's Valentine's Day as well as for other weekend dates. We've had a substantial increase in calls since the ad campaign."

"And how about the other weekend activities?" Adele asked.

"I confirmed with the band that's playing tonight," Macie said. "And Naomi's bringing two additional instructors for the yoga classes. Ava Day said they have eight bookings for manis, pedis, and facials from Silver Creek today. They're thrilled with the extra business."

"I'm glad we're able to send customers her way. She's done a fantastic job with her salon," Adele said.

"I have a feeling we'll be sending Ava even more business come this June. Guess who called me this morning?"

Since everyone else was looking at Ward expectantly, Tess allowed her gaze to cross the table.

"Brian," he answered, which meant nothing to her. "He's proposed to Carrie."

Around the table rose a lot of "So happy for the couple" sounds. They floated as lightly as soap bubbles blown on a warm summer's day and vanished just as quickly at Ward's next words: "They'd like to have the wedding here at Silver Creek."

"Oh," Adele said faintly.

"Have we recovered from the last wedding?" Daniel asked.

"My ears haven't." Reid made a show of tugging his earlobe. "They're still ringing from the bridesmaids' drunken karaoke set. The thing lasted until four A.M. Past even my bedtime."

"And the next morning, the makeup artist pitched a fit when all the ladies showed up with faces the color of pea soup," Quinn said. "And the hairstylist had to take twice as long because they kept moaning whenever the hairbrush came near. It was pitiful."

"Now, Quinn," her father said with mild reproof.

"It was," Quinn insisted. "Don't you remember how you had to threaten the groom's frat brothers with the police? They were trying to ride the steers. The dopes thought it'd be fun to race them," she explained for Tess's benefit.

Tess glanced at Daniel. His dark head was streaked with gray at the temples. Combined with his commanding air, he had the look of an ambassador. Even so, Tess had difficulty imagining this reserved man negotiating with a bunch of drunken wedding guests intent on riding his cattle.

"Oh, yes, it's all coming back to me now. That was a dreadful wedding! We had to air out the guest rooms for days afterward. They didn't tip the cleaning staff, either." Adele's voice was clipped and infinitely disapproving.

"Ha!" Quinn laughed. "You guys have short memories. That fiasco was nothing compared to the wedding before that one. Remember the screaming match that erupted between the bride and groom?" She turned to Tess. "The groom—a marine—on special leave from God knows what hellhole tour of duty, had returned just in time for the rehearsal dinner. Which was when he discovered, because his bride-to-be was silly or guilty enough to wear a spandex dress tight enough to make a

Kardashian blush, that she was four and a half months pregnant—"

"And the poor schmuck had been deployed for his tour of duty six months earlier. With no leave," Reid cut in. Shaking his head, he continued. "Yeah. I'd completely blocked that horror out. Ward was the hero that night. We were all worried the poor guy was going to lose it completely, but you talked him down. Once he was fairly calm, and not threatening to go on a rampage, you saddled up Rio and Sheikh and took him out on a trail ride past dawn. By then the guy was probably too tired to kill anyone."

"Dealing with the groom couldn't have been easy for you, Ward, especially since Erica had just—" With the abruptness of a car colliding into a brick wall, Quinn stopped. Sending her older brother an anguished look, she whispered, "Sorry."

Ward's expression betrayed nothing—the man could make a stone seem expressive. Whatever Quinn had alluded to when she mentioned this Erica person didn't seem to faze him. They could have been discussing the wine cellar's inventory or how many positive reviews they'd received on a travel website and he'd have shown more emotion.

It was the other family members' expressions that made Tess wonder. The worry in them spoke volumes.

And Ward Knowles was not a man who inspired people to worry about him.

Ward could hardly miss his family's collective consternation, but all he said was, "Let's get back to the important topic here—Brian and Carrie."

"Whom we love dearly and who will have a lovely, happy wedding—" Adele said brightly.

"Which might break our current rotten-nuptial streak," Quinn interjected.

Adele ignored Quinn's interruption. "Of course we'd be delighted to host the wedding here. Right, Daniel?"

"Brian's grown into a fine man."

His wife smiled. "Thanks in large part to you, darling," she said.

Daniel shrugged easily. "I'd say we all helped Brian when he needed it most. So, when can they get back to us with a date?"

"Already did, Dad," Ward said. "They'd like to have the wedding in June—this June."

"What? That's less than five months away," Reid said.

Ward nodded.

A heavy silence descended. Tess might be new to the hotel business, but she'd had plenty of experience working for an events company. She knew how difficult it would be to organize a wedding in such a short period. She glanced over at Macie Paulsen, who was in charge of the special events for the ranch. The redhead was looking distinctly unwell, as if the goat's milk cheesecake had turned to acid sludge in her stomach. Tess felt a spurt of sympathy for her.

Phil didn't look much happier. He'd already pushed his plate out of the way and pulled his iPad closer, fingers skimming its sleek surface. "Which weekend?" he asked, staring at the illuminated screen.

"Brian mentioned the first one."

Phil shook his head. "We're already more than half-full. How big a wedding are they planning?"

"Maybe they want an intimate affair," Adele said with a determined note of optimism.

"They're up to a rough count of sixty guests but haven't conferred with the mothers yet. Brian gave a ballpark figure of one hundred."

Quinn snorted. "So much for breaking our rotten streak. Man, I really hate weddings."

Adele looked at Ward with dismay. Then she turned

to her husband, and the two exchanged one of those silent communications shared between long-married couples.

With a tiny nod to Daniel, she told them, "We'll simply have to call the guests and ask them to rebook. Phil, please offer them a reduced rate for their troubles. And Macie, can you come up with a deluxe package to mollify them, a VIP tour of vineyards and some special spa treatments, perhaps? And you'll have to call the Lodge in Ukiah and see if the Strikers are willing to reserve a block of rooms. Same with the Hugheses' bed and breakfast and the Petersons' place."

"Uh, unfortunately I won't be able to arrange all that." Macie shifted in her seat. "I'm really sorry about this, Adele. I meant to approach you and Daniel first thing on Monday, I really did. It's just that I've been offered a position at a resort in Oahu. Grant is really excited about moving to Hawaii. He's pretty sure he can line up a ton of gigs playing at the resorts. And the surfing's so great there. Anyway, they've asked me to start at the end of the month. I said yes. Grant found us a really cheap flight out there—but we have to go next week."

No wonder Macie looked as if she wanted to cry.

Adele was silent and, though she was clearly thrown for a loop, Tess once again appreciated her new boss. If she'd been back at La Dolce Vita, Giorgio would be screaming at the top of his lungs. Perhaps throwing knives.

"I see." Adele's tone was measured. "This will require some adjustments on our part. We'll be sorry to lose you, Macie. But if you could start making calls about what perks we can offer so at least we've made some headway, that would be helpful. Phil, can you crunch the numbers and see what kind of reduction we can give on rates for the guests we're rebooking without it bankrupting us?"

"Okay." Phil pushed back his chair and sent a harassed look Macie's way. Her announcement must have caught him unaware, too. "Come on, Macie, let's see what we can accomplish before you fly off to the land of luaus."

There was silence until the two had left. Then Ward spoke.

"I'm sorry about all this. Obviously the timing's lousy. But you know how much Brian and Carrie love this place."

Adele waved off his apology. "Of course we do, darling. We'll figure out a way to keep the guests who need to be rebooked happy. It's too bad about Macie, though. She was good at her job."

"We'll need to find a replacement for her as soon as possible. But the real challenge will be organizing the wedding for Carrie and Brian. A wedding in early June requires someone working on it now," Daniel said.

"More like yesterday." Reid reached forward and swiped the last piece of cake from the platter.

Ward cleared his throat. "Mom, I know it's a lot to ask, but would you be willing to handle the wedding details for Carrie?"

"Why—I—" Adele floundered, at a loss for words.

"Unfortunately, Ward, that's not a feasible solution," Daniel said. "I told your aunt Lucy today that your mom and I would go help her and Peter ready the inn for their grand opening. I promised we'd go down there for a couple of weeks. And then there's the matter of a trip I've booked—"

Adele turned in her chair. "Oh, Daniel! Is it the one we discussed?"

"The tour of Andalusia?" He nodded. "Afterward we'll spend a week in Minorca. I've rented a cottage for us—just the two of us. Happy Valentine's Day, darling. I was planning to surprise you with it at dinner."

Ward watched his mother throw her arms about his father's neck with a cry of delight.

Damn, he thought. As soon as Brian and Carrie announced the early June date for their wedding and the high head count of guests, he'd known the logistics would prove tricky. But he hadn't suspected the business would become even more complicated than it already was. Who'd have guessed that Macie would be offered a new job, and accept it, and leave them in the lurch with no replacement? Even then things might have been manageable had his mother been free to take over. But Ward couldn't ask his parents to stay at the ranch simply so his mother could organize Carrie's wedding. Aunt Lucy and Uncle Peter's new inn was a family enterprise; a successful opening was key. Nor could he ask his parents to change their vacation plans, not when they'd spent so many years devoting themselves to making Silver Creek a premier guest ranch while simultaneously raising three kids. Their opportunities for private getaways had been rare.

But even the simplest of weddings—and destination weddings were never simple—required someone to coordinate the hundred and one details. Who else at Silver Creek could oversee them for Brian and Carrie? He glanced at his sister, who was sipping her coffee.

Quinn caught him eyeing her and lowered her cup to the table. "No way, José." She shook her head hard enough for the tip of her ponytail to swat her shoulders. "Your lovely Valentine present notwithstanding, I am not your wedding planner girl. I don't know the first thing about what goes into a wedding ceremony and I don't care to, either. All that sentimental goo gives me the hives."

No big news there, Ward thought. If there were a woman alive less interested in romance than Quinn, he'd be surprised. Her heart was too full of animals.

She'd been five years old when she'd taken in her first stray, an injured bunny who'd escaped a predator's maw. Now she was twenty-three, and the tally of adopted, rescued, and fostered animals she'd cared for had reached into the hundreds. Still, like everyone in the family, Quinn knew she was supposed to step up to the plate and pinch-hit when needed.

A little arm-twisting of his youngest sibling was in order, he decided. "Come on. It won't be so bad. Brian's like another brother to you—"

Her eyes narrowed to blue slits. "I will not bow to emotional blackmail or sexist assumptions that because I'm a female I'm the natural choice here. Since Brian's not only like a brother to you but also your best friend, why don't *you* spend the next few months listening to Carrie and Brian dither over invitations and whatnot—"

"Because I don't—"

His mother interrupted. "Stop, both of you. Ward, you're not thinking straight. Quinn would be about the worst person in the world to oversee this. Poor Carrie would never get the wedding of her dreams. And Quinn, there's no reason to look so pleased with yourself. Brian and Carrie are your friends. I expect you to do everything you can to help pull off this event. But it's obvious that neither you, Quinn, or Reid can take on the job of organizing things for Brian and Carrie when your father and I will be gone for so many weeks. The three of you will have even more responsibilities to manage, and handling the details of a wedding when the engaged couple is living on the other side of the continent is too time consuming. But I believe I have an answer to our problem—a brilliant one if I say so myself."

Thank God. His mother had saved their collective butts. Brian and Carrie would get their California country wedding and he wouldn't be forced to see to the details. "Really? That's great, Mom." He felt his face stretch in a wide grin.

She nodded. "Macie's announcement took me by surprise, so the obvious solution didn't immediately occur to me. The vision of a cottage in Minorca was pretty distracting, too," she added with a smile for his dad. "But then, while you and Quinn were squabbling, it occurred to me. We already have someone who's experienced at events planning."

Quinn straightened. "We do?"

From her voice Ward could tell she'd been worried she hadn't safely escaped being roped into wedding detail.

"We do," his mother confirmed. "Tess, would you be willing to take over Macie's position and handle the wedding details? And Ward, since Brian is your best friend, I think it's only right that you be the one to help Tess with the planning."

Ward sat stunned, silently marveling at his mother's genius. She'd not only figured out a way to avoid disappointing Brian and Carrie, but by effectively ordering him to help Tess, she'd also figured out a way to ensure they spent a considerable amount of time together. Yeah, it was pretty clever of her. Damn his mother's intuition and stubborn perseverance, he thought with an equal dose of irritation and amusement.

This was undoubtedly her latest attempt in her efforts to set him up with a woman. The campaign had started a few short months after his and Erica's breakup. Adele had suddenly begun insisting he accompany her to various events in San Francisco or Sacramento where, like a magician pulling an extravagant bouquet from the depths of a top hat, she would produce some female Ward "simply must meet."

To her annoyance he'd managed to resist the bevvy of marriageable beauties rounded up for his inspection. His mother's disappointment when he explained that he didn't want her matchmaking for him had been marked by pointed sighs and doleful glances. There, too, he'd resisted maternal pressure, refusing to whip out his iPhone and hurriedly dial one of those too-hastily-rejected women.

When none of her efforts bore fruit, his mother had switched tactics, dropping thinly veiled hints about how she and his father were getting old and how happy it would make them to see their children happily married. She was beginning to fear they would never experience the joy of grandchildren, of hearing the footsteps of little Knowles feet running through their home. From the way she carried on, she made it sound as if she and Ward's dad had one foot in the grave when, in fact, they had more energy than most people half their age.

He'd believed she'd given up the campaign, but in a flash of insight realized that her less-than-subtle hints had been extinguished just about when Tess arrived.

Mom was the mistress of sly, all right. In Tess she'd found a woman he couldn't either politely brush off, or bed and then politely brush off. Reid was the only guy he knew who possessed the extraordinary gift of being able to sleep with a woman, break things off, and still remain best of friends with her. Ward had no delusions about his own abilities. And obviously he'd still have to deal with Tess after he'd slept with her. Because even though he'd hardly spoken twenty words to her following the car debacle—Christ, he couldn't figure out why her nose was still out of joint over the death of that smoking piece of crap—the thought of what she might be like in bed had crossed his mind a few times a day.

Just because he was no longer interested in getting hitched didn't mean he'd taken a vow of celibacy. And he wasn't blind, either. Tess's dark eyes held secrets; her lush lips held promise. Sweet, mind-drugging promise.

And her gloriously plump breasts were the softest he'd ever touched.

Clever, Mom. Real clever.

"Uh, Adele, I'm not sure this idea will work."

Ward looked over at Tess. Thank God she'd made the objection. If it had come from him, his mother would have simply ignored him. She could be infuriatingly stubborn once she got the bit between her teeth—a trait Ms. Tess Casari shared. Tess's brown eyes might remind him of rich espresso but the looks she sent his way were anything but warm.

"Really, Tess? Why?" his mother asked, with the perfect mix of surprise and confusion. "You're detail-oriented and efficient. You have excellent style and taste and the good sense to know that neither has to cost an arm and a leg, which is crucial in planning a wedding. You couldn't find a sweeter bride to work with than Carrie, but she'll need guidance. I think you have the patience to help her and get the job done. And I thought you were interested in events planning. If things work out, we'd be happy to have you take over Macie's position permanently."

Ahh, the big carrot had been dangled, Ward thought.

"I'm sure this Carrie and Brian are both very nice people. And I would like to do events planning. It's more that I haven't really made a decision about how long I'll stay in the area—"

No surprise there, Ward told himself. Tess Casari didn't need to wear her absurdly high heels day in and day out to underscore that she didn't belong here. He imagined that once she replaced her death trap of a car, she'd head for some city where she could saunter down wide, smoothly paved sidewalks and dazzle the male population with those killer legs of hers. Why that thought annoyed him as much as seeing that Reid had presented her with a bouquet of flowers he refused to analyze.

"Oh!" Adele was silent for a moment. "I thought you were enjoying being at Silver Creek. And during your interview you mentioned about wanting to work in events planning." His mom wasn't above laying a little guilt trip now and then. Of course she usually only subjected her family to them—which only showed how much she'd come to like Tess.

"I do like working here, and yes, I would like to do events planning. And I would love the opportunity to be in charge of events planning. But planning a *wedding*—"

The desperation in that single word caught Ward's attention. Tess was very good at hiding her emotions—her cool dislike of him the exception—but, sharpening his gaze, he could detect the tension in the set of her shoulders.

Was it because she was still in mourning for her husband that she was resisting being in charge of planning a wedding? It was difficult to tell. Even if Ward hadn't been intentionally keeping his distance, Tess was reserved. Private. He'd never heard her chattering on about her life the way some women did.

As if realizing she might have revealed too much by letting the word "wedding" dangle in the air, she hurriedly continued. "It's just that I'm not sure I'm ready to handle all that a wedding involves on my own. I might not be up to the job."

Ward wasn't buying it. And from the expressions around the table, neither was the rest of his family. Tess might have been working as his mother's assistant for only a little over a month but he'd already noted her efficiency and attention to detail. He knew, too, that if his mother didn't believe Tess was capable of doing the job and doing it to Silver Creek's high standards, she would never have suggested it. The reputation of their guest ranch—not to mention Brian's and Carrie's happiness—was too important.

"As an events planner you need as much experience handling weddings as any other elaborate function, Tess." His mother's tone, eminently reasonable, was one Ward recognized. She employed it when she was determined to get her way. Few people could withstand it, not temperamental kitchen staff who sliced and diced with wickedly long knives, not brawny ranch hands who could rope and wrestle a full-ton steer to the ground, not beautiful, dark-eyed Italian women who walked with a mesmerizing roll of their hips on stiletto heels.

"Yes, I know that."

"Good. Then you should take this one on," his mother said. "Truly, this is the perfect wedding for you to cut your teeth on. Brian and Carrie couldn't be more adorable."

"Mom's right. It's highly doubtful that Carrie will morph into Bridezilla on you," Reid offered.

Quinn nodded and got into the act. "Yeah, Carrie's sweet. It's her stepsister Erica you have to worry about. She's something else—"

"Quinn," was all their mother needed to say for his sister to shut her overactive mouth with an audible click of her teeth.

The look on Quinn's face was too much. Christ, did his family really think the mere mention of Erica was enough to trigger a self-destructive bender? Hardly. He was just glad to have escaped the steel jaws of the matrimonial trap relatively unscathed.

"Tess, we know it's a lot to ask, but we would be so grateful if you'd agree to take over for Macie and handle the wedding for Ward's friends." When his dad added his voice to the chorus, Ward actually felt a moment of pity for Tess. No way was she going to be able to withstand the concerted campaign.

"And between Macie's files and mine, you'll have a detailed list of all the merchants you'll need to contact. And, of course, there'll be Ward to help you every step of the way." His mother graced the two of them with the brightest of smiles.

He wasn't fooled. That smile told him in no uncertain terms that he'd be banished to the doghouse if he didn't provide her protégé every assistance. He knew he should be irritated by this latest attempt to meddle in his life, but he figured this was a small price to pay in exchange for having a pretty terrific mother.

Now the only question was, how long would it take for Tess to recognize that further resistance was futile?

Chapter SIX

WHAT COULD SHE do but accept? Tess asked herself. Adele had been so generous in hiring her, a complete unknown, to be her personal assistant. She couldn't repay that kindness by refusing to work on this upcoming wedding just because she'd grown jaded about the institution of marriage. Surely she could handle the details and pull together a successful ceremony without being reminded of her own disastrous marriage. Plus, she'd be a fool to walk away from the opportunity to work as Silver Creek's events planner. She'd be acquiring the vital experience to run her own business one day.

"Okay, I'm in." She just hoped Brian and Carrie wouldn't be disappointed when they learned she had no previous experience as a wedding planner. She hadn't even planned her own.

The reaction around the conference table was immediate and unanimous. Even Ward smiled. Well, he would, she thought. The dark prince had once again gotten his way.

Reid's signature grin was wide. "I should have gotten you a bigger bouquet," he teased.

Adele, too, looked pleased as punch. "Thank you, Tess. I knew we could count on you."

Quinn pushed back her chair and rose to her feet. "I owe you big-time for letting me off the hook, city girl. I'll have to think of a suitable token of appreciation."

"There's no need, really." From what she'd observed, Quinn's tastes ran in a very different direction from hers.

"It'll be fun finding the right thank-you present." Turning to Ward, she said, "I'll head down to the corral and tack any of the horses still remaining."

Daniel, too, had risen from his seat. "Let me add my thanks, Tess. With you and Ward working together on the wedding, Adele and I will be able to truly enjoy our vacation."

Her working with Ward? She'd straighten out that misconception soon enough. The job would be stressful enough without having to deal with him.

Daniel extended a courteous hand to help Adele from her chair. "Darling, I think you and I should go check in on Phil and Macie. She might be getting an earful."

"Phil did look quite annoyed at Macie's surprise announcement. I'll be back in a few minutes, Tess, to do the tour of the public rooms. Then we can start going through the files of vendors and merchants so you have the best addresses. If you could give Roo our feedback on the desserts?"

"Of course." Tess nodded and then started stacking the empty plates next to her.

Across the table Ward mirrored her actions. *Oh, no.* She wanted him gone. "You really don't need to clear the—"

A single look stopped her protest in midstream. How was it that he managed to get his way without even opening his mouth?

"We have to talk."

That's what she got for finding fault with his silent commands. Now she'd have to listen to them. It only made her more annoyed that she liked the low timbre of his voice. There was a pleasing texture to it. It made her think of rich caramel sprinkled with grains of sea salt.

It didn't matter that she'd sampled her fair share of Roo's baked treats just minutes earlier. It was not a good idea to associate Ward Knowles with her favorite indulgence.

Banishing ludicrous thoughts of how Ward might taste, she made her voice as crisp and businesslike as possible. "Perhaps later. I don't want to keep Roo or your mother waiting." She gave him the smile she reserved for obnoxious clients and felt a surge of satisfaction when his eyes narrowed slightly. Score one for her.

"Let me clarify. We need to call Brian and Carrie so that I can introduce you to them. I'll have time this afternoon, once Quinn and I are back from the trail ride and have tended to the horses. How about meeting at three o'clock?"

"I'm sorry. There's the Valentine's Day tea. I told George and Jeff I'd help with the setup and wait on tables." Which meant she'd have to don a pair of blue jeans. Silver Creek's waitstaff dressed down, in crisp white shirts, blue jeans, and cowboy boots. This last was where she would draw the line. Self-respecting Italian girls from Queens did not own cowboy boots.

"With so little time until June, I'd expect you would want to meet your clients. You do plan to organize this wedding, don't you?"

She folded her arms across her chest and wished she'd worn her highest heels so she wasn't staring up at that squared jaw of his. "I told your parents I would. But I don't need you to perform the introductions for me. I'm perfectly capable of phoning your friends and discussing their wishes—"

"Which would be fine except that Carrie doesn't have

a lot of experience in this sort of thing. It'll be easier for the three of you if there's someone who can translate—"

Tess gave him a look. "She can't speak English?"

"Mainly she speaks astrophysics. She studies planet systems. Floral arrangements, wedding dresses, and menu selections not so much."

Tess felt her own universe tilt crazily. Just what had she gotten herself into? "Planet systems?"

Ward nodded. "Let's see if I remember the title of her dissertation. It was something along the lines of: 'The DEEP2 Galaxy Redshift and the Role of Environment in Galaxy Formation.' "

"Catchy." She frowned. "I didn't know we had a deep galaxy. I thought 'vast' covered it."

Ward gave a small smile. "Not that kind of deep," he corrected. " 'DEEP' stands for deep extragalactic evolutionary probe. She's doing a postdoc at MIT now."

"Of course," Tess said faintly as her mind whirred. And she'd thought she had trouble connecting with Quinn, whose world revolved around the animal kingdom. She always needed to remind herself that when Quinn spoke of kids she was actually referring to baby goats. A good wedding planner had to be able to understand a couple's vision and turn it into a memorable, beautiful wedding. What would she do if this Carrie person could speak only in quarks and black holes?

Suddenly, brushing Ward off didn't seem like such a brilliant idea—not until she was confident that she could understand Carrie's world and envision how she wanted her wedding.

Still, it was important to let Mr. I-Know-What's-Best Ward Knowles know that she wasn't a pushover. Nor was he the boss of her—at least not exactly. "Your mother may have suggested that you help me with the wedding details, but it's not necessary. I work better on my own."

He tilted his head. "Maybe so, but there's another reason why you and I will be working as a team on this wedding."

He really did have the high-and-mighty attitude down pat, she thought with a frown. "And that reason would be?"

"My mother. She's in matchmaking mode. I don't want her to suspect I'm on to her."

"What?" Of all the answers she'd expected, this one hadn't even made the extended list. "Matchmaking? Are you serious?"

"Afraid so. She can't help it. Some women needlepoint. Some garden. Others gossip. My mother matchmakes. She has a sentimental heart. Her fondest wish is to see her children married and to hear the happy squeals of grandbabies."

Unfortunately, Ward's words rang true. Tess had noticed that Adele seemed to get a little misty-eyed over young married couples that stayed at the ranch, especially when the women were expecting. She must not have drunk enough coffee, for the significance of what he'd said only then registered. "Wait, you mean she's trying to get you and me together? No, she can't be serious."

"I'm afraid so. Once she and Dad return from their trip to Spain I'll break the tragic news that sadly you and I were not to be."

"You can say that again. Never. Not in a million years."

Ward's dark brows rose. "My mother believes I'm a catch."

"A flaw common to many fond mothers, I'm sure. Much though I hate to disappoint her—"

"Other women do, too."

She smiled. "They probably haven't spent enough time in your company."

The corner of his mouth quirked in amusement.

"Probably not. Nevertheless, I'd like my mother to believe there's no need to trot another female in front of me for a few months. It grows tiresome."

"Wow. See, it's like I just said. If you'd only let those women see your extraordinary conceit—"

"Strangely enough many women are happy to overlook my character defects. Do you suppose it has something to do with my family owning a three-thousand-acre ranch?"

Such cynicism. But Tess wasn't going to be the one to inform him that his chiseled dark looks were far more likely the reason women were willing to put up with his lousy personality. They probably believed they'd be able to "change" him. Women could be so silly when it came to the opposite sex.

Of course, she was hardly one to feel superior to other women who were fools for love. She'd married David believing he was her Prince Charming. The fairy tale had lasted less than a month.

It was almost refreshing that she harbored no illusions about Ward's character. And she far preferred being annoyed with his sardonic attitude than acknowledging the faint twinge of sympathy she felt at his words. How awful to think a woman might be more interested in his wealth than in him. "Even if I didn't find you utterly unappealing, I make it a rule never to get involved with car killers or—"

"For Christ's sake. I did *not* kill your car."

"Gee, that's funny, because one minute it was running and the next—"

"It was not running; it was gasping," he corrected. "The mechanic down at Wexler's Auto Shop wept when he lifted your hood."

"Because he was looking at an avoidable tragedy."

"I'll say. Try replacing the oil in your car's engine next time."

The mechanic in New York had failed to mention her car would guzzle oil the way it did gas, but she wasn't going to admit the mechanic's negligence or her own ignorance to Ward. Instead, she glared at him. "So, to recap, even if I were interested in marrying a supremely arrogant, rude, and ridiculously rich man who owned a lot of cows and such, you'd be the last one I'd choose."

His smile was more a baring of teeth. "Excellent. Make sure you remember that. Let's plan on FaceTiming with Brian and Carrie after you've helped with the high tea."

Chapter SEVEN

THE GRAY MIST had cleared, but the morning was still raw when Ward stepped outside the main lodge and made his way back toward the barns and corrals. Nodding politely at two guests who'd just finished their morning runs and were walking in tight circles, shaking out their legs and stretching as they exhaled clouds of air, Ward turned up the collar of his jacket and tugged the coat closer against his bare neck.

Ward hadn't had time to check, but he bet that with the cool weather the number of last-minute reservations for the massage sessions and the yoga classes had spiked.

The high tea would be popular, too, with trail riders and yoga lovers alike. Tess Casari was going to have a busy day, he thought, picturing her crisscrossing the lounge and the adjacent bar where the tea would be served. The picture shifted to include the delectable swing of her rounded hips, and suddenly the morning air seemed balmy as his body temperature ratcheted up a few degrees.

He was a guy. Thinking about Tess's very enticing curves came as no big surprise. What was interesting was that he found her personality just as attention grabbing.

His mouth curved in an unconscious smile as he recalled their latest exchange. It was possibly the lengthiest conversation they'd shared. He was willing to admit he'd been entertained. Entertained, challenged, and intrigued. It was a combination he hadn't felt in quite some time. It struck him that he'd grown accustomed to women who tried a little too hard to please.

Tess was certainly different in that respect.

He'd decided it was only right to be up front about his mother's matchmaking plans. Though he didn't know Tess well, he could guess that she'd appreciate having someone meddle in her love life about as much as he did. Telling a beautiful woman his mother was trying to set them up was damnably embarrassing. It was tricky, too, as said woman might interpret the gesture as a come-on. He'd solved the problem by being about eight degrees more obnoxious than normal.

To his relief, she hadn't hesitated to point out the flaws many others were willing to overlook. What had she called him? Arrogant and rude.

She'd also called him ridiculously rich. She hadn't gotten the last bit right, probably confusing the fact that he and his family owned a lot of land with a swollen bank account.

The reality was more nuanced. Yes, the guest ranch was growing more and more popular and turning a profit. But most of the profits were then funneled into improving the lodgings and the ranch itself and paying the staff and wranglers' salaries.

Tess wasn't the first to assume Ward and his family were among the ranks of the wealthy. Erica, Ward's ex-fiancée, had been similarly mistaken. Until that fateful day when Ward decided it might be best to clear the air before Erica's remarks about how she'd like to start looking for a house on Nob Hill and a pied-à-terre in New York after they came back from their honeymoon reached his family's ears and they laughed themselves silly.

It had been an illuminating conversation for both Erica and him, one he should have initiated a hell of a lot sooner, but he'd thought she understood his character and what Silver Creek meant to him. But it soon became clear that words such as "heritage" and "stewardship of the land" didn't impress her nearly as much as "profit margin."

When Erica had finally realized that no amount of earnest persuading on her part was going to convince him to lobby his family to make radical and irrevocable changes to the ranch by selling off the cattle and sheep, building some first-rate golf courses, and turning Silver Creek into a premier resort, she'd cut her losses—with the cool precision of a surgeon.

Three months before they were to pledge their love and loyalty in front of a minister and assembled guests, she'd announced she couldn't marry a man who lacked ambition. By then he understood beyond a doubt that in Erica's world, ambition and success were judged in dollar signs. Still, it had hurt to know she could walk away from him so easily.

He'd heard through the grapevine that Erica was currently dating a Silicon Valley tech mogul whose company developed apps. Rumor had it he was readying an IPO that might make him one of the Valley's newest billionaires.

Ward wished her luck. He didn't blame anyone but himself for not having seen her character more clearly. He'd been fooled by the fact that she was often as sweet-tempered as her stepsister, Carrie. The thing was, Erica's brand of sweetness lasted only as long as everything went exactly her way. Since he'd believed himself in love with her, he'd done everything he could to keep her happy—that is, until he resisted her campaign to destroy a place and lifestyle the people he loved most in the world cherished.

Though he was grateful to have been saved from what would almost certainly have been a marriage rife with bitter resentment, Erica's rejection had nevertheless left a wound. Although covered with scar tissue, the pain lingered and was just sharp enough to remind him of the dangers of opening his heart again. He'd judged badly once. Who was to say he wouldn't be fooled twice?

Besides, the status quo was hardly terrible. He loved his work at Silver Creek, which on any given day entailed doing about a half dozen different jobs, and he enjoyed the company of women—on his own terms. He was looking for good sex and intelligent and fun company . . . with no strings attached. Admittedly, it was sometimes difficult to convince the woman in question that there'd be no deviating from this last item, but once he had, things went quite satisfactorily for both parties. He saw no reason to tinker with a near-perfect arrangement.

He supposed Tess Casari would label this as yet another example of his rude arrogance. It was a measure of her allure that Ward was even tempted to see whether he could convince her to give it a shot.

His thoughts had taken him the third of a mile down the ranch's private road to where the barns, round pen, and corrals were located.

Quinn was already in the corral, saddling Brocco, a dark bay gelding who was one of their beginner horses. Next to him, Gino, a sturdy pinto who was also bombproof—unfazed by anything that crossed his path—was saddled and dozing, his brown muzzle resting on the middle split rail.

"Hey," he said, unlatching the gate and then shutting it behind him. Balanced on the top wooden rail were three tooled saddles and a matching number of saddle blankets. He chose Aladdin's and lifted it off. Carrying it over to the flea-bitten gray standing placidly on the other side of Brocco, he shook out the striped saddle blanket and then settled it over the gelding's back. The saddle followed.

Quinn ducked under Brocco's neck to stand beside Ward. "Hey, yourself. So don't keep me in suspense. How'd it go with Tess? Is she really on board for handling the blessed nuptials?"

Ward decided it was only right to prolong her anxiety a few seconds more. It'd be character building—or something like that. Giving the saddle a final adjustment, he grabbed the cinch, drew it under Aladdin's belly, and then inserted the latigo through the cinch ring. He tightened the leather strap until the cinch was snug, threaded it through the saddle's D ring, and knotted it.

"Ward!" The pissed-off note in Quinn's voice was as sharp as the bite of the morning air. One should never overlook the simple pleasures in life. Tormenting younger sisters was one of them.

But Chester and Ion still needed to be tacked. If they didn't get the remaining horses ready, the trail ride would start late and affect the rest of the day's schedule. Normally starting a trail ride a few minutes late was no big deal, but with so many extra activities planned, there wasn't as much flexibility.

"You can breathe easy. She agreed."

"Yes!" Quinn cried as if her prayers had been answered. "I knew I liked Tess for a reason. You must be feeling pretty kindly toward her, too."

He grunted.

"Wow, that's eloquent. Is that really all you can muster by way of response after she's relieved you of a massive, months-long headache?"

"Are you going to saddle Chester or chatter?"

"Lucky for you I can do both." She turned to the rail

and hefted the thirty-pound saddle off it as if it weighed half that much. "And it's not chatter. This is a conversation, FYI. Your refusal to participate in it can only mean that you like Tess, too. I think it's those huge dark eyes of hers."

There were a lot of parts to Tess he liked. It remained to be seen, however, whether he'd do anything about his growing appreciation. "Did you fall on your head this morning? Oh, I get it, you're confusing Valentine's Day with April Fool's."

"Again, your evasion is so very telling."

Unfortunately, Quinn chose that moment to duck down and grab the cinch beneath Chester's barrel-shaped belly and missed the scowl Ward sent her.

"Listen, Sherlock. Tess can be as beautiful as the day is long." And yes, he'd noted the days were growing longer and Tess could knock the breath out of him just by walking into a room. Poetry in motion and all that. "I'm not interested."

"Ahh!" she crowed. "So you've noticed how pretty she is."

"Pipe down. You'll spook Chester," he warned, ignoring the fact that the horse didn't so much as twitch his ears when he spoke his name. The gelding knew the ropes. He was stealing a few winks before the morning ride started.

"She might be good for you. Have you thought about asking her out?"

Christ, was his sister ever going to shut up? This time he made sure she caught his scowl. His brow cleared as a thought struck him. "You know, you're sounding awfully like Mom."

"Who, me?"

Her expression was way too innocent.

"Yeah, you." Understanding dawned, and he shook his head at the enormity of her betrayal. "I can't believe it. I adopt a horse for you and this is how my kindness is repaid?"

She had the grace to look sheepish. "I figure it's like this. Mom will be so jazzed at the idea of you and Tess becoming an item, she'll leave Reid and me alone for a while. Now that spring is upon us and the birds are nesting, she's only going to get worse. And you *are* the oldest. Besides, Tess would be good for you. As far as I can see she doesn't seem the least bit impressed with you." She smiled sweetly.

"No, she doesn't, which could mean that she's as uninterested in going out with me as I am with her." Except, a voice inside his head reminded him, for those tantalizing flashes of feminine awareness he'd glimpsed in her eyes. The effect had been like adding a shot of brandy to espresso. Even now his blood heated at the thought. He ignored his reaction. "She doesn't even belong here. What in the hell is she doing in Acacia?"

"Mom told me she came here because her friend blindfolded her and stuck her in front of a map of California—after spinning her around a couple of times. You know, kind of like the game pin the tail on the donkey. Pretty amazing, huh?"

"Pretty strange. Why would I want to go out with someone who makes life plans based on a party game? Was she blitzed or is she just flaky?" From the covert study he'd been conducting he already knew she didn't drink much and wielded a laserlike focus on whatever task was assigned her. But there was no need to admit that to his sister.

"You did hear she lost her husband, right?" There was just enough censure in her tone to make him wince.

Christ. He couldn't imagine what losing her husband had been like for her, but he very much doubted Tess would want his pity. "Sorry, Quinn, you can lay off the guilt trip. No way am I going to be your sacrificial lamb. I like my life just fine as it is."

"Yeah, you're obviously happy. Come on, Ward, you do nothing but brood and scowl at spreadsheets—"

"Maybe because I'm trying to make this place profitable, despite the growing number of adopted animals on the premises—"

Quinn was on a roll and talked right over him. "And ever since Erica dumped you, when you do decide to date a woman, your internal timer begins ticking at 'Hello.' Two weeks, max, and then the poor thing is given what I'm guessing is a flawless speech about how you're not ready for a deeper commitment, blah, blah, blah. It's not healthy, Ward."

He paused, his hand flat against Ion's gray-and-black-patterned saddle blanket, and grinned. "That was good, Quinn. Unfortunately, you lack Mom's subtlety. You're going to have to refine that spiel if you don't want Reid in stitches when you try it on him."

When she rolled her eyes in exasperation, he grinned. "Have I told you recently how cute you look when you've been trounced by your betters?" he asked, knowing it would make her do a slow burn. "You remind me of that Chihuahua you fostered, all bulgy-eyed and wiggly." Oh, yeah. This last would keep her seething for a good half hour. "'Fraid you'll have to drop the topic of my love life, kid. It's showtime."

Chapter EIGHT

WITH THE HELP of Jim and Mitchell, two of the wranglers, they got the guests mounted on their assigned horses, checked the length of their stirrups, and adjusted the cinches with an on-time departure. Since Quinn, Ward, and Jim were taking the group out, they made sure to memorize names as they chatted with the guests and got them settled in their saddles. And when they introduced themselves, Quinn and Ward stuck to first names only so as to maintain a casual and easy atmosphere during the trail ride. Often guests became distracted upon hearing "Knowles" attached to their names. Visions of cozying up to one of them in the hopes of getting a perk or VIP treatment obscured the view they should be concentrating on: the landscape they were riding through.

They headed out at an easy walk, following the tractor tracks along the fence line, allowing the guests to grow accustomed to the horses beneath them. In the lower pastures, sheep and newborn lambs dotted the rolling fields. Adjacent to them were the quarter horses the Knowleses trained. In addition to the trail horses reserved for the guests, Ward's family had another twenty they were bringing along. Some would be kept as cutting horses; the rest sold as pleasure or competition horses. When Ward and the other riders approached, both sheep and equines meandered toward the fence, their curiosity roused by the passing horses.

Ward rode next to a couple visiting from Kentucky. Madlon and Kirk Glenn were spending two weeks touring the northern part of the state. They'd started their trip in San Francisco, visiting museums and taking in the sights, before renting a car to tour the Napa and Sonoma vineyards. They were wrapping up their California trip at Silver Creek. Since both husband and wife seemed genuinely taken with the ranch, Ward was happy to field their questions. Acting as ranch historian as well as riding instructor was part and parcel of leading a trail ride.

"What kind of sheep are these?" Kirk asked him.

"The breed's called Lincoln."

"So they're from England? From the look of them I'd have guessed Jamaica," Madlon said.

Ward laughed. "They do look like Rastafarians, don't they? Those dreadlocks they're wearing? When we sheer them later they'll produce a superior quality wool. There are a fair number of artisanal spinners in the region. The blanket underneath your saddle?" He pointed his gloved finger at the black, gray, and red–striped pad extending beyond the fender and the saddle skirt. "It's woven from Silver Creek's sheep by Clover Stiles. She owns The Fold, a yarn store in Acacia. She also knits sweaters, scarves, ponchos, and the like using our wool."

"How wonderful. And the horses?" Madlon pointed to a group grazing by the fence. "That silver one's a beauty."

"Yeah, that he is. That's Bilbao. We're training him to be a cutting horse. He's three, so he'll be filling out a little more through the chest and withers, but do you see how he's a little smaller than Rascal, the chestnut grazing next to him? Both Rascal and Bilbao are quarter horses, but cutting horses generally have a smaller build. Rascal's more a pleasure horse, like Aladdin and Ion, the horses you and Glenn are riding."

"This is so interesting. May I ask another question?"

"Sure." He was more than happy to talk about the ranch and its mission, especially if it kept his thoughts from wandering in the direction of a certain New Yorker. He wondered why she'd never once asked to come out on a trail ride—

Madlon's voice broke into his musings. "It's kind of funny, but I just happened to notice that all the trail horses are males—"

Her husband's laughter cut off the rest of question, but Ward had gotten the gist of it. "Shame on you, Pug, for checking out other guys' equipment!"

Madlon blushed at her husband's teasing. "I noticed, that's all. It stuck out."

Her husband whooped again.

Ward fought a grin. "You're right, all our trail horses are geldings. We've found the rides go better with single sex horses, especially as we often have novice riders. Mares are great. They're actually harder workers—"

"Of course they are. That applies to females of *all* species," Madlon said.

"True. But when a mare goes into heat she sometimes gets a little tetchy and even gelded horses get distracted—" And just like that, an image of Tess and her huge dark eyes, saucy ponytail, and exquisite curves popped into his mind. He had no doubt she would do her best to clock—or geld—him if he were foolish enough to ask if she was in heat. And no, he wasn't usually what Quinn would call a chauvinist jerk; he just wanted to have a reason for the inconvenient attraction plaguing him. Pheromones could explain it.

Kirk clucked at Ion, who'd stopped to swipe a dried

nettle, one of his favorite treats. "So how long has the ranch been operating?"

"The Knowleses have been raising quarter horses and cattle since 1915. The sheep and the pear orchard you see over there"—he extended his arm across the tracks to the rows of pear trees lining the other side; in two months' time their branches would be covered in delicate white blossoms—"are the newest introductions. They're part of an ongoing effort to diversify Silver Creek's land use. All the farming and ranching done here is organic and sustainable."

"It's wonderful." Madlon patted Aladdin's gray neck as if congratulating him for being part of such a wonderful enterprise. "And when did the Knowleses decide to open Silver Creek to paying guests?"

"Thirty-three years ago." Three years before he was born. "Daniel and Adele Knowles, the current owners, recognized that they had to take the ranch in a new direction. It was their decision to decrease the number of cattle in order to make the ranch sustainable. They were some of the first ranchers in the area to switch to grass feeding. But to afford those changes they also realized they needed a steady revenue. You're it," he said, flashing a smile.

"Happy to be of service," Kirk said. "So far this is money well spent."

"In the beginning, Adele and Daniel had help from Lucy Knowles, Daniel's sister. But then she married, and she and her husband Peter decided to buy an inn in Maryland, where Peter's from. Now they're opening a second in South Carolina, near Aiken."

"Might be worth a visit on our next vacation, right, Kirk?" Madlon glanced around again at the lambs lying on the short-cropped field and gave a happy sigh. "I paint. Do you think I could come back here in the afternoon with my sketchbook? I'll be careful not to disturb the babies."

"Pug's a really good artist. I've been trying to encourage her to set up a website and sell her works online," Kirk said.

"It shouldn't be a problem," Ward replied. "So, 'Pug.' That's an unusual nickname."

Madlon laughed cheerfully. "Isn't it? My brother gave it to me when I was little. It stuck."

"Well, it's a good thing you don't look like a pug. But that's a funny coincidence. I was telling my sister earlier how much she reminded me of a Chihuahua. She, too, may find herself with a canine nickname."

"Beware the wrath of an aggrieved sister. My brother ended up with a lot of frogs in his bed. Lots of them," Madlon said.

Ward grinned and tipped his hat. "Duly warned."

They'd reached the wooden gate that led to the higher pastures. The leader, Ward shifted in his saddle to check on the other riders behind. Quinn, astride her black Appaloosa, Domino, was in the middle of the pack, talking to a young couple from Oakland. When she saw him turn in his saddle, she gave a thumbs-up sign. Imagining how she'd retaliate if he began calling her Chi-chi, Ward grinned, then let his gaze travel to the last riders. Taking up the rear, Jim gave a casual wave. The riders he was supervising were doing fine, too.

Turning back to his own group, he said, "I'll open the gate. After everyone passes through it, we can pick up a trot. About three-quarters of a mile further on, we'll start loping. You all ready for a quicker pace?"

Karen and Hope, a mother and daughter who were visiting from Oregon, their weekend stay a Valentine's present Hope had arranged for her mother, nodded in unison, Karen adding, "Ready as we'll ever be. But boy am I looking forward to the hot stone massage later this afternoon." Karen was riding Brocco and was probably the greenest of the group. But she looked game and athletic.

"Don't worry, you'll do great. Brocco's a smooth ride."

Ward squeezed his legs around Rio's girth and the seven-year-old gelding moved into an easy ground-skimming trot, his muscled neck curved in a delicate arch and his black mane rising and falling in time to the two-beat gait. They passed the upper pastures where the Angus cattle roamed, the herd smaller now that the pregnant cows had been moved closer to the barns for calving season.

The terrain grew hillier. The open, brownish gray fields were topped by a soft gray sky but ahead, about a mile farther, the grassy meadows met a dark line of tall cypress that marked the beginning of the state preserve. The trails that wound throughout the forest offered hours of riding.

Ward closed his hand on his reins and raised his arm. The horses, all well-trained or "made," slowed to a walk behind him. Once again, he shifted in his saddle but this time addressed the entire group. "All right, folks, you ready to enjoy a nice, easy lope for this next stretch?"

Excited answers of "Yes" and "You betcha" floated on the breeze. He looked over at the woman named Corinne who was riding Gomez. The man next to her, astride Miro, was Allen. "They'll take good care of you," he assured them. "These two have been riding the trails all their lives. They know their job."

"I can tell Gomez is a good horse. He's been slowing down whenever I ask," Corinne said.

"Don't worry about me, but Silver Creek's chef had better be prepared for some seriously hungry guests," Allen added.

"Jeff Sullivan, the restaurant's chef, likes nothing better than guests with serious appetites. And the ranch is serving a high tea this afternoon." Tess would be volunteering her services then. He might have to check on how she was faring. It would get her back up, but riling her was a lot of fun. He wondered whether she even owned a pair of jeans. Tess Casari in snug jeans would be a sight to behold.

"Okay, let's ride." He closed his legs and opened his left hand slightly, relaxing his grip on the reins. Rio surged forward into a fluid lope. Behind him came the rich snorts as the other horses also picked up speed. The air was soon filled with the pounding of hooves on the hard earth, the jangling of metal bits and the creaking of leather, some of the best music in the world.

A ray of sunlight pierced the cloud cover and landed on a ribbon of silver that meandered its way down the fir-topped mountain and then over the open land. It was the creek for which his family's ranch was named. As Ward drew the cool air deep into his lungs, he knew he was about the luckiest man alive to have a job that allowed him to work the land he loved.

Women came and women went but this love remained.

Chapter NINE

THE HIGH TEA was hopping, the chatter animated, the guests' appetites voracious. And Tess's arms were aching. This time out of the kitchen, her tray was laden with a pot of jasmine tea, two cups, a small pot of lavender honey, and a saucer of sliced lemons. That was just the beverage portion of the order. The tray also held a plate piled with coconut macaroons and chocolate-dipped strawberries—by far the most popular item on the menu. Another plate had a pyramid of tea sandwiches to make Tut proud. In all, it was a lot to balance as she threaded her way through the lounge to her destination, a couple in their thirties.

"Here you go." Carefully she lowered the tray and began transferring the dishes onto the round table in front of them. The couple were trim so they mustn't always eat like professional linebackers. They "oohed" appreciatively as she presented them with their order.

"Thank you. This looks divine."

"Yeah, it does," her partner agreed, already reaching for a salmon and pumpernickel sandwich.

"Well, enjoy. And let me know if you'd like anything else," Tess replied with a smile.

"We will, don't you worry."

In the public rooms, the tea might be all that was decorous enthusiasm, but behind the kitchen's swinging double doors, Roo was bitching a blue streak. Since the pastry chef was an Aussie, her curses were colorful, but apparently Roo didn't feel they were adequate to the task of reacting to the unexpected popularity of the day's tea, which she was in charge of so that Jeff and his staff could prep for dinner. During Tess's last trip into the kitchen Roo had demanded she provide her with some good Italian swear words. Teaching someone from Australia's Northern Territory to pronounce Italian was like eating spaghetti with a toothpick.

Roo didn't seem to notice any problem. She rattled off Tess's harried offerings of *che coglione, figlio di una mignotta,* and *vaffanculo* with cheerful violence as she whipped together extra sandwiches. Strangely enough, the mangled obscenities went perfectly with her five-foot stature, pixie features, teased hair, Cleopatra eyeliner, tattoo sleeves, and piercings.

Across the gleaming stainless steel kitchen, Jeff and his sous-chef, Chris; his prep cook, Carter; and his line cook, Mack; were already dicing vegetables for dinner. When he worked, Jeff liked to rock out to whatever was on someone's iPod. From what Tess could surmise whenever she hurried into the kitchen to drop off dirty dishes with Tim, the dishwasher on duty, and pick up a new order, the playlist du jour was composed of the Red Hot Chili Peppers, Alice in Chains, and the Deftones.

None of these were especially Tess's favorites, but she wasn't stupid enough to criticize any of the kitchen staff's musical tastes, not when three of the men behind the counter were wielding wickedly sharp knives. Jeff Sullivan's temper was equally sharp. Mainly he used it to eviscerate any fool less than anal with the plating.

To Tess he'd been quite sweet since he'd wrung a promise from her that she'd make him a home-cooked

Italian meal. She was going to prepare her mother's signature comfort dish: baked penne with tomatoes, cream, and five cheeses. A second helping of her mother's dish risked a week of wearing crisis pants and loose sweaters, but every bite was worth the gazillion calories. To complete the meal Tess planned to make two of Mrs. Vecchio's dishes: a tart green salad of arugula, endive, shaved parmesan, and lemon vinaigrette, and a dessert of a crostata with fig jam. Anna had promised to email the recipe for the crostata.

Jeff loved the idea of sampling recipes from Anna and Tess's mothers, claiming that home cooking was the real thing and that these dishes should form the backbone of any restaurant. The Silver Creek chef knew his *cucina italiana*. He'd interned at one of Tuscany's top restaurants. And he'd obviously picked up some key vocabulary during his internship. As Tess passed through the swinging doors, the Nine Inch Nails were wailing and, from their respective stations across the wide aisle, Jeff and Roo were engaging in a seriously competitive swearing smackdown.

It was all a little much. She passed the dirty china and cutlery to Tim and nearly groaned in relief as their weight was removed from her tray. With each roundtrip, the loads had gotten heavier. By now it seemed as if they weighed a ton. She dreaded the idea of tipping a tray over by mistake and sending teapots and baked goodies flying in the middle of Adele and Daniel's desert-hued lounge. She'd gotten out of waitressing shape, but then, whenever she'd served at the events catered by La Dolce Vita, she hadn't been hefting six-cup teapots and stacked plates—merely light-as-air appetizers and pastries. With a wince she shook out her arm and then jammed her fist into the small of her back. It, too, ached.

"Here's your order, Tess," Roo broke off swearing long enough to tell her.

"Great." She eyed the tray. Chocolate-dipped strawberries, apple tartlets, sandwiches, and tea for two. The order was for a couple seated at the small table by the window. Ignoring her aching arms, she lifted the tray. From behind, she felt a whoosh of air as the kitchen door swung open, but assumed it was Liz, another of the servers. She turned and nearly slammed into Ward.

"Careful there." He reached out a hand to steady her, which, of course, did nothing of the kind.

"Thanks," she muttered and then pressed her lips together so they wouldn't betray the trembling feeling his touch engendered. Readjusting the tray, she made to step around him. She was careful not to look at him again. He'd changed into a black button-down shirt and black jeans and looked far too good.

"Almost done?" he asked.

She realized with a start that it must be almost time to call his friends. "High tea hasn't slowed down yet. As much as I'd love to hang around and chat, we have some ridiculously hungry guests." She left the kitchen, quite pleased that Ward Knowles was going to have to cool his cowboy heels.

In the lounge, she crossed Gordon, one of the regular servers, and exchanged a comical look of dismay with him as she wended her way to the opposite end of the bustling lounge. The spacious room was filled with the buzz of voices and the clinking of china.

As she approached the couple by the window they straightened in their armchairs. Anticipation lit their faces. With a professional smile she began placing their order on the circular glass-topped table, lowering the teapot first and then the cups and saucers around the outer rim of the tray. The trick was to keep it balanced even as her arm muscles quivered in relief from the lightened load. Last came the chocolate-dipped strawberries, tartlets, and sandwiches.

"Mmm. This looks amazing, doesn't it, Kirk?"

"Just the ticket. We rode out this morning on a long trail ride."

"The most lovely trail ride," the woman volunteered. "Then after lunch I spent an hour and a half sketching the lambs. Kirk brought his camera and took pictures. You can see why we've worked up an appetite. The lambs are so precious. You've seen them, of course."

Tess took the fifth on that one. "Hmm, well, you've certainly had a busy day."

"And we're looking forward to a busy night." Kirk wiggled his eyebrows. "Dancing and such. The such will be particularly fun, won't it, Madlon?"

His wife replied with an easy, comfortable laugh.

Tess's smile warmed. She liked their open affection for each other. It reminded her of how Daniel and Adele interacted. Under other circumstances she might have lingered at their table. But she'd noticed a group of four that had just settled onto the sofa and wingback chairs across the room and Gordon was still in the kitchen, so she tucked the tray beneath her arm. "Enjoy the rest of your Valentine's Day."

"Hard not to, at a place like this."

"You, too, my dear," the woman named Madlon offered kindly.

"How about a sandwich, Kirk?" She picked up the plate and smiled at her husband.

"Thanks, love."

Tess told herself not to be envious of the couple, who not only were enjoying this Valentine's Day together but from the looks of it would also share many more.

She and David hadn't lasted long enough to celebrate a single one.

* * *

She could barely suppress her irritation when she returned to the kitchen and found that Ward was still there. He was standing behind the counter next to Roo, loading up a tray of strawberries, savory biscuits, and nut brittle. It was the iced tea with sprigs of mint that was the giveaway. A couple had ordered iced rather than hot tea because they'd just finished a yoga session and wanted something cool to quench their thirst.

"That's my order." At this point she didn't care that she sounded like one of the grumps in her old neighborhood who shooed kids away from playing on the sidewalk outside his house. Then it occurred to her that the grumpy geezers wouldn't dare shoo someone like Ward away, which didn't improve her mood one iota.

"That it is," he replied, unfazed by her tone. "And the sooner we get it out, the sooner you and I can conference call with Brian and Carrie."

"Good luck with that. A party of four just came in." To Roo she said, "They want two plates of sandwiches, four red velvet cupcakes, the nut brittle, and four granola scones."

Roo rattled off a string of new vocabulary words. "Did I get that last one right?"

"No, it's *'pezzo' di merda,* not *pozzo.*"

Tess saw Ward's dark brows shoot up in astonishment. Her mood lightened a shade.

"Right. *Pezzo.* What's the matter with these people? Seating for dinner starts at six!" Roo tried out another couple of curses for good measure.

"Yeah, well, this party went horseback riding this morning. Now they want to eat like horses."

"Generally when people come to stay at a working ranch, they partake in ranch activities."

"Huh. Go figure." Tess thought about what activity she'd like to indulge in: a long hot soak for her abused muscles. But then she met Ward's eyes and an entirely different activity suggested itself. The gunslinger outfit—black on black—emphasized his muscled build. He looked strong and dangerous and all too virile, and it had been far too long since she'd felt a man's touch.

But it wasn't going to be this man touching her. Not now, not ever, no matter how much her body might plead otherwise.

Damn, why was her life so complicated? Why did she keep being attracted to men who were totally wrong for her?

She was now convinced that the reason David had fallen for her was that she'd been absolutely wrong for him since she symbolized everything his parents weren't. Rebellious, David hadn't been content merely to date her. The perfect way to thumb his nose at his parents had been to marry her, the proof their outrage at having their name connected with a Casari rather than a Cooke or a Campbell. But once the novelty of marrying her and the appeal of royally pissing off the elder Bradfords had grown old, David began to view their marriage as a prison. He'd broken free and never looked back.

It was impossible for her to know exactly how great a role his illness had played in the destruction of their marriage. Things had gone bad so quickly it was hard to believe he also hadn't experienced a change of heart—that when marriage no longer appealed, he simply decided to ignore the vows he'd uttered.

Ward wasn't like that. He obviously took his responsibilities seriously. But just because Ward might differ from David in terms of temperament, that didn't make him any more suitable.

She could console herself that at least with Ward she wasn't stupid enough to confuse basic physical attraction with any chance of a happily ever after. And while she might get twitchy and bothered any time she looked at him for longer than ten seconds, at least she saw his flaws—his bossy high-handedness—with crystal clarity. Surely that was progress.

All she had to do was carefully monitor the number of seconds she allowed herself to look at him and she'd be okay. She figured five was her max. Six and she might start trembling and quivering as everything went all warm and fluttery inside her. And she'd have to be careful not to let him stand too close, because then she'd be feeling a lot more than warm and fluttery. More like sizzling and aching.

She suddenly realized that that's exactly what had happened—that she'd been staring at him, drowning in his blue-green gaze, mooning over his lean cheeks that were now shadowed with the hint of stubble and thinking how they'd feel beneath her fingers.

Her own cheeks flamed red. Horrified that she'd been lost in a man trance for Ward, she made to grab the tray, a move Ward immediately blocked by holding it. She tugged and nearly growled in frustration when it wouldn't even slide a measly inch toward her. "Do you mind? The guests are waiting for their food."

"You've been relieved of duty."

"What? Are you nuts? I can't leave Gordon and Liz to handle the bar and the lounge by themselves."

"You won't. I've arranged for a replacement. Ah, here she is now. Took you long enough."

Tess spun around. Quinn was dressed in a clean white tuxedo shirt and slim-fitting jeans. Her hair was pulled back in a thick ponytail. This time she'd bothered with a brush. "Sorry. Had to wash up. All set and ready to serve, Roo."

"Then haul this tray out to—where are these guests sitting again, Tess?"

"They're sitting on the matching wingback chairs underneath the flower arrangement, the one with pussy willows—"

"The humungous one?"

"Yes. But really, Quinn, I can—"

"Got it. Off I go. Ta-ta for now. Say hi to Brian and Carrie for me." She lifted the tray and balanced it. The effort came with a grimace. "You must be stronger than you look, city girl. You're going to owe me, Ward."

"No, I won't. Get going before their iced tea melts."

"Yeah, yeah. What I do for love," she muttered before pushing through the swinging doors.

Tess turned to Ward. "That really wasn't necessary."

"Yes, it was. I don't want to keep Brian and Carrie waiting and the sooner we can get the ball rolling, the sooner we'll know how many additional guests their parents want to invite, which is the biggest headache logistically speaking and one that will affect not only the number of extra rooms you need to book, but the food and entertainment, too. And Quinn's just giving you grief. She knows she's supposed to lend a hand whenever and wherever. It's our job description."

Mr. Ward Knowles, High and Mighty Ruler of the World, was back, Tess thought with relief. If she could just focus on how much he annoyed her, surely she'd be able to ignore how attracted she was to the rest of him.

Chapter TEN

"WE'LL CALL BRIAN and Carrie from my office. I texted Bri earlier and told him to expect our call," Ward said.

"All right." Tess turned and exchanged goodbyes with Roo and Jeff and rattled off a few more pungent Italian oaths for Roo's ever-expanding vocabulary, and they left, Ward following her down the hallway lined with enlarged photographs of Silver Creek in the different seasons. The carpeting muffled the sounds of their steps and the light was soft, making Tess's white peasant blouse the brightest object in the space. Ward watched the metronome sweep of Tess's thick ponytail against the white cotton as she moved.

Damn, but she was a fascinating mix of contradictions, he thought. She possessed a lighthearted mix of spunky grit, intelligence, and humor. He'd seen it as she joked with Roo and Jeff and exchanged cheerful insults with the kitchen staff while whisking in and out of the kitchen with the energy of a V8 engine. But beneath her banter and can-do dynamism, Ward detected a deep well of reserve.

He wondered about it. Of course he knew about her husband. But he sensed there was more that pained Tess and that she guarded those secret wounds carefully. He wondered with whom she would share those secrets.

She obviously had guts. What had it been like for her to leave everything behind and come to a place like Acacia, where she knew not a soul? It made her sparkling cheerfulness that much more impressive. He couldn't help but be intrigued.

The genius of his mother's plan to set him up with Tess was increasingly clear. Better not to think about Tess's spirit, mind, or heart and what unknown events had shaped her. If he was to think about her, he should concentrate on the way she filled out her jeans.

Because Tess in a pair of jeans was a pretty damn fantastic sight. Though he appreciated her dresses and the fine view they offered of her legs, the jeans she'd opted to wear to serve tea hugged all her curves, right up to her truly excellent ass.

It was a good thing that he was behind her, so the view of her lush breasts offered by the scooped neck of her peasant blouse was hidden from him. Otherwise he'd be in danger of losing it altogether. Her butt was distraction enough. He imagined cupping those sweet cheeks and letting their weight fill his palms.

God, Cupid must be laughing his chubby head off. This was not how he'd planned to spend Valentine's Day, spinning erotic fantasies of Tess Casari.

Any further sexual daydreams vanished when he saw Tess reach behind to knead the small of her back with her fist. Again. The first time he'd caught the involuntary gesture (and no way would the Tess he knew ever willingly show vulnerability) was in the kitchen. That was when he'd decided she needed relief, pronto. The second she passed through the swinging doors, he'd whipped out his cell and told Quinn to get down to the kitchen on the double.

When Tess had returned, her tray was stacked with

dirty dishes. Yet still she moved with grace and managed to dredge up another Italian curse for Roo's entertainment. It was only when she slowed down long enough to scowl at his presence behind the stainless steel counter that he realized she was wearing the same sexy heels she'd had on earlier. The shoes did fine things for her legs but he couldn't imagine how she'd survived wearing them to serve high tea to a bunch of famished guests.

He'd probably be weeping from the pain.

Which had made him all the more determined to stop her from taking another tray out to the guests. Luckily Quinn arrived before he had to take any extreme measures, like tying Tess up. But he'd known by the snooty angle of Tess's cute little nose that she was not pleased with his tactics.

As if that was anything new.

In an effort to keep her distance, Tess had never ventured inside Ward's office. As it was she saw him whenever he dropped by Adele's office. Those encounters were unnerving enough. No need to tempt fate by stepping onto his turf.

Ward's office had a more modern feel than Adele's. Yet the pieces were made of beautiful open-grained woods instead of the typical glass-and-steel furnishings common to many contemporary décors. His desk was large and square, and Ward had positioned it at an angle so that when he was working he could look out the windows onto the gardens. Past the gardens and landscaped shrubbery Tess spied the stone walls that surrounded the outdoor swimming pool and the terraces where guests could sun themselves. Beyond that she could see a few of the one- and two-bedroom cabins, but really only because she knew they were there. The architect and landscape designer had done a brilliant job of making the structures nearly invisible. Walking along the winding paths and coming upon one of the cabins hidden by dwarf pines and other shrubs was a little like discovering a magical wooden fort.

From the room checks she performed with Adele, Tess knew the cabins' interiors were as appealing as their exteriors. Adele, who'd selected the furnishings for each guest room and cabin at Silver Creek, knew how to achieve an appealing rustic elegance in the quarters. Guests could sleep on cloudlike beds and soak in oversized tubs and never know that less than a quarter of a mile beyond, cows munched, sheep bleated, horses galloped about, and goats did whatever goats do.

If Tess were one of the ranch guests, she'd be happy to keep those critters forever at a comfortable remove.

Ward had walked directly to his desk to turn the computer on. "Take a seat while I get hold of Brian and Carrie."

For once she was happy to follow his commands. Wordlessly she sank into the carved wooden chair facing the desk. It was surprisingly comfortable. Then again, after the day she'd had, a rocky ledge would have felt like heaven. She wiggled her toes inside her shoes, but her feet screamed for more relief. Surreptitiously she eased them out of her shoes and nearly groaned aloud.

While Ward clicked computer keys she stole a quick peek at the strong lines of his face. As a guilty indulgence it was better even than the bite of the chocolate-covered strawberry she'd filched in the kitchen. Though Ward had gotten his hair cut, a lock of it fell across his wide brow at a rakish angle. He really was dreamy looking, she thought with a trace of wistfulness. Too bad he was Mr. Wrong.

She heard the miked sound of a man's voice and quickly shifted her gaze to a bronze sculpture of a horse running with its legs outstretched.

"That you, Ward?"

"Yeah, Brian. How's it going? Did you break the news to the families? I imagine there was much weeping on Carrie's side."

Tess's gaze slid back to Ward's face, which was now creased in an easy grin. He was even more handsome right now, happily joking with his friend. A pang of homesickness pierced her. She missed Anna.

Ward's friend laughed, then answered, "Surprisingly no. Carrie's dad didn't even threaten to drive up to Boston and run me off with a shotgun for presuming to ask for his daughter's hand."

"Miracles never cease."

"Yeah. I gotta tell you, bud, I've never felt so lucky. Or so happy. So, were Adele and Daniel okay with our having the wedding at the ranch?"

"I think we're going to be able to accommodate you."

"Fantastic news. Thanks, buddy. Hold on just a sec, Carrie's coming. She was in her study. Guess what she was reading up on today?" Tess hadn't even met Ward's friend Brian yet, but she could hear the grin in his voice. "The article was called 'Fluorescent Excitation of Spectral Lines and Close-Coupling.'"

"Of course it was." Ward laughed

"Awesome, huh? Admit it, I have the sexiest fiancée in the whole world. Hey, hon, it's Ward. He's got great news. We can have the wedding at Silver Creek."

"Oh, yay! I'm so excited. Hi, Ward!"

"Hey, Carrie. Listen, I've got someone I want you to meet. Her name's Tess Casari and she's our new events planner. If you guys hit it off, she'll be coordinating your wedding for you. Let me turn the monitor around so we can all see each other."

At his words, Tess ran a quick, nervous hand over her hair, which she'd pulled into a ponytail to serve the high tea. But her bangs, long though they were, hadn't stayed.

She fiddled with a thick lock, tucking it behind her ear. Then she made herself fold her hands over the notebook she'd grabbed from her office so she could take notes. She'd spent some of the morning jotting down ideas and making lists but still . . . what if she blew this?

Ward turned and must have seen the panic she was fighting back. "Relax. You'll be fine. You look fine, too."

She felt her eyes widen in surprise. He hardly knew her. How could he have any sort of confidence that she could handle the minutiae of organizing a destination wedding? And he thought she looked fine?

"Astrophysicist and political science junkie, remember? And they're both about as nice as can be." Dropping his long frame into the chair next to her, he flashed a smile at the computer screen, where Tess saw two people sitting on a sofa, holding hands, and grinning widely back at her.

Ward's deep voice was laced with amusement as he continued. "So, this is a little unusual, but Carrie and Brian, I'd like to introduce you to Tess Casari, my mother's right-hand woman and our new events planner."

She didn't want to admit that Ward had been right, but she took an instant liking to Brian and Carrie. They were a darned cute couple. Brian, with dark reddish hair and freckles and ears that stuck out just the teeniest bit, had the sort of boyish looks that made her want to grin right back at him. Carrie was equally appealing. Her gold blond hair fell past her shoulders and her large eyes were cornflower blue.

It was pretty clear from the way they sat squeezed together on the large sofa that they were over the moon in love. Before they'd even exchanged hellos, Brian had lifted Carrie's hand and kissed it. Tess didn't think he even registered the gesture.

She had never thought of herself as especially jaded,

but while the four of them were all roughly the same age, she felt about a thousand years older than Brian and Carrie.

But this meeting wasn't about her. So she shut the door on painful memories of how quickly her own giddy happiness at marrying the man she loved had turned into confused anguish and heartbreak, and injected every ounce of warmth and enthusiasm into her smile that she possibly could.

"Hi, Carrie. Hi, Brian. Congratulations on your engagement. I hope the two of you will be very happy together."

"Hi, Tess. It's so nice to meet you. Brian and I are so grateful that you'll be handling the wedding details. I already know that I'm going to love your ideas. If you work for Adele you've got to be good at your job. She's amazing, isn't she?"

"Yes, she is," Tess agreed. She drew a breath. There was no way she could do this job without being completely up front with Ward's friends. "But I think you should know right off the bat that I don't actually have experience in planning weddings on my own—"

"Not to worry, Carrie. Mom's giving Tess her files, which contain contacts and notes, and I'll be serving as Tess's second lieutenant. We'll make sure your wedding goes off without too many hitches."

Tess had noted an air of delicacy about Carrie. Combined with her enormous blue eyes and sweet disposition, certain men would probably scale mountains or act like Lancelot in her service.

Ward obviously fell into that category. It had taken less than three minutes for his protective impulses to be triggered.

Carrie beamed. "Whatever Tess and you do will be more than good enough for us, Ward. We just know having it at Silver Creek will make our wedding a beautiful and happy event, right, Brian?"

For an answer Brian kissed her hand again.

Tess stifled a sigh. These two lovebirds clearly had no idea how much planning—days and months of it—went into making an event "beautiful and happy."

"We'll do our best for you," she said. "I'll start on Monday to give us as much time as possible to make all the arrangements. So first off, I'm going to give you a little homework." Perhaps someone who spent her time studying galaxies would like the concept of homework assignments. "Do you have anything to write with that's handy?"

Nodding eagerly like the model student Tess assumed she'd been, Carrie reached for a notepad lying next to her on the sofa. Brian had leaned in the opposite direction. When he presented her with a pen, Carrie smiled as if she'd been given two dozen roses.

"Ready," she said happily.

"Okay. First, you're going to have to think about your wedding dress. Once we have an idea about its style, we'll be able to figure out what flowers would look best in your bouquet and in the floral arrangements."

Carrie glanced up from her notepad, her previous elation slightly dimmed. "I'm afraid I don't have a lot of fashion sense. Generally I ask Erica, my stepsister, to shop with me. She's got incredible taste."

"Well, I'm sure she'd love to go bridal gown shopping with you to help you choose the perfect dress."

Carrie's gaze shifted to Ward and an odd expression crossed her face. Tess wasn't sure but it seemed to contain equal parts worry and embarrassment.

"That's a fine idea," Ward said, which struck Tess as strange, because of course it was a perfectly fine idea for Carrie to ask a family member to help her find a wedding dress.

She cast a sideways glance at Ward. For once she could read him. The tight line of his jaw told her the casual reassurance he'd given Carrie masked something not so casual. Abruptly she recalled the comment Quinn had made earlier at the staff meeting about Carrie's step-sister being somewhat less than wonderful.

Well, she knew firsthand no family was perfect. Here was the first wrinkle to iron out. "Or, if you prefer, I can email you pictures of dresses I think would suit you along with the addresses of the shops where you can try them on. You can bring your phone with you when you go to the boutique. The salesperson will be happy to take your picture so we can decide together which one looks best on you."

"You'd do that—hunt down wedding dresses for me?"

"Of course. I love shopping."

"Really? I don't. I just get overwhelmed. Completely overwhelmed. Gosh, that would be so helpful. I only wish we could do the same thing with the food. We've been to some of our friends' weddings. The menu, the cake, it's all kind of beyond me. I'm not much of an eater. I mean, I eat—it's simply not that big a deal to me what the meal is. I'm not terribly sophisticated when it comes to food," she confessed.

"Basically, if the food at the wedding is better than what Carrie and I can cook, we'll be happy."

Carrie turned to Brian. "I'm not *that* bad."

"No, of course not. You do an excellent microwave." He grinned.

Okay. Her first wedding clients were the kind who zapped pizzas in their microwaves and pronounced them "delish." Ward had been right about Carrie needing guidance. Well, she could do better in that department than Giorgio Bissi, her old boss. He would either have rushed the computer on Ward's desk and started screaming that they were imbeciles or he would have simply gotten up out of his chair and stormed out of the room.

"Luckily, I like to eat almost as much as I like to shop," she told them with a smile. "Why don't you send me a list of the foods you like best—steak, lamb, fish, chicken—as well as your favorite vegetables and desserts. The wedding cake will probably be yummy no matter what combination of cake and filling you choose, but if you hate any particular flavor, let me know. Generally it's the design of the cake that people get worked up about. I'll take your preferences and brainstorm with Jeff and Roo, the chef and pastry chef at Silver Creek, or the caterer if we need to hire one, and design menus for the different meals. Will you be able to come out to California for a tasting?"

"I hope so, but we haven't had a chance to look at our schedules yet. We might manage a quick weekend."

"It'd be great if you could," Ward said. "Something tells me that we won't have that much time to hang out during the wedding weekend."

"We'll get to work on it then," Brian promised.

"Depending on how many people you invite we may have to arrange for an outside caterer. I'll ask Jeff and Roo to give me a number they feel comfortable working with." She jotted down a note to talk to them ASAP. "And we'll need an estimate of your numbers for printing the wedding invitations—and I'll be happy to help you choose the font and style," she said with a smile, already guessing that this would be another challenge for Carrie.

"Did your parents have an idea about the number of guests they'd like to include? We may need to reserve additional blocks of rooms in other local hotels and B&Bs," Ward said.

"I think we better reserve some extra rooms anyway. Some members of my family will need to be lodged as far apart as possible—my parents, for example," Brian said with a grimace.

"And your mom and stepdad, Carrie, have they got a big list?" Ward asked.

She sighed. "I'm afraid so. Once Mom got over the shock of our wanting to have the wedding at your place, she began counting the number of people who simply had to be included, so it's safe to assume we'll be more than the sixty Brian and I hoped for. I'll get our lists coordinated and email you the number as soon as I can."

It didn't come as a surprise to Tess that Carrie's mother was inflating the guest list. She must be so happy for her daughter. Tess checked her notes and saw another item she'd have to get busy on. "Have you made any decisions about your wedding party?"

Brian answered first. "I'd like to have Paul, my brother-in-law, and Reid as my groomsmen. Ward has agreed to be my best man. Always stepping in when I need you, bud."

Tess shot a quick glance at Ward. An embarrassed flush stained his cheeks. Who'd have thought Ward Knowles could blush? With an effort, she bit back her mirth and prompted, "And how about you, Carrie?"

"Well, I'd like Hannah and Grace—those are Brian's nieces—to be my flower girls. They're six and eight."

"That's a perfect age."

"They're adorable."

Tess smiled. "Even better. And for your bridesmaids?"

"Well, I'd like to have Brian's sister, Allie—she's Hannah and Grace's mom—be one of my bridesmaids."

Tess nodded and wrote down Allie's name. "Anyone else?"

There was a pause. "Well," Carrie hesitated, looking terribly uncomfortable. In a rush she continued, "Ward, I'm so sorry about this. But Erica called to wish Mom and Benjamin a happy Valentine's Day and so, of course, heard our news. Well, she immediately assumed that I would want her as my maid of honor, which is fine and doesn't really bother me except that I know how difficult—"

"I can handle it."

"Really?" She seemed to melt against the sofa cushions. Her relief was short-lived, however, for a frown appeared between her brows. "I'm embarrassed to admit it, Ward, but I'd been trying to figure out a way to avoid having her in the wedding party. I didn't want to make things hard for you. But, of course, I couldn't come up with one. If I ask Allie, then I have to ask Erica. It would hurt her feelings not to—"

"Don't fret, Carrie." Ward's voice had dropped a register, and Tess suddenly wondered how much practice he'd had at soothing females. Was this Erica one of them?

Okay, so she'd learned something here. This couple came with some interesting family dynamics. Brian's parents—divorced presumably—feuded and perhaps even erupted into full-scale war; Carrie seemed to have a sister who caused problems. Was she a drama queen? A bitch to end all bitches? It would be nice to know sooner rather than later so she'd be prepared to deal with any unpleasantness, but Carrie was unlikely to provide the necessary details.

The answers would have to wait for a little while. Until then, best to get back to the business at hand.

"Well, it's great that you've chosen your attendants. Once you select your wedding dress you can decide what style of dress you want for your flower girls and your sister-in-law and stepsister."

Carrie smiled weakly. "Erica will have a very definite opinion about what she wants to wear."

"Okay." Erica clearly intimidated her stepsister. But

Tess didn't like the idea of Carrie not having her preferences respected on her own wedding day. She decided that if she sensed Carrie was being bulldozed by Erica, she wouldn't hesitate to stand up for her client. What did she care if the stepsister didn't like her?

Obviously Ward wasn't alone in having his protective instincts roused by Carrie, she thought. Or maybe a part of her was rooting for this couple to have everything she hadn't had with David: a beautiful, special wedding followed by years of laughter and love.

She offered Carrie and Brian a bright smile. "I think we've covered the essentials for now. I'll be emailing you lots of stuff to look over in the next few days, and I'll be expecting lots of lists with preferences and ideas in return. You'll probably feel a little overwhelmed at first, but once you've decided on the major items, things will get easier." For them, at least. She'd have to hustle big-time to organize a wedding in such a short period.

She continued smiling as Carrie and Brian thanked her repeatedly, saying how awesome she was and how comfortable they felt with her already. She waited as they exchanged a few more words with Ward, and Brian promised he'd check his and Carrie's schedules for a free weekend. She closed her notebook and waited silently as Ward stood, went to the computer, and clicked the keys. The screen in front of them went momentarily blank, then a photograph appeared of the main lodge in summer, the front flower beds awash in color and the trees heavy with dark green leaves. Adele had the same screen saver.

She waited until Ward turned around. "So what's the deal with this Erica person?"

It would have been too much to hope for that Tess wouldn't pick up on the fact that any time Erica's name was mentioned everyone fell over themselves in apology, Ward thought with a resigned sigh.

Tess was not only perceptive, she was a careful listener. With Brian and Carrie she'd have been doubly attentive since she was trying to get a sense of them and their families. Even if Quinn's morning fumbling hadn't clued her in, Carrie had made it crystal clear that Erica was a touchy subject.

"Erica? Not a big deal at all. Carrie's just feeling a little awkward because Erica and I were engaged." If he spoke as if he wasn't bothered by having to address the subject then maybe they could talk about something fucking else.

Anything else.

"Excuse me? You were what?"

He crossed his arms. "You heard me. We were engaged to be married and then she decided it wasn't a good idea so she broke it off." He'd kept his voice level, and when he was finished speaking he gave her a long look, daring her to follow up.

Stupid of him to think she'd back down. "Are you kidding me? What in God's name are Brian and Carrie doing, asking to have their wedding here when you and Carrie's stepsister—"

He cut her off with a bored drawl so she'd understand how uninteresting the topic of Erica was. "Because Brian is my best friend and some of his happiest memories are linked to Silver Creek. And because, as I've said before, the fact that I was engaged to Erica really has no bearing on this situation at all. Now, if we're finished here, there are some pregnant lambs I should check on."

For a moment he thought she'd continue questioning him. To his immense relief she gave a short nod.

"I'm sorry if you thought I was prying. I'm simply trying to understand the dynamics of this wedding, which are turning out to be a *little* more complex than I'd expected."

"Everything will be fine. You were great with Carrie and Brian. I'm sure you'll figure out how to give them a terrific wedding celebration. Erica is not a factor."

The look she gave him was patently skeptical. He waited, expecting her to rise from her chair and leave his office, and was puzzled when she remained sitting. She'd never lingered in his presence before. He frowned at the perversity of women. Frankly he was tired of dealing with the opposite sex, and that included the ones he'd been involved with as well as the ones that, in his saner moments, he was trying to keep his distance from. He wanted to go check on the sheep and then go home and down a couple of ice-cold beers.

Then he caught her slight movement and finally understood. Naturally she was trying to hide it, wriggling in her chair as surreptitiously as she could. Slowly he let his gaze travel down the length of her jean-clad legs, past the bend at her knees, to follow the sharp angle where her feet were tucked under her seat and moving busily. Cocking his head, he grinned.

One of those feet was bare.

On impulse he dropped to one knee. Ignoring her squawk of surprise, he reached under the seat and located a leather pump hiding just beyond the chair's rear legs. For a moment he lingered, enjoying the fact that his head was maybe eight inches from her lap. Enjoying, too, that she was equally aware of his proximity to a very special place.

Easing his weight back slowly, he held up the shoe and regarded it. Damn, he thought. That was a hell of a heel. Arousal coursed a fiery path through his bloodstream.

He lifted his gaze. A very gratifying blush had stolen over her olive complexion. It was a stunning combination.

"I lost it. The shoe, I mean." Her voice held a breathless awareness.

What had he been thinking? This was way better than a cold beer.

He smiled. "Indeed."

"Can I have it back?" She held out her hand imperiously. The effect, however, was spoiled by the fine trembling that seized it.

"Certainly." His free hand slipped beneath the chair and snagged a delicate ankle. He tugged a resisting limb up and toward him. It was no contest. He'd had a lifetime experience wrestling cattle and sheep. One feisty, squirming Italian beauty wasn't going to deter him.

Holding her delicate foot in the cradle of his hand, he studied it gravely. Of course she wore nail polish the color of a full-bodied wine. Of course she had a fine, high instep that made him want to open his mouth and draw his teeth along the arch, made him wonder whether he could make her moan and her body tremble with the same desire that was spiking his blood. Damned if he wasn't tempted to bring said foot and the body attached to it tumbling into his arms with one good tug.

Because one good tug on that navy bow-tied ribbon would be all it would take to loosen the front of her peasant blouse. He wanted to see if her lush breasts tasted as sweet as he'd imagined.

He wouldn't have thought it possible, but his body grew even harder. And though he was fairly certain that if he applied himself, he could have a very gratifying moan tumbling from Tess's lips, he realized that, however tempting it was, this was not a good idea.

Carefully he brought the shoe to her purple-tipped toes and, raising his gaze to hers, slipped it carefully back on her foot. In a voice rough with suppressed need he said, "Happy Valentine's Day, Tess."

Standing, he forced himself to walk toward the door,

away from temptation. But he couldn't resist a backward glance. Yup, she looked amazing. Most of all he liked the stunned look on her face, as if his touch had rocked her world just as thoroughly as she'd rocked his. "You know, cowboy boots are a hell of a lot more comfortable. You might consider a pair."

If only for his own peace of mind, he added silently as he left the office, because he wasn't sure he could take much more of the infinitely tempting Tess Casari in her sexy-as-hell shoes.

Chapter ELEVEN

DAMN, DAMN, DAMN. The refrain had become a constant loop in Tess's head that she couldn't block for the simple reason that she couldn't stop thinking about Ward. That moment in his office when he'd held her foot in his calloused hand had packed a sensual wallop the size of Mount Everest, causing everything inside her first to seize tight and then to quiver as a fierce, reckless want consumed her.

All he'd done was hold her foot and now she couldn't stop fantasizing about the other places on her body she wanted his hands.

Worst of all, however, was the painful longing that had pierced her heart when he knelt before her and carefully guided her foot into her shoe as he wished her a happy Valentine's Day. It was ridiculous, she knew, but Ward, with that one casual, throwaway gesture, had made her feel like Cinderella when the prince placed the glass slipper on her foot.

It didn't seem to matter how many lectures she gave herself about no longer believing in fairy tales and not wanting to have anything to do with handsome princes. In that moment Ward had managed to resurrect the secret, silly, romantic longing she'd believed she'd vanquished: that one day she might be a princess in someone's eyes—loved, prized, and cherished.

After the debacle of her short-lived marriage, she'd been sure all that mushy sentimentality was a thing of the painful past. Ward's gesture made her realize just how susceptible she still was to those foolish hopes and desires.

She hated feeling vulnerable and off-kilter, with no one to confide in. As fond as she was growing of the Knowleses and her coworkers at the guest lodge—since she avoided going near the barns, she didn't really know any of the ranch hands—she could hardly discuss Ward with them, could she?

Besides, of all the Knowleses, she was closest to Adele. She couldn't talk to the man's mother about the devastating effect he had on her. Indeed, she couldn't mention Ward at all, not even to rag about his role in her car's demise anymore, if Ward was right about Adele indulging in a little matchmaking—a notion as crazy as any Tess had heard.

Ward was not the kind of man who needed any help in attracting a female.

Having no one nearby to confide in made her miss New York even more than usual. The haven of Anna's apartment, where she and Anna would curl up on the sofa and talk for hours, seemed farther away than ever. And with the time difference, scheduling their chats was tricky. They either had to talk at an ungodly predawn hour for Tess, or super late at night when Anna finished working at La Dolce Vita.

But with Anna she could get the whole Ward situation off her chest and thus hopefully succeed in getting him out of her mind. She only wished that when Anna gave one of her outrageous responses, she could reach across the sofa cushion and poke her in the ribs in rebuke.

Which was precisely what she would have liked to do

when Tess phoned Anna the following evening. First she brought Anna up to speed on how Adele had suggested she take over for Macie and that she plan Brian and Carrie's wedding with Ward's help. Then she told her about the FaceTime meeting and how it turned out that Ward had been engaged to Carrie's stepsister. She finished with her account of the shoe incident.

Anna had crowed with delight at the news that Tess was being given the chance to be Silver Creek's events planner and reacted with the same shock Tess had felt when she heard about Erica. But it was the shoe business she zoomed in on like a heat-seeking missile.

"Oh my God, Tess! I love that Ward got your juices flowing just by holding your foot. You know, I read this article about how erotic an experience it can be when a man makes love to your feet."

"He wasn't making love to my feet. He was just putting on my shoe!"

"Well, he was putting it on expertly, wasn't he? And just think how good it would have been if he had decided to nibble on your toes and lick your arches."

With a groan Tess dropped her head back against the pillows of her bed. But instead of the ceiling's wood panels, there, projected in high-def, she saw an image of Ward holding her naked foot in his strong hands. His chiseled features stern with intent, he drew her foot toward his lips. She tried to resist, but it was, of course, futile. As his mouth closed about her big toe, Tess was enveloped by fiery heat. Lavalike, it flowed through her as he sucked her sensitive flesh and then raked his strong white teeth over it.

She groaned again. "You are so evil."

Anna laughed. "I know. It's why you love me. But seriously, Tess, this is great. After the hell David put you through, making you feel like you were a failure on every level, you need a guy in your life who'll help you get your groove back. Why not Ward Knowles? He sounds like a good candidate. Remember that saying about if the shoe fits—"

"Not funny. Have you forgotten that his family owns a decent chunk of Northern California? A little out of my league—and I've already learned how well that works."

"But that's what makes Ward perfect. He isn't pretending to like you—he's just a guy who wants to play with those cute little toesies of yours and maybe a couple of other body parts as well."

"If your mother could hear the things you say—"

"She'd be at Mass every day and twice on Saturday. I know. Speaking of which, Mom saw yours yesterday after service let out. Yours was on her way to visit Chris and was bringing the flowers you sent. Mom said she looked pretty good. Less hollow eyed."

Tess hoped her mother's improved demeanor was because she no longer had to worry so much about whether she and her dad would be able to continue with Christopher's care. It would be nice to know she'd helped with that. There was so little they had ever let her do.

"That's good. It makes me feel a little less guilty for not being there to visit Chris with her."

"Which is ridiculous. You have to live your life, Tess. Your mom's great, and her devotion is remarkable, but the path she's chosen isn't one many would or could take. And though she may not say it, I don't honestly think she'd want you to make that sacrifice."

It was a conversation they'd had before. In her heart, Tess knew Anna was right, but that didn't make it easier to push aside the ever-present guilt that accompanied thoughts of her family.

"I miss you, Anna."

"Ah, sweetie, I miss you, too. But this is good. You're being challenged in all sorts of ways. I think it's high time you acknowledge that I was super brilliant in insisting you go to Acacia."

Tess snorted. "The jury's still out on that one, oh wise one. Tell you what, I'll send you some of Roo's organic jasmine tea so you can start reading leaves, too."

"You'll thank me one of these days, Casari. Tell Adele I'll hunt for one of those necklaces in a deep blue. It's nice to know someone appreciates me in California."

"Email me your mom's recipe for her crostata, and maybe I'll decide to forgive you for sending me to a place where most of the inhabitants walk on four legs."

"The critters are behind fences, right? Just stick to your side and all will be good."

"If you were in my shoes, you wouldn't be so sanguine. These aren't critters. They're beasts."

"If I were in your shoes, I'd be concentrating real hard on a certain two-legged male beast. Ciao, *cara*."

Tess was busy over the next couple of days helping Adele go through the rooms, public and private, looking for damages in the wake of Valentine's Day weekend and shadowing Macie to get up to speed on how events were planned at the ranch. Once she was done with those tasks, she searched the Internet for hours, bookmarking images of wedding dresses, bouquets, floral arrangements, and wedding invitations. When her eyes grew tired, she'd wander into the kitchen and brainstorm with Jeff and Roo about what dishes they could propose to Brian and Carrie for the different meals during the weekend of the wedding.

She had no idea why Ward, who was supposed to offer assistance, had chosen to pull a disappearing act. She was fine with not seeing him. Really. It was just that it might have helped to get a good, 100 percent obnoxious dose of the Master of the Universe version of the man. It would combat the scorching visions running through her head of him doing wicked and wonderful things to her feet and all points north on her body.

Ward's whereabouts remained a mystery until Reid happened to wander into her office. She was studying pictures of wedding dresses that might suit Carrie and had lined them up on the floor, her desk being too small a surface. After scouring the Internet she'd found twenty beautiful gowns that weren't outrageously priced and that Carrie could buy in Boston or New York. She'd already done a first edit, whittling down the number to fifteen, but her goal was to cut at least five more before she sent Carrie the attachments. She already knew that too many choices would overwhelm the bride-to-be.

The rap on her open door had her glancing up from where she was kneeling in front of the row of pictures. She was surprised at how disappointed she was to see Reid rather than Ward.

"Oh, hi," she said. She returned her attention to the pictures. Yes, that one could go, she decided, pulling it from the line. The dress was too severe and a bit too white for Carrie's complexion.

"What have we got here?" Reid stepped over the line of pictures to stand beside her. "You picked some good ones." He studied the dresses in silence for a moment, then squatted beside her and tapped his finger on the gown she'd placed in the center. "This is the one."

Okay, he'd picked the gown she herself had decided would look best on Carrie. The full-length strapless gown was fashioned in antique white, a soft, flattering color. Constructed with an overlay of lace and organza decorated with crystal sprig appliqués, it was floaty and romantic and would enhance Carrie's delicate beauty.

She looked at him accusingly. "You know, you are almost too perfect. You're good-looking, charming, and you have decent fashion taste." No way was she going to stroke Reid's ego even more by admitting the truth: His taste was excellent. "Are you some kind of alien or super cyborg?"

He grinned. "Sorry to disappoint, but no. I just happen to like women and have devoted myself to the study of them. In their clothes and out of them." He leaned close and dropped his voice to a confidential whisper. "If it makes you feel better, I have been known to leave the toilet seat up."

"Thank God. Now I can sleep at night."

He rose to his feet and held out a hand to help her up. They stood a moment, both looking at the pictures spread out on the floor. "Yeah," he said with a nod. "That's definitely the dress for Carrie, though I guess she would look pretty in a couple of the others, too." He leaned down and tapped three photos with same confidence he'd shown earlier. "The trick will be to get her to pick that one, though. Get Ward on it. He has a way with her."

She was beginning to suspect that Ward was as talented in getting his way with the opposite sex as Reid. She pushed the thought aside and culled four more photos of dresses that on closer inspection just didn't seem right for Carrie. "Your brother doesn't seem to be around."

Reid's normally carefree expression turned serious. "One of our ewes had difficulty lambing. Our foreman Pete was dosing a colicky horse with mineral oil and walking him in the corral so Ward dealt with the birthing. After Pete, Ward's got the best hands on the ranch."

Tess wasn't surprised to hear that.

"It was a tricky delivery—the ewe had stopped pushing—but Ward managed to draw both lambs out of her with no harm to mother or babes," Reid said.

"So sheep sometimes give up in the middle of labor?"

Reid nodded. "Yeah, when there's a problem or the lamb is really big. It was probably for the best that this ewe did stop pushing, since the lambs were twisted around each other. But Ward got them straightened out. Then, just when we thought we were in the clear, animal-wise, Mitchell, one of our wranglers, found one of our cows. Dead. Dad and Mitchell took samples. Ward's with them now, waiting for the vet to arrive. We hope he'll be able to determine the cause of death and rule out any infectious diseases. A dead cow is not a good day for us. We sure as hell don't want any more to die."

"No, I can't imagine you would," she said quietly. Though the Knowleses appeared to own a lot of cows and sheep, obviously having one of them die wasn't good. It would be awful if whatever had killed the cow affected the others.

"Anyway I came by to see whether you'd like to join us. Ward, Phil, and I are meeting with a marketing firm. They're pitching ideas about expanding our reach. Ward thought it might interest you since you're taking over Macie's responsibilities. Ward may be a bit late, depending on when the vet shows, but after the meeting you can tell him you've found a dress for Carrie."

"I'd be happy to join you, but I'm not going to add to Ward's workload by asking him to convince Carrie this is the dress for her. I can do that on my own."

Reid nodded. "Go for it. He was really pleased by how well you and Carrie got along. Brian and Ward are best friends, so in Ward's world that means it's his job to make Carrie happy."

"He seems pretty good at it." Then, succumbing to curiosity, she asked, "So what's the story with Brian and Carrie anyway? I would have thought they'd realize it's kind of awkward for Ward to host their wedding after Carrie's stepsister called off her and Ward's wedding."

"So you know about that."

"The weird way everyone acted whenever Erica's name was mentioned was kind of a giveaway," she said drily. "Of course, it didn't occur to me that she and Ward were once engaged."

"Ward's better off without her. Even Mom thinks so."

Tess couldn't hide her surprise. "If you all feel this way about her, that makes Brian and Carrie's decision awkward not just for Ward but for your whole family."

"We're just pissed on Ward's behalf. Seeing his heart get trampled by Erica wasn't pretty. But you don't have to worry about a thing. He won't let what happened affect anything to do with Brian and Carrie. He's too good and loyal a friend—to Brian especially—so if they want their wedding here with Erica as maid of honor, he'll make it work for them."

"Why? And what makes Brian such a special case?" She felt justified asking because she needed to understand the dynamics of a situation that involved the key players in the wedding. The fact was, however, she really wanted to know what made Ward tick.

"Ward almost got himself killed for Brian."

She stared in shock. "What?"

"It happened the fall of Ward's junior year of high school. Acacia's too small to have its own high school. The town where the district school was located was having problems with gang violence. Brian had just moved to the area so he didn't know what streets to avoid. Ward was driving home and saw the new kid—Brian and he were in the same class—surrounded by a group of toughs. They probably planned to mug Brian, which wouldn't have been hard since he was scrawny as a scarecrow back then, mainly freckles and bones. Ward jumped out of his car and ran over to try and prevent him from being beaten to a pulp, only one of the hoods had a switchblade, was high, and stupid as dirt. He freaked when Ward called out that the cops were coming. Instead of running he decided to take out Ward with his knife. Had it gone any deeper, Ward wouldn't be here today."

"My God. That's some story." She pictured a younger Ward lying on the sidewalk of some town and bleeding onto the pavement. With a shudder, she folded her arms tightly around her middle.

"Yeah. Ever since then, Ward's been Brian's protector. I guess almost dying for someone forges a damned strong bond. Then, too, Ward probably feels a little guilty because he's got a family who loves him. Brian's family isn't so great. When he moved here, his parents were going through a really ugly period. They divorced soon after. Brian ended up basically living here for the remainder of high school and college. He always says the time he spent at Silver Creek represents the best memories he has of his youth. And Carrie's family, though basically nice, has its difficult members."

Reid didn't need to say the name for Tess to understand he was referring to Erica.

"As I'm sure you've already figured out, Brian and Carrie aren't as strong as Ward—though not many people are. They're both incredibly kind and fun, and Carrie's sweet as anything, but they unconsciously lean on Ward because they know he won't let them down."

"He sounds like an amazing friend."

"Yeah, he is." Reid's voice rang with love and Tess knew a moment of envy that her own brother would never be able to speak of her like that. "So there you have it, the reason we're willing to risk annoying a lot of guests who booked their stay at the ranch just so Brian and Carrie can get married exactly when and how they want. We love them, sure. But we love Ward a whole lot more."

Reid checked his watch. "The guys from the marketing firm should be rolling up about now. Meet you in the conference room in a few?"

"Yes, sure," she answered distractedly, her head too full of what Reid had just told her.

She almost wished she hadn't learned about Ward's bravery or his generosity to his friend at his own expense. There were times—more and more of them—when she forgot the traits in his personality that had previously irritated her so thoroughly. She could no longer dismiss him as overbearing and arrogant when she now possessed a fuller and more nuanced portrait of him. One that was terrifyingly attractive.

He was proud and high-handed, certainly. But he was also caring. And he was one of the sexiest men she'd ever encountered—and she'd lived in New York, for Pete's sake. If she had even a dollop of sense she'd be even more cautious around him. A man like Ward was too dangerous.

Chapter TWELVE

WARD COULD HARDLY walk into a business meeting with the sweaty muck of birth and death ground into his jeans and skin. In addition to avoiding the long commutes on congested highways like so many in California, being able to grab a quick shower when he needed it was another perk of living where he worked. The pelting hot water did more than wash off the dirt. It helped ease some of his black mood at having lost a cow. But it didn't lessen his impatience to hear the lab results, and Gary Cooney, their vet, had left only a few minutes ago.

Dressed, he jogged to the barns. Quinn was in the lambing pen with Holly, both women holding the ewe that had delivered the twin lambs so that the smaller one could nurse. The stupid thing had yet to accept it. She kept running it off whenever it approached her udder.

"How's she doing?" he asked.

Her arms locked around the ewe's shorn and wriggling body, Quinn grimaced. "She's still rejecting it. I vote to bring Sooner in here. He'll teach her to care for her babies in a hurry." Sooner was Quinn's sheltie. Another of her rescues, the dog had come to her because its owners hadn't quite understood that herding dogs, even the ones with the silky coats and cute ears, liked to herd more than they liked to sit cooped up in apartments twenty-three hours out of twenty-four. The sheltie had originally been named Cookie, but Quinn had changed it to Sooner as he tended to find a herd and hold it sooner rather than later.

Ward eyed the struggling sheep. Damned if he was going to save her lambs only to have her starve one of them. "Fine by me. Frank getting the van ready?" he asked Holly.

Holly was holding the newborn lamb and had her head pressed against the sheep's flank, the better to see that the newborn was actually latched on to its mother's teat and suckling.

"Yeah," she replied, her voice muffled. "He and Quinn are leaving for the rescue shelter at two."

"So if all goes according to plan and the horse loads well, we should be back at four P.M. I can't wait for him to see his new home, Ward."

He nodded. "If I'm not around, ask Pete to make sure the corral is free so the horse can have a chance to acclimate. Okay, I'm officially late for this damned meeting, which means I have about thirty seconds before Phil starts texting. If you need me—"

"Unless you can speak sheep we don't need you," Quinn said with a grunt as the ewe struggled to free herself. "Go. But tell Mitchell to send Sooner in here."

Meetings like today's were a necessary evil. Ward far preferred executing the ideas that came out of them than sitting and listening to some PowerPoint presentation. So he wasn't too distressed at being ten minutes late—Reid could fill him in if anything important had been addressed.

Much to his surprise, the meeting hadn't even started

yet. He entered the conference room to find the two guys from the Porter Consulting Group, a marketing firm based in San Francisco, chatting casually with Phil while Reid stood over by the window, talking on his cell. Ward went over to shake hands with Ted Dulchek and Michael Parenti and to make it clear they could start without further delay.

"Oh, we're waiting for Tess. I sent her to get us some coffee and biscotti. Might as well take advantage of her area of expertise," Phil told him with a faint smirk.

Excusing himself, Ward crossed the room to where Reid stood. His conversation finished, Reid slipped his cell into his jeans pocket. Ward cocked an inquiring eyebrow at his brother.

"I know." Reid turned back toward the window so his voice wouldn't carry. "Sending off the only woman in the room is a dumbshit move. Here's my take on it. Phil's been watching too many episodes of *Mad Men*—the early ones. It's also possible he's engaging in a power play. You know how touchy he can be. I'm guessing his nose is out of joint because he didn't get to have any input in choosing Macie's replacement. But before I could countermand him and simply call Roo to have her send some coffee and cookies in, Tess was up and out of her seat. She's got that New York power walk down."

Yeah, Ward had witnessed how much ground her stride covered. Those legs worked. "Phil better get over his pique. I don't want to lose her." Ward spoke just as quietly despite the fact that he was good and pissed. "So, do you want to have the pleasure of telling Phil to get his head out of his ass or shall I?"

"Though I know how much you would enjoy the process, it'd better be me since I was an eyewitness to his idiocy."

"Good point. Remember to mention that there are sexual discrimination laws in the workplace."

"No worries."

"If only." He massaged the back of his neck and realized he'd neglected to towel dry his hair. The top of his collar was damp. "Dad and Pete are out checking the rest of the herd for any signs of illness."

"Yeah, Mom told me. I was just speaking to her. She hasn't heard anything from Dad. Gotta hope no news is good news, but I'll saddle Sirrus and ride out after I tell Phil to grow up."

"I'd tell you to go now, but you're the expert on equine tourism. They may have questions about our competition."

"At least we can start now. Tess is here." Reid nodded in the direction of the door. "Oh, while we're on the subject, Tess, efficient as always, has found some terrific dresses for Carrie. One's a gem. She might need help getting Carrie to recognize which one it is. I suggested she enlist your help, but she told me she wasn't going to bother you. I figured you'd want to know."

As soon as Reid had pronounced her name, Ward pivoted, his eyes seeking her out. She was rolling a trolley laden with a coffee carafe, cups and saucers, and a plate of Roo's biscotti into the room.

"You thought right. I'll drop a heavy hint in Carrie's ear. It'll cross one item off Tess's lengthy to-do list. Now if we could only pin down the number of guests Carrie's parents are adding to the list." He could have been speaking Swahili or gibberish for all he knew or cared. Every particle of his being was focused on Tess.

Forty-eight hours had elapsed since he'd seen her, since he'd cradled her slender foot in his hands. Yet it took only one long, sweeping look; today she'd pulled her hair back in a bun and was wearing a fitted orange and purple top and a slim beige skirt with her ever-present high heels. And damned if desire didn't slam him with the force of a two-thousand-pound bull when he recognized them as the very same shoes he'd slipped back on her delectable foot on Valentine's Day.

He walked over to her. "Thank you for bringing the coffee."

Her gaze met his and, to his infinite pleasure, a blush stole over her cheeks. "I, uh, figured you might need a jolt of caffeine. Reid told me about the cow. I'm sorry."

He couldn't help but be pleased that he'd been on her mind, especially when thoughts of her preoccupied him so often. "I appreciate it. And I'm glad you came to the meeting. I'll be interested to hear your ideas."

The flush on her cheeks deepened. "I doubt I'll have any. I haven't been here that long."

He'd come to know one thing about her: She rose to challenges. It was discovering the bits and pieces of her character—her strength, her intelligence, her sense of humor, even her careful reserve—that attracted him even more than her temptress looks. With each discovery, Ward wanted to uncover more of her secrets.

"That's why your ideas will be interesting. You've been here long enough to observe how things are done and yet you're still new enough to detect areas for improvement." He smiled as he threw down the gauntlet.

They settled into their seats with their coffees and stared at the projection screen. Within minutes it became clear to Ward that the central theme of the pitch, complete with the requisite slick graphics, charts, and tables, was that the key to success lay in increasing traffic to the guest ranch's website. Phil, in addition to earning the "Dick of the Week" award, was also a numbers geek. Nothing made him happier than staring at pie charts. He listened to the presentation with a beatific expression, nodding sagely, smiling, and then nodding some more. Tired and annoyed, Ward had a sudden vision of Phil stuck on someone's dashboard, an executive bobblehead. Nope, it wouldn't sell, because Christ, who would want to buy something so boring?

It went without saying that using social media to expand their reach was vital in this day and age. But surely his family needed to do more than simply commission a photographer/videographer, make their website as easy to navigate as possible, and then remember to hire the Porter Group to write some excellent ad copy for them, Ward thought.

He reached back to rub the tense muscles of his neck. So far nothing in the presentation was making him optimistic about increasing occupancy and revenue. On the verge of interrupting Michael Parenti, who was presenting this segment of the pitch, Ward caught himself as a new slide flashed onto the screen. The header read: "Definitive Content: Educate Your Guests and Tell Your Story. Be Unique."

All right. Now they were talking. "Anyone have thoughts on the best way to educate our guests about what makes Silver Creek Ranch special?" he asked.

"Well, that would be in the ad copy we'd put on the website," Phil said.

"I don't think that's enough. We need a more dynamic medium." It was small of him, Ward knew, but he was happy to shoot Phil's answer down. He was still royally pissed at the way Phil had treated Tess.

"You might want to consider expanding your social media presence to Facebook and Twitter," Michael said.

Phil's expression turned mulish. "Twitter? What, do I look like Justin Bieber?"

Ward heard Reid mutter something under his breath about both Phil and Bieber. It was safe to assume the comment was not flattering to either man. Then he glanced at Tess. She was busy writing on her notepad. While she might know zip about ranching, she had worked in the service industry in New York City. He was willing to bet she was a little more clued in than Phil. "So what media would you choose, Tess?"

She didn't hesitate. "Definitely Facebook and Twitter, and I'd also consider Pinterest."

"Pinterest isn't a serious revenue driver," Michael said.

"Maybe not. But you're looking for ways to show how unique Silver Creek is, right? Pinterest allows you to create great boards. You could make a collage of all sorts of things that make Silver Creek Ranch a wonderful place to visit, whether it's the cabins, Roo's pastries, the animals, that sort of thing." Tess shrugged. "Then it's a question of people repinning, just as they might retweet."

"And how do you feel about Twitter?" Reid asked her.

"Well, I've noticed you and your family don't spend a lot of time looking at your cellphones, but a lot of the rest of the world does. Tweets are easy to blast out and can cover a lot of different topics in a day."

"So, better than blogs in that respect?"

"Well, there's that guy who did the *Waiter Rant* blog awhile back, which was pretty entertaining, but that's not what you're looking for. Twitter and Pinterest are also cheaper than print advertising—not that you want to give up the glossy magazines," she added with a glance at Phil.

Score another point for Tess, Ward thought with a dose of pride. She'd noticed Phil's addiction to *Condé Nast Traveler*.

"Okay, so Twitter, Pinterest—these are definitely things we're going to want to investigate to expand our clientele base," he said.

Michael cleared his throat. "But unlike the website, where you can have someone manage it, those two media work best if you have someone on the premises handling them."

"We'll find someone." Already Ward was figuring out how best to approach Tess with the idea that she be in charge of tweeting news about the ranch and posting images on Pinterest.

It occurred to him that his mother must have been just waiting for the opportunity to promote Tess. Like him, it would have taken her only a couple of days to appreciate her smarts. And she would have realized, too, that this quality would make Tess a lot more interesting to him than the other women she'd selected in her matchmaking efforts.

He had to give credit where credit was due. His mother had hit the jackpot. Tess was a hell of a woman: sexy and intriguing. The question was whether it would be smart to pursue this growing fascination. A better question was whether he cared about being smart.

Michael clicked to the next image. This one read "Develop Appealing Special Offers and Update Them Regularly."

Catchy, real catchy, Ward thought. Good thing the ad copy these guys wrote was better than their PowerPoint headers.

It was Ted Dulchek's turn to speak. "We're aware of the inroads you're making with respect to special promotions. Phil told us what a success Valentine's weekend was and how you've already received rebookings from it. The challenge will be to create special offers during nonholiday, off-season periods."

"Some of the guest ranches offer themed stays. Cowgirls' weekend, tours of local wineries, and the like," Reid said. "I'm building a relationship with several of the local wineries to see whether we can work out a mutually beneficial package—something along the lines of a weekend stay here and enology courses."

Ted nodded. "Both of those could certainly appeal to an important target audience. Women love the idea of getting away with their girlfriends and doing something different, like taking a course in wines. I'm sure learning how to be a cowgirl for a weekend . . ."

Tess had just finished drawing a box around the words "cowgirls' weekend," ready to write down whatever ideas Ward and Reid might fire off about what such a package might include—other than lots of women, horses, and, well, ropes and stuff, when she realized that five pairs of eyes were focused on her. "What? I mean, excuse me. Did someone say something?" She took care to avoid looking in Ward's direction in case she got distracted by the way his damp hair curled at the ends.

The corners of Reid's mouth had lifted. "As the only woman present, you'll have to be our resident expert. How would you feel about you and your best friend coming here for a cowgirls' weekend?"

She nearly choked on the horrified laugh that threatened to erupt. As if she and Anna would ever want to spend a weekend pretending to be cowgirls. She pressed her lips together until they hurt. Even then it took a few seconds before she could trust her mouth to speak.

"Uh, the wannabe cowgirl thing isn't exactly my cup of espresso, if you know what I mean, but I'm sure there are plenty of other women who might enjoy it"—next time she went to church she'd confess for that whopper of a lie—"especially if you included a deluxe spa package, and I mean the works, and convinced Roo to do a dessert night where she invited the women into the kitchen and offered some baking demonstrations. Oh, and there'd have to be dancing and drinks." With those extras, if a girl like her was shanghaied into such a ridiculous event, she wouldn't find it a total loss. If the girl had any brains, she might even figure out how to avoid getting on the back of a horse entirely.

Her answer had caused Ward to cough loudly, forcefully.

Okay, did she care that he now realized beyond a shadow of a doubt that she had no clue what cowgirls liked to do—except maybe find handsome-as-sin dark-haired cowboys with gold-flecked eyes—which, by the way, wasn't exclusive to cowgirls?

It was strange to discover that the answer was *yes*. She did care what he thought. What had happened to her determined disdain? Had hearing about his rescue of Brian and seeing firsthand how generous he was with his friends obliterated it? That was reason enough for her change in attitude but she worried there was more to it than that.

Luckily she had no chance to analyze her feelings further for Reid spoke. "Your version of a cowgirls' weekend is"—his face split in a wide grin—"a tad unorthodox, but actually that might work to our advantage. It'd be a distinctly unique take on the theme. We would stand out from the other guest and dude ranches. What do you think, Ward?"

Oh Lord, now she was going to have to look at him. Her pulse quickened.

Ward's expression was enigmatic. He was not a man she'd ever want to play poker with, especially when her thoughts kept circling back to what it would feel like to thread her fingers through the damp, silky thickness of his hair. She'd lose the shirt off her back to him within minutes—and wasn't that a disturbingly appealing image?

Blindly she reached for her coffee cup to hide behind, lowering it only when she heard him say, "Phil, how about getting to work figuring out when we can fit a cowgirls' weekend into the calendar? Tess, would you mind consulting with Quinn on this? Between the two of you, I bet you'll come up with a terrific package."

Good grief. Now she was going to have to hold her own against Quinn, cowgirl extraordinaire.

Chapter THIRTEEN

THE MEETING BROKE soon after. Ward thanked Michael Parenti and Ted Dulchek for coming out to Silver Creek and asked them to draw up an estimate for revamping the ranch's website. Then he turned to Phil.

"Would you and Reid mind seeing Ted and Michael out? There's something Reid wants to go over with you before he rides out to check on the cattle. I need to talk to Tess about Brian and Carrie's wedding."

Tess, who'd been quietly sidling out of the room, stopped in her tracks and tried to remember how to breathe. Oh Lord, she was going to be alone with Ward.

"Really, I can handle this on my own." She hoped the asperity in her voice masked the fact that her pulse was beating triple time. Somehow, despite her repeated assurances, Ward had marched her back to her office, a small space that had shrunk two sizes now that he was standing in it. When she breathed she caught the soapy clean scent of him. It was making her lightheaded, and she was terrified she might say something irrevocably stupid, like, "Goddamnit, kiss me."

Indifferent to her condition, Ward stared down at the row of dresses spread out on the sisal rug. "Of course you can. But the sooner we get Carrie to choose her wedding gown, the sooner we can move on to the attendants' dress. So, which one is it? This one?" His booted foot pointed to the one Reid had also unerringly chosen.

It was ridiculous. Was there something in the Acacia water or the vegetables they grew at Silver Creek that was the reason both Knowles brothers possessed good looks and fashion sense? She crossed her arms over her chest and, bristling with defensiveness, demanded, "So why that one?"

"It's romantic. All that poufy stuff will look good on her."

"That's tulle," she said, happy to be able to tell him something.

He arched a brow. "Tulle, burlap, whatever. It works." He checked his watch. "Carrie'll be home from the university by now. Let's call her." His tone was brisk and all businesslike as he pulled out his cellphone, so she nearly dropped the photocopies she'd gathered up from the floor when he said, "So your wedding dress, did it look like one of those?" He nodded to the papers fluttering in her hand.

Overcompensating, she tightened her grip and felt the papers crease. With an effort, she made herself relax. "My wedding dress?"

His thumb paused to hover over the keypad of his cell. "Yeah, what was yours like?"

"I, uh, just wore a pretty dress. David and I were married at city hall."

He looked surprised. "Oh. I'd have thought you'd go for that sort of thing—"

Sadness pierced her that David hadn't understood that about her, or perhaps hadn't cared. Yet Ward, who knew her far less well, already did.

"We eloped. There was no need for anything formal."

He nodded. Perhaps it was because she sensed he

didn't intend to pursue the topic or press her for answers that she suddenly felt compelled to explain. "David and I decided it would be better if we skipped a church ceremony and save my parents the expense."

"I'm sure you took his breath away."

It was she who was robbed of breath. The quietly uttered compliment took her completely by surprise. Luckily she didn't have to respond. Ward had raised the phone to his ear. His stance relaxed, his expression calm, he betrayed none of his thoughts. But she wasn't stupid. She knew he was fully aware that she'd just revealed more about herself in the last five seconds than she had in the past six weeks.

She didn't have the time to worry or obsess about what he might think of the insight he'd gained, however, because Ward began speaking.

"Hey, it's me. Yeah, everything's fine here. Listen, is Brian there? Out at the gym? No, that's perfect. I don't want him barging in. Guess what—Tess has been searching high and low for wedding dresses and thinks she's found some you'll really go for. Yeah, we only hire the best. Care to open your computer? She's sitting down to send them to you as attachments. Once you've got them up on your screen, Tess can fill you in . . ."

It took only twenty minutes for Ward—with a few carefully inserted suggestions from her—to help Carrie winnow the dresses down to five and drop the subtle hint that the frothy lace and tulle one was extraspecial. "Tess, Reid, and I think you might just look as stunning in it as one of those galaxies you study, kiddo."

And she'd thought Reid was the one with the silver tongue. It was just one more opinion about Ward she'd have to revise.

"You'll know which is the gown that's perfect for you when you slip it on," Tess said.

"I can't wait. This wedding stuff is far more fun than I ever dreamed it would be. Of course, that's largely thanks to you, Tess. And you, too, Ward, for providing Tess as our planner and for giving us such a beautiful place to hold the wedding. I can't wait to call my mom and see if she can drive up to Boston so we can go shopping on the weekend. Oh! I have some good news: Our minister said he'd be happy to fly out and perform the ceremony. He's such a great guy. And Mom said she'd send me the list of guests she and Dad want to add tomorrow. She says it probably won't top forty but she simply must invite them." As she pronounced the word "must," Carrie raised her hands to make twin air quotes. "Since it's a destination wedding she's sure that many of them will decline."

Both Ward and Tess smiled, remaining scrupulously polite rather than voicing their skepticism. Destination weddings were sometimes a great draw, with the guests deciding to expand the wedding event into a longer vacation trip. In her excitement over the dresses she'd selected to try, Carrie didn't notice their silence. "And Mom and Dad think Brian and I should come out to Acacia and meet you, Tess, so we can go over all the wedding details together. My dad is giving us his miles. I'm so happy," she said and laughed.

"That's terrific. It will give us a chance to make lots of decisions." Tess's mind was already whirring as she compiled a mental list of the essential items she could have them decide on during the visit: the photographer/videographer, the makeup artist and hairstylist, the floral arrangements, and the wedding cake and menu tasting—essentials that couldn't be properly considered talking over the phone or using FaceTime.

But there was one topic she could address now. And

the sooner she got the specifics down, the sooner she could draft the wedding invitation to send to Carrie and Brian for their approval.

"I did want to float one idea I had," she said. "I looked up the lunar calendar and it's supposed to be a full moon on that Saturday. I thought it might be nice if you chose to have the dinner and dancing alfresco. Dancing under the stars with your husband might be a lovely way to celebrate the start of your and Brian's new life together."

"Dancing with Brian under a full moon after we've just said our vows? I think I'm gonna cry."

Tess smiled and made a mental note to stock boxes of Kleenex in preparation for Carrie's visit to Silver Creek. "So do you think you'd like to schedule the wedding ceremony for five in the afternoon?"

"Yes, and I'm sure Brian will love the idea. If we have it at five o'clock we don't have too long a wait to start celebrating. Brian does love a party."

"Well, just let me know as soon as you can so I can create a mock-up of the wedding invite for you. The invitations need to go out ASAP."

"Yes, ma'am," Carrie replied, saluting. "Mom's going to love you."

They said goodbye shortly after that so Carrie could call her mother with the news about the dresses.

"You handled that like a pro, Tess."

Feeling the weight of his gaze on her, Tess busied herself closing the windows of her computer, staring at the vanishing icons as the screen went blank as if in wonder at such a sight.

"Well, it'd be kind of pathetic if I had no aptitude for my self-professed dream job. And don't breathe easy yet—there's still plenty of opportunities for a screw-up of epic proportions." She certainly didn't plan to make one, though.

"Duly warned. At least I can rest easy knowing I won't

have to take Brian out for a midnight ride when he finds out Carrie's pregnant with his best buddy's—his ex-best buddy's—child."

"Huh?" Then, remembering the staff meeting where Quinn and Reid described one of the previous horrible weddings they'd had to host—or police—she said, "Yeah, you should be spared that fun."

"Speaking of fun, I was wondering whether you'd like to be responsible for doing the tweets and Pinterest board."

She rose from her chair, fighting the urge to jump out of it. "I don't think that'd be such a good idea."

"Hmm. Why not?" With a lazy kind of interest he watched her pace the confines of her small office.

"Because to do it right, you need people like you or Reid or the guys who work on the ranch to take pictures. It shouldn't be just the guest lodge." She paused. "How about Quinn?"

"Not a good risk. Can't trust her not to tweet something totally inappropriate."

Damn. She knew that. The first time she'd met her, Quinn was wearing a shirt that had "There are more horses' asses than horses in the world" emblazoned across it.

"At least she knows something about the ranch—"

"Moreover, Quinn would lose interest in tweeting in about three days, max. In case you haven't noticed, we're not that technologically oriented a family."

"Well, what about one of your hands?" She really did not want to take this job on.

He cleared his throat. When he spoke, his voice was all patience. "The thing about ranch hands is that they're generally using them—so it would be kind of unreasonable to expect them to carry around iPhones so they could type texts and snap pictures."

"See, I didn't know that. That just shows you how ill-suited I am." A bit of a stretch, but she wasn't going to let go of that line of argument. It was her lifeline.

"One of the best ways to learn is by doing."

So said Mr. Cowboy–Business Executive–Ranch Heir, she retorted silently. She didn't have to say yes, she told herself.

"Out of curiosity, is there a reason you don't want to do the job?" he asked.

"Other than the fact that overseeing the event planning for Silver Creek and handling Carrie and Brian's wedding is already pretty time-consuming?"

"The tweeting one hundred and forty characters and taking pics would take maybe half an hour out of your day—"

"Which is not an insignificant chunk of time when I'm organizing a destination wedding. And if we're exchanging philosophies here, buster, I'd argue that everyone has their area of expertise. Mine doesn't cover the great outdoors and four-legged creatures. I have no interest in taking pictures of sheep and cattle." Her lofty tone told him he could stick that in his pipe and smoke it.

His slow, knowing smile had her stiffening. "I get it. You're scared of animals."

Scared spitless, but darned if she was going to admit that. "Don't be ridiculous. I just don't know much about them. Not everyone grows up surrounded by animals that bleat and moo, you know." Or have really big hooves, she added silently.

He cocked an eyebrow. "What about ones that woof and meow? I know you lived in the city, but didn't your family even have a dog or a cat?"

"We couldn't. Chris—"

She stopped. Being in Ward's company was turning into a bare-your-soul fest, except it seemed like she was doing all the baring.

"Chris? Who's that?"

All right. Maybe this would shut him up. Better still, maybe the pitying look she'd seen on so many other faces would steal over his and she would be the one to stop talking. She quit her pacing and turned, watching him as she presented the bald facts. "My older brother, Christopher, suffers from severe autism. In his case it presents with frequent, uncontrolled outbursts. When Christopher still lived with us, my parents—my mom principally, since Dad was at work for most of the day—couldn't risk having a pet for fear that Christopher might have an episode near the pet and it would react by trying to defend itself."

"I'm sorry about your brother. I've read that sometimes animals can help people afflicted with autism."

Her nod was more a jerk of the head. "I know. Some patients at Chris's facility get visits from therapy dogs. They tried with him, but it had the opposite effect. He becomes severely agitated. If Chris gets upset for too long, it gets kind of intense and not in a good way, and he has to be given extra medication, which no one wants." She realized that at some point in her explanation she'd folded her arms across her middle. Her fingers were digging into her elbows. She made herself relax her hands.

"Your brother's condition must have been rough on your family."

"Yeah. Sometimes early detection and therapy can really help, though even then it's a question whether as adults they'll be able to live independently. Unfortunately with Chris he'll never be able to live outside an institution. But at least he's in a good facility and it's close enough for Mom to visit him every day. When Chris was still at home, keeping him safe was a full-time job for her. Now she can help Dad a little with the bookkeeping for his construction company. It's a tiny operation, but still." She shrugged. "So to make a long story short, the only animal I got to know as a kid was the Angottis' dog, Caesar. I don't know what kind he was. He looked like a dirty mop with teeth. Caesar used to hide behind a bush in the front yard, lying in wait as I walked to and from school. Every day, he'd race out, those sharp teeth bared, and try to bite me."

"We don't have any dogs of that description on the ranch."

"That's good, 'cause that was one nasty, vicious beast. He made Dracula look friendly."

A grin pulled the corners of his mouth. "Listen, I really want you to do the Twitter/Pinterest posts. I think you could make them fun and appealing, and generate interest in the ranch. How about we make a deal? You do the tweets and take the snapshots, and I'll look around for a decent used car—one that won't catch fire after a few thousand miles."

A car. It would liberate her from those hellish taxi rides with Ralph Cummins. The prospect was so enticing she ditched any snarky replies that contained "car killer" in them. "How about you just give me the money and I find my own car?"

"Nope. I'll do the looking. You seem to know as much about automobiles as you do animals—barely enough to fill a thimble."

He didn't seem fazed when she narrowed her eyes.

"So, how about it? You do the Twitter stuff; I'll put out some feelers out and find you a decent car."

When she still hesitated, he added, "I'll owe you big-time, Tess."

"Oh, all right," she said with a show of reluctance so that he wouldn't think she was the world's softest touch.

"Thanks. So, we better get you acquainted with the ranch and its creatures large and small. Let's start with the least scary animals imaginable—the newborn lambs. Before you know it we'll have you roping steer. Come on."

She gaped at him. "What, you mean now?"

"No time like the present." His grin was cheerful and, she thought, evil. "I'd recommend changing into some jeans, though. You want me to pick you up at your cabin?"

"No! No," she repeated somewhat less hysterically. The last thing she wanted was to have Ward filling her cabin with his presence. "I'll meet you down at the, uh, barn."

"Barns," he corrected. "The sheep are in the smaller one on the right. See you in a few."

"Yeah, in a few," she echoed weakly. Oh God, she thought. This was going to be a mistake. A big mistake.

Chapter FOURTEEN

A STRANGER IN a strange land, that's what she was. Tess was on foreign ground. Literally. She had never stepped on a floor covered with inches of straw before, never inhaled the scents teasing her nostrils. She guessed they must be some combination of hay, wool, and manure, this last ordinarily sufficient to revolt her, yet for some reason she didn't find the scent offensive, just odd. Certainly it was no worse than being passed by a New York garbage truck at high noon during the month of August when the temperatures climbed into the triple digits and the stench of rotting refuse was strong enough to make one's head spin. Nor was it worse than descending into the bowels of New York and stepping into a crowded subway car full of perspiring bodies. As for the sounds, well, of course, she'd heard them before, but only on TV when she was channel surfing and happened to venture into Animal Planet territory or other stations where nature programs could be found. But the exchange of these lambs' tiny bleats, answered by the lower, longer ones of their mothers, was like listening to a fascinating if indecipherable conversation.

She loitered just inside the half-lit barn, staring at the different wooden pens that divided the space. Lambs and sheep slept in some of them; in others the lambs were half-buried under their mothers' bellies, nursing while the sheep systematically picked at hay out of a feeder—Tess had no idea whether there was a specific name for the contraption. Once again, Ward's notion that she should be the one tweeting about the ranch's goings-on struck her as pure, unadulterated craziness.

"There you are. Come over here. I'll introduce you to the newest members of our flock."

With a start, Tess looked over to one of the pens at the far end of the barn. She had assumed Ward was elsewhere, doing something in another barn. Only now did she realize that he'd been crouching in one of the pens, tending to a lamb or sheep.

Though his features were indiscernible in the darkened interior, the amusement that laced his voice was clear. "I'll be right next to you to protect you from the wee vicious beasties."

"Ha. So funny," she muttered.

She never should have told him about Caesar, the four-legged fascist. She picked her way carefully toward him. She'd changed into shiny patent leather boots that had the distinct advantage of being waterproof so she could wipe them down once she was safely back inside, but she still didn't mean to get them covered with sheep droppings.

"Climb over the rail." He held out a hand. Unthinkingly she grasped it, and the heat of his calloused palm transferred to her and spread until she felt hot and bothered all over. The man was an inferno, she thought dazedly. Suddenly she pictured not only his large hand engulfing hers but his naked body wrapped about her, and more heat flowed through her, as unstoppable as a river cascading down a mountain. What would it be like to have his hard length entering her?

Her cheeks burned. This was too much, she thought,

panicking. One innocent handclasp and she began imagining the two of them having sex? What was wrong with her? She'd gone through sexual droughts before and it had never made her nuts.

As soon as she'd swung her other leg over the rail, she released his hand. Hurriedly she began unbuttoning her peacoat.

"It's hot in here," she said as if needing to justify her action.

"Body heat."

"Excuse me?"

"The sheep and lambs' bodies generate a lot of heat."

Relief made her weak-kneed. If he was going on about sheep and lambs then maybe he hadn't noticed how she'd reacted to his touch. Right after Carrie liking the dresses she'd found, this would be the best news of the day.

"So come meet these little guys. They've just eaten so they're kind of sleepy. Here, this one could use some cuddling."

She stared at the lamb. Even in the soft light, its wool seemed snowy white against the gold-yellow of the straw. Its eyes were funny, not round but slightly slanted, and its ears stuck out like handlebars on a bike. It regarded her placidly, its eyes blinking and black nose twitching.

"Sit down. That's right. He's curious so he'll come over to sniff your scent. You can hold him if you like."

She'd held a cat in her arms before but never imagined enfolding a hooved creature in her lap. But the lamb was small, barely bigger than that nasty dog Caesar had been. It had stepped toward her, its nose outstretched and nostrils quivering. She wrapped her arms about it and felt its heart hammering against its ribs. Luckily Ward didn't ask her anything because she was too filled with awe to speak.

She stroked the soft warm wool covering its body. When the lamb's legs suddenly buckled, and it landed in her lap, she caught her breath. Slowly she released it with a sigh of wonder. "It's so sweet."

"Congratulations, Tess. You've officially passed the lamb test. To celebrate, you get to name this little guy—actually gal."

"It's a she?"

"Yeah."

"And you're not going to eat her, right?"

"Our sheep are raised for their wool. Now that her mother is letting her nurse, she should have a nice long life. All our stock live the best lives we can give them. When the cattle go to market, we use the most humane practices available. Quinn wouldn't be able to sleep at night otherwise. But we do raise the cattle for beef. It's a fact of life on a cattle ranch."

"It's okay. I like meat. It just would have been weird if this little sweetie ended up on my plate. Her name should be"—she didn't have to rack her brains; the name came unbidden—"Angie."

"Angie she is then." He cocked his head. "I think that must be Quinn and Frank, one of the ranch hands, returning with Quinn's new adopted horse. They'll be turning him out in the nearest corral. Can you bear to leave Angie to take a look?"

Almost too embarrassed to admit that she, who a mere twenty minutes earlier had been essentially anti-animal, was now unwilling to relinquish this tiny lamb with its bowed neck sleeping so innocently in the shelter of her arms. "I wouldn't want to disturb her."

"Her belly's full and she's warm. We'll put her right next to her brother and mother." The straw rustled as he crossed the small pen. He bent over her. His breath mingling with hers, he carefully scooped Angie out of her lap. The scrape of his fingers seared through the denim covering her inner thighs.

"There. I've got her." His husky voice caressed her as thoroughly as his touch had. "You okay?"

No. She was not okay. Something huge had happened in this simple barn filled with the plaintive bleats and sleepy calls of sheep. Ward had given her something precious. A connection she never would have made otherwise. It was something mundane for him, part of his everyday life. To Tess it was like opening a door and showing her a world.

Of course she was bowled over by the experience of holding an adorable woolly baby animal. Such trust and gentleness was extraordinary. It was the man who'd brought her to this unlikely place full of animal noises and odors—full of animals—who she now saw in a whole new light.

"Why wouldn't I be all right?"

"Okay. Then let's take a look at Quinn's new project."

The shock of leaving the cocoonlike world of the lambs and sheep in all their pungent woolly cuteness and stepping into the raw February afternoon to the agitated snorts of a horse, whose ears swiveled and tail swished, vividly reminded Tess of all the reasons she preferred to keep a safe distance from big animals. Especially the ones that outweighed her by a factor of ten and who possessed huge teeth and enormous hooves.

This was definitely one of those. And for all the fear it roused in her, she also felt a wave of pity for the creature. It had obviously been terribly abused. It looked skeletal, the dull coat stretched tight over its bones. More distressing still—if such a thing was possible—were the gashes covering its coat.

"Holy crap," she whispered, staring at the wounds. "What happened to it?"

"Most likely it was whipped." Ward's voice was flat. "Stay here, okay?"

If she hadn't been so disturbed, she might have attempted a pert response about how nothing would have induced her to approach the horse, but all she could do was nod.

She watched him walk to where Quinn was standing and holding the line of rope attached to the horse's halter. To Tess, the rope seemed far too short. Ward didn't seem alarmed by the fact that as he approached, the horse had begun tossing its head and pinning its ears. Even she knew that was a bad sign. But if anything, Ward seemed calmer than ever, which was saying something since the man personified cool reserve.

She could just make out his low-pitched words. "Who's this guy? I thought the horse I adopted for you was a gray. Given up for adoption when the owner lost her job."

"Glory? Frank and I already turned him out in the corral. He's lovely. He's got the potential to make a great trail horse. This one's Tucker. I couldn't leave him, Ward. He's so scared and hurt. He arrived at the shelter three days ago. Betsy Collins, the woman who you consulted about adopting Glory, told me the police found him wandering near a highway. I'd love to get my hands on the sons of bitches that did this to him."

"Quinn, you realize you may never get this horse to trust a human again?"

"Maybe, maybe not. But at least I can give him the life every creature deserves."

Ward nodded. "I'll call Gary Cooney. Tucker will have to be quarantined until Gary clears him."

Quinn nodded. "I thought I'd put him in a makeshift pen next to the goats. Jim went to set it up for me. That way Tucker will be at a safe distance from the other horses, but he won't be lonely. And it'll give him a chance to get used to my comings and goings."

"Just make sure you don't allow anyone to use the shovel and pitchfork or barrow you use to clean the pen. Not until he's been cleared and vaccinated. And have someone with you when you're cleaning it out. I don't want him attacking you. Damn, those cuts make me sick."

"I'll make him better." Quinn's voice was fierce.

"I know you'll try your hardest, kiddo. Here's Frank with the grain bucket. The fact that Tucker's near starving may make it easier to get him into the pen. Here, Frank." Slowly Ward extended his arm for the bucket.

It took twenty minutes to get the horse to the makeshift metal enclosure, with Ward sprinkling bits of grain on the ground, the horse taking tentative steps forward, and Quinn offering a steady stream of praise. Not once did either Knowles show the slightest impatience with the animal. Though its quivering didn't cease, it stopped snorting quite as frequently to track Ward's hand each time it delved into the black rubber bucket.

Ward was right. The horse's hunger was even more powerful than his fear of humans. The knowledge was profoundly disturbing.

Unable to quell her curiosity as to what Ward and Quinn intended to do with Tucker, Tess followed at a safe distance until they reached a smaller barn constructed of the same weathered wood as the others. Attached to it was a fenced enclosure. Inside it a half dozen grayish brown goats with white markings were milling around. No, they were playing around, on a kind of a jungle gym, Tess realized with a start. One of the goats was butting a tetherball; two others were standing on top of a huge cylindrical hay bale. There was even a balance beam of sorts—a log set on concrete blocks—but no one seemed interested in crossing it at the moment.

The second they spotted Quinn and Ward, the goats on the hay bale jumped down and scrambled to join the others trotting over to the fence. Once there, they stuck their white and brown noses though the gaps in the fence. One energetically rose on its hind legs to peer over the top rail. A chorus of *maa*s filled the air.

The noise had the horse's tail rising up at a funny angle.

Uh-oh, Tess thought.

Ward stepped into the metal enclosure that was adjacent to the goats' pen and about half its size. He shook the bucket, redirecting the horse's attention to him.

Next to Ward, Quinn slowly took in the rope as the horse approached tentatively, its ribs heaving from panic and fear. When the horse had cleared the entrance, Quinn passed the rope to Ward and then quietly slipped through the rails of the pen as one of the ranch hands closed the gate. At the clank of metal the horse reared suddenly, and Tess's nerves leapt just as violently.

Ward never lost his cool. He kept hold of the rope as the horse pawed the air. When it had all four hooves back on the ground, Ward once again rattled the bucket. The horse stretched its nose and neck out as far as it could, perhaps hoping it could inhale the grain like a vacuum cleaner, but refused to take a step nearer. Still shaking the bucket, Ward somehow managed to close the distance between them. Just before he poured the grain onto the ground, he extended his free hand and unsnapped the rope attached to the halter. As the grain bounced on the hard dirt and the starved horse lowered his head to eat, Ward stepped back, rope in hand.

It was all done so fluidly. Tess had no sooner understood what Ward was about than he was ducking through the metal rails of the makeshift corral with the same quiet and calm he'd demonstrated throughout. He must possess nerves of steel, she thought.

Not so her. Tess could feel her heart slamming against her ribs. She was almost more scared now that Ward was safe and visions of what could have happened to him streamed before her.

As soon as Ward was on the outside of the corral, Quinn disappeared into the barn. She emerged with an armful of hay. After chucking it over the top rail of the pen, she went over to where Ward was watching the horse. Noticing Tess for the first time, she smiled. "Hey, city girl. Glad to see you down here."

Ward turned. "It's all right to come closer, Tess. I promise you Quinn's new horse won't be coming near us. I doubt he'll let any human near him for a while."

Since she'd already figured that much out for herself, she walked over to them. As she approached, Quinn stepped sideways so Tess could stand between her and Ward. "So what do you think of Tucker? It's criminal what they did to him."

"Yes, it is. I don't know a thing about horses. But I guess I'd have to say that Tucker's lucky to have met you."

Quinn angled her head. "You know, I like you more and more. So did you take a look at Glory, the horse Ward got me? He's a sweetie. I'm going to take him on some test rides. I think he's going to make a good trail horse. Now that spring is nearly upon us, maybe you'd like to go on one."

She had to nip this one in the bud before any of these horse-crazy people got ideas. "A trail ride? I don't think so. You ever heard that saying, 'One ought to try everything once except incest and folk dancing'? Well, I'd rather try folk dancing than horseback riding."

Quinn snorted then succumbed to full-throated laughter. On Tess's other side, Ward ducked his dark head, but she caught the smile stretching across his face.

"Riding's way better than folk dancing. Right, Ward?"

"And way, way better than incest." Ward's drawled response provoked another snort of hilarity from his sister. "Tess is going to be tweeting about the ranch for us, Quinn, so why don't you take her around and introduce her to Alberta, Hennie, and the others? I've got to hunt Pete down and find out whether any more cattle have sickened. Oh," he added as he turned away from the rail. "Tess and you need to brainstorm activities for a cowgirls' weekend at the ranch. You're to supply the ideas that don't involve nail polish."

Quinn's grin was wicked. "So he's got you planning a cowgirls' weekend, huh? Sounds like my brother wants to broaden your horizons."

That's what she was afraid of.

Chapter FIFTEEN

"Hi, Mom. It's me. I didn't call too late, did I?" Tess had dialed her parents' number immediately upon returning to her cabin. Still in the clothes she'd worn to see the sheep, she paced the small sitting area that in one corner was equipped with a sink, a small stove top, and a tiny fridge.

"No, I was just washing the floor before I went upstairs." Maria Casari washed the kitchen floor every night. Cleaning offered Tess's mother the semblance of control in a life that was filled with so much she could neither fix nor straighten. "Your Papa's upstairs. He told me you got a letter in the mail today. He said it looked businesslike." Tess heard her call loudly, "Frank, it's Teresa. She's on the phone." There was a long pause and then she returned on the line. "Sorry. He must be watching that show of his."

"It's okay. I can talk to him later in the week. I wouldn't want to interrupt. He might not figure out who dunnit otherwise."

"Maybe I should go get the letter—"

"No, I'm sure it's not important." She paid her bills online, and the bank where she'd set up the fund for

Christopher had her cell phone number and email address.

"What if it's from—"

"It wouldn't be. David's parents have no reason to contact me." The Bradfords had made it clear they had no wish to communicate with her ever again. Perhaps the letter from the lawyer informing her that David was proceeding with a divorce had found her at last. She hardly wanted to read that and dredge up those painful memories. "How are you, Mom?"

"Chris had a good day. Jay let him play on the computer for a half hour in the afternoon and there were hot dogs at lunch."

"I know hot dogs are his favorite." It was useless to point out to her mother that she hadn't answered Tess's question about how she was doing. It would only sadden her. Besides, how Chris's day went did dictate the quality of her own.

"And how are things with you, Teresa?"

"They're good. You know that couple I told you about, the one I'm planning the wedding for? I found some dresses for the bride and she seemed really excited about them. And I've been given a new responsibility as events planner and promoter. They want me to post stuff about the goings-on at the ranch. Today I went down to the barns. I held a newborn lamb, Mom."

"Your great-great-grandparents were farmers."

"Really? I didn't know that."

"Well, your great-grandfather was the second son so he went into the city and got a job in a bank. He and his wife lived in the city. His older brother's family eventually sold the farm. So this family, the Knowleses, they have many sheep?"

"I don't know the exact number. It seems like a lot."

"And they have cows and horses and goats, too?"

"Yeah. I met the goats, too. They weren't quite as

adorable as the lamb but they were pretty funny. One, her name is Hennie, likes to hit a ball with her head. The goats are dairy goats. And I have to say the cheese they make is delicious. Speaking of cheese, I got Mrs. Vecchio's recipe from Anna so I'm all set to make my Italian dinner for the chef here. He's going to love your baked penne."

"Don't forget the gorgonzola. It doesn't have the right pep without it."

"I won't. I miss you." She thought of the banter Quinn and Ward had exchanged, the love they—Reid included—had for one another. There was so much Chris would never know. "Will you tell Chris I miss him, too?"

"Of course." There was a short silence on her mother's end. Then she spoke. "Teresa, these people, this place—your papa and I think it's good you went there."

Tess swallowed the thick lump of emotion clogging her throat. "Thank you, Mom."

Ward was in a tack shop on the outskirts of Hopland. He had a fairly long list of items to pick up. Topping it was a dozen saddle blankets that had been woven with Silver Creek wool in a deal his father had negotiated several years ago with Clinton Stiles, the owner of the tack shop, and his sister, Clover, a weaver who owned The Fold in Acacia. Per their agreement, Clover bought wool from Silver Creek at a reduced price and wove a certain number of blankets for the ranch. The rest Clinton sold in the tack shop. Clover used their wool to make other items as well, spinning it into yarn and knitting sweaters and whatever else struck her fancy.

Acacia had an artsy, homespun feel to it; its townsfolk liked the idea of wearing sweaters and scarves from sheep that were raised a few miles down the road. Tourists got a kick when they heard the wool came from the biggest ranch in the area. Ranch guests bought them as souvenirs.

Normally Ward would have picked up the blankets in town at The Fold, but Clover was away, exhibiting her work at a wool festival in Oregon.

Another item on his list was for Quinn. She wanted him to pick up a new bosal because she'd decided that if Tucker ever agreed to let her on his back she'd try him in a hackamore rather than a bridle with a bit. Ward figured if anyone was going to convince Tucker that humans were worthy of a ride, it would be Quinn.

The vet had cleared Tucker of having any communicable diseases. As soon as she got the green light from Gary Cooney, Quinn had turned the gelding out with Harper and Bristol, two of their mellowest dudes, so docile and laid-back that it was the common joke that all they were missing in life was a sofa, a bag of Doritos, and a bong.

Whenever Quinn passed by, they'd mosey over to the rail for a scratch and tickle and then follow her around the corral, just hoping for some more of her lovin'. Tucker, ever watchful, must have noticed that they had no fear of this human. By now Quinn could stand next to him without him rearing or pawing. Yesterday she'd even been able to apply the ointment Cooney had prescribed to Tucker's gashes. The progress with Tucker thrilled Quinn.

The autopsy results from the veterinary lab had determined the cause of death for their cow: redwater, a bacterial disease that colonized in the liver and then attacked the other organs. Mature cattle that contracted redwater could be healthy one day and dead the next. The diagnosis had come as something of a shock since they'd vaccinated the herd last spring. But Gary Cooney believed that perhaps the vaccine had worn off. His recommendation was to move to a six-month schedule for the vaccine. The loss of a healthy cow stung, but so far she was the only one to have contracted the disease. And at least redwater wasn't infectious like brucellosis or leptospirosis, which could spread to other animals.

Having selected a nice braided bosal, Ward had everything he'd come for, but instead of going to the register to pay up, he found himself in a different section of Clinton's store. The boot section. The women's boot section, to be precise.

His eyes traveled along the rows of cowboy boots, their hues as varied as a rainbow, their stitching running the gamut from plain to intricate. He skipped the ones made of snakeskin, ostrich, and lizard. They weren't made for doing more than showing off on a Saturday night. Besides, he couldn't see Tess being too happy about wearing snakes.

Aha, that was the boot for her, he thought. A Lucchese with whorls of purple stitching against distressed brown leather. The stitching made him think of the purple nail polish decorating her very pretty foot. The image of it remained fresh in his mind.

He grabbed the boot off the wall. "Do these run true to size, Clinton?"

"Yeah." Clint nodded slowly. He did many things slowly. "I've heard tell they're real comfortable. 'Course they're Luccheses, so what would you expect? They're not cheap," he warned.

"You got 'em in a size eight?" He'd caught a glimpse of the size of Tess's high-heeled pump and somehow that piece of information, along with the rest of the things he'd learned about her, was seared in his memory.

"Might have." He ambled off in the direction of the stockroom.

Ward sat down on the wooden bench, the sample boot in hand, and waited for Clinton to return.

Yeah, these would look good on her, he thought. They were beautifully constructed and in a color just funky enough to appeal to her city girl side. Most important, the intricate stitching didn't impede their function. And he wanted these boots to be functional.

He realized that he'd begun a campaign of sorts with respect to Tess. And just as he would a business plan for the ranch, he intended to pursue this campaign thoroughly and successfully.

The idea had been born the afternoon she'd shared a few reluctant comments about herself: her lack of a formal wedding; her neighbor's nasty dog, Caesar the ankle biter; her brother Christopher's autism. Her admissions had revealed a depth of pain that to Ward seemed all the more poignant for the effort she took to conceal it. Obviously a lot of things that should have been joyous in her life weren't—he now strongly suspected her marriage had not been the happy union he'd initially believed; certainly her brother's illness had taken a terrible toll on her family.

The new assignment he'd given her of tweeting and creating a picture board of the ranch on Pinterest fit in neatly with his plan. He wanted to introduce her to the animals that were the heart and soul of Silver Creek.

She'd already come a long way in the past week. The sheep were her favorites. Every day she went looking for Angie. A stunned smile would spread over her face when the lamb would come over. And while she was obviously leery of Tucker, Quinn's rescue horse, she nevertheless stopped by the corral to see how he was faring.

Despite her professed disinterest, it was easy to see that Tess's fascination with the animals on the ranch was growing. He intended to nurture that fascination. The next step in his campaign was to get her astride a horse. These funky purple-stitched boots would forestall the first excuse she'd use: that none of her shoes or boots were suitable for riding.

Knowing her as well as he did, he could guess what her second ride-avoiding attempt would be: a smart-aleck comment about how she'd rather have a car to drive than a horse to a ride. He had an answer for that, too. It was all in the timing, and he was planning with the precision of a general going into battle—because he knew Tess was going to do her damnedest to avoid getting on the back of a horse.

That his mother had orchestrated it so that Tess and he would work together no longer irritated him. He wouldn't change his mother—not even her matchmaking proclivity—for anything. Besides, he was willing to admit that something about Tess had gotten to him the moment he spotted her behind the wheel of her smoking clunker. She'd been all huge, dark eyes and raw courage, and graced with the softest breasts he'd felt in a long time.

"You're in luck, Ward. We got a pair in size eight. Good thing, because Luccheses are special orders."

Clinton's mellow drawl was as startling as the blare of a sixteen wheeler. Ward straightened on the wooden bench with a jolt. He had no idea how much time had passed while he'd been reliving the sensation of his arm brushing against Tess's lush rack. It could have been minutes; it could have been hours.

Clinton opened the cardboard box and pulled the tissue paper back for Ward's inspection. "That's going to be one happy lady."

Ward surely hoped so.

Walking along the winding gravel path that led to her cabin, Tess slowed when she spotted the large cardboard box resting against the cabin's door. Had Anna mailed her something? she wondered. She'd already sent the blue resin necklace she'd found for Adele—perfect timing since Adele and Daniel were due to leave the next day for South Carolina. They'd be spending ten days with Daniel's sister and brother-in-law, helping them ready their inn for its grand opening. From there they would fly to Spain for their romantic getaway.

No, the box couldn't be from Anna. It was way too big—unless she'd decided to send a good-luck cooking pot to bolster Tess's nerves for the meal she was making for Jeff and Roo and their kitchen staff the following night.

Curiosity had her quickening her pace. Surprise had her widening her eyes. There was no address or stamp on the wrapped brown paper; there was only her first name written in black ink. But she recognized the bold angular script. A flutter of excitement burst inside her.

Ignoring the damp cold of the afternoon, Tess plunked herself down on the stoop next to the box, hauled it onto her lap, and tore open the wrapping. Her breath came out in an "Oh" of astonishment at the box's contents.

They were fantastic, she thought as she trailed her fingers over the surprisingly soft leather. Admittedly cowboy boots weren't her usual style, but maybe it was time to branch out and recognize that craftsmanship was craftsmanship. Prada couldn't have done better. It amazed her that Ward had gone and bought her a pair of boots. She lifted one out of the box and peered at the size stamped inside. Eight. Damn, the man was good.

Obviously she'd have to try them. She'd been planning on changing into jeans anyway. It was cold out and Tess had yet to take her daily picture of Angie, who'd started to have a fan club of sorts among Silver Creek's Twitter followers. And Reid, when he'd stopped by her office bearing a much-appreciated cup of coffee, had mentioned that the night before, a sorrel mare (she didn't admit she had no idea what "sorrel" meant) had given birth.

According to Reid, the foal was a great going-away present for Daniel and Adele. They'd been waiting for this maiden mare to deliver. A newborn foal would make a great addition to the collection of images she was posting on Pinterest.

Boots and box in her arms, she scrambled to her feet.

Chapter SIXTEEN

NO LONGER CONVINCED that the animals were determined to stampede her, Tess had grown somewhat more comfortable going down and observing them. She'd even become accustomed to the bustle of the barns in the afternoon, when the hands herded the sheep and young lambs into their barn for the night to protect the young lambs from the freezing night temperatures and predators. Holly and Frank Boone, a married couple who'd worked at Silver Creek for the past ten years and had begun dispensing information whenever Tess was in their company for longer than five minutes, informed her that coyotes had started making a comeback in the area. The thought of Angie or her brother, Arlo (Quinn had named him that), being dragged off by a coyote horrified her.

When she arrived at the barns, the flock of sheep and lambs was being herded into the sheep barn by Pete and Frank and two of the dogs. The dogs were keeping in line the strays that didn't understand that the sound of Holly rattling a bucket was a good thing, the promise of hay and other delicious feed. She was pretty sure Angie, Arlo, and their mother weren't that dim.

Tess would have followed the woolly herd but, glancing to the left, she noticed Quinn, Daniel, and Adele standing by the large corral.

They were watching Ward. He was on horseback, riding a horse whose coat made her think of blue steel as it moved through the dull light of the late afternoon.

She had no idea what he was doing, only that it was complicated and exceptionally beautiful. It involved the horse surging from a stop into a full-out run only to stop again, sometimes stopping so quickly that the horse seemed to sink on its hind legs as its front hooves slid forward in the soft dirt. It looked as if the horse was going to sit down on its muscled rear.

Ward and his horse must have known what they were doing, because they never went barreling through the wooden fence as she half-expected each time they raced from one end of the corral to the other. From what she could tell, this was a standard move, for though Quinn and her parents were watching attentively, Adele hadn't slapped her hand over her eyes in fright.

Tess recovered her breath only to lose it again; Ward's full-tilt racing and stopping on a dime ended, to be replaced by an equally improbable move. His horse started spinning around in a tight circle, his rear hooves pivoting in one spot. How it could whirl like a twister was incredible. Even more astonishing was that, through it all, Ward remained motionless in the saddle.

It was an extraordinary spectacle, but she couldn't say she was sorry when the horse ceased its supersonic circling. As seamlessly as the spinning had started, it stopped, and the gray horse was standing stock-still, its hooves perfectly aligned. Ward leaned over to pat its neck with his gloved hand.

Next to her, Quinn spoke. "So, did you film that?"

To her surprise, Tess realized that she had indeed trained her iPhone on Ward. She supposed she'd gotten so used to taking pictures and short videos during the past week that it had become second nature, no conscious thought necessary. "Yeah."

"Don't stop recording. Reid and Carlos are bringing in the steers now, so Ward can give Bilbao some practice working the cattle. Bilbao's still learning."

"You mean Ward's not done yet? That was like a warm-up?" Tess whispered incredulously.

Quinn grinned. "Pretty much. Ward was working on Bilbao's rundown and reining techniques. Now Bilbao's going to track and trail one of the cattle. He's getting good at it. I think he's been watching Sirrus, Reid's horse."

Quinn's voice had risen as the air became filled with the lowing and heavy stomp of cattle. Daniel moved away from his place at the fence to open the gate to the corral and waited as a dozen or so black and red cattle entered it, followed by Reid on a light gray spotted horse with an inky black mane and tail. Carlos, another of the hands, was also on horseback, but instead of entering the ring, he dismounted to stand by Daniel.

A big mooing mass of hooves and swishing tails, the cattle trotted into the corral, which suddenly seemed to have shrunk in size. And though Reid was now in the ring, too, Tess couldn't keep her eyes off Ward.

He had kept Bilbao on the far end of the corral when the cattle entered, but now that they were clumped in a patchwork of red and brown hides he moved his horse toward them. Tess didn't know what he and Bilbao were supposed to do. She had no idea what tracking and trailing involved, but she could tell that Bilbao was behaving differently. He walked straight into the cattle clustered together and broke them into two groups. She assumed that Ward told him to follow the smaller group that trotted into the center of the ring, for that's what the horse did.

For a second she couldn't figure out what was happening, why the horse and the cows just seemed to be standing still in the middle of the ring. Then it became clear. Bilbao had fixed his attention on one of the steers, staring down a reddish brown one with a funny clump of hair sprouting between its ears. If she'd had to describe it, she'd have said Bilbao was giving the steer the evil eye. Then he shifted, lowering his dark gray head and moving forward with a menacing intent. She was reminded of how the sheepdogs slunk low to the ground when they were herding a stray sheep. The difference was, Ward's horse was about two thousand times bigger than those dogs. Nonetheless it nimbly mirrored the steer's every move as it dodged and feinted, trying to get around the horse and back to the herd.

Bilbao wasn't letting it. As he had earlier when Ward was "warming" him up, the horse sank back on his haunches, moving his front legs from left to right with incredible speed, refusing to let the steer pass. Blocking him the way a guard would in basketball. Tess had a sudden fond memory of the days of not playing basketball in school with Anna. Sister Louisa would have loved to have had Bilbao on defense.

The horse had some crazy moves, all right. Throughout it all, Ward never interfered, just flowed with Bilbao's rapid shifts, their bodies moving as one.

Then Ward must have given him a signal, for Bilbao's head, which had been stretched low to the ground the entire time, rose. He stood, his hooves aligned perfectly, looking beautiful and superior, and making it abundantly clear that he could no longer be bothered to summon any interest in something as bovine as a cow. Released, the steer galloped back to the herd.

Even if she lived to be a hundred Tess doubted she'd ever be as cool as Bilbao had been for those brief minutes.

* * *

Ward had noticed Tess standing next to Quinn when he ended Bilbao's run with the steer. He was glad the young horse had performed well and put on a sterling show for her. He didn't usually show off, but Tess had him doing things he'd never have done before.

Like buying cowboy boots for a woman.

He wanted to see whether she was wearing them. For some reason seeing them on her felt more important—more urgent somehow—than when he'd slipped the big sparkly diamond on Erica's finger. The realization was startling, considering that he'd been set to share his life with Erica, considering how much he'd thought he'd loved her. At the moment, though, he didn't care to analyze what his feelings signified. He simply had them. Period.

He waited as Reid took a turn with Sirrus. They were brilliant. Reid was an exceptional rider and Reid's gelding just loved working the cattle. Ward fully expected Bilbao to become as cow smart as Sirrus. Quinn was convinced Sirrus was teaching the younger horse his best moves. She could be right, because he got better and better with every training session they had with Reid and his horse.

As soon as Sirrus had released the steer and it had run back to the herd, Ward and Reid guided their mounts toward the cattle, moving them to the gate where Carlos and their dad were waiting.

"I'll take Bilbao for you, Ward, and ride the herd back to the pasture with Reid and Carlos," his father said.

"You sure?"

"Absolutely. I'm leaving you all with a lot of work starting tomorrow. This is the least I can do. Besides, you looked like you were having so much fun on Bilbao. I'd like to see what tricks you've been teaching him. And if we ride for long enough, your mother may have finally finished her packing. I can't even see the bed she's got so many outfits." His grousing was affectionate.

"Fine by me. I've got some stuff to do and I'd like to sneak another peek at the new foal." He slipped his boots out of the stirrups, swung his leg over the saddle, and dropped to the ground. "I think that colt may prove almost as smart as this guy here." He gave Bilbao a hearty pat on his neck.

"The foal's a beaut, all right. He's already begun kicking up his heels and racing around his dam. Quinn wants to name him Rush. As in Gold Rush."

"Yeah," Ward said with a nod. "That's a good name."

Already in his chaps, Daniel nimbly mounted Bilbao. Gathering the reins in his left hand, he clucked and Bilbao moved into an easy lope down the track. "Smooth as whiskey," he called.

Coming from the man who'd not only taught him how to ride at age three but who for years had trained all the cow horses on the ranch, that was high praise indeed.

Pleased as he was by his father's approval, right now he was more eager to discover whether he'd won a certain woman's favor.

She was wearing them. And he wasn't the only one who'd noticed and who was delighted by the sight of Tess Casari in a pair of fine leather cowboy boots. It could be argued, however, that his sister's and mother's pleasure was of a different order than his. In addition, theirs was mixed with a healthy dose of speculation. Like bookends, they stood on either side of her, staring down at her new footwear.

"They're beauts, Tess. Luccheses, right?"

Ward saw her nod. "Um, yes."

"And the stitching?"

Tess bent over and pulled the leg of her jeans up to her knee. Her back to him, Ward was given a very fine view of her heart-shaped ass. He wondered whether he should say something but then decided no. He was enjoying the view too much.

"Sweet." There was a hint of envy in Quinn's pronouncement. "Those boots are the real deal, right, Mom? Real cowgirl gear."

"Very chic cowgirl gear and perfect for you, Tess. Did you get Ralph to drive you to Clinton's shop?"

Ward decided the time had come to save Tess from any awkward explanations of how the boots had found themselves on her very sexy feet. "Dad took off on Bilbao for a ride. You can get the rest of your packing done in peace, Mom."

At the sound of Ward's voice Tess spun around on her new heels. Any faster and she could give Bilbao lessons. A rosy bloom colored her cheeks, and she couldn't quite meet his gaze.

She was damned adorable when flustered. He bit the inside of his cheek to keep from grinning.

His words provided an excellent distraction. "Oh, good!" his mother exclaimed. "Your father simply can't understand how difficult packing for two back-to-back trips can be. I'm thrilled to be going, of course, but I do feel bad about leaving you all with so much to do. You, especially, Tess."

"I like being busy. Really. And Carrie and Brian's wedding promises to be a whole lot easier to plan now that they've found a free weekend to come out and meet with the vendors."

"It's a shame Daniel and I will miss them. You'll send our love, won't you, Ward?"

"Will do."

Quinn, an indifferent packer and equally indifferent to the topic of Carrie and Brian's wedding, wasn't so easily sidetracked. "We were just admiring Tess's new boots. Have you checked 'em out, Ward?"

He let his gaze travel down to the pointed brown leather tips peeking out beneath her jeans. "Sharp. Good to see you now have the right kind of footwear for your new responsibilities documenting life at Silver Creek. Speaking of which, I was going to head over and take another look at the new colt, Rush. Catchy name by the way, brat. You ladies care to join me?"

"I'll say hi to the little guy later. It's Tucker time now. I'm going to let him look at the bosal you bought me at Clinton's. I guess Clint's been getting lots of business from us." Ward returned her sly smile with a bland one. "Oh!" she said excitedly. "Guess what. Tucker let me groom him with a soft brush after lunch." Justified pride rang in her voice.

"That's wonderful," their mother said.

"It is," Ward agreed. "I noticed his cuts are beginning to heal. It'll be interesting to see what he looks like after he's gained another hundred pounds or so."

"He'll be a beaut. And Glory's doing real well. As sweet as I suspected. Perfect trail horse. Okay, time's a-wasting. Ciao, y'all." She sauntered off with a wave.

"I'll have to postpone my visit to Rush, too. I need to take advantage of not having your father underfoot and constantly interrupting so I can finish packing. But you should definitely go with Ward, Tess, and take photos. People love pictures of newborn foals." His mother smiled with innocent brightness.

It looked like his mother, the indefatigable matchmaker, wasn't going to let up until she stepped onto the plane for South Carolina, Ward thought with amusement.

With Adele gone, Tess found she could no longer ignore how delicious Ward looked. "Delicious" might sound excessive, but it was the only word that properly described how he looked in worn blue jeans and chaps. Since she'd started coming down to the barns, she'd seen the other hands wearing chaps, but those cowboys hadn't made her heart thump painfully or feel as if she should suddenly start fanning her face.

Ward wore the kind that zippered down his long muscular legs, hugging them. Made of dark tan suede, they didn't have the fringes or ornamentation that she'd noticed on some of the ones worn by the wranglers. There was nothing to distract her eyes or to keep her gaze from zeroing in on where the chaps buckled, framing the bulge of his sex. Her internal thermostat soared just from *not* looking at that particular spot.

But the brim of his hat was angled downward—the better to study her new boots, she assumed. With his gaze shielded, she found the temptation impossible to resist. Yup, his crotch was truly the finest eye candy: yummy and calorie free.

Oh, yes, he was fine. He could probably star in one of those calendars. Twelve Months of Ward Knowles. It'd be an instant bestseller on account of its broad appeal. After all, he could do hunky businessman as well as hunky cowboy. It was really a toss-up as to which version was more devastating.

And to think that just a few months ago she'd pooh-poohed the appeal of a virile cowboy.

But maybe it was just one virile cowboy who'd changed her worldview.

He raised his head and, though she couldn't quite see his eyes, the smile that played over his mouth made her think he'd figured out where her own eyes had repeatedly strayed. "So, you like the boots."

"Yeah. I do. I can't believe you bought them. Can I pay—"

His mouth pursed as if he'd tasted something sour. He tipped his head back so that their eyes locked. "This was a present."

She'd insulted him. It was one thing to exchange barbs with him when he was being bossy and domineering, another when he had shown his generosity. "Then thank you," she answered quietly. "They're pretty darned snazzy."

"And functional. They'll get the job done and look good doing it. Like you." He didn't give her time to let the compliment go to her head. "Come and meet Silver Creek's newest resident."

Quinn had named the foal Gold Rush because, Ward said, he would end up the same color as his mother, whose coat was a lovely reddish gold, with a pale blond mane and tail. The baby horse was beautiful. Comical-looking, too, his ridiculously long legs like the stilts the revelers used during Carnevale celebrations. While his mother munched noisily on grain, Rush had alternately pranced and dashed around the pen—showing off, Ward explained with a soft laugh. The sound had Rush's fuzzy ears swiveling back and forth.

Abruptly exhausted by his performance, the foal had sunk slowly, awkwardly, onto his knees by his mother's hooves. He lay quietly, his tiny nose moving the straw with each exhalation. Slowly his large eyes closed and he slept.

Tess snapped a final picture. She'd taken dozens, recognizing they'd be a hit with the growing number of Silver Creek Ranch's followers. Although Rush was adorable, her heart belonged to Angie and her twin brother, Arlo.

They left mother and foal napping in the barn.

"What time are your parents leaving tomorrow?" Tess asked.

"They've got an early flight out of San Fran to Aiken. Reid's driving them. On his way back he's got appointments at some vineyards in Sonoma."

"I'll have to make sure I post these pictures tonight then so your parents will have something to enjoy while they're waiting for their flight." She slipped her iPhone into her jacket pocket.

"Good idea. Knowing Mom, she'll pass around her phone. I'd lay odds she'll get a good portion of the airport to sign up to the ranch's Twitter account."

"She's a talented woman."

"Mm-hmm, and determined. So, you done for the day?"

"No, I've got to head over to the kitchen and give Jeff my shopping list."

"Is this shopping list for the Italian home-cooked meal Jeff's been talking about?"

"Word's spread, huh?" Tess wasn't surprised. Ward and his family often wandered into the kitchen: Adele to discuss the menu; Reid to consult on wine pairings; Ward and his father to exchange insults about their favorite soccer teams; Quinn to plan the kitchen garden and occasionally wait on tables.

"It's superseded the ongoing debate of who's going to advance to the European finals this year."

"That's a nontopic. Italy will win the cup. So the dinner's the number one topic? Now I know I'll burn it." She paused, acutely aware that her heartbeat had accelerated before she'd even voiced her next words. "Are you busy tomorrow? You could join us if you aren't."

She prayed she'd managed to sound casual enough. And the invitation was entirely justified. The man had just given her a pair of seriously great boots.

"How could I pass up a chance to eat homemade Italian food—burnt or otherwise?" His smile set off tiny sparks of desire inside her, as bright as a hundred sparklers streaming through the night, and she knew that burning the dinner would be the least of her worries tomorrow night.

If he smiled like that again, it would be she who caught fire.

Chapter SEVENTEEN

IT TOOK A mere four hours after Adele and Daniel's departure for the first crisis to strike. Tess was going over the wedding invitations for Carrie and Brian one last time, checking for typos before she emailed the file to the stationer, when Anita Garcia, the head of housekeeping, rushed into her office in a state of hysteria.

Tess spun around in her chair to stare in dismay at the older woman's pale face. She hurried forward and placed an arm about her bowed, heaving shoulders.

"Anita, what's happened? Are you all right? Do you need a doctor?"

Tess's Spanish was good, but Anita's distress made her speech nearly incomprehensible. All Tess could gather was that there was something terribly wrong with one of the cabins—she wasn't sure but thought it was Mariposa or Monterey. The "M" was the only decipherable sound.

Ignoring the visions of ax murderers or rabid wolves dancing in her head, Tess ushered her out of the office. Maybe a glass of water or a cup of bracing hot tea would calm Anita, and they could get to the bottom of this.

They met Ward in the hallway. His frown told her he'd heard the commotion from his office.

"*¿Qué pasa,* Anita?"

At the concern in Ward's voice, Anita's face crumpled and she raised a fist to her mouth.

"It's something to do with one of the guest cabins. I was thinking a glass of water might help."

"Yeah, or whiskey. *Todo estará bien. Prometo.*"

In the staff room they sat Anita down on the sage twill sofa while Tess hurried into the kitchen for a glass of lemon water.

When she returned, Ward was crouching by the sofa, listening to Anita's choked whisper. He rose as she passed Anita the glass.

"Anita says the Mariposa Lodge was trashed by the guests who checked out this morning."

"I told Roo about Anita. She's sending Heather in with some cookies to sit with her until she's feeling more herself."

Heather, one of Roo's assistants, came in before Tess had finished her sentence, bearing a plate of Roo's finest baked goodies.

"Thanks, Heather," Ward said.

"No problem. I was due a break anyway."

Ward turned back to her. "I'm going to check out the lodge."

Anita lowered the glass of water and spoke, her voice somewhat calmer. "I came to you, Teresa, because Señora Knowles and you have been checking the rooms—"

"I'll go take a look at it right now," she assured Anita. "I hope they didn't break anything."

The housekeeper lowered her head, mumbling something that Tess didn't even bother to interpret. They'd find out what had upset her shortly.

* * *

The door to the one-bedroom cabin was ajar and Anita's cleaning cart was parked against the cedar siding.

"She must have hightailed it out of there," Ward observed. "Maybe I should go in first."

"Be my guest," Tess said with an exaggerated sweep of her arm. She wasn't nearly so worried that an ax murderer would attempt to machete her or a wild beast devour her with Ward by her side.

"Such hospitality." His grin matched her attempt at lightheartedness.

Ward stepped inside and she followed, nearly slamming into him when he stopped abruptly. "Oh! Sorry! I didn't—" she began, only to have the rest of her sentence die away. Like Ward, she stood mute before the sight that greeted them.

Holy cannoli.

Except it wasn't cannoli she was looking at, but thick chocolate and bright raspberry smears covering the walls. And that was just the beginning. Her gaze crisscrossed the wrecked bedroom, and it was like running her eyes over the weekend's dessert menu. In addition to the chocolate and raspberry coulis streaks, there was mocha whipped cream, lavender frosting, and what must have been mango ice cream. A veritable smorgasbord.

It was one thing to be identifying the foodstuff. Quite another to realize that the streaks weren't random. They were prints. Human body prints. Naked human body prints. Smeared yet recognizable, they covered the walls and armchairs. Even the rugs. The unmade bed, with its formerly snow-white sheets, had seen a whole lot of dessert. She couldn't begin to imagine what the bathroom looked like. At least the marble was washable. . . .

"These two guests must have some kind of sweet tooth." Her voice was a stunned whisper.

"Jesus, this gives a whole new meaning to the term 'action painting.' They damn well better leave a positive review on TripAdvisor."

His comment had her bursting into appalled laughter. Ward's own, lower and rueful, joined hers.

When she was finally able to control her hilarity, she offered, "They obviously appreciated the room service."

"I'll say." The corner of his mouth lifted in a crooked smile. "And they must have liked the room—they certainly made good use of it."

"Every square inch."

"Do you think we should tell Roo that we now have positive proof her molten chocolate cake is orgasmic?"

She muffled a snort. "Or that her mango-ginger ice cream has decidedly stimulating properties?"

Ward shook his head. "No, we'd better not. She might try to outdo herself. I'm not sure we can afford any more such enthusiastic responses."

"I'm not sure that any could top this couple's."

"They certainly were creative."

"Yeah." Tess stared at an orange body print of a woman's very round breasts. The outline was especially striking against what had formerly been an ecru wall. She'd gotten good at memorizing the different paint colors for when she had to contact Walter, the ranch's handyman, after she or Adele discovered walls that had been scuffed or dinged.

The damage done to the cabin was going to require a lot more than one of Walter's touch-ups. Tess decided it was far better—and safer—to fixate on the amount of paint and soap Walter was going to need rather than obsess about the naked woman who'd been pressed up against the wall . . . backward and forward.

"Have you got your phone? I left mine in my office when I heard Anita."

"Sure." She drew her phone from the pocket of her belted sweater and passed it to him. But instead of calling someone—Walter, for instance—he began taking pictures of the walls and furnishings.

"These are for the lawyer," he said in answer to her unspoken question. "We need to document the destruction so he can pursue damages if the guests balk. Oh, and even though these photos will be on your camera, I don't think they should be included in your tweets or posted on your Pinterest board."

"A shame. If anything has a chance of going viral, this would be it. Then again, my mom just convinced our priest, who's big on sheep and cuddly lambs—the whole flock thing, you know—to follow my tweets. I'd rather not cause him to have a heart attack."

Ward gave a bark of laughter, then they fell silent once again, staring at the destruction around them.

It wasn't often one chanced upon the aftermath of an all-out, all-you-can-eat sexual binge. The sight was surreal. Grotesque, yet strangely and most definitely arousing.

Never had Tess been more acutely aware of Ward's intense masculinity. Or his strength. He could have her stripped bare and pressed against that wall, driving into her slick, aching heat in seconds. And she'd be urging him on, wrapping her legs against his pumping flanks, digging her nails into his broad shoulders.

She wouldn't need to have her body slathered in sweet cream or frosting, however. Far more important would be the feel of his hot flesh rubbing against hers, the scratch of the dark stubble shadowing his cheeks against her lips, and the salty, masculine taste of him as she nibbled and licked her way over his body. Her breath hitched, her body tightening in unbearable need.

It was pointless to deny it anymore. She had the hots

for this man. Serious hots. Walking into this room that, thanks to its previous occupants, screamed "sexual marathon," had brought her simmering need to a full, insistent boil. There was no ignoring the heat rising from her . . . or from him. The space between them sizzled with awareness.

He'd shoved his hands in his pockets. He was in businessman mode today, dressed in a midnight blue dress shirt and gray trousers, every inch of him as sinfully handsome as he'd been the day before in jeans and chaps, the brim of his dark beige cowboy hat pulled low over his brow.

Urban or country, it didn't matter. She'd be too busy shucking his clothes off as fast as she could. She wanted the man underneath.

"You know I'm attracted to you."

For all their casualness, his words, spoken in a low, husky voice, sent a thrill of pleasure skipping down her spine. It danced at the base, radiant.

She swallowed. "I know."

"So, are we going to do something about this thing between us?"

She glanced at his chiseled profile and then looked away quickly lest he read too much in her expression. She could do this—keep it physical, she told herself. They would be satisfying an intense physical attraction.

There'd be nothing deeper between them.

Nothing that involved her heart. She couldn't trust that organ. It had misled her so disastrously with David.

"I think we'll have to."

He gave a short, decisive nod of his head. She couldn't help but note that he, too, seemed determined to keep his gaze averted. "Good to know."

* * *

I think we'll have to. It had taken every ounce of Ward's self-control not to jump Tess the moment she'd uttered those words. Of course he'd have to have dragged her outside first. No way would he have touched her in that room.

He was a healthy male; he'd instantly envisioned Tess and him reenacting every sexual position so graphically imprinted on the walls of the guest room. He'd come up with a dozen more ways to pleasure Tess as well, but nothing on earth would induce him to try a single one in a room marked with others' leavings.

The effort cost him. He wasn't sure how he got through the next several hours, but he must not have blundered too badly. He couldn't recall anyone looking at him cross-eyed . . . though, truth be told, his eyesight had gone kind of hazy. Sexual anticipation blurred his vision.

To clear his head and make the hands of the clock move forward to the hour when he could legitimately find Tess and drag her off somewhere private, he took Rio out to check on the cattle in the far pasture, glad it was a Monday and that Mitch and Rick would be leading the trail rides for the few guests staying at the ranch. He wasn't in the mood for chitchat and was pretty sure he'd bite the head off anyone who interrupted him imagining Tess naked and underneath him.

It was Quinn who reminded him that this was the day Tess was cooking her Italian dinner. Since he'd ridden Rio hard and then had to take extra time cooling the gelding down, he'd been sure he had to suffer only an hour or so more before getting Tess to himself. The realization that he'd have to share her with a room full of foodies over dinner made him growl low in his throat. He didn't want to eat food, damn it. He wanted to taste Tess.

Quinn was used to his surlier moods, so she just lifted a brow. "Gee, I kind of thought you'd be looking forward to Tess's special dinner. Since you went to the trouble of buying her those truly kick-ass boots I assumed you'd grown markedly more intelligent about the opposite sex."

Ward merely shot her his most withering look and lifted his saddle off Rio's back. The gelding's coat was still damp so he snapped a lead rope onto Rio's halter and began walking him down the gravel road.

Annoyingly, Quinn fell into step beside him. Though his sister wasn't as tall as he was, she had pretty long legs, so she didn't have to work too hard to match his stride.

"I wish I could come to dinner just for the entertainment value of watching you two try not to look at each other. It's hysterical."

"Don't you have somewhere else to be right now?"

"Nope. Not until tonight. I'm taking over for Reid so he can enjoy the tastings he's scheduled at the vineyards. I've got barn duty. Pete told me Bianca's giving signs she's ready to foal. A big dinner would just make me sleepy."

Ward set aside his irritation with his sister to say, "You'll call me if she does foal."

"Not likely—not unless she's having trouble, that is. I'm not going to interrupt your evening with my favorite city girl. What's that saying? The one about how food is the language of love?" she asked, batting her eyes.

An image of the Mariposa cabin flashed before his eyes. If the saying Quinn quoted was true, those guests must certainly have been feeling the love. Ward didn't know exactly how deep his feelings for Tess ran. He admired and liked her. His physical attraction was obvious and had only increased since he'd begun spending more time with her. He'd invested a hell of a lot of thought into buying her boots. He wanted her around. He wanted to be inside her and make her cry as she came. That might not add up to love, but it was a lot more than he'd felt for a woman in a long time.

And it made the biting need to make love to her all the sharper.

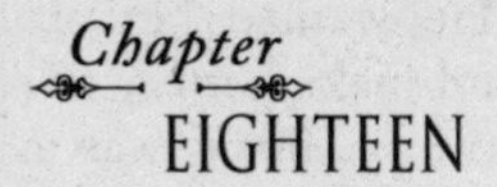

Chapter EIGHTEEN

ANYONE WHO CLAIMED that cooking for a room full of professionals was fun was as mad as Alice's hatter. Still, Tess thought she'd been handling the dinner preparations fairly well, even with Jeff watching her every move—her every slice, measure, and mix of ingredients—with eagle-eyed intensity until she was ready to scream that it was just *dinner*.

To make matters worse, the recipe had to be doubled to serve the entire kitchen—Jeff's and Roo's staff combined. The math didn't present too much of a challenge—or it wouldn't have if Jeff hadn't been rattling off questions about where her mother liked to buy her ingredients and how long the recipe had been in the family.

In sum, there was an awful lot of penne to boil and cheese to grate. She couldn't help but worry that one false move and instead of Romano cheese she'd be adding skin and blood to the recipe. Not a pleasant thought. The same fear gripped her while she was shaving parmesan and slicing asparagus for the salad. When she finished the prep work with her fingers still attached and intact, she was nearly giddy with relief.

Not a good state to be in when Ward entered the kitchen. Her giddiness made her even more susceptible to his presence than usual. A roaring filled her ears, as if the kitchen had magically transformed into a stadium filled to the rafters with screaming fans. Yet oddly, everyone in the kitchen—Roo had come over to watch her prepare the fig crostata with the same unnerving intensity as her colleague—and Heather, Gordon, and Chris, who were crisscrossing the space, preparing the last of the dinner orders, faded to near invisibility. They became mere shades the second she saw Ward.

He'd just showered. His hair was damp and curling at the ends and his jaw was freshly shaven. With her senses askew, she somehow knew that despite the distance separating them she would only have to breathe deeply to catch his clean, soapy scent. It would fill her like a physical thing.

Her fingers sank into the ball of dough she'd let chill for an hour in the massive walk-in refrigerator. It was cool and slightly sticky against her skin, and she realized then that the rest of the dinner would be like this: torturous reminders of the scene she and Ward had happened upon this morning. As she spread the thick, sweet, grappa-spiked fig jam, she imagined that she wasn't applying it over the flattened dough but rather over Ward's quivering muscles. Her hand shook.

"Wow, if I weren't so eager to taste your mom's baked penne, I'd suggest we skip straight to dessert. That crostata looks really delicious, doesn't it, Ward?" Jeff said.

"Yeah, it does." His voice was like a low rumble of thunder, intense and thrilling.

"I think I'm going to have to eat a couple of slices at least. One plain and then a second drizzled with heavy cream. Whipped might be tasty. Not strictly traditional, but sometimes rules need to be broken. What do you think, Tess?"

"Mm-hmm." The sound was far too close to a moan. She hadn't prayed in a while. Now seemed like a good time. Please, no more speculating on the merits of heavy cream. Make that no more food-related questions, period. She couldn't take another food fantasy without turning into a babbling idiot. "Uh, I could use a really big glass of ice water."

"Worked up a thirst?" Roo asked her.

"Kind of." If drinking it didn't cool her down, she could always dump it over her head.

The dinner Tess had prepared was delicious. The food was flavorful, nicely presented yet unpretentious. After the hard ride he'd put in on Rio, Ward would normally have enjoyed seconds and been happy to hang out with Roo and Jeff and the kitchen staff, all food lovers and great people to break bread with. But as he polished off course after course, he was consumed by one thought: He might not be responsible for the consequences if he didn't get Tess alone. Soon.

Ward wasn't sure if anyone around the long table, which Heather and Chris had set up and decorated with white linen cloths and votive candles and sprigs of rosemary and lavender in bud vases, noticed how quiet he and Tess were throughout dinner.

They were having too good a time.

The wine, a Montepulciano d'Abruzzo supplied by Ward, was flowing, Jeff had his iPod playing a mix of Dean Martin, Paolo Conte, and Frank Sinatra in tribute to the meal Tess had prepared, and Heather and Chris had already felt compelled by the tunes and the deliciousness of the baked penne to get up from the table and perform a laid-back swing dance.

They'd be a sight to enjoy, too, except Tess was finishing her fig crostata. Ward twirled the wine in the bowl of his glass and concentrated on not snapping the stem between his fingers. He wanted that mouth on him. He wanted that sweet pink tongue trailing and lapping, those white teeth nipping and scoring. Any path she chose to travel along his body was fine with him, but he wanted the explorations to begin now.

And he intended to return the favor, lick for lick, nibble for nibble.

Tess finished the last bite of her crostata, and he was torn between cursing and groaning in relief that the sensual torture-pleasure of watching the loaded fork slip past her parted lips was finally at an end.

He rose from his chair and circled the table, his step determined. Woe to anyone who tried to come between him and Tess, distract him with chitchat, or quiz her about whether adding fresh figs to the crostata would improve the dessert. He just might toss them into the corner of the empty dining room. He stopped by her chair and held out his hand. "Let's go."

"I—we can't just *leave*!" Her voice was high pitched with anxiety.

His gaze swept the table. Roo, Jeff, Chris, and Liz merely smiled . . . Cheshire cat smiles. Okay, so maybe they had noticed how quiet and edgy he and Tess had been throughout the meal. Or else they'd heard a whisper about a budding romance; Silver Creek was a hotbed of juicy gossip. For all Ward cared they could have read about him and Tess in the local paper. All that mattered was being alone with Tess. Starting now.

"Yeah, we can." He reached down and took her hand. "Night, all."

"Night," they echoed amiably.

"Thanks for the delicious meal, Tess," Jeff said, raising his glass of grappa in salute.

"Don't you need me to—" Her voice was strained. Nerves, he thought. He was feeling pretty edgy himself.

"You cooked. We ate. Ergo, we clean up," Jeff said.

"Yeah, those are the rules," Roo confirmed.

Before Tess could find any other topics to discuss, Ward tugged her hand and led her out of the low-lit dining room, past Natalie working at the front desk, who barely bothered to glance up from her computer screen, and into the night.

Chapter NINETEEN

COLD DARKNESS ENVELOPED them. Or maybe it just seemed cold because her body was flushed with arousal. She wasn't wearing a coat, and her skin, already tingly with excitement, broke out in goose bumps. Her breasts, tight and achy from rubbing against the lace of her bra with each hurried step she took, distracted her the most. She bit her lip hard to keep from whimpering.

"Are we marching off to battle?" Please let him think it was the maniacal pace he was setting that made her breathless.

He stopped abruptly and managed a laugh. "Sorry, it's just—ah, the hell with it." And he hauled her into his arms, his mouth swooping down and claiming her.

As a first kiss it was brutal. Raw. And absolutely wonderful. His mouth was hot, a fiery explosion of need that drove away the chill and had her pressing against him, opening her mouth wider and tangling her tongue with his, seeking, demanding all he could give her.

He responded with a low growl of approval, and pulled her even closer. Tess could feel the frantic pounding of his heart. It beat in time to hers. When at last they separated, their mingled breath formed a cloud of desire in the dark night.

"Wow." Dazed, it was all she could manage.

"Yeah. Your place or mine?"

"Yours." She made an effort to pull her thoughts together. "Your bed is bound to be bigger."

"Have I told you I like the way your mind works?" He'd already resumed walking, moving at the same urgent clip as before, practically towing her along. "I'm looking forward to discovering a whole bunch of new things to like about you."

She tried not to trip. "Gosh, you're really upping the stakes here. Hope you're not going to be disappointed." She almost managed the flip tone she normally employed. Almost but not quite. Could he detect the thread of uncertainty in it?

He paused long enough to let his gaze travel over her. Its weight caressed. If she'd been a cat, she'd have purred. As it was she had to stifle her moan.

She saw a quick flash of white as he smiled. He obviously had excellent hearing. "I don't think we have anything to worry about."

Ward had left a few lights on. The ranch-style house, built from timber and stone and with the same design principles as the main guest lodge and cabins, had large windows and a flowing spaciousness to it. As with the other structures on the property, it pleased the eye.

It could have been a shack for all she cared.

Right now she had much more serious things to consider, such as how much she liked its owner. How much she liked his kisses, too, their raw power as elemental as a storm ripping through a summer sky. Their intensity left her breathless. Enthralled.

She barely noticed the softly lit living room decorated with comfortable-looking armchairs and a matching sofa, or the large stone fireplace. Ward didn't seem interested in showing the space off, either. His hand wrapped about hers, he marched her past it and into the adjacent room. His bedroom. A flick of the switch on the wall illuminated two lamps on either side of a massive platform bed.

Given the speed at which Ward was operating, she knew that he could have them naked and entwined on that slate blue comforter in a few deftly orchestrated seconds.

He turned, and she knew he was going to kiss her again and that if he did, the tempest that was Ward's touch would sweep her up and she'd be lost. Perhaps even more thoroughly lost than when David entered her life.

Her raised hand stayed him. She needed to lay down the ground rules. Make him understand. Otherwise there'd be no way she could do this.

"Listen. I haven't done this in a while. Not since David. I should have, but I didn't."

He raised a dark brow in surprise. "Should have?"

"Yeah. When our marriage went bad, when David left, I was thrown off balance for a while." No need to go into the details of her crying jags, the terrible confusion, and the despondence of those early days. "So I didn't want to get involved." Her attempt at a casual shrug failed. It was as jerky as a marionette being ruthlessly yanked. "And when David got sick, and called me from the hospital, when he slipped into a coma, well, that was a terrible period. I was with him in the hospital, but I wasn't the same person he'd married. I couldn't be. After he died, I just wanted to escape, leave everything that had happened far behind."

"I can't imagine what you went through. I'm so sorry," he said as he raised his hand and cupped the side of her face. The tenderness of his gesture made her heart ache and swell with sudden yearning. She ignored it. To give in to silly romantic desires would be disastrous.

Physical, she reminded herself. She had to keep this physical.

"Ward, I didn't tell you this to have you feel sorry for me. That's the last thing I want. What I need is for you to understand that I'm not looking for anything serious or permanent. I'm not looking for love. I don't need any promises." Her voice lowered to a whisper. "I just want this." She laid her hand over his and drew it down to her breast.

His eyes held hers for a long moment. She met his gaze squarely, and stiffened her spine so she wouldn't tremble.

It must have convinced him. He gave a sweetly crooked smile. "Okay. I think I can work with that."

He closed his fingers, kneading her breast lightly, sending lightning shooting through her. The moan that tumbled from her lips was caught as he covered them with his own. His tongue entered, rubbing, circling, arousing her beyond belief. With his free arm he drew her flush against the hard muscled length of him. Like a brand, he seared her, body and soul, marking her as his.

She'd seen ample evidence of his clever and quick hands. It shouldn't have surprised her when her blouse and skirt fell to the floor without her even noticing that he'd been working the buttons and fastenings. Caught in the raw pleasure of his kisses and the roaming caresses of his hands as he stroked her and fondled her, she simply accepted her extraordinary good luck at being with a man blessed with superior moves. She kissed him like she was starving.

But then he stepped back, and the absence of his hands on her made her body shake from want. Her aching nipples, pebble-hard, strained against the lace of her bra, begging for his touch.

He took his time, looking his fill. The bright gold glitter in his eyes told her he approved of the deep lavender bra and matching panties she'd chosen. Slowly his gaze traveled down her legs to the cowboy boots she'd elected to wear. She'd told herself that the boots would be super comfortable to cook in but as she'd pulled them on before heading to the main lodge, she'd acknowledged the truth. She was wearing them for him.

His smile was wolfish. Hungry and ever so predatory. And for the first time since coming here she wasn't in the least freaked out at being in the presence of a wild animal.

"Very nice." Even as he spoke his long fingers skimmed the valley between her breasts and found the bra's front clasp. A *click* and it opened. Slowly his fingers trailed over her skin to drag the satin straps off her shoulders. The bra fell away.

"Very, very nice." His quiet voice was a husky rasp, low and thrilling. "You're even more beautiful than I imagined." His hands cupped her breasts, and, at his touch, she groaned aloud. His smile widened, white and wicked. Slowly he lowered his head, bringing his mouth to her aching nipple. He suckled, drawing it deep into his mouth, scoring its tight bud with his teeth, and then lavished the same exquisite care on her other breast. She arched, crying as pleasure pooled deep inside her, as her muscles quivered with arousal.

As he drove her wild with his tongue and teeth, raining kisses over her, Ward's fingers slipped inside the elastic band of her panties. Inch by inch he dragged the lacy material down her legs. Crouching, he guided the panties over her boots, held her as she stepped out of them, and tossed them away.

Rocking back on his heels, he studied her. There was no way she could quiet her heaving breasts. Or stop her body from trembling, silently begging for the caress of his hands, the wet heat of his mouth. Impossible. She needed him so.

He didn't seem to mind. "You know, I think we've moved beyond nice to mind-blowing," he said in a low-pitched voice that caressed like velvet. "We'll leave the boots on . . . for now."

He walked her back to the bed, an erotic waltz in which the fabric of his clothes brushed her naked body. Each graze ratcheted up her arousal. Heat pulsed in her core as everything inside her tightened and throbbed in reckless want.

The backs of her knees met the padded edge of the bed.

Exquisite though it would have been to let herself fall backward and have Ward follow her down onto the mattress and continue his sensual torment, she stopped. "My turn."

For a second she thought he might continue with his expert seduction. Then he smiled a crooked, beautiful smile. "Far be it from me to argue with a naked lady."

She laughed, grateful that he was funny and smart. And, as she went to work on the serious mission of getting Ward even more naked than she was—because she was determined to divest him of every article of clothing—she added "completely gorgeous" and "outrageously sexy" to the list of things to be thankful for.

Unbuttoning his shirt, she dragged it off him, then paused in hushed appreciation. There was something to be said for the country life. Muscles sculpted from ranch work contoured his broad shoulders, molded his chest, and created mouthwatering ridges down his abdomen.

Then she saw the scar. A jagged, puckered line, it ran down his side and toward his navel. It was thick and hideous looking and at the sight of it an invisible fist squeezed her heart. Reid hadn't exaggerated. Had the blade from that hopped-up gang member sliced any deeper, this amazing man would probably have died.

She traced the horrid thing with her finger. "This must have hurt."

His breath whistled as his abdominals jumped beneath the pad of her finger. "Like hell. But I was very brave."

She swallowed but couldn't manage the same light tone. "No doubt. You got this when you came to Brian's rescue, right?"

"Someone told you, huh? Figures." He gave a slight, impatient shake of his head. "Look, it happened a long time ago. I'm fine. I've even been told by Quinn that the scar lends character. The ladies seem to agree. They're all quite impressed."

She recognized the distraction for what it was. After all, she was an expert at avoiding certain topics. But because she was feeling very indulgent, she decided to let him think he'd succeeded. "They are, are they?" She arched her brows.

"Mmm-hmm, though I like to think that the scar's not the only thing that impresses them."

She let her gaze travel over his naked torso. No, it wouldn't be. For Pete's sake, the trail of dark hair that began just below his navel and disappeared behind the waist of his trousers was enough to make her knees go weak. "Well, I guess I'll have to take a closer look and see whether I can discover anything remotely impressive about you."

"I was hoping you'd say that. And, sweetheart, I think you'll find it's close at hand."

"Oh, yeah? Would that be this hand?" She let her fingers travel down the silky dark line that bisected his abs.

"You're on the right track."

"I think I'll be the judge of that." Reaching his belt buckle, she flicked it open and then drew the zipper of his trousers down, letting her knuckles rub the rigid length of his erection.

Ward's ragged groan was the sweetest sound.

His penis was clearly delineated. Thick and long, it strained against the cotton of his black briefs. Her breath grew shallow. With a yank she pulled the waistband of his trousers down his lean hips.

"Impatient?" he asked, a hint of laughter in his voice.

"Yes. Do you have a problem with that?"

"Can't say I do. I'm feeling a little desperate myself. Here," he said and began helping her, shucking off his boots and socks then his trousers and briefs with a speed that would have been comical if it weren't so gratifying. So very gratifying.

Eager and proud, his penis jutted out. In response her body grew wet and tight and needy. She wanted him inside her, deep inside her, filling her.

She reached out to stroke him, but he stopped her with a rueful shake of his head. "Sorry, Tess, but I'm on a really short fuse here. Touch me and I'll explode."

"Really?" She loved the idea that he was this aroused. "That might be fun."

"This will be a lot more fun, I guarantee." He pushed her lightly and, as she fell onto the bed, followed her down. Their bodies met in a kiss of heated flesh that left them both moaning.

"Hello, you," he said as he settled his hard length over her.

The alignment was near perfect.

"So glad we could meet this way." She wiggled just a little so his shaft pressed against the juncture of her thighs. He gave a strangled curse and closed his eyes for a moment.

When he opened them again, they burned with intensity. "I think it's time we get to know each other better." He lowered his lips to hers and kissed her slowly, thoroughly, as he rocked his hips, rubbing his shaft against her clitoris. "Lots better."

She ran her palms over the taut muscles of his butt, urging him closer. "That would be nice. Do you have anything particular in mind?" Lord, he had a really fine ass.

His kiss turned rougher, a little wild with need, and that was really fine, too, she thought. When his hands moved to her breasts, cupping and squeezing, and teasing their tight sensitive peaks, she pretty much lost all ability to think. Except to acknowledge that she'd never felt so good before or wanted someone inside her so much.

Trailing his mouth along the line of her jaw to her earlobe, he caught it between his teeth and nipped the soft flesh then licked away the sting.

"Ward—" His name was a plea as her body convulsed beneath him.

"Here's an idea." His whisper fanned the shell of her ear. "Why don't you lift those long legs of yours and put those cowboy boots right here?" With her legs gripping his waist, he jacked his body up to kneel on the bed. "Mmm-hmm, yeah, very nice," he said, looking down at her naked and open to him.

Wrapping an arm beneath her hips to support her, he rubbed the broad head of his cock against her, gliding ever more easily as she coated him with wet heat. His brilliant gaze never left hers and he held her fast even as she writhed and bucked in need.

"Please, Ward, I want you. I want you in me now." Her voice was frantic and she was beyond caring.

His smile was primitive. "How about this?" He pressed an inch forward.

She hooked her boots together to draw him closer. "I have it on good authority that these are kick-ass boots," she warned.

"Then, in the interest of self-preservation—"

With a single powerful thrust he embedded himself. Crying out with pleasure, she arched off the bed, drawing him even deeper.

For a second neither of them spoke. She knew he, too, was absorbing the incredible sensations rolling through them.

"Better?" he whispered, brushing her lips slowly.

"Oh, yes." It wasn't just better, it was magical. On fire for him, she shimmied her hips and clenched him tighter.

"Christ, Tess. You are incredible." His sensual teasing was at an end. His face, all hard planes, was stamped with fierce arousal. With a flex of his hips, he withdrew and then rocked into her, penetrating her more. He did it again, driving deeper still.

She moaned as her core began to contract helplessly about him, her entire body trembling with need. "Ward, please, I—"

He grabbed her hands and pulled them above her head. Linking their fingers together, he whispered hoarsely. "I've got you. Hold on."

He moved with a controlled force that thrilled, fulfilling every sensual promise of his strong athletic body. Each surge had her moaning in ecstasy, her body arching beneath his, her toes curling inside her boots as her hands clutched his fiercely, frantically; each withdrawal had her whimpering at the loss.

His kisses, wickedly plundering, as irresistible as the barely leashed wildness of his body driving into her, consumed her with equal passion. He took her higher and higher, filling her with undiluted ecstasy.

Together they climbed, coming ever closer, their whispers turning to broken moans and helpless gasps.

"Ward?" she managed to gasp.

"Yeah, babe?"

"Whatever you do, don't ever stop."

He brushed his lips over hers. “Never, Tess.”
He was as good as his word.

Much, much later, Ward removed Tess’s cowboy boots, too.

Naked, they slept as they’d made love, bodies pressed together and entwined. Breaths mingling, hearts matching beat for pounding beat.

Chapter TWENTY

WARD AWOKE A happy man, a very happy man.

Hard not to be when Tess was sleeping half-draped over him, her bare leg sandwiched between his and her breath sending her long, dark bangs tickling his chest with every exhale. He lay with his arm looped possessively about her, listening to the nesting birds stir outside his still-darkened window and herald the March dawn with energetic chirps. Spring was sweeping winter away. Change was in the air.

Ward definitely approved of the changes that had occurred last night. He shifted, drawing Tess even closer against him, and smiled when her nipples pebbled against his chest. She was so beautiful and so incredibly responsive.

It came as no surprise that the sex between them had been fantastic. The sight of Tess with her long legs and deliciously lush curves clad in nothing but the cowboy boots he'd bought for her, had nearly blown his mind. The pleasure they'd found in each other's bodies had been equally stunning. Tess was a passionate woman, generous and uninhibited.

But there'd been something else he discovered. When he'd been deep inside her body, their gazes locked as she trembled convulsively around him, he'd felt somehow like they belonged to each other. It was a sense of connection that went beyond the merely physical. The memory made him shift slightly so he could press a kiss against her head and breathe in the scent of her sleep-warmed skin.

Whether Tess would admit what had happened to them was anything more serious than a long, thrilling bout of five-star sex was another question. Actually, he was pretty sure she'd deny it with her usual tough-cookie sass. Now that he'd begun to put together the pieces of the puzzle that was Tess Casari he understood why she might be even more commitment shy than he was. Though there were still some gaping holes in the picture, certain details were becoming clear. The most troubling one was how hurt she'd been by her late husband.

Tess was the sort of woman who should be looking for the warmth, joy, and love she'd enjoyed in her marriage. It was becoming terribly clear that her marriage had provided few of those things. Her words to him the night before had made it plain her marriage had destroyed the hopes she'd carried in her heart entering it. The evidence had been there, audible in the strained catch of her voice, visible in the shadows lurking in her eyes.

It had made him want to draw her into his arms and kiss away the hurt, soothe her with murmured words.

But then she'd continued her speech, informing him that she didn't need his pity, nor did she want promises of forever. And another part of him, the part that, ever since Erica had returned his engagement ring with a "Thanks, but no thanks," was determined to avoid emotional entanglements, had heard Tess's words with a surge of relief. He was off the hook, messy emotion-wise.

What man determined to remain single wouldn't feel

like he'd been given a prettily wrapped gift were a beautiful, desirable woman to tell him she wanted only to have sex with him, no strings attached?

Guilty as charged, he'd been more than willing to agree to a plan that so neatly meshed with his own MO.

But after last night he didn't think that what they'd shared could simply be described as two people having a bang-up time scratching each other's itches. Sex with Tess went way beyond that, into a new territory.

In case he needed yet another sign that whatever had happened last night wasn't nearly as simple as Tess had decreed it should be, he wasn't remotely ready to utter the words "Thanks for the great time last night. Let's do it again sometime."

He wanted more with her.

It was still early but Ward, taking care not to disturb her, rolled out of bed and pulled on his jeans. In the kitchen, he flipped on the coffee maker and then decided to go one better and fix her some toast from a loaf of seeded whole wheat.

As he waited for the coffee to finish dripping and the toaster to ding, he looked out the window. There was just enough light to make out the roof lines of the barns, the fences demarcating the corrals, and the jagged outlines of the mountains in the distance. His home. His life.

Ward would be the first to acknowledge what a great life it was. He lived in one of the most beautiful places in the world. He loved the people around him. His family was healthy, supportive, and remarkably nondysfunctional. He could handle their bouts of nosiness and interference knowing they were fueled by love.

Perhaps that was the reason he'd been able to resist Erica's demands, her however-many-step plan to transform him from a rancher and hotelier into someone who tended his financial portfolio and God knows what else.

After Erica moved on to far greener pastures, he'd taken stock and recognized that, all things considered, he was still one lucky bastard.

He wondered whether he would have come to the same conclusion had it been Tess who walked out of his life.

A few days later, Tess was in her office, clicking through the sample wedding portraits the photographer-videographer had sent to showcase her talent. Tess had already booked an appointment with Liz Reading, the photographer, so that Liz could meet Carrie and Brian, but as their visit approached—they were due to arrive Friday midday—Tess was compulsively double-checking all the vendors and merchants she'd preselected for the couple.

She felt fairly confident about Liz Reading, though. The photographer used settings to great effect in her pictures. That would mean a lot to Carrie and Brian, since their wedding would be held in such a beautiful place. Tess clicked on a night shot. Locked in a tender embrace, a bride and groom stood at the edge of a lake where a flotilla of votive candles bobbed in the blue-black water. Liz Reading had caught the moon's reflection so that its path led across the water, waiting for the couple to take their first steps together.

How lovely, Tess thought a little mistily.

A lot of things were striking her as lovely, and it was easy to pinpoint when she'd shed her disenchanted attitude. It coincided with the hour she'd removed her clothes for Ward and stepped into his arms, naked except for the cowboy boots he'd given her. Funny that a man she'd labeled as proud and rude should be the reason for the glow that now seemed to touch everything around her, illuminating herself as well.

Her cell rang and she answered with a distracted "Hello?," her gaze still fixed on the computer screen in front of her.

"Oh my God, your cowboy's gone viral!"

She straightened in her chair in surprise. "Anna?"

"Who else? Okay, maybe I'm exaggerating a bit about the video going viral, but it's pretty sensational. Have you checked the numbers, the reach?"

"No, I haven't. Phil, who handles reservations and is a big back office numbers cruncher, likes to be in charge of that stuff. And things have been pretty, um, busy around here. Lots going on."

In all honesty, Armageddon could have been unfolding and Tess probably wouldn't have noticed. In the three days since she and Ward had first made love she'd yet to catch her breath. She lost it every time Ward kissed her, touched her, or simply looked at her. That lazy gleam in his eyes drove her wild. Even when he wasn't nearby, he occupied her thoughts—invaded them with the same confidence he did everything else. It left her dazed and happy and smiling.

She hadn't smiled so much in . . . never.

"Well, I think your boss is gonna be pleased with the buzz you've created. And let me tell you, now that I've seen him in action, I've got to admit the raw material is mighty fine. Who knew watching a guy on a horse keep a cow away from its buddies could be so darned exciting?"

Tess could list a whole bunch of things Ward could do that were even more exciting. For instance, watching him walk toward her and knowing he was going to take her hand or perhaps slip his arm about her waist and draw her close while his lips unerringly found the pulse at the hollow of her neck could cause her heart to skip and desire to flutter deep inside her. Not just desire but bone-deep happiness—the feeling as beautiful as a flock of birds taking flight, their beating wings caught in a ray of light.

She was so happy she was loopy with it, but at least she had the sense not to blurt out how incredible Ward was. She didn't want to be charged with deviating from the "It's Just Sex" route, which anyone listening to her—Anna especially—might quickly suspect.

She wasn't deviating so much as skirting, a fine but important distinction. She was doing her best to navigate the treacherous territory she found herself in, enjoying every moment with Ward yet still keeping her head and heart. Not an easy task when he made her feel so special, when he was so much more than she'd expected as a lover.

Of course he was stupendous in bed. Anyone who could move as he did, who was graced with his hands and mouth and who possessed any kind of appreciation for the female body, would be pretty hot between the sheets. Or against a wall. Or on a dresser, driving into her to the accompanying beat of the metal handles jangling against the drawers. But Ward could probably blow a woman's mind in a tent on the lumpy ground—he was that talented.

Though wonderfully impressive, his sexual prowess wasn't what truly made her have to work so hard at remembering the ground rules she'd laid out for them. It was the little gestures that most likely anyone else but Tess would have assumed was her due, such as bringing her coffee in bed. He would not only do that, but after passing her the steaming cup, he'd stretch out beside her and talk, sharing bits about what he had to do that day on the ranch and at the guest lodge and then asking what was on her agenda. And while they talked, his arm would find its way around her shoulders to caress them. Then his fingers would comb through her tangled hair, stroking it and toying with it. Simple sharing, simple touching.

No man had ever thought to bring her coffee before, not even David. In hindsight she saw that all too soon he'd been far more interested in orchestrating and controlling their time together. He'd always needed to be the star, the bright focal point. Dazzled as she'd been, it hadn't occurred to her to question the dynamic.

"Ward's good at a lot of things," she finally answered, knowing she had to say something in response to Anna's comment. Though she tried to make her tone stoutly loyal rather than dreamy, her friend was too perceptive.

"Oh, boy! You did the deed, didn't you? Oh, I am so proud of you, *cara*! So maybe it's time to say *'Mille grazie,'* for sending you to a place where you'd find a cowboy dude to tear up the sheets with."

Anna was never going to let her forget the role she'd played in landing Tess in Acacia. "Thank you, Anna," she said obediently.

"You're welcome," she replied, all graciousness. "Now I understand why you haven't been monitoring the stats on your tweets. Share time, girlfriend. You don't have to give me all the spicy details of what you and your cowboy have been up to, just ninety-nine percent of them. My phone's fully charged so you can start . . . now."

Tess laughed. "First of all, may I remind you that Ward and I are employed full-time? With his parents gone, Ward's got even more to do at the ranch and the lodge." Which made how attentive he was to her in and out of bed all the more gratifying.

"Teresa Elisabetta Casari, are you going to make me board a plane?"

"Nothing I'd like better."

"Me, too. I miss you. God, I might even have to sign

up for that cowgirl weekend so I can see some of this wonderful machismo in action."

"I'd love it. Phil and Reid have decided to hold it on the last weekend in July. Say the word and I'll reserve a cabin for you."

"So you'll be staying through July then. That would bring your stay at Silver Creek up to, wow, six months, right?"

The question made Tess pause. Quickly she tallied the months. Back in January she would have laughed herself silly at the suggestion that she might want stay half a year or even longer in this place. Now there was so much she wanted to do and so many opportunities, both professional and personal, to explore. She felt like she wasn't just getting experience as an events planner; she was growing as a person.

She shied away from considering how her new relationship with Ward would factor into the equation. To probe deeper would violate the "It's Just Sex" rules.

Anna was still talking. "Late July, huh? I have tons of vacation time but I'll have to check the schedule with Giorgio. If that weekend doesn't work out, I'll arrange another one, perhaps a romantic getaway for Lucas and me. He'd look so fine in a pair of chaps." She sighed lustily. "So, Tess, won't you dish just a teeny bit to get me through the rest of day until Lucas comes home?"

Tess took pity on her. "Okay. The video getting all the buzz? Ward's a zillion times sexier in the flesh—I mean in person."

"Of course," Anna said, her tone as solemn as the grave.

"And, well, he's very detail oriented."

"A good thing in a man."

"And, okay." She drew a breath. "He's made me coffee in bed for the past three mornings."

"Very nice."

Trust Anna to understand. "And when I told him that I didn't need any special treatment, he smiled and said, 'That's why I like doing it.' "

"Oh! I like him!" Anna exclaimed happily. She was silent for a moment. "Do you think he has any Italian in him? Hmm, probably not," she said, answering her own question. "But we could make him an honorary Italian."

"He liked your crostata."

"That settles it then. So you've been busy as the bees and the birds—"

"Like I said, only after work." But Ward didn't waste a moment of their time alone, Tess thought with a smile. "The guests have been behaving themselves—no medical emergencies, dramas, or destroyed rooms—but there's a lot going on at the barns. Another foal and three more lambs were born."

"Yay. You know, I'm really enjoying the ranching life, especially when I don't actually have to walk into a barn. So we'll be getting pics of the baby animals on Pinterest?"

"They'll be there," Tess promised. "We may hold a contest so that our followers can choose a name for them." She and Quinn had come up with the plan. "And one of the guests who stayed here, her name's Madlon Glenn, did these great paintings of the sheep and lambs in the pastures. She's given me permission to post them."

"Cool. How's the wedding taking shape?"

"Brian and Carrie are coming on Friday. I've been busy finalizing all their appointments for the weekend." If there was a drawback to Brian and Carrie's impending arrival it was that she and Ward would have less time together. But maybe it was for the best. It would prevent her heart from straying into forbidden territory.

"They're seeing all the vendors in one weekend?"

"Yeah. I can't bank on them coming again before the wedding so this is my best chance to ensure they have a real say."

Anna whistled. "Big weekend for them and you."

"I'm looking forward to meeting them both. I just hope they're happy with how I've arranged things."

"Why wouldn't they be? You've done an amazing job seeing to all the details long-distance and with practically no time."

"I suppose. It's just that Carrie and Brian are so close to Ward. I want everything to go smoothly. Perfectly." And she wanted Ward and his family to be really pleased they'd placed their faith in her.

"You're forgetting rule number one. Nothing ever goes perfectly in this business. There's always some disaster—"

"Don't even mention that word!"

"—lurking. But don't worry, you're super good at dealing with them. Giorgio was always impressed by how calm you'd remain when chaos erupted."

It was a lesson Tess had learned from being around her brother, Chris. It never helped to add to his agitation.

"Maybe," she replied. "But it's much easier to remain levelheaded when it's not your flub-up, your too-stupid-for-words miscalculation."

"Nope. I just don't see that happening, *cara*."

"That crystal ball of yours better be telling the truth."

"You dare to doubt my powers? Oh my God, look at the time! Okay, off to make myself pretty for my urban cowboy. Ciao," Anna said.

Tess glanced at her watch and nearly leapt from her seat. That was the thing about talking with Anna. An hour conversation with her best friend flew by as if it were propelled by jet fuel. She had to get down to the barns.

Ward had told her he had a surprise for her at the horse barn and that she should wear her jeans. The boots were now an assumed necessity. She had to go change. Grabbing her iPhone in case there was something worthy of photographing, she hurried out.

Chapter TWENTY-ONE

SHE'D EXPECTED TO find Ward in the horse barn, perhaps standing quietly in one of the large stalls and watching the newest foal nurse. Instead she spotted him in the open area in front of the corral—she had no problem recognizing him in his dark beige cowboy hat, even with the brim pulled low. She could have picked Ward out of an arena filled with studly cowboys dressed in denim and the requisite Stetson. There was just something about him. He was standing beside a man dressed in a plaid shirt and khakis. The stranger was leaning against a little silver car.

Ward looked up at the sound of her footsteps on the gravel. "Hey," he said. "Tess, this is Mike O'Roarke. He has a car for sale."

Mike stuck out a hand for Tess to shake. "Yeah. My brothers and I convinced my mom to turn in her driver's license. She turned eighty last week. And her car doesn't really suit us—we need truck beds and horsepower to haul heavy loads so we've been looking for an interested buyer."

"Oh." Tess felt equal parts excitement and bewilderment. This was not what she had been expecting when Ward told her he had a surprise for her. She'd kind of hoped it involved a dark corner in the hayloft. "I'd be happy to look at your mom's car."

Mike stepped aside. "Here she is," he said, gesturing at the compact. "She's six years old, but only has forty thousand miles on her. Mom really only used her to get groceries, pick up the mail, and drive to the doctor's and such. But we put new radials on her last December and she's been well maintained—"

"With regular oil changes," Ward finished.

Tess shot him a look, but it wasn't nearly as fierce as it might have been. The man was amazing. How had he managed to find a car for her on top of all his other responsibilities? She tried hard not to stare at the very cute, shiny, undented car before her. She couldn't believe it was six years old. It looked almost new. On the heels of that thought came dismay. No way could she afford a car this nice.

The men were looking at her expectantly. She realized that she was probably supposed to go kick the nearly new tires and then maybe ask to see under the hood to verify that an engine was actually inside. But she remained where she was.

"Something wrong, Tess?"

Ward's question brought a flush to her cheeks. "I was just thinking—this car looks really nice. How much are you asking for it, Mr. O'Roarke?"

"Mike," he corrected. "We'd like to get three thousand for her. But Ward told me that you're really in need of a car, and that you've been relying on Ralph Cummins. No one should have to ride with Ralph more than once in his or her lifetime. So I'd be willing to shave off a couple hundred."

She could handle that price. "I think that sounds doable."

Mike smiled. "Okay then. You want to take her for a test drive?"

She let her gaze travel over the car. It really was adorable.

"Sure," she replied at the same time as Ward laid a hand on her arm and said, "Would you mind waiting an hour, Mike? Reid's around. I'm sure he's up for a beer or two. Tess and I were about to go riding."

"What?"

Tess was still in a state of shock twenty minutes later. Mike had gone off to find Reid, and Ward had guided her into the corral, where he was fiddling with the saddle on one of the two horses tied to the rail, a big dark horse that looked as solid as a tank. And to Tess twice as big.

"So, you ready?"

"Haven't I had my surprise for the day? The car is great. You can stop there."

Ward laughed infuriatingly. "I'd like to introduce you to Brocco." He patted the horse on the neck with a hearty slap that it acknowledged by blowing heavily out of its nostrils. Tess wasn't charmed. "He's going to be taking you on a trail ride this afternoon—after you take a couple of turns in the corral."

Forget charmed, she was horrified. She didn't want to be introduced to this shaggy behemoth of a horse, let alone ride the thing. She'd come a long way in the animals-aren't-going-to-bite-or-stampede-me department, but there were limits.

Still, she'd have to let Ward down gently. It would be awful to hurt his feelings.

She gave him a bright smile. "Thanks, but I'll pass. After I take a ride in my new car—you know, the reliable, inanimate object—I have to get back to planning the whole cowgirls' weekend with Quinn. But my research is complete. I've learned more than I ever thought about what cowgirls like to get up to on a ranch. No need to get on a horse's back. Though he certainly is, um, impressive."

The corner of Ward's mouth lifted in amusement. "Brocco is the bravest, gentlest soul you'll ever meet. I tell you, Angie's rabid in comparison."

She fought a grin at the image of sweet fuzzy Angie as a rabid beast. "I don't think you should talk about Angie that way. There must be some law against defaming lambs."

"Just stating facts. Brocco's the perfect horse for you to learn to ride on. I want to show you how much fun riding is, Tess. You're going to love it."

She shook her head. He was doing an excellent job selling the idea, but she was skeptical to the marrow of her bones. "I know as much as I need to about riding. I see the guests limp into the lodge after a trail ride and hear them groan as they sit down, complaining about their sore backs, legs, and butts." She raised her brows. "Those being the only body parts they're willing to mention in public."

He rested his elbows on the top rail and leaned forward, the brim of his hat nearly grazing her forehead. His eyes gleamed wicked and intent. "And what if I promise to kiss every sore inch of you, kiss you and make you all better?" he asked in a husky tone, and just like that, all the oxygen left her brain in one big *whoosh* as she imagined his mouth moving carefully and slowly over each tender spot, bestowing hot, healing kisses. She knew he'd be most thorough in his ministrations.

She eyed the horse named Brocco dolefully. "It must be snowing in hell."

He grinned. "That's my girl. You won't regret it."

Since the day Tess had rolled up to Silver Creek in that smoke-belching disaster of an automobile, Ward had recognized she had pluck and grit in spades. Even had the car she'd driven been brand-spanking new, Ward didn't know many women who'd have the courage to pack up and leave their city, job, friends, family, and connections for a completely new life where she knew not a soul. Moreover, she didn't boast—she simply shrugged the subject of her coming to Acacia off by saying that she'd needed a change.

Her explanation was too simple. Lots of people wanted to change their lives; few had the guts to pull up stakes and test themselves as she had. He thought of her traveling alone for thousands of miles in that piece-of-crap car, which was most likely held together with duct tape, superglue, and coat hangers. That she'd made it past New Jersey was a miracle. His blood ran cold thinking about what could have happened to her had she broken down on some isolated stretch of road.

And she continued to face her fears. Right now she was staring the biggest one—physically, at least—in the face.

"You ever patted a horse before?"

She made a face. "Like the horses that pull the carriages through Central Park or the horses the mounted police ride? Those things are huge, bigger even than Brocco here, and by the way, I think I'll need an escalator to get on top of him."

She tended to run off at the mouth when she was nervous, which only proved how brave she was because she hadn't ducked through the corral's rails to gain the safety of the other side.

"Won't need one," he answered. He probably sounded annoyingly cheerful to her, but being around her made him happy. He'd begun to realize it wasn't only when he was making love to her that he felt this extraordinary sense of rightness. It was there whenever she was near.

"But first things first," he continued. "Let's have

Brocco meet you. It's just like with the lambs, Tess. You want Brocco to learn your scent and get a good look at you. Come stand a bit to the side of his head. A horse's eyes are set wide, so it's easier for him to see you when you stand here." He drew her toward the gelding and stepped behind her, resting his hands on her hips in a show of support—and because he simply wanted to touch her.

As Tess let Brocco blow a warm gust of air over the back of her hand, Ward rattled off some information for her to store away in that clever brain. "Brocco was born on the ranch. He was a big bruiser even as a colt, so better suited as a pleasure horse than for cow work. He's eighteen, so by now he knows the trails backward and forward. He's a good guy—loves his job as a trail horse. You can trust him. How about climbing into the saddle?"

Her shoulders rose as she drew a breath. "Sure, why not? God, I can't even see over his back." She was craning her neck.

"Which makes the view that much better. You're going to be surprised by how much you enjoy this."

"Can I get that in writing?"

Ward hid a grin as he unlooped Brocco's reins and then walked the gelding into the center of the corral, Tess walking stiffly by his side.

"I'm going to give you a leg up but first, this," he said, and he angled his head and kissed her, his lips moving persuasively over hers. He kept kissing her until he felt her relax by incremental degrees.

When their lips parted she managed a tiny smile for him. "Is this standard service for all nervous novice riders?"

"No, ma'am," he drawled. "You're getting the special package."

"Music to a New Yorker's ears."

He laughed and pressed his lips to hers once more. Before she could get nervous again he said, "Give me your left leg." Cupping her shin, he said, "Ready? One, two, three."

He boosted her up in the air. Although he wouldn't term her landing exactly graceful, she nonetheless managed to swing her leg over and settle into the saddle.

"Ward, this is really high off the ground. Where's the seat belt?"

"No need for one. See these parts of your saddle?" His hands framed her front and back. "This is your pommel and cantle and they're shaped nice and high. And see this horn here? If you feel you're losing your balance and need something solid to hold on to, just grab hold of it."

"That I think I can do."

He gave her thigh a pat and felt the muscle beneath her tight jeans leap in response. If he hadn't been determined to get her comfortable and confident on Brocco, he might have let his hand wander, discovering what other places might quicken beneath his touch. Later, he promised himself. Later he'd peel her out of those jeans and sweater and indulge himself, kissing and stroking her as she writhed and arched beneath him, urging him on, her moans of pleasure fueling his.

Right now he had the responsibility of encouraging her to discover an entirely new pleasure: the thrill of being carried on Brocco's broad back. It was up to him to orchestrate it perfectly.

She didn't know how he did it, but whenever the fear started to overwhelm her, Ward was there, immediate and reassuring, telling her what to do with the horse, his voice as soothing as if she were cradled in his strong arms.

With his coaching, she let her legs relax and lengthen, and loosened her death grip on the saddle horn protruding from the center of the saddle.

She actually thought she was doing a good job keeping the terror of riding the huge horse at bay when Ward announced that now that she and Brocco had executed two perfect laps of the corral they were going to head out on the trail.

"Are you sure about that?" she asked, her voice shrill. "What if he decides to run off somewhere, like to the nearest grain store?"

"He's not going to go any faster than a walk today. You can trust him."

"You're sure we won't go any faster than this?" She was babbling but that was the least of her worries.

"I promise."

She drew a calming breath. She believed him. It was simple. It was amazing. Yeah, he'd shamelessly seduced her onto Brocco's back with that irresistible line about kissing all her aching parts (of which she guaranteed she'd have at least a hundred), but she'd known even as she relented that Ward would keep her safe. In the wreckage of her marriage to David, her ability to trust had been severely damaged. Yet Ward, whom she'd initially pegged as high-handed and arrogant, had been the one to restore it. He was a proud man. But she now understood that his pride went hand in hand with a profound decency and honesty. If he told her she'd be safe with Brocco, then he'd do everything to make that so.

In which case she might as well try to relax, especially since her muscles were threatening to cramp big-time.

She made herself concentrate on the foreign noises: the heavy clop and scrape of Brocco's hooves on the dirt path as they followed the line of fenced pasture. She marveled at the sounds he made—the round, wet snorts, the grunts that emanated from deep in his belly. Combined with the jangle of the metal bit and the creak of the leather saddle, they made oddly fascinating music.

Slowly she learned the rolling rhythm of Brocco's walk and unbent herself enough to move with it by rocking her lower back. Her grip around the saddle horn remained tight, but she no longer clutched it like a panicked child.

Astride Rio, Ward walked abreast of her, and she figured that the horses must be used to this. Their necks swayed and their heads bobbed in an easy sync. They passed fields dotted with cattle in small and large clumps, some with tails swishing as they grazed. A few lay on the earth dozing. They looked like black and rust-red boulders against the afternoon sky.

The cattle made her think of the video she'd made. "My friend Anna called me earlier. Apparently the video I took of you and Bilbao when you were keeping that cow away from the rest of the herd has gotten really popular. You're a hit."

"Bilbao's a fine horse."

"I don't think the people following my tweets know any more about horses than I do. I meant you personally are the hit."

"So that explains Phil's euphoria. He said he'd no sooner posted the dates for the cowgirls' weekend on the website than he was deluged with emails and calls."

Something in Ward's voice made her glance at him. Not even the shadow of his hat could conceal the red flag coloring his cheek. Wonder of wonders, he was embarrassed. Who knew the man could be cute as well as sexy as all get-out?

She couldn't resist teasing him. "Guess there must be a lot of women hoping you're part of the weekend package."

"Christ, I thought this Twitter business would be about increasing the number of bookings—"

"And not the number of women looking at pics of yummy hunks doing cowboy stuff? The two go hand in hand."

After grumbling something under his breath, he said, "I'll figure out a way to get Reid and Quinn to handle the activities that weekend. It shouldn't be hard to twist their arms."

Enjoying herself thoroughly, she managed to shrug without jerking on the reins, something Ward had said was a no-no in riding. "Fine. You want to cause a riot and have a bunch of irate women post lousy reviews on TripAdvisor because they didn't get to bat their eyelashes at the star of their cowboy fantasies, that's your business."

A muscle twitched beneath his stubble-shadowed jaw. Then he ground out, "I'm calling for an immediate moratorium on pics or videos of me. Stick to Reid."

"He *is* a lot prettier."

Distracted, she hadn't realized how far they'd traveled—Brocco's gait covered a lot more ground than she'd have guessed—and suddenly she became aware that the terrain had changed dramatically. They'd entered the forest, surrounded by the trees she'd previously seen only from a distance as a dark green smudge covering the mountains.

She glanced up. Pale bands of light sliced the thick canopy. The tree trunks reminded her of the columns in a cathedral, their towering lines arching overhead as their branches joined. Cool moist air hung heavy in the hushed quiet. Even the horses' hooves were muffled. She'd never seen trees so tall, so massive, so numerous. As a setting it was beautiful and a tiny bit unsettling. Yet Brocco's pace remained steady. If he wasn't nervous, surely she could remain calm. Awed but calm.

They didn't speak. For Tess, speaking of the mundane would be akin to desecration in such a place. To voice what was growing stronger in her heart was impossible, too. Because though the trees had probably survived for centuries here, she feared that what she felt for Ward might not—that somehow the love she sensed taking root in her heart would be destroyed by as-of-yet unseen forces. She reminded herself of the promise she'd made—to keep things physical, to avoid thinking of a relationship that involved commitment and love—and rode on next to the man who had given her more than he could ever guess.

Chapter TWENTY-TWO

WARD WAS NOTHING if not diligent in searching out all the spots that were sore from Tess's first horseback ride. After test-driving Mike O'Roarke's car, which she decided she loved because its driver's seat felt like heaven rather than like a saddle, they'd gone to his house where, with a take-charge authority she was coming to appreciate in a whole new way, he'd stripped her out of her clothes and then shucked his own before scooping her up and carrying her to the tiled walk-in shower.

Under the pulsing hot jets, he'd commenced his first round of ministrations. Caressing her with soap-slicked hands and the rough cat-tongue lick of the washcloth, he kneaded her muscles with long, sure strokes, massaging them until they felt as pliant as warm putty.

He didn't stop there. Wrapping her in a fluffy bath towel, he carried her to the bed. Laying her upon it, he followed her down and turned his attention to spots that ached just for him.

Heat pooled low and urgent in her belly with each knowing glide of his strong fingers, with each quick nip, and each slow, dragging lick of his tongue as he unerringly found the spots on her body—the inside of her elbows, the hollow behind her ears, the side of her breasts, the point of her hip bones—that sent silver streaks of pleasure coursing through her. Her moans turned to whimpers of need.

She felt him smile against the sensitive skin of her inner thigh. He'd been working his way up it, alternating between kisses, licks, and playful bites, a triad designed to drive her mad. "Oh God, Ward," she panted, spiraling ever closer to the edge. "Please, whatever you do, don't ever stop."

"Bossy bit of goods, aren't you? Lucky for you I like you bossy."

Actually, she wasn't all that demanding and she considered herself reasonably sane. But Ward summoned aspects of her character that no one else could, and she'd never been so greedy or so wild for a man's touch before.

Not even with David. In the beginning his lovemaking had been sweet and satisfying. And then, after they'd married, neither of those. But even when things had been right and happy between them, their lovemaking hadn't compared to how she felt when wrapped in Ward's embrace: beautiful, desired, and special.

Ward's mouth was meandering ever closer to the V of her legs, bringing him tantalizingly near to where she wanted him most, then pausing, retreating. Tormenting her so deliciously. "More?"

Digging her fingers into his wet hair she tugged and arched her back in supplication, in blatant invitation.

"I'll take that as a 'yes.' "

Slowly he drew his finger down her cleft and inserted it into her slick heat.

She tightened around him. "Just so you know, I'm planning a serious retaliation," she managed to gasp.

"I can't wait." His low laugh washed over her like a hot wind running before a storm. He closed his mouth over her as his fingers worked their magic and summoned waves of pleasure to crash over her. She came with a piercing cry.

And then, when he pulled her into his arms and ran his hands gently over her, pressing soft kisses into her brow until her tremors had ceased, something far more powerful stole into her carefully guarded heart.

The ring of Ward's cellphone woke him from the near catatonic slumber he'd fallen into after making love to Tess. The woman gave as good as she got and she'd been fiercely creative in torturing him with her mouth before driving him nearly insane while she lowered herself slowly inch by inch onto his throbbing cock.

As was her wont, Tess was sleeping draped over him, her lush curves and silky hair the most exquisite blanket imaginable. He managed to grab the phone off the bedside table without dislodging her or even disturbing her much. She simply burrowed closer and mumbled drowsily against his sternum.

He answered the phone with a smile. "Ward here."

"Hey, buddy, it's me."

"Brian, how are you?" He kept his voice as low as possible.

"I'm good. We can't wait to see you."

"Same goes. You and I get to do the fun stuff, like choose the wines and champagne with Reid and listen to demo tapes of the bands. Tess has found some good ones."

"Sounds right up my alley."

"You'll also get to taste the cakes and decide on the menus for the meals. And maybe smile for the photographer. But the other items on Tess's list are basically girlie—flowers and stuff."

Brian cleared his throat. "Speaking of girlie stuff,

Ward, there's a development. I wanted to give you a heads-up."

Ward stilled, and it seemed as if the gentle inhale and exhale of Tess's breath against his throat was the only movement.

"It's Erica." Brian sighed. "She heard that Carrie and I were coming to see you this weekend and wants to join us, saying that as her stepsister and maid of honor she'd love to help Carrie decide things. I'm sorry, Ward, but we couldn't figure out how to say no. Carrie hates to make her feel left out."

Damn, he should have guessed something like this would happen since Erica was an expert at pushing buttons and Carrie was the world's softest touch—with Erica in particular. She carried a goodly amount of guilt at being the child who'd gotten to live with Erica's father, Carrie's mother being his second wife.

"When's Erica coming?"

His voice must have sharpened, for Tess raised her head from his chest to blink at him, her deep brown eyes coming into focus. Damn and double damn.

"Her car's in the shop. She's going to meet us at the airport."

"You mean she plans on being here the whole weekend?" He couldn't hide his incredulity.

"We haven't seen her in a while, since she didn't come east for Christmas. She seems to think this will be a great bonding experience for her and Carrie."

Ward coughed. Because it was that or snort in disgust. Tess was now fully awake, her elbows propped against his chest and following the conversation. He was sure she could hear Brian's every word.

"Ward, I'm really sorry—"

"It's not your fault." Family was family, after all. It wasn't like Ward didn't bend over backward for his own. Then again, they'd never act like Erica. "Did it even occur to her that we might be booked?"

"She was sure you wouldn't be."

Ward ground his teeth.

"She called your reservation desk. She's got a cabin—nowhere near ours, thankfully."

Dull pain throbbed in his jaw as he said, "Then I guess we'll be seeing the three of you tomorrow."

"Can't tell you how sorry I am about this. Awkward as hell."

"Yeah. Good thing I love Carrie and kind of tolerate you. See you tomorrow."

He clicked the phone off and met Tess's gaze.

She didn't beat around the bush. "So your ex-fiancée's coming for the weekend."

"Looks like it."

She sat up, and he scowled but didn't attempt to draw her back down, though he did rest his hand possessively on her naked thigh.

"And she's going to help Carrie in her decisions?"

He gave her credit for trying to be diplomatic when she could have used words like "horn in" and "bully" and not been too far off the mark.

He sighed. "Brian's my best friend. I want his and Carrie's wedding to go smoothly and be the happiest event we can arrange for them. I'd also like to impress the roughly hundred guests that will be in attendance in the hopes that some of them may decide to come back and enjoy a stay at Silver Creek on their own. Or spread the word about the ranch to their friends and acquaintances. Word of mouth is still our best promotional tool. If I object to Erica's coming she's going to throw a hissy fit. And she might not be over it by the wedding date."

"Sounds like a charmer, your ex."

He cocked his head. "And your husband was faultless?" He'd learned a lot about Tess in recent days. That drowsy lambent period between bouts of making love was an especially good time for subtle interrogations and accumulating facts about this woman. He now knew about Nicco Bandinelli, the first boy she'd kissed in sixth grade, and about the men she'd dated before meeting her husband, David. They'd been strings-free affairs because she was too busy working at La Dolce Vita and most guys wanted to date women who were free evenings. He'd managed to conceal his annoyance over their existence and the fact that he and Tess also had a so-called strings-free thing going on by reminding himself that what mattered was that she was with him now. There was plenty of time to ease her into accepting a deeper commitment, of getting her to admit she cared for him.

He also had a far better insight into just how difficult it had been for her family to cope with the unending stress and heartache of her brother Christopher's disability. Though she never articulated it, Ward thought that it must have led to a pretty difficult childhood for her. With the bulk of her parents' energy going to caring and worrying over Christopher, there'd been precious little left for her. Another person might have resented being relegated to the role of all-but-invisible child, yet Tess had instead accepted how taxed the elder Casaris were. Not many people would have that kind of sympathy for their parents.

He'd managed to glean bits and pieces of information about her marriage to David, enough to grasp that it had soured very quickly. And then there'd been his illness, a cancer of the brain that she learned about only after he had called her from the hospital. But she often remained tightly guarded when it came to talking about her ex-husband.

Like now.

A flush had stolen over her cheeks. "You're right. No one is without fault."

He looked at her, her hair a tangled mass about her shoulders, her breasts soft and round and just the right size for his large hands. As he gazed at her, the dusky rose of her aureoles puckered, her nipples hardening into delectable buds.

"I don't know about that," he said, smiling slowly. "From my vantage point you look perfect." Inside and out, he added silently. He'd learned his lesson with Erica. Looks didn't matter if he couldn't admire the character within.

She gave a quick shake of her head and lowered her gaze. "I'm not perfect at all. Far from it. There are a lot of things I've done that I regret. Don't put me on a pedestal."

He leaned closer, put a finger under her chin to lift it, and was taken aback by her troubled eyes.

"Okay," he said and touched his lips to hers in a light, soothing kiss that was all too brief.

She drew back and though she managed a smile he sensed the effort behind it. It frustrated him that he had no clue what in her past could cause her such unease and cast such a shadow.

Before he could probe for answers, Tess swung her legs over the edge of the bed and stood to gather her jeans, sweater, and underthings.

He glanced at his watch. It was just past six o'clock. "Do you want to grab some dinner?" They could talk then.

She shook her head. "I'll get something later. First I've got to call my mom before it's too late back east. Christopher had a dentist's appointment today and that's always rough for them both. His teeth aren't good but he can't be fully anesthetized because of his meds."

"You can call her from here, you know. I'll go to another room so you can have some privacy."

"Thanks, but no. I'll call her from my office. I've got some work to do."

"Don't tell me you're going back to do more for the wedding." At her quick nod, he frowned. "You're kidding. You've gone over every vendor, every appointment, menu, floral arrangement, and table setting, every minuscule detail—"

"And something tells me that your ex-fiancée is going to be a whole lot more exacting about all of them than Carrie and Brian could ever be."

"I don't see how it'd be possible to find fault. You've worked your butt off for this wedding."

"What kind of events planner would I be if I didn't? Look, I don't know Carrie and Brian as well as you do, but I like them, and I don't want their weekend here to be stressful because I haven't anticipated something that Erica might point out that would make their wedding even better. I want them totally confident that this is the wedding they want—doubts can set in too easily otherwise."

"You don't need to work on it tonight, though—"

She cut him off with a quick shake of her head. "Yeah, I do. This is my job, what you're paying me for."

In the course of the conversation she'd somehow managed to put on her matching red panties and bra, trimmed with black lace. It was like a reverse strip tease. Unfortunately he'd been so distracted by the conversation he hadn't been able to enjoy the sight of her shimmying into the scraps of lace and silk. He realized it showed how much he cared. To date he'd yet to behold Tess in her sexy lingerie without becoming 100 percent focused on getting her underneath or on top of him as quickly as possible.

He rose to his feet and walked over to her. Bringing

his hands up, he gently pushed back her tangled hair, tucking her bangs behind her ears before cupping her face and kissing her deeply, thoroughly. At last he felt her tension seep away.

"Thank you," he said huskily.

This time her smile came more easily. "You can thank me once we get through this weekend."

Chapter TWENTY-THREE

TESS AWOKE FRIDAY morning with eyes grittier than a sandlot and a brain that felt shrink-wrapped from staring at her computer screen for too many hours the night before as she reviewed websites and studied her notes.

Oh Lord, she was really not looking forward to this day, she thought as she walked up the path from her cabin to the lodge. But there was no way to avoid it. She'd simply have to put imaginary blinkers on and pretend that Ward's ex-fiancée wasn't there. The entire weekend was supposed to be about the engaged couple and ensuring she was organizing the wedding they truly wanted. She couldn't waste the finite number of hours she had with Brian and Carrie obsessing about what had made Ward fall in love with Erica Marsh. Or comparing herself to Erica.

She needed to remind herself that she and Ward had a very defined relationship, composed of two essential ingredients: great sex and a good time. No complications allowed. Expecting Ward to announce his eternal devotion and ask her to live happily ever after with him ventured into forbidden territory.

Her head understood this. She simply had to convince

her foolish heart to get with the program. The problem was that with each passing day her heart grew fuller with everything that was Ward: his passion, his smile, his fierce tenderness . . .

She was almost at the front entrance to the lodge when a voice came out of nowhere, causing her to nearly jump out of her skin.

"That's some stern look you've got on your face, city girl."

"Quinn! You scared the daylights out of me."

Standing with her shoulder propped against the timbered wall of the lodge, Quinn straightened. "You walked right past me. Sorry I scared you, though I guess it's appropriate to be scared since I'm about to abduct you. Come on, we're going into town."

"I wish I could, but I've got—"

"See, that's the thing about being abducted. You don't really have any say over the matter. This way, Tess," she said. "The getaway car awaits."

Tess knew herself to be pretty scrappy when the occasion called for it, but she was under no illusion that she could best Quinn, who could toss hay bales like they were pillows.

Quinn cocked her hip. "I only have to whistle and Reid will be out here as extra reinforcement. And Mom knows all about the intervention, so don't try any lines about not wanting to disappoint her."

She wondered where this so-called intervention was supposed to take place. There were no clues to be had from Quinn's appearance. She was dressed in her usual work attire: faded jeans that molded her long legs, cowboy boots, and a crew neck sweater over a T-shirt. Her blond hair was pulled back in a knot at the nape of her neck. The outfit might be casual, but a woman who looked like Quinn could get away with wearing it to a

Park Avenue Fortune 500 company boardroom meeting or dinner at Per Se.

Seeing that those places were three thousand miles away, their destination was more likely the general store's luncheonette or perhaps Spillin' the Beans. Grabbing a plateful of scrambled eggs or slugging a triple-shot latte suddenly sounded appealing. She could use some extra energy today.

"Okay. Where are you taking me? And can we take my car?" She loved her new car. It was so zippy and cute. Even better, it never coughed or wheezed.

"Sorry, but no. Time is of the essence." Victorious, Quinn grinned and looped her arm through Tess's, marching her toward her red pickup truck, which was parked on the other side of the courtyard, pointing down the graveled drive. "And our destination is Ava Day's salon."

"But why? I've already arranged for her to come to the ranch this afternoon to do a consultation and makeup session with Carrie."

Quinn shook her head. "This isn't for Carrie. It's for you. We have a nine o'clock appointment. Mom and I are treating you to a facial, blow out, and mani."

Tess dug in her heels. "Quinn, I can't be gone that long—"

Quinn was as strong as she looked, and physics was on her side, her forward momentum propelling Tess along. "Oh, yes you can. Ward told me how you went back to work last night. You're more than prepared. What you need is some pampering so that you're refreshed. And looking your best. Especially now that Erica's coming," she added under her breath.

Great. Just what she needed: Independent confirmation that Erica spelled trouble for the Brian and Carrie–centric weekend. To make it worse, Quinn had added a whopping dollop of worry that Tess would come up short in the looks department, too. She would have loved to be the rare individual who could rise above such superficial concerns—more like Quinn, who was indifferent to her beauty—but unfortunately she was as insecure as most women when it came to the daily low-level beauty pageants they participated in with one another.

A very thin veneer of silver could be gleaned in the gloomy, ominous cloud that was Erica Marsh. Since Quinn had mentioned Erica, Tess didn't have to embarrass herself by being the one to bring up the topic of Ward's ex-fiancée. "So, what's up with Erica coming here?"

They'd reached the pickup truck, and Quinn walked Tess around to the passenger's side. Opening the door, she swept the Western tack catalogs and leashes lying on the front seat to the floor, clearing a small, dog-hair-covered space for Tess. Tess glanced at her off-white skirt and groaned inwardly. This day wasn't going at all as planned.

"I don't know. Really, I can't figure her out. You know those sorts of people whose motivations just seem so out there, almost incomprehensible, because they're so radically different from your own? That's the way it is with Erica. I love Ward like anything, and it was awful to see how hurt he was when Erica called off the engagement—though he did his best to hide it, stoic macho dude that he is—but between you and me and the dashboard I'll say it. I am so glad that Erica didn't become a part of our family. She's beautiful, smart, talented, and a user. She spent all this time with Ward and never cared enough to understand him." Her voice was laced with disgust. "I have to stop talking about her or it will ruin my day."

Quinn circled around the hood of the truck and

climbed in to the driver's seat. "Hop inside, or we'll be late for Ava."

Tess stared again at the seat in dismay and made an attempt to brush off the animal hairs clinging to the fabric upholstery, but gave up when they only floated in the air to resettle in essentially the same spots. Her own car was as neat inside as outside.

Stifling a sigh, she climbed into the truck and tried to block a mental image of a thousand and one black and brown dog hairs affixing themselves to her rear.

If she had to choose, though, she'd pick worrying about being covered in dog hair over the prospect of dealing with Ward's ex-fiancée any day of the week.

It was a testament to Ava Day's skills as an aesthetician that Tess's worries and fear receded during her deluxe pampering session. Seated in adjacent chairs, she and Quinn had tremendous fun ribbing each other and letting Ava and her assistant Ricki fill them in on town gossip.

When Tess voiced astonishment that Quinn was getting her hair and nails done, Quinn had laughed. "You aren't the only one who needs to be well armed to confront Erica, city girl. With just a look she can make me feel like something Pirate dragged in."

Recalling some of the gruesome carcasses she'd seen Quinn's cat parade around with in his mouth, Tess felt the latte Ricki had fetched for her from Spillin' the Beans shift uncomfortably in her stomach.

Before Tess could respond to that depressing bit of information, Quinn continued. "You know, I think it may be time I quit calling you 'city girl' now that you not only can feed Alberta and Hennie and the rest of the goat gang without looking like you're about to faint from fear, but you're also proving your chops as a rider. By all reports you did a fine job on Brocco. We're all real proud of you. We might even succeed in turning you into a cowgirl."

Tess locked eyes with her in the oversized mirror in front of them. "Ever heard the Italian expression '*L'anno del mai e il mese del poi*'?"

Quinn grinned as she repeated it in a fairly decent accent. "No. Can't say I have."

"Translated, it means, 'The year of never and the month of then.'"

"You are so deep, CG. Around here we like to remind stubborn mules like you to never say never. Oh, and when Erica starts in on you—and I'm willing to bet my saddle she will once she figures out you and Ward are an item, which will take her all of about thirty seconds—just remember, we're on your side, pal."

That Quinn liked her and considered her more than just someone who worked at her family's ranch moved her beyond words. Tess recalled the loneliness she'd felt upon arriving in Acacia, her sense of disorientation. She'd come a long way. Not only was she accepted and liked, but she also recognized how much she admired the Knowleses and everyone at Silver Creek Ranch for trying to preserve the land and the way of life they loved. Quite a discovery for a girl born and bred in Queens, New York.

To her dismay, Tess discovered shortly that the best facial and complimentary neck massage in the world could relax someone only so much.

"Holy crap. What are they doing here already? Their plane must have landed early," Quinn whispered loudly as they entered the main lodge.

Tess followed the direction of her gaze. It took all her years of working with La Dolce Vita's demanding New York clientele to maintain her easy smile when she walked into the lounge and saw the woman sitting next to Ward on the sofa.

Erica Marsh was beautiful. A flaxen-haired princess to Ward's dark prince charming, they made a perfect match.

Erica's identity was obvious. After the numerous FaceTime chats Tess had conducted with Brian and Carrie, she instantly recognized the couple on the loveseat perpendicular to Ward and Erica. Plus, they were holding hands . . . whereas Erica was sitting close enough to Ward that her straight blond hair brushed his shoulder when she turned her head at the sound of her and Quinn's approach.

Another muscle in Tess's neck reknotted. Erica had azure blue eyes reminiscent of a quiet sea at night.

Ward was already on his feet. "Here they are now," he said and stepped forward to meet them with as relieved a smile as she'd ever seen on his face. "Tess, I'd like to introduce you in person to Brian and Carrie. Their plane landed early. And this is Erica Marsh, Carrie's stepsister."

While she and Quinn exchanged hellos with the trio, Ward positioned himself next to Tess so that she was flanked by two Knowleses. The show of support would have helped if she weren't so very conscious of being inspected by Ward's ex-fiancée. She wondered how many dog hairs were sticking to her skirt and felt another muscle tighten.

Focus, she reminded herself. She turned to Carrie. "How great that you arrived early. Quinn and I were just in town at Ava Day's Salon. She's so looking forward to meeting you to discuss your hair and makeup and what services your bridal party would like."

"Oh, Carrie, I was hoping you would use the Mercer Street salon, where I go," Erica interjected. "I told my stylist, Nicole, that I was sure you would."

Carrie flushed. "Yes, I know you mentioned her to me but—"

"But Ava is right in town and while Nicole does superb work, she was going to have to charge Carrie to make the trip up here. Carrie wanted to keep the expenses down so that she could offer a spa package to you and Brian's sister in addition to your hair and makeup," Tess said.

"Of course, that's fine. It was simply an idea I had." Erica's smile could be described only as angelic. "I do so want you to look beautiful."

Tess soon learned this was Erica's favorite MO, to smile as she thrust the verbal dagger home. Because of the sweetness of her expression, it took a moment for her victim to realize what had happened. Carrie, who actually was sweet—though a bit unworldly given her fascination with far-flung galaxies—was no match for her.

While the group finished the coffee and biscotti that Gordon had served them, and Tess went over the schedule of appointments for the afternoon, Erica alternated between chatting brightly with Ward and undermining Carrie's choices for her wedding. Wasn't a DJ a better choice than a band? Was Carrie sure the navy bridesmaids dresses she'd selected would coordinate well with her own bridal dress? She was exceptionally good at slipping comments into a conversation when Ward's attention was diverted by Brian so that neither man witnessed the damage she was inflicting. Tess deflected them as much as possible, politely defending Carrie's choices. The game was tiresome, Erica alone enjoying it.

Weirdly enough, Tess was actually relieved when Erica decided to include her in her well-aimed barbs. It gave Carrie a reprieve. And Tess was better equipped to deal with Erica's subtle and not-so-subtle digs.

Erica's decision to shift the focus of her cutting remarks was at first surprising. Then not so much. And when Tess understood what was going on—what Erica really wanted out of the weekend—she knew the under-the-radar attacks would eventually escalate.

The first of the day's appointments was with Roo and Jeff for a tasting of the menus. It wasn't scheduled for another hour, so Brian asked Ward to show them the newest additions to the ranch.

They walked down to the barns. It was a beautiful spring day, in the low fifties. The grass had already turned a bright green. Masses of daffodils danced in the light breeze. Steve, one of the gardeners who tended the plants and shrubs around the main lodge, had told Tess that any day now the cherry trees would burst into bloom.

Tess was walking next to Carrie, pointing to the wide expanse of lawn where the wedding tent for the dinner would be, with a dance floor set up just outside of it near the gardens, which would be in full bloom. If rain was in the forecast, the tent could be enlarged with extra pieces to protect the dancers and the band. Every now and again, Tess would catch snatches of Erica and Ward's conversation. Except for that brief moment when Ward had been introducing Tess to them, Erica hadn't left his side. From the way she let her arm casually brush his as she chattered animatedly one would never guess she'd jilted Ward.

As they approached one of the corrals where several horses were nibbling on shoots of grass, Erica pointed. "Don't I recognize that horse, Ward?" she asked, resting her other hand on his sweater.

Tess looked to where she was pointing. It was that or fixate on Erica's hand, which had yet to move from Ward's arm.

"Maybe. That's Bilbao." Ward stepped sideways, forcing Erica to drop her hand. Tess's spirits lifted marginally.

Carrie and Brian went over to the railing so Brian could take a picture of her with the horses as a backdrop. Then they switched places, Brian mugging for the camera with a wide grin.

Erica spoke again. "Oh! I remember now. Wasn't Bilbao the one you were training in that tweet? Such marvelous riding, Ward. All my friends were talking about it. Who took the video? You, Quinn?"

Quinn had accompanied them down to the barns, making sure to announce, however, that she would be peeling off to go work with Glory and Tucker. Tess couldn't blame her for wanting to flee.

Quinn shook her head. "No, Tess took it. She's doing the Twitter thing for us. The Pinterest account too," she added.

"Really?" Erica turned to look at her with an assessing gleam in her eyes. "I thought you were just the events planner."

Tess ignored the "just the events planner" jab. "The tweets are to drum up interest in the ranch and some of the events we've scheduled for later this summer."

"Quite the go-getter, aren't you?" Erica said. A light glaze of condescension coated her words.

"It's not all that difficult to promote the guest ranch using social media. It's beautiful here."

Her answer was casual, meant to show Erica that she wasn't interested in being drawn into a competition. The tactic might have worked if Ward hadn't decided to voice his support.

"Tess has been doing an amazing job for us. She's an invaluable member of our staff."

Although she and Ward had both been behaving with strict professionalism—it went without saying that any PDA on the job would have been unacceptable—Ward's approbation held just enough warmth to register as something more than businesslike. And since Erica had a stake in the matter, she noticed.

Erica's glance traveled between them. The smile Tess was beginning to despise curved Erica's lipsticked lips.

"It must be gratifying to have such an appreciative employer."

"I'm not Tess's employer," Ward corrected, which was true. Even though she reported to him, she'd been hired by Adele.

"That's what I've always loved about you, Ward. Your modesty."

Oh, wow, thought Tess, stunned by Erica's audacity. She'd dumped him and now she was using the "L" word. And since Tess had paid attention in Sister Katherine's ninth-grade English class, she knew Erica had used the present perfect rather than the past tense. Meaning said love wasn't over.

Standing beside her, Quinn muttered, "Obvious much? Give her another ten minutes and she'll start singing the lyrics to Whitney's 'I Will Always Love You.' "

Tess stifled a snort at the absurd image. "Behave," she whispered. Of its own volition, her gaze strayed to Ward. How would he react to Erica's pronouncement?

He was frowning, his brows drawn in a dark line. It would be so great if he burst into laughter.

But before Ward could respond to Erica's comment, Brian called him over to snap a picture of Carrie and him together. Naturally Erica wandered over too, and a mini photo shoot ensued.

Then Erica's bright voice summoned her. "Tess, would you mind taking the camera so the four of us can be in the picture at once? It'll be fun to post them on FB."

"And then she can show everyone how cozy she still is with her ex-fiancé," Quinn said with a roll of her eyes. "I'm sorry to abandon you, CG, but I don't want to keep Tucker waiting. He's gotten used to our lunchtime sessions. He eats, I groom."

Tess was amazed at the progress Quinn had made with the gelding. He already looked like a different horse from the abused, half-starved creature who'd arrived in late February.

"It's okay. Have fun with Tucker," she said.

"I'd wish you the same, but I'm thinking that's impossible." With a wave, she called out a cheery goodbye to the rest of the group before sauntering off toward the farther corrals.

With a sigh, Tess went over to the rail to document the happy foursome. Somehow with every frame she clicked, Erica always managed to be next to Ward, her head tilted just a little toward him, her smile shining with happiness.

Tess didn't need a zoom lens to see what was going on. Erica was interested in rekindling her relationship with Ward. And the moment she understood that there was something between Tess and Ward, she'd decided to up the intensity of her campaign to win him back. The melting glances she sent his way became more frequent, as did the compliments she sprinkled into her observations about the ranch. Tess had to suppress a snort of disgust when Erica oohed and ahhed over the "darling lambs." One would think all she dreamed of was being a rancher's wife.

It was difficult to judge whether Ward was falling for the act. He had his poker face on. But could she blame him if he did find himself softening toward his ex? Erica was lovely, and Ward had obviously found her lovable.

Tess tried to imagine how she would feel in his place. She wasn't sure she'd have been particularly clear-eyed if David had ever chosen to reenter her life after storming out of it. How would she have reacted if he'd behaved as if he still felt something for her?

Would she have recognized it was just another game—that he was trying to win her over because he could? Or would she have been charmed and seduced all over again? Not simply by his clever lines, but by the fantasies she'd spun in which he returned to her, begging her to forgive him his idiocy.

Missing him as desperately as she had, she'd imagined plenty of such scenarios between bouts of crying over him or cursing him for having left her heart in ragged pieces.

Would she have forgiven the hurt he'd inflicted, and fallen all over again?

She wasn't sure, to be honest. Everything with David was complicated by unanswered questions. Had marriage to her really been akin to a prison sentence for him? Or had his abrupt sea change been the result of the malignant tumor growing in his brain?

What Tess remembered most vividly was David's undeniable charm. It was a trait Erica possessed, too. Tess could see how she could have won Ward's heart with her bright intelligence. Then there was her beauty and the confidence that came with her perfect blue-eyed blond looks.

Could Erica win him back? At the thought, a band squeezed her heart, because she couldn't answer with any of Erica's abundant confidence. And though she'd never felt as close to someone as she did to Ward, or as awed by the sensations storming her as when she was in his arms, she had explicitly told Ward that she wanted to avoid a complicated relationship, that she wasn't looking for an emotional commitment.

He'd accepted those rules all too happily.

She knew he liked her. Perhaps even a lot.

But he'd loved Erica.

The weekend could not end soon enough.

Chapter TWENTY-FOUR

"Ward, do you think we'll have time to ride this afternoon? I'd love to go over some of the old trails with you," Erica asked, smiling at him over the assortment of pastries and wedding cake in the lodge's dining room.

Ward fought the urge to growl his reply that he had an even better idea. He'd love to stuff her into Ralph Cummins's taxi, slam the door, and instruct Ralph to hit the gas and not slow down until he reached Palo Alto, where Erica was currently living. Once the taxi was out of sight, he'd go down to the bottom of the road to Silver Creek Ranch and lock the gates. With a padlock.

Instead, he shoveled in a forkful of the wedding cake Roo had baked and pretended not to hear. He'd been doing a lot of that.

The lunch was supposed to be devoted to sampling the menu Jeff and Roo had devised for the wedding dinner, complete with hors d'oeuvres and a mini version of the wedding cake that Ward was currently masticating. The Silver Creek chefs had gone all out for his friends. The broiled salmon seasoned with bread crumbs, lemon, and garlic butter was delicious, as were the pan-seared boneless chicken breasts stuffed with sundried tomatoes and goat cheese, and the vegetarian option, a spring vegetable risotto. He wasn't much of a dessert man, but the moist yellow wedding cake with its rich white chocolate buttercream frosting was unbelievably good.

If the rest of Brian and Carrie's wedding was just as amazing, it would be a smash. And damn, it would be nice to break the lousy streak of luck they'd previously had holding weddings at Silver Creek.

Seated next to Carrie and Brian, Tess was doing her best to make it happen. She'd helped them narrow the choices of hors d'oeuvres down to the most interesting and tastiest, being sure to keep some traditional favorites so that everyone would be happily. She'd done the same with the side dishes and salad.

He, too, was helping when he could. But each time he opened his mouth, Erica seemed to think that it was her cue to speak as well. Only instead of pitching in with an opinion for Bri and Carrie that might actually guide them, she preferred to engage him exclusively. Like a spring stream after the winter melt-off, she babbled questions and gushed with coy invitations to take an intimate tour for two down Memory Lane.

It was leaving a bad taste in his mouth.

Moreover, his deaf and mute act weren't having the desired effect. When he ignored Erica, she either repeated the question or appealed to Carrie or Brian.

This time, she resorted to the latter tactic. "Wouldn't it be fun to go riding, guys?" she said with a bright smile.

Brian smiled affably. "I'd be up for it—depending on whether Tess and Ward think we have enough time. What's next on our schedule of events?"

"The photographer will be arriving in forty-five minutes. Then Ava Day is coming to do a hair and makeup consultation."

"I doubt I'll want to go riding after I've just had makeup applied and spoil whatever Ava's managed to do with this ridiculous mess." Carrie fingered her thick, wavy hair, which Ward had never noticed anything ridiculous about. It was pretty and shiny, with hints of coppery red and gold mixed with blond.

Of course, he now had a distinct preference for brunettes with long bangs that ended in a sexy hook just above the jaw.

Tess smiled at Carrie's comment. "Ava will love your hair. I can't wait to see what kind of style she suggests for you."

"And while Carrie's having her consultation, you and I have an outing with Reid," Ward told Brian, who perked up at the news, sitting straighter in his chair. "We're going to one of the local vineyards. Reid likes the wines they're producing, and their prices are reasonable. He's just negotiated a deal with them so I think they'll offer a nice discount for your wedding."

Brian grinned. "I can totally get behind that plan."

Ward gave an answering grin. "Thought you would."

"I think I'll accompany you guys to the wine tasting," Erica said. "You don't mind, Carrie, do you? You don't need me to advise you on your hairdo, and I'd enjoy bringing home a new vintage to share with my friends. Remember how much fun we used to have going to vineyards, Ward?"

Wasn't there some sacrosanct maid of honor code that forbade them from ditching these key sessions? Ward wondered. He quickly looked over at Tess, but she'd reverted to the Tess of old, damn it. Polite and reserved, she revealed none of her thoughts.

Would a little show of jealousy be asking too much? Surely she'd noticed that if Erica continued any further down her chosen road, she'd soon suggest that for old times' sake he and she should have a sleepover tonight. Pajamas optional.

If Tess was carefully masking her thoughts, Carrie was like an open book.

"Feel free to go with the guys, Erica. I'll be fine with Tess and Ava."

Bri, too, was easy to read. He looked crestfallen at the prospect of his future sister-in-law tagging along but then rallied with a "Sure, great!" that rang a shade too heartily. To cover the slip, he quickly raised his cup of cappuccino to his lips and drained it.

While it pleased Ward no end that Carrie liked Tess so much, and while he was relieved that Erica's selfishness hadn't hurt her feelings or caused any problems for Tess, he was nonetheless tempted to put a wrench in Erica's plans. It'd be easy. He could simply say this was a guys-only expedition, part of Reid and his pre-bachelor-party gift to Brian, and that after the vineyard they would be heading to a strip joint.

He reluctantly abandoned the idea. The last thing he wanted was to have Erica gush about how fun watching pole dancers with him would be.

Amazingly, ditching her stepsister for a wine tasting wasn't enough for Erica. She immediately returned to her earlier demand.

"So what about taking a horseback ride tomorrow? Surely there must be some point in the day when we can go. I mean, it's not like this wedding is such a big or complicated affair."

At the other end of the table, Tess's lips tightened, her only sign of irritation. He tried to imagine Erica ever showing such self-discipline and couldn't. Indeed, he couldn't picture Erica ever working as hard on an event as Tess had without loudly soliciting praise.

He honestly couldn't remember if Erica had always been so self-centered or whether it was so obvious now because he was viewing her through the crystal-clear lens of disenchantment.

Tess had opened her notebook to answer Erica. "Tomorrow Carrie and I will be meeting with Samantha

Nicholls, the floral designer. Her place is in—" She paused and flipped through her notes, searching. "Sorry, I'm not from around here. Oh, yes, here's the address. She's located in Mendocino. Adele thinks she's fabulous, so it's worth the long drive."

"Obviously, you can't be from around here if you think that's any kind of distance," Erica said. "So where are you from?"

"New York."

"Oh, where'd you work?"

"I worked at a full-service events company called La Dolce Vita."

Erica smiled. "It must be one of the smaller ones. I've never heard of it."

All right, he'd had it with Erica's crap. "My mother was quite impressed with the company and how well the boss spoke of Tess. It's why she hired Tess."

That stopped her.

Tess sent him a look of silent thanks, then shifted her attention to Carrie. "Our appointment with Samantha Nicholls is in the afternoon. Phil Onofrie, who's in charge of reservations, was hoping to go over the guest list with you tomorrow morning. And George Reich, the restaurant's manager, wanted to show you his ideas for the table settings so you have a sense of what might work for centerpieces when you meet with Samantha—"

Erica cut in. "Can't this Phil Onofrie meet with us another time? After all, he's an employee."

Carrie and Brian looked appalled at the carelessness of Erica's comment but remained silent. They probably knew from experience how little effect their protests would have.

Ward wondered where he could find a short pier to suggest Erica take a long walk off it. What could possibly make her think he'd tolerate these kinds of comments? His voice carried the icy censure she deserved.

"Yes, and as an employee Phil has a legal right to a day off. It happens to be on Sunday."

Tess directed her words to Carrie, her own cut to Erica. "I'll speak to Phil and see whether he can make a Sunday morning meeting before you leave."

Considering that she was getting her way, Erica should have looked much happier. Then again, she didn't like any resistance to her plans. Shifting her attention to Carrie, she said, "It'll be fun to go for a trail ride, won't it?"

But even mild-mannered Carrie was proving contrary. With a small laugh, she fiddled with the spoon resting by her coffee cup. "Actually, I'm a little nervous at the prospect. I haven't been on a horse in years. Graduate school and working on my doctorate didn't leave a lot of time for riding. I may not even remember how to make the horse go." She turned to Tess. "Do you ride a lot?"

"No, not at all. I don't ride."

"Not true," Ward said. "Tess has got the walk down pat and was a quick study at neck reining. I plan to have her loping by June."

He loved Tess's blushes. "Don't believe him, Carrie," she said, shooting him a quick admonishing look then shaking her head when he grinned widely. "Ward's exaggerating big-time. I very much doubt I'll ever graduate from a walk."

"I'm not going to attempt anything faster tomorrow, either. I have no desire to be married in a body cast," Carrie said.

Tess laughed. "Especially when you have one of the loveliest wedding dresses anyone will ever see."

"And no matter how many hooks and buttons and layers her dress has, I figure it has to be easier to remove than a body cast," Brian joked. "So yeah, sweetheart, you stick to a walk, okay?"

"Will you come for the trail ride with us?" Carrie asked Tess.

"Oh, I—"

"I'm sure she'll have other things to do," Erica cut in. "Tweeting perhaps," she added under her breath. Ward wondered whether she'd intentionally said it loud enough for him to hear. Likely, he decided.

For once Brian spoke over Erica. "That's a great idea, babe. Tess certainly deserves some R and R this weekend after all her hard work."

Ward grinned, knowing that ordinarily Tess would hotly protest the notion that riding could ever be restful or relaxing. "I second the motion," he said.

And with Tess present on the trail ride, he'd have one more reason to ignore Erica's attempts to re-insinuate herself in his life, let alone his affection. That ship had definitely sailed. Not a speck of white canvas to be spied on the horizon.

But he couldn't flat-out tell Erica to stop wasting her breath, not if he wanted to keep the weekend from blowing up and making things awkward for Brian and Carrie. That left him with resorting to avoidance tactics. It wasn't a strategy he particularly enjoyed but it did have one bonus. It involved keeping Tess close at hand.

He was counting the hours until his hands could actually make contact.

Chapter TWENTY-FIVE

ERICA MARSH, TESS decided, did not improve upon further acquaintance. She just got bitchier. Whenever possible, Tess tried to avoid that vulgar insult; the *Wizard of Oz* slant to the term "witch" was just so much more colorful. But likening Erica to a female dog—and, in this case, one in heat—sadly fit. How else to characterize Erica's constant need to assert her superiority over other women and her ceaseless efforts to attract the opposite sex—a certain dark-haired, broad-shouldered alpha male in particular?

It had been a relief the day before when Erica, freshly changed into a sheer gauzy dress that would soon leave her shivering (perhaps part of a plan to get Ward to remove his jacket for her), went off with the men to the winery, leaving Tess and Carrie to spend the next two hours with Ava Day.

But while Erica's departure was welcome, Tess had found her attention straying during Carrie's session with Ava, wondering how often Erica was reaching out to touch Ward or press against him.

At least Ava was perfect with Carrie. She'd enthusiastically admired the photo of the wedding dress Tess produced, suggesting an updo that would flatter Carrie's delicate bone structure and compliment the romance of the strapless embroidered tulle-and-silk gown. To make the hairstyle even more stunning, Ava proposed adorning Carrie's hair with miniature ivory rosebuds to match the hue of her wedding gown.

For the makeup, she and Carrie had agreed that a natural look would work best. After brushing and curling Carrie's hair and pinning it into the style Carrie had picked, Ava applied her makeup, using a light foundation to even out her tone and then adding eyeliner, mascara, and a creamy gold eye shadow to highlight her blue eyes. The lightest of rosy blushes and lipstick finished the look.

She stepped back and nodded to Tess, who was acting as her assistant. With a flourish worthy of Vanna White, Tess produced the mirrors Ava had brought with her makeup tools.

"Have a look." She gave one mirror to Carrie and then stepped behind her with the other.

"Oh my God! I look fantastic!"

Tess nodded, her smile almost as wide as Carrie's. "You do. You really do. Best of all, you still look like you."

"Tess is right. I don't think a groom likes it when his bride is so made up she looks like someone else. He's nervous enough. Now, Carrie, let me rearrange your hair in another style so we don't give anything away to Brian."

"Okay. Just give me another sec to admire myself." She twisted in her chair and craned her neck to catch all the different angles. "Ava, I just love it. I really do."

"You have great hair. It's got lots of body. Just take good care of it between now and June. No crazy diets. Also, use plenty of sunblock." She tapped the picture of Carrie's dress. "Strapless gowns and tan lines don't mix."

"Thanks for the tip. I'll make sure I wear sunblock

and a hat tomorrow when we ride. Maybe Quinn has one I can borrow."

"Oh, you're going riding? The countryside is so beautiful this time of year," Ava replied.

"It was my stepsister Erica's idea. I think she wanted to take a trip down memory lane this weekend. She and Ward used to ride a lot."

"They were engaged, right?" Ava had unpinned Carrie's hair, and the reddish gold locks tumbled down her back. Deftly she made two French braids along either side of her head and then wrapped the ends in a loose bun at the nape of her neck.

"I like this look, too." Carrie angled her head, admiring Ava's handiwork in the mirror. "I could never manage a style like this on my own." Returning to the topic of her stepsister, she said, "From the minute we climbed out of the car, Erica hasn't stopped looking at Ward. I think she may be regretting that she walked away from the engagement."

Although Tess had guessed that much herself, to hear it confirmed by someone who knew Erica so well made her stomach clench in a knot that rivaled the twists and loops Ava had created with Carrie's hair.

"I would imagine Ward would be a hard man to get over," Ava said. "Don't you, Tess?"

She managed a casual smile. "Yeah, I think he would be." She knew it with a certainty that reached down to her marrow and to the depths of her heart.

By Saturday morning the likelihood that Erica was having second thoughts about ending her relationship with Ward was all too clear to Tess. Erica behaved as if every minute should be spent glued to Ward's side and sulked when she couldn't. Tess did her best to ignore her but that became next to impossible when Erica began to take her frustrations out on Silver Creek's staff.

Tess, Carrie, Brian, and Erica had gone down to the corrals for the trail ride Erica had insisted upon. They were to meet Reid and Ward there. Instead, they were met by Frank, who told them that Ward and Reid were running late. A steer, which Tess now knew was a castrated male, had gotten a nasty gash in the side of his neck. Today was a day off for Pete Williams, the foreman, and Gary Cooney was at the veterinary hospital, operating on a dog that had been badly bitten in a fight, so Ward and Reid had to tend to the injured animal themselves.

Just then an angry bellowing had filled the air and they'd turned toward the source. There were Ward and Reid, astride their horses, herding the hurt steer into the corral nearest the cattle barn. Tess had seen the dark red blood matting the steer's black hide and foreleg, and her stomach had heaved.

Working as a team, the brothers sent their lassos sailing through the air, catching the steer's rear hooves and bringing him to the ground. With the animal tied, bellowing furiously in anger and fear, Ward held its head down while Frank hurried toward them with the veterinary first aid supplies so Reid could clean and stitch the wound. Tess saw Ward's lips move, but couldn't make out what he was saying to Frank. The other man nodded and then jogged out of the corral to where the four of them stood watching.

"Ward said that you should go on and get mounted so that you don't lose time. He and Reid will be along shortly."

Erica resisted. "No. I'm going to stay and watch."

Tess had discovered that she was the kind of person who always had to state her own desires, and make sure everyone understood that they trumped all others.

But Brian wasn't having any of it. "Listen, Ward's organized this trail ride for us, and even though he's in the midst of dealing with an emergency, he's making sure we get to have our fun. So why don't we do as he asks and go get on the horses?"

Hearing his words, Tess felt her opinion of Brian rise. She liked him—he had a sweet, freckled, all-American boyish air with just enough Dennis the Menace mixed in to make him funny as well as endearing. She liked him even better now that he was standing up to Erica and sticking up for his best friend.

With an impatient shrug Erica relented. But as they made their way back to the horse barn, she made sure to telegraph her annoyance by maintaining a sullen silence. If only the silence had lasted.

In the corral closest to the horse barn stood four horses, saddled and bridled. They wore halters, too, with ropes attached to posts.

One of the ranch hands—Tess remembered his name was Jim and that he and Quinn were good friends—came out of the barn. He was young, maybe twenty, thin as linguini, and affable, imbued with the good-natured friendliness Tess had discovered was the hallmark of Silver Creek's wranglers. As Quinn had explained one day when Tess was taking some pictures of the horses being groomed with some special tool that helped them shed their winter coats, the guests helped pay for the four-legged animals on the ranch, so one of the wranglers' jobs was to keep the guests happy and smiling. Offering great horseback rides along beautiful winding trails was one way of achieving that goal. Being pleasant and unfailingly polite was another.

"Hey, Tess. Ward told me to saddle Brocco for you." Turning to Brian, Carrie, and Erica, Jim said, "Hi, you must be Ward's friends. I'm Jim. We've got your horses ready, too. Let's see." He checked the white board attached to the side of the barn, which had all the horses' names written in marker on it. Tess read Brian's name next to Chili, Carrie next to Major, and her own name next to Brocco. Erica had been given a horse called Nate.

Jim was pointing them out. Chili was a reddish horse, a sorrel, she remembered Reid telling her. Major was almost as big as Brocco but a paint horse, white with brownish black splotches all over. She'd never really looked at Nate before. There were so many horses, it was difficult to know them all. To Tess's untrained eye, Nate looked pretty nice, his coat a dark gold with a black tail and mane.

But Erica apparently found something lacking. "Nate's a beginner horse, isn't he?"

Jim looked surprised and Tess immediately felt sorry for him. "Nate's the greatest, a good—"

"I'm not a beginner. I have no intention of plodding at a walk for two hours. I want a real horse to ride, not a La-Z-Boy recliner on four legs."

Erica probably wasn't the first rude person Jim had been forced to deal with at Silver Creek, but he probably hadn't expected one of Ward's friends to behave this way. He raised his cowboy hat and ran a hand through his ginger hair before settling the hat back on his head. The gesture provided crucial time to formulate a tactful response. "Ward picked these horses, so—"

"He was being overly cautious. I can handle a horse with a little personality and drive. Really."

Even with the brim of Jim's hat lowered, Tess could see the ranch hand's unhappiness. He shifted his weight from one foot to the other, then asked, "And when was the last time you rode?"

Erica didn't skip a beat. "Two weeks ago."

"Really?" Carrie asked. "I didn't know that."

"Carrie, you can't expect me to tell you everything I

do." That blasted smile was back. "Darryl and Pam Welch invited me to ride at Glenoaks. Pam takes lessons there."

"Oh, I thought you went cruising with them."

"We did both. They're like me—they love challenging themselves." Dismissing her stepsister, she fixed her attention on Jim. "Please saddle another horse for me. I refuse to ride a horse that looks like he has one hoof in the grave."

"Erica, there's no call to be rude," Carrie said.

Erica ignored her.

Tess looked at Nate. He was standing with his eyes half closed, having a pleasant doze in the spring sunshine. She wished he'd wake up and bite Erica in retaliation for her snarky comment, but he seemed supremely unaffected by the humans' presence. And Tess bet Ward didn't let horses who bit anywhere near Silver Creek's guests.

"Don't worry about Ward. I'll explain the switch to him," Erica's lady-of-the-manor tone was breathtaking in its presumption.

Stiff-legged, Jim stalked over to the relaxing equine and uncinched the saddle, pulling it off his broad back.

"You can ride Ziggy." He gave a terse nod toward a white horse that was tied to the post as well, but unsaddled. Ziggy had his nose to the ground, his wide nostrils blowing as he searched the ground for stray bits of hay. "I just finished brushing him."

Ziggy must have passed whatever equine test Erica felt qualified to give. Personally Tess thought it just as likely she was satisfied with the new horse because she'd decided she'd look better perched on top of a snowy white steed than a dark gold one. Erica paid a lot of attention to accessories that enhanced her looks.

When Erica gave her stamp of approval with a careless nod of her blond head, Tess breathed a sigh of relief.

At least now Erica would quit treating Jim so insultingly. She wondered how Erica thought she could possibly maintain such a posture around Ward. Had she never noticed the respect and appreciation the Knowleses showed all the employees at Silver Creek, from the upper echelons of the guest lodge's management to Lexi Carter, a high school sophomore who worked after school and on weekends, helping Quinn with the goats and the kitchen garden?

Jim made quick work of tacking Ziggy, then led the horse over to the mounting block. After checking the cinch, he waited while Erica climbed the wooden steps, put her booted foot into the wooden stirrup, and swung her leg over the saddle. Then Erica gathered the reins in her right hand, clucked, and guided Ziggy into the center of the corral. Without a word of thanks.

Jim watched her and the horse walk away and gave a short shake of his head.

He turned to Carrie. "You're going to be riding Major. He's a super nice horse."

"I'm sure of it." Carrie's tone was effusive, making up for Erica's rudeness. "Thanks for getting the horses ready for us, Jim. And I'm sorry about my stepsister. She is a pretty good rider."

"As long as Ward's okay with the switch, no harm done."

Chapter TWENTY-SIX

WARD'S AND REID'S booted feet rang along with their horses' hooves on the drive as they walked up to the horse corral.

"Cooney may have to insert a stent into that cut to drain it," Reid said.

The vet would be coming after he'd finished operating on the dog. "Maybe, maybe not. The wound looked pretty clean by the time you finished sewing it up. You did a good job," Ward said.

"Thanks. I hope Frank and Carlos can find whatever cut him. I don't want to play tailor again any time soon."

With Sirrus and Rio huffing and snorting behind them, they walked in companionable silence. "So, you feel like taking the lead on this ride?"

Reid laughed. "That's a good one. You mean so I can have the pleasure of riding with Brian and the delightful Erica? After yesterday's extravagant display, do you really think she's going to let you get away with hanging back with Carrie and Tess?"

Embarrassment washed over Ward. At the winery they'd visited, Erica had given "obvious" a whole new meaning. It hadn't taken long for Ward to begin hoping the tasting room's manager would think that Erica simply couldn't hold her alcohol, ignoring the fact that they were sipping the vineyard's cabernet rather than seriously imbibing.

"Okay, Romeo," he drawled. "Time to quiz the expert on women. So what's with Erica's nonstop giggling and hair flicking?"

"You left out the lip licking and the finger trailing down the V of her dress. Those are dandy, too."

"Don't remind me." Ward gave a heartfelt groan. "She never did this stuff when we were engaged."

Reid shrugged. "Never had to. She had you right where she wanted you, ready to walk down the aisle to happily ever after. Then something shinier must have caught her attention and she decided to go for it."

"That would be the Silicon Valley techie. Where the hell is he when I need him?"

"My guess is that he slicked away."

Ward laughed at the term. His laughter faded at his brother's next words.

"Or she came to her senses and realized that you were pretty and shiny after all. A worthy pursuit. That video of you did show you at your silent cowboy best. It's amazing what women will project onto an appealing male form."

"You going to night school in female psychology? I thought you were more focused on the female physique."

"Both are fascinating," Reid replied easily. "Whatever Erica's motivation, you, brother mine, are most definitely in her sights."

"It's embarrassing."

"I imagine it would be. And I feel really sorry for you. But not sorry enough to forgo the pleasure of riding next to your other woman—and, oh yeah, given Erica's competitive personality, I'd have to posit that Tess may be yet another reason why Erica's determined to show you the love." He laughed and shook his head. "Damn, I'm glad I'm not in your boots."

"Fuck you," Ward said mildly. "Someday all that smooth loverboy charm's going to come back to haunt you. And when it happens, I'm going to be the one laughing my ass off."

They'd reached the corral. Brian, Carrie, and Erica were already mounted. Ward's gaze sought out Tess, finding her by the corral's railing, talking to Jim. At the sound of their approach, her head turned in his direction. Her expression was a mix of pleasure and worry.

"All set?" he asked, wishing he could wrap his arms about her and kiss away her nervousness. At the end of their ride on Thursday, he'd thought she was gaining more confidence in Brocco and in herself.

"Oh, yes, I was just about to get on Brocco. Is the steer all right? It looked and sounded like he was in a lot of pain."

"The cut was nasty," Ward conceded. "But most of that bellowing was probably to tell us how insulted he was by my sitting on his head and Reid jabbing him repeatedly with a needle. No self-respecting steer will tolerate a double insult like that."

"Then I guess it's safe to say that steer possesses a healthy dose of self-respect."

He smiled. "Yeah. So, we're good to go?" His gaze swept over the corral. Brian and the women had walked their horses over to the water trough. But instead of Nate's buckskin haunches standing between Major and Chili, he saw Ziggy's white coat and silver tail.

"Why's Erica on Ziggy, Jim?"

"I'm really sorry, Ward. Nothing I said seemed to convince her."

He sighed. Christ, he didn't want to deal with any bullshit this morning.

His silence gave Jim the wrong impression. "I know I

shouldn't have switched horses for her, but she insisted you'd be fine with it."

Of course. Why should Erica stop being a pain in the butt just because they were about to go for a trail ride, the activity she'd lobbied for? Jim shouldn't have given in, but chewing him out wouldn't help matters.

"Don't worry about it this time," he said. "But next time you're confronted by a mouthy guest, stand your ground. Be polite but firm."

"Don't look now, but here comes the mouthy guest in question," Reid said.

After offering Ziggy a drink, she had steered him away from the trough. Spotting Ward and Reid, her smile widened and she nudged her mount toward them with her boot heels.

"Tell me what happened," Ward asked Jim.

The younger man raised his shoulders in a helpless shrug. "No clue. She took a disliking to Nate. Decided he was a beginner horse."

"Jim did his best to convince her that she should ride Nate, Ward." Tess spoke in a quick rush since Erica was closing in on them.

"I know you're not to blame, Jim," he said.

Okay, he thought assessing the situation. So Erica would be riding Ziggy. He was a good horse, but it was spring and sometimes even the most seasoned horses succumbed to spring fever. They got just a little jumpier and friskier. His mother liked to use the term "fizzy." Ward had chosen Nate for Erica because he'd been ridden a number of times during the week and had been rock solid on each outing.

Though he was tempted to haul Erica off Ziggy's back and tell her it was Nate or nothing, he had a hunch she'd figure out a way to make that backfire just to score a point, such as listing every trail ride they'd ever been on together. He had no desire to listen to such a recitation.

Besides, a confrontation would only embarrass everyone. And if they didn't head out soon, they'd be late for Carrie's meeting with George Reich, which had been scheduled for before the lunch crowd descended.

Erica reined Ziggy to a halt in front of them. Her smile was all satisfaction.

He got right to the point. "We assign horses to riders here for a reason, Erica."

"Don't be silly, Ward. You've seen me ride. I know what I'm doing on a horse."

Erica was an okay rider, but, like many others, her opinion of her abilities was inflated.

Stacy Westfall she was not.

It wasn't the first time they'd dealt with guests who thought they were hot shit in the saddle when, in fact, they were dried turds. He would simply have to control the environment as much as possible by making their stints at a lope short and sweet. If Erica complained even once, he'd whip out his bandana and gag her.

Turning his back on Erica, he said to Tess, "Let's get you into the saddle. Brocco was out on the trail yesterday so the stirrups may need to be adjusted. If you'll hold Rio, Jim, I'll help Tess mount."

He gave Rio's reins to Jim, and he and Tess walked over to where Brocco was standing.

Tess waited while he unfastened Brocco's halter and checked the cinch.

"Ready?" he asked.

He couldn't point to the moment when touching Tess or getting a smile from her had become a key means to lifting his spirits or beating back the lousiness of a day, but he accepted the power she now wielded. Even now, just catching the scent of her shampoo as he stepped closer made him happy. So happy that he felt a smile tug the corners of his mouth.

"I guess so." She patted Brocco's neck—the gesture

showed him he'd been right in thinking her confidence around horses was growing—and nodded. He grabbed her bent jeaned leg—his smile growing—and boosted her up. She'd gotten smoother about settling into the saddle. Yeah, he was damned proud of her. She found the stirrups, and he checked their length.

"They actually look good. How do they feel?" he asked.

"Okay—"

Whatever else Tess had planned to say was cut off. "Wow. I didn't realize you offered the deluxe treatment, Ward. A leg up and stirrups checked? Isn't the mounting block good enough for Tess?"

He glanced up from his position in front of Brocco's large diamond-shaped head. Erica was smiling at him, but even from this distance he detected the tension behind the effort. If she forced the smile any more it might crack.

"Any complaints, take it up with the owners," Ward replied. After making sure that Tess was holding the reins properly in her right hand, he walked back to Jim, who passed him Rio's.

"Thanks, Jim. We'll be back in a couple. You and Quinn taking the guests on the eleven-o'clock ride?"

"Yeah. It's not a big group, just twelve riders. We'll probably take the lake trail," he said, referring to the lake that was fed by Silver Creek and formed part of the forest preserve.

Ward swung himself into the saddle. "Good day for it. Have fun. Reid and I will take care of the horses after we come back."

Jim nodded and escaped to the sanity of the horse barn.

Reid was already astride Sirrus. "So, Erica and Brian, you're going to ride with me. We'll be taking some excursions on connecting trails to do some loping. When we feel like walking we'll rejoin Carrie, Tess, and my geriatric older brother."

Ward looked at Reid to signal his thanks but his brother already had Sirrus heading out of the courtyard at a brisk walk.

The morning suddenly got a whole lot better from Ward's point of view. "All right," he said with a smile. "Let's ride."

He was going to have to think of a way to repay Reid when this ride was over, Ward decided. For all of Reid's razzing over how determined Erica would be to remain in Ward's company during the ride, his brother was doing an outstanding job blocking her every attempt, taking full advantage of the number of trails that crisscrossed one another over the ranch's rolling hills. After having publicly boasted of how she longed to ride at a faster pace, Erica couldn't exactly protest whenever he suggested they peel off on a side trail to trot or lope.

And when the five of them were together, it was easy for Ward to keep his attention primarily fixed on Carrie and Tess. The two of them were clearly enjoying themselves. Carrie had been extolling the beauty of the day—easy to do with the spring sunshine warming the air and scenting it with the fragrant notes of fresh green grass and pine. For the first time since their arrival, Carrie's enthusiastic comments drowned out Erica's, saving Ward from having to fend her off.

Still, he grinned in relief when once again Brian and Erica followed Reid down a trail that crossed Silver Creek, the distant sounds of their hooves on the wooden bridge music to his ears.

Carrie, chattering away with Tess, didn't even notice. "I fell in love with this place the summer I came to visit

Brian. My sophomore year in college. Brian and you were juniors, right, Ward?"

"Yeah."

"Adele and Daniel had been giving Brian gainful employment since high school. But just because they'd opened their hearts to Brian didn't mean that they had to open their home to some girl from Greenwich, Connecticut."

"I did vouch for how cute you were, Carrie."

"I cannot thank you enough. Because who knows whether I'd have gone into astrophysics—I'd been thinking of majoring in math—if I hadn't come out to Silver Creek and lain in the meadow with Brian. We spent hours staring up at all the stars glittering down on us. No houses anywhere, no lights, just those points of light. It got me to imagining what might lie beyond."

"That's what you were doing with Brian?" Ward teased. "Reid and I were always sure you two were exploring far more than the celestial heavens."

Carrie giggled, blushing under the hat she'd borrowed from Quinn. "We weren't always stargazing," she conceded. "But this place is magical. I just don't know anything like it back east. Do you, Tess?"

"Certainly not near Queens, New York, I don't."

"So do you feel this way, too—this incredible awe at being surrounded by so much nature? Has it made you fall in love?"

Unlike Carrie, Tess wasn't wearing a cowboy hat. As soon as Ward understood where Carrie's question was leading, he slowed Rio's walk further to observe her reaction.

Her laughter sounded a bit forced, as colored with embarrassment as her cheeks. Her response betrayed an equal self-consciousness.

"In love?" Her gaze darted to the right, connecting with his, then ricocheted back to stare fixedly between

Brocco's cocked ears. "I—uh, well, I'm a city girl through and through."

Carrie looked across to Ward. "Looks like Tess needs a little convincing. I'd recommend taking her out to the meadow at night so she can appreciate the wonders of nature." She grinned.

"Hmm, the evenings are warming up." He was set to say more to see how much Tess's blush could deepen when the sound of horses loping up the trail reached him.

And all hell broke loose.

Reid was in front, followed by Brian and then Erica. The men pulled their horses back from a lope down to a walk, but Erica, either because Ziggy had been trailing a bit and she wanted to catch up or because she wanted to get back to the group as quickly as the others and not miss any of the exchanges, waited to slow down. Not an expert rider, she misjudged the distance—and like a speeding driver tailgating the car ahead, her belated attempt to slam on the breaks failed.

Ziggy, his head jerked high by Erica's yanking on the reins and ears pinned back, rammed Chili. Chili was one of their best trail horses, but no animal likes to be plowed into, and he reacted with a buck, his rear hooves doing their own slamming—right into Ziggy's chest.

Ziggy squealed in pain and reared, throwing Erica off balance. Lurching frantically to stay in the saddle, she overcompensated, falling onto his neck. With a cry she grabbed his mane.

These five seconds of frightened chaos might have ended with no further incident if, at that exact moment, a doe and a buck hadn't burst through the underbrush on the side of the trail with a crash and the snap of young branches, landing in the horses' midst.

Already panicked, Ziggy lost it completely. Normally mellow when confronted with the deer, rabbits, and even bobcats that sometimes crossed their paths, this time he spooked, jumping sideways. The second his hooves touched the ground, he wheeled around and was gone, tearing down the trail as if the hounds of hell were chasing him.

It all happened so quickly. And since Reid was riding in front of Brian, he missed the mayhem. Ward, facing the opposite direction, saw the nightmare unfold.

The second the frightened Ziggy spun on his haunches like a circus pony and took off down the trail, Ward spurred Rio forward. He was already at a gallop as he passed Reid. "Keep Tess safe!"

Tess's heart pounded as loudly as the sound of Rio's hooves thundering down the trail as he and Ward flew after Erica. It pounded not just from the fright of seeing Erica's and Brian's horses shy and spook, or from having two large deer burst out of the undergrowth like two disturbed extras from *Bambi* (a movie she'd honestly never liked because of all the wild critters), it pounded from the crystalline revelation: She'd fallen in love with an extraordinary man.

She might never come to love *Bambi* but she suddenly knew without a doubt that she loved Ward Knowles. He was an amazing man, a true hero, a modern-day knight in jeans and a cowboy hat, racing off to save a damsel in distress.

Another thing she realized was that she pretty much loved Brocco. He'd stood still, his hooves never leaving the ground during the pandemonium. It was as if he'd heard Ward's shout to Reid—that he keep Tess safe—and decided to do his part. She was going to filch a carrot from Quinn's cache and feed it to him once they got back to the barn.

With Brocco she could easily show her appreciation

and the depth of her affection. Ward was a different matter.

Even if she could screw up the courage to show how deeply in love she'd fallen with Ward, there was a little problem. The man of her heart was racing off to rescue the wrong damsel. When he returned fifteen minutes later—fifteen minutes that felt more like fifteen hours as Tess listened to Reid talk soothing nonsense to calm a rattled Carrie—Erica was seated in front of him on Rio, leading a limping Ziggy behind them. Despite her scare, despite Ziggy's injury, Erica's eyes shone with what Tess could interpret only as joy. And why not? After all, Erica was back once more in Ward's arms.

Chapter TWENTY-SEVEN

FOUR HOURS LATER that special glow still illuminated Erica's face. More irritating and depressing was how it amped up in wattage when Ward and Brian appeared at the tail end of Carrie's meeting with Samantha Nicholls at her Mendocino floral shop, Seaside Lilies.

The meeting had gone well. Since Samantha had come recommended by Adele, Tess hadn't really worried it wouldn't. Samantha had done her homework and suggested a mix of peonies, roses, and calla lilies for Carrie's bouquet that suited the romantic style of her wedding dress. Fortunately Samantha had visited Silver Creek during the summer, and so she knew which flowers would be in bloom and was able to suggest arrangements for the tables' centerpieces that would echo the ranch's gardens.

It was Samantha's job to be helpful; it was seeing Erica fulfill her role as maid of honor with immense good cheer that caught Tess by surprise. The glow resulting from Ward's gallant rescue had done more than color her cheeks; it had mellowed her personality. Not a single silky-smooth criticism passed her lips. When asked for her opinion on the bridesmaids' bouquets and the men's boutonnieres, she offered ideas that actually suited the style of the wedding. More surprising, she then went on to make the frankly brilliant suggestion that Samantha create several hanging decorations of star flowers for the tent that could be suspended over the diners, combining the theme of stars and flowers. The idea perfectly encapsulated Carrie's vision for her wedding.

Riding ensconced in Ward's strong arms had obviously brought out the best in Erica, Tess thought as Carrie sprang out of her chair and hugged her stepsister.

"That is so brilliant, Erica. I love the idea," Carrie said.

If Erica was revealing an admirable best side, all glowing sweetness and light, Tess was feeling impossibly dull. The only positive thing she could say about herself was that she had just enough self-restraint to keep her petty thoughts about Erica's transformation to herself. Unleashing them would only show Erica how much it had rankled to watch her ride back to the ranch, safe and secure in Ward's arms.

While Carrie was greeting Brian and then excitedly listing the flowers Samantha was going to use in the centerpieces and larger displays, along with Erica's idea for a hanging installation, Ward chatted with Samantha, who wanted to know when Adele and Daniel were returning from their trip so that she and Adele could confer about the flowers for the Mother's Day weekend they were holding at the ranch.

Erica had sidled next to Ward and entered the conversation easily by praising Adele's eye and excellent taste. Tess, unable to take much more of Erica's triumphant niceness, especially when she found herself agreeing with the other woman, decided a hasty retreat was in order.

She scooped her purse off the stool that stood next to a long wooden workstation and, exiting the glass conservatory that served as Samantha's studio, glanced at her watch.

It was four o'clock, but after the morning they'd had it felt much later. For each hour since Ward's dramatic rescue, Erica must have recounted the tale of his bravery three times over. With every recounting her voice grew a little more breathless.

By now Tess could recite the story herself, visualize Rio racing after Erica's terrified horse and, as they galloped neck and neck down the winding trail, see Ward leaning over and grabbing Ziggy's bridle and bringing the animal under control. She could hear Erica, who'd lost her reins as well as her stirrups, sob with relief as she slowly unclenched her fear-frozen fingers from Ziggy's long mane. Apparently, when she'd slid from the saddle her legs had been too shaky to hold her. So, of course, Ward had lifted her onto Rio's back and shepherded her to where the others waited in worried apprehension.

Tess thought her head might explode if she had to hear the story again. She took a deep breath, hoping to empty her mind of every last image of Erica curled against Ward's broad chest as Rio carried them back to the barn.

She looked around her, not really seeing the grounds of Seaside Lilies. She drew another breath and caught the hint of the sea's salty tang in the air. But its freshness couldn't chase away the pounding inside her head. Opening her handbag, she looked inside, rummaging through the jumble of her keys, cell, lipstick, compact, hair elastics, and her ever-present notebook filled with the decisions Carrie and Brian had made over the weekend. Where was the darned aspirin?

The sound of the others' voices had her abandoning her search. She'd get some aspirin in her cabin. She must have some there.

"There you are, Tess. I hope we didn't keep you waiting," Carrie said. She had her hand wrapped in Brian's bigger one and looked happy. That was good. So far, Carrie, bless her generous nature, had been pleased by all the wedding plans put forth.

"No, I was just getting some fresh air. I've never smelled the Pacific before."

"You'll have to take some time off and do some exploring. The northern coast is amazing," Brian said.

Tess smiled past her headache. "Yeah, maybe."

They made their goodbyes to Samantha and walked toward the cars, Brian's rental car and Ward's. Erica had naturally positioned herself next to Ward so Tess maintained a space between herself and the foursome.

"Hop in, Tess," Ward said. "I don't want us to be late."

She glanced over at him in confusion, unable to think of a single thing they might be late for.

"For our appointment," he prompted.

"You guys have another appointment?" Brian said.

"Yeah." Ward was already drawing his car keys from his jeans pocket. "Luckily it's not far. We'll meet you back at the ranch."

"So what's this fairy tale about a meeting?" Tess stared out the windshield as she spoke. They were on Route 1, going God knows where, and the scenery was beautiful. Almost as magnificent as the man steering the car. "Erica knew you were lying by the way."

"Ask me if I care. I wanted to spend some time alone with you."

She focused on the first because the second made her too happy. "Yeah, well, she's working awfully hard to make you care, isn't she?" She brought her hands together and turned slightly toward him. When she spoke she made her voice go gooey with admiration. "Oh, Ward, I've never seen anyone ride like that. I don't know what would have happened if you hadn't been able to grab Ziggy's reins and slow him down."

He shot her a glance that was a mix of irritation and amusement. "Knock it off."

Her voice turned even more treacly. "Yes, Ward, I'll do anything you say, Ward."

"So, what would you have liked me to do, let Ziggy run off with her?"

"Yeah," she admitted. Abandoning her cloying tone, she slumped back into the padded leather of the front seat. God, she hated being jealous, but she couldn't seem to shake it or temper her dislike for Erica—not even when she could see qualities to admire in her. "And maybe she could have run into Sasquatch and he could have made her his mate, kind of like in *King Kong*."

"I don't think Sasquatch would have her. Too high maintenance."

Tess didn't think so, either, but she refused to abandon her funk. "Wouldn't work anyway since she'd probably figure out a way to get you to rescue her from Sasquatch, too. *Porca puttana,*" she muttered under her breath.

"You know, you are incredibly sexy when you get all Italian fishwifey."

She tossed her head. "Save the sweet talk for Erica. I have a headache."

Suddenly Ward pulled off the road. As the wheels bounced over a rutted dirt drive, she looked around her in surprise, seeing nothing but the gnarled limbs of trees softened by fuzzy spots of bright green leaves beginning to unfurl. "Hey, where are we going?"

"A little nature appreciation."

"Oh, please, after Bambi and friend made their appearance on the trail, I think I've appreciated all the nature I need to for today."

He didn't answer but merely grinned as he negotiated the ruts and potholes left by the spring rains. Ahead, Tess saw a clearing, a meadow filled with tall grass and delicate yellow wildflowers. Then beyond, nothing but sky.

She opened her mouth to repeat her question, but Ward had already turned onto the field, cut the ignition, and opened his door. Moving quickly, he circled around to her side. Pulling open her door, he held out his hand. She could hear the sound of the surf now, a slow rumbling roll followed by the thunderous crash of waves slamming the rocks. The meadow ended in a cliff overlooking the sea. Searching, her eyes met his, and a thrill shot through her at the intensity of his blue-green-gold-chipped gaze.

He took her hand. Wordlessly he led her around to the front of the Jeep and backed her against the hood and lifted her onto it. The warmth of the engine penetrated her cotton skirt. He moved closer, stepping between her legs, which of their own volition opened in a V of welcome.

"God, you're beautiful."

"As beautiful as Gina Lollobrigida?"

"Gina who?" He frowned. "Christ, Tess, you're more beautiful than any movie star or celebrity. You're you. Unique. And you drive me crazy with need."

"Good answer."

They stared at each other, the excitement building as surely as the heat flaring between their bodies. The sea air around them seemed charged. Heavy with moisture, it caressed. She stilled, waiting for his next move while her heart revved with wild joy.

Deliberately, he lowered his hands to the hood on either side of her hips. Leaning over her he brushed his mouth against hers, then caught her lower lip with his teeth, nipping lightly. The teasing bite had her mouth opening with a ragged moan of need that he fed with a sure thrust of his tongue that dove deep into her mouth. He kissed her with a hunger that was fierce, dark, and wonderful.

"What are you doing?" she whispered, aware that her hands were gripping his button-down shirt, clutching it like a lifeline.

"What I've been dreaming of doing for about thirty-six hours."

"You've been dreaming of kissing me on the hood of your car for thirty-six hours?" she was amazed she could tease him while her body was on fire for him, every cell of her being seeming to cry out for his touch, his possession.

"I've been dreaming of kissing you on a car, in a saddle, in a bathtub, against a barn, you name the place, and you and I have been there—and doing a whole lot more than just kiss. I've missed you, Tess. If you shut up, I'll be happy to show you how much." His hands had slipped beneath her skirt to travel slowly up her thighs. The touch of his work-roughened palms made her simultaneously melty and twitchy, which sounded weird but felt spectacular, like nothing else in the world.

She wrapped a hand about his wrist, halting his progress. "Are you suggesting what I think you are?"

"Most definitely." His other hand, the one free to roam, flirted with the elastic of her panties, dancing along the inside of her thigh. She fought the urge to squirm, to pant, to give him anything he wanted.

"Here—where anyone can come across us?"

"Not a lot of folks out here." The tip of his finger brushed her curls, and her damp flesh strained, desperate for contact.

"I don't want you to think I'm easy." Which was funny since she was ready to do just about anything to have his hands caressing her, to have his mouth devouring her, to have his solid weight pressing down on her, and his rock hard heat filling her.

His mouth moved to her ear and, tracing the curve of it, hit a couple thousand erogenous zones in one slow lick. "You, easy? If only." He laughed. His breath, a warm cloud against her damp skin, set another frothy wave of pleasure rolling through her. "Had you been remotely easy I would have figured out how to have my satisfyingly wicked way with you about fifteen minutes after you drove up in that sputtering wreck."

His touch was driving her straight toward bliss. Hearing his words, happiness flooded her. "So you already liked me back then?"

"There were parts of you I liked immediately. I'd be happy to give a guided tour right now, showing you each and every one. But first let me set your mind at ease. You made it quite clear that you were not easy. I can only tell you how very grateful I am that you've relented even a bit. Now, darling, would you mind slipping off those panties?"

She declined with a slow shake of her head, electing instead to lean back with her elbows propped on the hood. Then she smiled. "Why don't you do it instead?" She paused and added in a whisper, "With your teeth."

Darkness had settled over the ranch by the time they returned. Ward parked by his house and together he and Tess walked along the path to her cabin. He held her hand. Their progress was leisurely. He often slowed their pace even further, bringing her to a stop so he could kiss her lingeringly.

After their passionate interlude by the cliff, the raw hunger that had driven him had mellowed to a slow savoring. But each kiss, each taste of Tess's sweetness, was like a distillation of what they'd shared. It reminded him of the strength of her legs wrapped around his pumping hips as he thrust deep inside her in a rhythm as elemental as the ocean just beyond the cliffs, of her hands clutching him close, urging him on while her inner muscles clenched his straining cock. His heart had pounded at the beauty of her expression, at the sight of her dark eyes bright with joy and desire and passion.

The memory of her touching him, too, was equally vivid. She really had driven him crazy, cupping his balls and stroking his shaft as her mouth wreaked its own hot mayhem, licking and nibbling him until he was ready to explode from the need to plunge into the wet warmth of her body.

Even at its rawest and raunchiest, making love with Tess was like poetry. Fucking poetry.

With an inward grin, he decided not to share this observation. Tess might not recognize it for the sincere compliment it was.

Damn, this woman made him happy.

His happiness had become crystalline when Tess came in his arms, crying his name in a shattered voice. As she trembled from the aftershocks of her orgasm, only his soft kisses, easy murmurs, and gentle petting could restore her. At that moment, he'd felt not only happy, but also essential.

This time when he raised their clasped hands to press a kiss against the delicate ridge of her knuckles, he saw a flash of white in the deepening gloom. She was smiling—as happy as he was.

"You sure you won't come to dinner tonight?" he asked, kissing her hand again before lowering it.

She shook her head. "No. I know Carrie and Brian would be okay with it—they're so easygoing. But for you to have to explain my presence to Erica at a dinner that's social rather than wedding-related, well, that would just be awkward. I think I'll turn in early. It's been an action-packed day."

"That it has."

He could kiss her until she changed her mind about dinner. As tempting as the plan was, he abandoned it. She was right about how Erica would behave, and he wanted to protect her from Erica's antagonism—an antagonism that would be that much more pointed if Ward forgot himself, as well he might following the kind of afternoon he and Tess had shared.

He wouldn't be able to see her face lit by the table's candles and resist reaching out and tucking a silken bang behind her ear: a casual touch, but one that would scream possession to any who witnessed it. He didn't want to deal with Erica anymore this weekend.

He squeezed her hand as he came to a halt. "They'll be gone tomorrow." The comment was as much for him as for Tess. He loved Brian and Carrie but he wanted them gone so he could have Tess to himself. Angling his head he covered her mouth and kissed her slowly, thoroughly. When he drew back, they were both breathing a little raggedly. "How's the headache?" he asked, skimming the side of her face with his free hand.

She gave a little smile. "What headache?"

His own smile spread. "I'm that good, huh?"

"Maybe it's that *I'm* that good."

"That you are, Tess Casari."

She rose onto her tiptoes and kissed him. "Glad you've been paying attention."

"Very close attention," he said, slipping an arm around her back and drawing her close. He lowered his head to kiss her until they both forgot the need to breathe.

A voice in the dark stopped him. "Ward, is that you?" Erica said. "So you're back. We were beginning to wonder. Brian and Carrie sent me out to find you."

Ward doubted that very much. He stepped back, but kept a hold of Tess's hand. Erica had interrupted a private moment. After her idiotic behavior this weekend—she couldn't really believe there was a snowball's chance in hell that he and she would ever get back together—he was damned if he was going to pretend Tess wasn't important to him. Maybe now she would recognize the futility of her campaign.

He was still steamed at the stunt she'd pulled, demanding Jim switch horses for her when he wasn't around to put the kibosh on her riding Ziggy. His anger was directed at himself as much as at her. He should have insisted she ride Nate, who had been out more than Ziggy the previous week and so would have been less likely to spook. Being far lazier than Ziggy, Nate certainly wouldn't have taken off down the trail at a gallop. Or continued for nearly as long.

Ward could only thank God no one had gotten hurt because he'd let Erica have her way.

Tess spoke. "I should go, Ward. I need to call my parents before it's too late for them."

"Okay." Reluctantly he released her hand.

He could feel Erica's sharp gaze penetrating the gloom. He knew that his shirt was still untucked and Tess's hair looked like a family of squirrels had taken up residence in it. Her skirt was a little worse for wear, too, he thought with a smile. Busy as he'd been dragging off her panties with his teeth and then kissing his way back up her naked legs, he hadn't bothered to remove her skirt (probably for the best, as they'd been making love out in the open). It had as many wrinkles as a crumpled piece of paper.

Were only half the evidence of what he and Tess had been up to this afternoon visible, Erica might well ask herself why she'd never emerged so rumpled and disheveled following a bout of sex with him. Good question, and one Ward would have been more than happy to answer. It was because she'd never inspired anything close to the white-hot passion Tess ignited in him with a single sultry look.

"I'll see you tomorrow," Tess said. "Phil will be here at eight-thirty to meet with Carrie about the guest list."

"Right." He didn't want her to go. "You've got dinner?"

"Jeff boxed up some leftovers from the wedding menu. Best doggie bag ever," she told him cheerfully. "Bye, Erica."

The evening air was nowhere near as chilly as Erica's voice. "Goodbye."

He listened to her footsteps recede down the path and thought of how much he'd enjoy eating leftovers with Tess in her cabin. But he couldn't ditch Brian and Carrie on their last night.

"Are you going to the guest lodge?" Erica asked.

He hadn't forgotten Erica was standing there, watching him watch Tess. He'd merely hoped that if he ignored her she'd go away. "No, I have to change."

"Do you mind if I come to your house? There's something I'd like to say. It's important."

His parents hadn't raised him to be rude or openly insulting to women. And he needed to remember that at one point he'd thought Erica should be his wife. He should be nice to her out of gratitude for disabusing him of that foolish plan.

"I can spare a few minutes."

* * *

He entered the house and flipped on the interior lights by the front door and gestured for Erica to precede him. As she stepped inside the living room, she glanced about, surveying it.

"It's just as I remember. You haven't changed it. I'm glad," she said.

He remained silent. He could care less what she thought of his décor.

He dropped his keys in a shallow red and black ceramic bowl that a local potter his mother admired had made. The discordant jangle of the metal rang in the space left by his silence.

Erica turned toward him. She'd already dressed for dinner in a dark blue dress that hugged her slender frame. Her gaze flicked over him, and the fine lines around her eyes deepened as she saw the evidence of the afternoon's activities. He remembered Tess grabbing fistfuls of his shirt and tugging him down to cover her, and he bit back a smile.

"Ward, I wanted to apologize again for insisting I ride Ziggy. It was foolish of me. I think I overestimated my skills. And I'm so sorry about Ziggy coming up lame. But he seemed better after the ice was applied. That's a good sign, isn't it?"

He nodded. It was pointless telling her that the numbness from the ice was probably what had made Ziggy's leg feel better. Tomorrow morning would be the real test. As for her claim that she'd already apologized for her idiotic behavior, he didn't recall her actually saying anything remotely contrite—there had just been a lot of noise coming from her mouth. At least she was making the attempt now.

She'd been standing before him with her hands clasped,

a pose that reminded him of a schoolgirl sent before the teacher. At his nod she smiled in relief and stepped forward, her hand outstretched.

"Thank you for being so understanding," she said, touching his arm lightly. "I know that if you hadn't been so quick to react, things might have gone very badly."

Now she was back to repeating the ridiculous comments she'd made earlier about his quick reflexes and valor. The only reason he'd been the first to go after her was that, unlike Reid, Ward had actually witnessed the events unfold like a row of dominoes knocking one another over, ending with Ziggy bolting, Canada-bound.

He shifted his stance slightly so that her hand no longer had contact with his arm. "I accept your apology. If that's all, Erica—"

"Actually, I do have something else I wanted to say. It's about us. This weekend has made me realize that my foolishness extends to more than switching horses. I made a terrible mistake when I broke off our engagement, Ward. I'm so sorry that I threw away what we had. I'm even sorrier that I hurt you."

Oh, shit. He'd be lying if he said there hadn't been a period following Erica's walking out on him when he had imagined scenarios in which she would come back, her blue eyes swimming in tears of remorse, to ask his forgiveness and admit to a change of heart.

The reality wasn't nearly as sweet as the imagining. Because the possibility of their ever reuniting was a chimera—he recognized it as such even if Erica wasn't willing to admit the reality. He'd learned too much about her and, more important, too much about himself to believe it would ever work. He wanted a woman he could trust, heart and soul.

"Erica, you're getting caught up in the emotion of Carrie and Brian's wedding plans. It's too late—"

"I'm not, and it's not too late. I know it isn't. Especially now that I've had a chance to see things more clearly. I was stupid to take what we had for granted, not to recognize how special it was, how wonderful you are. But I'm going to make it up to you."

"What about that guy you were with?"

"What? Oh, Landon? He wasn't right for me."

So it hadn't worked out between Erica and her high-tech mogul, Ward thought. That would explain why she was suddenly impressed with his supposed virtues.

"Listen, Erica, this idea of yours, that somehow we can get back together, is frankly delusional. It won't work. We can't go back, and even if you're no longer in a relationship, I am."

"You mean with Tess? But Ward, what you and I had—it was real, not some office fling. Tess, well . . ." She gave the smallest of dismissive shrugs. "She's not right for you."

He could have replied that if what Erica and he had together was so real, why, then, had she walked away from the engagement? He could have added, too, that for him, being with Tess actually felt a damned sight more "real" than what he'd "shared" with Erica, which was kind of interesting since Tess went out of her way to insist that she had no interest in a serious relationship with him.

But he made neither point because, basically, he didn't particularly want to talk to Erica about anything, let alone his feelings for Tess. He settled for, "Sorry, Erica. The answer is no. I have no interest in rekindling a relationship with you. End of story."

He'd spoken the words in a flat tone. To his amazement she smiled and then leaned in and kissed the corner of his mouth. He froze, wondering if she really had lost her friggin' mind.

"I'm not going to give up on us, Ward. I'm the woman

for you. I'm going to convince you of how right you and I are together. You'll see," she said with cheerful confidence.

Ward was still shaking his head after the muted thud of his front door shutting had melted away. Damn it, this woman really did not know when to quit.

Chapter TWENTY-EIGHT

TESS AWOKE THE next morning groggy. She had slept poorly, plagued by troubled dreams inspired less by the fatigue from the whirlwind meetings she'd arranged for Carrie and Brian and more by the distressing telephone conversation she'd had with her mother. Like so much in the Casaris' lives, it centered on Christopher. According to her mother, the past couple of days had been bad for him, to the point where the floor supervisor had warned her that they would have to contact Christopher's doctor to increase the dosage of his medication. Her mom thought Chris's outbursts were a result of seeing the dentist, but the supervisor wasn't convinced. Her mother was praying Chris improved by next week.

The news was depressing. Her brother had been doing relatively well. But the problem with Christopher's condition was that every period of stability brought false hope. It led them to believe that somehow the doctors had at last hit upon the right dosage and combination of meds and therapy for him. Their elation was soon dashed.

Tess knew that while upping his meds might temporarily lessen Christopher's violent outbursts, it opened the door for new problems. The antipsychotic drugs weren't without side effects, and Christopher already suffered from severe gastrointestinal problems.

The quiet despair in her mother's voice was terrible to hear. So often her mother did her utmost to hide the fears she lived with. Tess knew the reason. Her parents didn't want her life to be marked by the all-consuming worry that darkened theirs. Keeping her at arm's length from their troubles was their way of showing their love and their regret that she could never claim their attention.

She could never blame them for their chosen method of dealing with a thirty-four-year-old tragedy. But the strain in her mother's voice made her feel terrible for being at Silver Creek, a beautiful place and far from the unending worries her parents faced. The guilt was impossible to suppress, even though her mother had assured her repeatedly how happy she and Tess's dad were that she was doing well at the guest ranch and that the job as events planner was so fulfilling.

In the wake of their conversation, she couldn't help but think that setting up an account for Christopher with the Bradfords' money had, in the end, achieved little. Yes, it had eased the financial burden for her parents, but the emotional weight that came with caring for him—a weight equally taxing—hadn't been lifted. She'd witnessed the same with David's parents when for weeks on end he'd lain unresponsive until not even the machines attached to him could keep him breathing.

The sole bright spot in the conversation had been in getting her mother to agree that should Christopher's condition deteriorate, she'd let Tess know so that she could arrange to come help.

With another family this concession might seem normal, only to be expected; with Tess's it was huge. But for all their sakes, for Christopher's, especially, Tess hoped her mother wouldn't need to make that call.

She'd been walking along the path from her cabin to the main lodge, hardly aware of her surroundings. Ward's voice broke into her abstracted daze and, blinking, she saw the pale pink of the rhododendron bushes that seemingly overnight had come into bloom.

Ward was dressed in a pair of wheat-colored jeans and a blue-checked shirt. He was freshly shaved. By now Tess knew his schedule well. He'd have been up for hours, helping with the animals, checking on the steer's cut, Ziggy's leg, and the newborn calves, foals, and lambs. Today, he'd have awakened even earlier to shower and change in time for this last meeting with Brian and Carrie.

"Hey." He smiled as his gaze traveled over her face. "You okay?"

"Yeah. Phil said he'd be here at eight thirty so I thought I'd head up to the lodge." It was just past eight o'clock.

"Everything else okay?" he asked. Something in her voice or expression must have struck him as off.

She put an effort into her smile. She wasn't used to sharing her worries about Christopher with anyone, except perhaps Anna. Tess remembered the day her dad and mom had moved Christopher into the private facility. She'd gone to stay with the Vecchios. In Anna's pink bedroom she'd sat on Anna's bed and hugged a teddy bear and wept.

"I'm fine."

He didn't look entirely convinced. "Your family all right?"

Just when she thought she couldn't fall in love with him any more, she tumbled a little deeper. "Yeah. Mom's worried about Christopher."

He wrapped an arm about her shoulders and drew her forward, pressing a kiss against her temple. "You don't have to be at the meeting, you know. Phil and I can go through the guest list—"

"And miss out on the popovers Roo's baking this morning? Not likely," she replied lightly. "Did you check on Ziggy? How is he?"

"Still limping. The area around his ankle is puffy and warm, but at least he didn't bow a tendon. That's an injury that can take a lot longer to heal. I'm hoping that with rest and icing, he'll be able to go back out on the trail in a week or so."

"And how was dinner?" she asked as they began heading up the path. Ward had lowered his arm, but they walked close enough for her shoulder to brush his upper bicep—and close enough for her to see the muscle in his jaw clench at the mention of dinner. "Did it go all right?"

"Yeah."

She hazarded a guess. "Erica?"

Bingo. "The woman doesn't know when to quit." His tone was exasperated.

"Poor you," she said without sympathy. "So how many new ways did she find to describe your total wonderfulness?"

"Frankly, I lost track."

"Wow. I hope you're not expecting me to compete."

"No. That's what I like about you. Your refreshing honesty when it comes to my character."

"Yes, I see you all too clearly. Warts and all."

He grinned. "Much better. Damn, I'm starving. I hope Roo made her strawberry butter to go with the popovers."

"Was the barbecue not good last night?" Jeff and Chris, his sous-chef, had prepared a barbecue with sweet potato fries, roast vegetables, a field salad, and cornbread as sides. The menu was what they'd be serving on Friday night for the wedding guests. Dinner would be buffet style, relaxed so the guests could mingle and dance to the swing band Tess had booked for the evening's entertainment. For those who didn't eat meat there would be vegetarian chili. Dessert would feature an array of fruit tarts and ices.

"Brian had thirds of the barbecue, so I'd say it passed his taste test—and he loved the two micro beers Reid chose. But listening to Erica catalog how wonderful I was killed my appetite."

"The things you suffer."

He swooped down for a kiss, never breaking his stride. "I'm hoping you'll ease my pain later today."

"I have the afternoon off."

"Exactly," he replied, with a smile in his voice that she couldn't help but return.

"It'll be fun to have someone help me do the laundry."

He gave an exaggerated wince. "Not quite what I had in mind. But perhaps I'll be able to interest you in some other activities afterward. I've been told I'm wonderfully persuasive."

"Wonderfully cocky, too," she said, adopting a prim tone that would have made the nuns at her school nod approvingly.

"That I am. And let's just leave my wonderfulness at those two qualities, okay?"

She laughed. "If you insist." Never mind that she, too, could list a whole bunch of other ways in which Ward was wonderful; a man as confident as he was didn't need a recitation. But it irked to find herself once again in complete agreement with Erica.

Chapter TWENTY-NINE

Even though checkout time wasn't till noon, there were a number of guests already in the dining room, presumably those with long drives ahead of them or early flights to catch—or those who wished to squeeze in a trail ride or run before leaving. On Sundays the kitchen offered a buffet breakfast as well as menu items—including popovers. When Ward and she entered, several guests stood along the long table set up at the end of the dining room, helping themselves to yogurt, homemade granola, scrambled eggs, sausage, and bacon.

She saw Brian, Carrie, and Erica at a table for six. Brian and Carrie were talking animatedly.

Erica wasn't. She was staring at the entry to the dining room, obviously on the lookout for Ward. Her expression flickered when she saw him with Tess, but by the time they reached the table—Ward stopped to speak to a number of the guests to say he hoped they'd enjoyed their stay—her expression was serene.

Like Carrie, she was dressed for traveling, though Erica had chosen a navy silk polka-dotted shirt that Tess could tell was expertly tailored, while Carrie wore a more casual light pink cardigan top.

Erica's hair fell loose past her shoulders in a smooth blond curtain. As Ward and Tess approached, she flicked it back in a practiced move and smiled.

"Good morning," she said.

"Good morning, everyone," Ward answered for them while Tess ignored the sensation of being sized up by Erica. Her gaze traveled over her, calculating exactly how much Tess had spent on her multicolored, ribbed sweater dress with its blocks of purple, tan, orange, and gray, which she'd accessorized with the chunky necklace Anna had bought her and her favorite pair of pumps. It consoled her that whatever price Erica arrived at would be much higher than what she, a devout sales shopper, had actually paid.

Luckily she'd had the sense to wear a businesslike outfit even to a Sunday breakfast meeting. But even dressed professionally it was hard to appear as self-possessed as Erica—harder still when she now knew that the other woman had spent most of last night riffing on Ward's wonderfulness.

In just how many ways had Erica enumerated his bravery, intelligence, humor, and sizzling-hot sexiness? This thought was followed by another: After dinner, had Erica offered to demonstrate her appreciation of him even more concretely? Actions spoke so much louder than words.

She had to stop this, thought Tess. She was becoming small and jealous and she hated that.

They were just about to settle into their seats when Phil arrived. Ward introduced him, and Carrie made sure to thank him for arranging to come to the ranch on his day off.

"No problem," he said, obviously pleased that Carrie was so considerate. "Silver Creek has the best breakfast in town anyway."

"Why don't you sit next to Carrie, Phil, so that you can go over the guest list with her without all the cups and glasses getting in the way?" Ward suggested.

"Okay." Phil pulled out his chair, and Ward sat down next to Brian.

Tess made to sit in the chair next to him, but Erica stood up from her own. "Tess, you should take my seat. I'll sit beside Ward."

"Erica, it's not necessary for—" Ward began.

"I just thought that Carrie would like to sit next to her so they can talk about the guest list."

It was annoying how Erica managed to make her self-centered plan sound altruistic, thought Tess, as she sat in Erica's vacated seat. Rise above it, she told herself. Ward's ex-fiancée would be gone soon.

Luckily, Liz, who was serving their table, came over to their table bearing two large stainless steel coffeepots. She placed one pot on the table and then circled the table filling their cups from the other.

Inhaling the rich aroma of black coffee, Tess felt some of her previous grogginess dissipate. She took a slow sip. Oh yeah, much better, she thought.

Finished pouring, Liz said brightly, "What can I get everyone?"

"First off, let's have two baskets of popovers for the table," Ward said.

"Mmm, yes," Erica said. "I have yet to taste popovers as good as the ones here at Silver Creek. Can we have that amazing jam and butter, too?"

"Of course. And Roo's made an incredible honey butter. It's got a dash of cinnamon and cayenne. I'll bring that out, too." Liz scribbled on her pad.

Brian and Carrie decided on the coddled eggs with ham and cheese; Phil wanted the breakfast burrito; Tess went for the feta and spinach omelet; Erica held off on her own order until Ward told Liz he'd have the western omelet and then chose that, too.

Tess wondered whether she'd take her coffee black as Ward did to underscore how well matched they were.

Her petty thoughts were interrupted by Brian, who began clinking his coffee cup with the bowl of his spoon. "May I have your attention, please, before my mouth is too full with the best breakfast in California. I want to thank you, Ward and Tess, and you, too, Phil, for all the time and effort you've already put in to planning our wedding. Tess, the ideas you've given us have been so terrific, I find I'm actually looking forward to the ceremony. Almost as much as I am to the honeymoon. Phil, thanks for emptying this place out so that our friends and family can take it over. Ward, thanks for giving us a basement rate on this shindig so that Carrie and I don't feel like we've completely drained Carrie's mom and stepdad's retirement fund. Thanks, too, for being my best friend all these years." Grinning, he raised his cup. "Finally, here's to hoping you'll be in my shoes in the near future. With a little spiffing up, you'll make a decent-looking groom. Don't you think so, Tess?" Grinning, he gave her a knowing wink.

As remarks went, Brian's veered into the red zone of the gaffe meter. No sooner had the words left his mouth than he seemed to recall his future sister-in-law's presence and the uncomfortable fact that if she hadn't opted out of the engagement, she and Ward would have already tied the marital knot and the four of them would be well on their way to being one happy family. His freckled face took on the hue of a tomato.

Tess's gaze flew to Ward's. He wasn't a loyal friend for nothing. His expression was amused, revealing no embarrassment or pain.

But Brian wasn't let off the hook. Erica's light laugh

filled the air. "Funny you should mention the idea of Ward having a go at marriage, Brian. Ward and I were talking about just that subject last night. I told him I'm planning to prove beyond a shadow of a doubt that I've seen the error of my ways. Perhaps we'll be having another wedding here soon."

Here was the answer to her unspoken fear: Erica had done a lot more than praise Ward. She'd gone further, paying him the highest compliment by telling him she wanted to marry him. She was willing to say the words to join them forever. For richer, for poorer, in sickness and in health.

Tess's throat tightened as panic and remembered hurt roiled inside her. What could she do? What could she say to match Erica's declaration when her heart still harbored the pain of her last marriage? She knew how quickly a marriage could sour. If she were to fail at one again, her heart might never mend.

Yes, she'd fallen in love with Ward, but did that mean she was ready to consider marriage? Could she brave the risk?

Around the table, everyone had gone silent. Tess couldn't bear to look over at Ward. What if once again he showed nothing but his professional poker face? She might scream.

Then, just as the silence threatened to become terribly awkward, Phil cleared his throat. "I'd love to look at the guest list so I have a better sense of the VIPs and the MIPs and make sure everyone's properly placed."

Tess could have kissed him.

Carrie sank back against her chair in patent relief. "Oh, of course! I've got it here, Phil." She leaned over to grab her bag and placed it on the table. "But what are MIPs?" she continued as she opened the bag and delved inside, searching. "I've heard of MPs but not MIPs."

He grinned sheepishly. "Sorry about that. It's my term

for middling important people. Sometimes they cause more headaches than the VIPs."

"Oh." Carrie's tone was distracted. She'd begun pulling stuff out from the depths of her bulky shoulder bag. First came a large calculator that could probably compute math problems Tess had never heard of. Next, a textbook that Carrie must actually be reading, because why else would someone carry around an inch-and-a-half-thick tome entitled *Active Galactic Nuclei*? After that followed a composition notebook, a laptop, and a bulging wallet stuffed with receipts. As item after item piled up on the table, Carrie looked increasingly panicked. "I was sure I had the list with me—"

"Could it be in your computer?" Tess asked.

Carrie shook her head. "Oh no. That's my work laptop. My other one is back in Boston." She looked up, distress etched on her face. "I'm so sorry. I must have forgotten the guest list back home."

Tess said, "It's okay, we can—"

"Not to worry, Carrie," Erica cut in. "I've got the guest list right here." She produced a stapled sheath of papers from her own handbag with a smile. "Christine called when you left from Boston and asked me to bring along a copy. Just in case you left it on your desk under a pile of books."

"Guess Mom knows me pretty well. Though, in my defense, I've been working on this problem, trying to figure out a model for the covariance matrix of the real-space—"

"Of course you were," Erica interrupted with practiced ease, which Tess thought was a shame. It would be neat to know what a covariance matrix was and what "real" as opposed to "fake" space was. Then again, there was an awfully good chance she wouldn't understand a word of Carrie's explanation.

Erica passed her stepsister the stapled papers. "Here you go."

"Thanks." Carrie tucked a lock of reddish gold hair behind her ear. "Okay, Phil. Confession time part two. I didn't really look at the list Mom sent and honestly I don't know who falls into the MIP versus VIP category. If it helps, Brian and my friends are solid MIPs—but easy-going ones. They'll be happy wherever they are. Mom and Benjamin's friends, not so much."

"Not to worry, Phil. I've got a pretty good idea of who is where in the pecking order," Erica said.

"Oh, good."

Tess understood Phil's relief. There were few headaches worse than dealing with the fallout of guests who created a holy stink because their "consequence" had been overlooked and they'd been booked in a room that failed to reflect their elevated status. It was like a maître d' sticking a megawatt movie star or a billionaire hedge fund manager at a table next to the bathroom. A big oops.

Phil prided himself on the attention that was paid and the little extras that were provided to the VIPs who came to stay at the ranch. But Googling every guest on the list would have taken time he really couldn't spare now that the high season was just around the corner.

Carrie looked like she'd just passed a really difficult exam. "Okay, then, I'll read the names out loud and Erica can tell you whether they're used to penthouse suites and champagne." She scanned the first page, then flipped to the second. "Gosh, there are a lot of names—"

Tess could hear the note of panic in Carrie's voice. Everything had gone so well this weekend; Tess wanted this last planning session to be equally easy so that Carrie could go back to Boston and focus on those covariance matrix things, free of any wedding-detail worries.

"Let's begin with those who've accepted," she suggested.

"Oh, right. Well, there's us. I guess Bri and I get to be VIPs—isn't that nice—and well, all our sets of parents."

Brian spoke up. "I think to keep the peace we should put my parents in separate hotels. The less contact the better."

Phil made a notation on his iPad.

"That should go for my Dad, too," Carrie said. "I think Mom and Benjamin would be less stressed if Dad and Sarah, his girlfriend, were staying elsewhere."

"Sarah . . ." Phil's fingers hovered over the screen.

"Richards," Tess supplied, remembering the name from her notes.

Across the table Ward smiled at her. How could she not smile back? It went a little way toward easing the pain that Erica's announcement had caused. Of course, Erica, ever watchful, noticed the exchange.

They went through the list of family members, deciding that Brian's sister, Allie, and Paul and their two young daughters, Hannah and Grace, should be put in one of the two-bedroom cabins at Silver Creek. Tess would arrange for babysitting for when the girls tired of the festivities. With Allie and Paul's accommodations arranged, Carrie continued down the list of people who'd been prompt in accepting, with Erica conferring VIP status on a few of the guests invited by Christine Greer Marsh and her husband, Benjamin Marsh.

It was done with such exactitude that Tess wondered if Erica spent her free time memorizing the *Social Register* as well as every *Forbes* list ever compiled. The data stored in her head was impressive—and a touch scary as well. Phil, however, was entranced. His fingers flew over the screen to keep up with the annotated bios she supplied.

Carrie's mother and stepfather seemed to know a lot of important people. Other than the fact that they lived in Greenwich, Connecticut, Tess wouldn't have necessarily guessed that about them. Carrie was so modest.

It made Erica's attitude and her subtle digs more understandable—if not excusable or defensible. Tess now saw why Erica acted as if she were just a little more special than anyone else.

Once they'd sorted out the column of guests who had accepted into ultra-important and somewhat-less-important categories, Carrie began reading off those who'd yet to RSVP.

Phil, recognizing he had an info gold mine in Erica, wanted to know how they ranked, too, so that he could place them in the appropriate cabins or rooms in the Ukiah hotel and B&B as their replies came in.

They'd gone through a half dozen names when Liz arrived, armed with two yellow-and-white-checked linen-covered baskets. Tess sniffed the air, catching the scent of warm popovers, and suddenly she was famished. She let her attention drift as Liz set the baskets on the table and then placed medium-sized ramekins next to them.

"Okay, I say we hit the pause button for a second and enjoy at least one popover before we continue," Ward said.

Brian was already reaching for the basket, flipping the napkin over so that the delicious steam escaped. "Amen to that," he said offering a popover to Tess and Carrie.

Even Phil consented. Setting aside his iPad, he passed the popovers to Erica and Ward and then helped himself.

Roo's popovers were so good, they were inhaled. First helpings were followed by seconds in a stunningly short period of time. The large baskets empty, the tubs of flavored butter depleted, the dinners exchanged guilty glances.

"I don't know how you live with food like this on a daily basis," Carrie said to Tess. "It's too good."

"Jeff makes a salad that's almost as delicious," she said. "And I don't eat breakfast here."

"The bread Roo sends over for our morning toast is ridiculously healthy," Ward said.

Erica scowled, not liking the "our" in Ward's sentence. Tess understood he was making it clear to everyone—Erica above all—that he and Tess shared breakfast.

Tess's eyes locked with Ward's. In them she saw warm approval swiftly turn to something hotter, and she knew he was thinking of what their breakfasts led to when Ward wasn't on early morning barn duty.

They might have continued staring at each other had one of the guests not stopped by their table to say goodbye to Ward and thank him for the wonderful trail rides. The rides had made the man, who looked to be in his early fifties, determined to take up riding again.

Ward stood to shake the man's hand and said that he hoped he'd soon be returning to Silver Creek. There were miles of trails still to explore.

Listening to them, Tess felt her smile grow. She loved how Ward conducted himself around the guests. It was a side of him she'd begun to see fully only after she'd started spending time down at the horse barn and corral, where he mingled with the guests who'd signed up to ride. He was always cordial and willing to answer their questions about the ranch. His open love for the property, its horses, and the livestock was evident in his every word. The guests responded to his obvious attachment and enthusiasm, quickly adopting his attitude as their own.

While Ward and the man discussed places to ride near Santa Monica, where the man lived, Erica turned to her stepsister. "Shall we continue with the guest list, Carrie?"

"Better go ahead before the rest of breakfast arrives, babe," Brian said.

"Okay." Carrie wiped her fingers on her napkin and picked up the list. "Now, where was I? Oh, yeah. The Bradfords, Edward and Hope. Wait, I know them." She paused, frowning in recollection. "Wasn't Edward Bradford Benjamin's boss or something?"

Tess froze in her seat. The Bradfords? No, it couldn't be—

"Yes," Erica said. For a horrible moment Tess thought Erica had read Tess's panicked thoughts. But then she continued. "Dad was VP of one of his companies when we lived in Boston. He left the company when he met Christine and decided to move to Greenwich to be near her. But he and Mr. Bradford have remained friends. I'm sure the Bradfords will attend if their schedule permits. Though now that I think about it, maybe they won't. Their only son died recently so perhaps they won't want to endure the socializing a wedding requires. Remember when Dad and Christine went to that funeral in Boston last December, Carrie? It was for the Bradfords' son."

"That's right. I remember we had dinner with Benjamin and Mom afterward. Benjamin felt terrible for the Bradfords. They were shattered. So VIP category for them, Phil."

Oh God. Just when she'd hoped the past was behind her, it reared its ugly head. The news that the Bradfords were friends of Carrie's family came as a violent shock . . . yet it shouldn't. Some worlds had less than six degrees of separation. More like three. New England's wealthy elite was one of them.

Connections were one thing—and Carrie's mother and stepfather were obviously well connected. What rocked her was the idea that they had been asked to attend David's burial when she, his wife, had been barred from paying her last respects, from saying a last goodbye.

Hurt and humiliation flooded her once more. Choking her.

Carrie looked up. "Are you okay, Tess?"

"Of course. I swallowed my coffee too quickly. It burned." She tried a smile, fighting the dizziness that had assailed her at the mention of the Bradfords. She reached for her ice water and took a deep gulp. "There. All better now," she said, patting her trembling lips with a napkin.

Across the table she met Erica's inquisitive gaze.

Somehow she got through the rest of the breakfast. It was easier once Ward sat down again, for Erica shifted the focus of her attention to him. Tess hadn't liked how carefully Erica had studied her, with a kind of microscopic intensity, following the mention of the Bradfords. Tess wondered how much of her inner turmoil she'd inadvertently revealed. Fortunately Ward appeared to notice nothing amiss, engaged as he'd been talking to the guest.

The conversation flowed around her, Brian reminiscing about his high school and college summer jobs at Silver Creek, lifeguarding at the pool, weeding the vegetable gardens, and bussing in the kitchen. His stories were funny; Brian told a good tale. Tess managed to smile at the appropriate moments as she moved her omelet around her plate.

Carrie happened to glance at her watch. "Oh my God, Brian, we've got to get going or we'll miss our flight. I still have a couple more things to throw in my suitcase."

They all rose from the table. "The weekend's gone way too fast," Brian said.

"Yes, it has. Good thing you'll be back before long," Ward said.

Brian smiled. "Damn straight. Thanks, Phil, for dealing with our guest list. Maybe we'll get lucky and all those who have yet to reply will decline."

Tess hoped Brian's wish came true. Even the possibility of facing the Bradfords again made her sick.

Brian and Carrie hurried out. Erica turned to Ward. When she smiled like that, she was stunningly beautiful, Tess thought.

"Luckily I'm all packed," Erica said. "But my suitcase is rather heavy and doesn't have wheels. Would you mind helping me with it? The staff must be very busy."

She was stunningly beautiful and extremely clever, Tess added silently. Erica of course knew Ward would be unwilling to further burden his employees during peak check-out time.

Ward gave Erica a long look, then shrugged. "Sure." To Tess he said, "I'll meet you in a few minutes at Brian's car, okay?"

She nodded, secretly relieved to have a few minutes alone. If she didn't compose herself, Ward might guess that something was wrong. And where would she start if he asked? The list was growing longer by the minute, starting with his ex-fiancée's declaration that she intended to win back his heart, and ending with the awful prospect of her former in-laws appearing at the wedding where, if they were to catch sight of her, they would doubtless spit in her eye. The middle of her list was just as distressing. It consisted of all the ways she'd fallen in love with Ward and all the reasons she wasn't yet ready to voice to him what was in her heart.

Even though Carrie had said that she still had a few belongings to stow in her bag, she and Brian met Tess by the rental car first. Carrie was growing nervous at the prospect of missing their flight. She'd told Tess she taught a large lecture class on Monday mornings. Once again she checked her watch. "Should I call Erica?"

Brian wrapped his arm about her shoulder and squeezed it. "No. Believe me, Ward's not going to let her make us late." He pressed a quick kiss against her brow. To Tess he gave a lopsided grin. "Actually I'm glad we got you alone. I wanted to say sorry for the remark I made earlier. For a while I was concerned that Ward was having trouble moving on after the break-up. Now it seems as if it's Erica. But you don't have anything to worry about, Tess—"

"Oh! Here they are," Carrie exclaimed happily.

Tess turned to see Ward and Erica walking up the path together. They made a striking couple, his compelling dark looks a perfect foil for her blond beauty.

"Hey, guys," Brian called out as they neared. "We were about to send out an APB for the two of you."

Erica glanced up at his words and perhaps because she wasn't watching the path, or perhaps because this was just another part of her grand plan, she stumbled sideways into Ward, who reached out to steady her with his free hand. "Careful, Erica," Tess heard him say.

"Thanks. You're always there for me, aren't you?" There was only one word to describe the smile Erica gave Ward: dazzling.

Ward must have reacted by moving. Or maybe Erica just choreographed it all impeccably. Which one it was didn't really matter. What did matter was that she teetered again on her heels and lost her balance. Pitching forward, she landed against Ward in a graceful arc, and somehow her hands found their way around his neck. Her lips found him too. She kissed him, open-mouthed and for far too long . . . So long that her kiss became *their* kiss.

* * *

"Listen, Tess, you can't still be mad about that damned kiss."

"I hadn't realized there was a time limit." Her voice was tight.

"Yeah." He gave her a crooked smile. "It elapsed about forty minutes ago."

She didn't return his smile. She couldn't. The image of Ward and Erica kissing still sickened her. It had unlocked all the jealousy and misery she'd felt when David taunted her with the other women he picked up for sex. She remembered how she'd cried and wailed and stormed with him not to hurt her like this. She'd even begged.

They were in Ward's laundry room, the oddest place for a fight, especially as it was a nice laundry room, clean and bright, with lots of countertops. Determined to ignore Ward, she'd made good use of the space over the afternoon. She now had piles of laundry neatly stacked and she was still adding to them.

Doggedly she smoothed the shirt she'd pulled out of the dryer and folded it, running her hands along the warm cotton edges, pressing down with her weight so that he wouldn't see how they trembled.

She thanked God for the laundry. It gave her something to do, something to focus on rather than rewinding the image of Erica pressed tight against Ward, kissing him for far too long, so that when it finally ended Brian had whispered an appalled, "Oh, shit."

Personally, Tess thought that didn't even begin to do justice to the situation.

She pulled out another shirt from the dryer and began folding it with machinelike precision.

Standing next to her, Ward sighed and shifted, propping his hip against the washing machine, which was churning and sloshing with another load. He'd left her for an hour or so to check on Ziggy and the wounded steer, doubtless hoping that when he returned she'd have calmed down. In a sense, she had, but it was less a calming down than a shutting down, her way of blocking out the hurt.

"I'm sorry you're upset, Tess. There's no cause."

She spared him a quick glance before returning to her task. "Of course not. Why should I be upset if your ex-fiancée not only announces publicly that she wants you back, but then proceeds to give you mouth-to-mouth resuscitation? Talk about trying to revive love. Were you even going to mention that last night she wasn't only interested in talking about your exceptional wonderfulness? That she'd also decided to tell you how much she longed to walk down the aisle with you? Interesting that you skipped over that part of the evening's discussion." Abruptly she stopped and clamped her mouth shut. No, she wouldn't do this. She *couldn't* do this.

"Tess, I hate that we're fighting over Erica. I'm sorry she kissed me. But it's not fair to act as if I'm complicit in any of this."

She maintained a stony silence.

He raked a hand through his hair in frustration. "Tess, it takes two to tango. I am *not* getting back together with Erica. Do you remember those women I told you about—the ones who were more attracted to what Silver Creek represented in dollar signs than they were to whatever qualities I might possess? Well, Erica was one of those women."

"What do you mean? You said she broke off the engagement."

"Yeah, she did call it off." Bitterness tinged his voice. "But only after I made it clear that I wouldn't go through with her nifty idea to sell off our livestock so we could turn the pastures into world-class golf courses and go looking for fat-cat investors to make Silver Creek into a resort like any other in America. The pot of gold she envisioned from these decisions would go toward some nice properties she wanted to live in—in San Francisco, New York, God knows where else. Once she realized I would never try and convince my family to change the ranch so she could lead the pampered life she'd envisioned, she decided I wasn't worth marrying. Once I realized what really fueled her desire to be Mrs. Ward Knowles, I was only too glad to let her go."

"Maybe she's seen the errors of her ways—"

"I'm fairly sure she has, especially now that it seems she and her rich Silicon Valley boyfriend have split. I actually think you're partly to blame in this business too."

"Me? What are you talking about?"

He grinned because her question had come out as a shocked squeak. "You're doing such a great job promoting the ranch and raising its profile, she's probably figured out that it's not necessary to sell off the cattle and sheep to make this place turn a profit. I wouldn't be surprised if she's calculated exactly how many well-organized events like Brian and Carrie's wedding and the cowgirls' weekend it would take to increase the ranch's revenue. Of course, Erica's also probably still laboring under the delusion that somehow that money would ultimately be used so she and I could jet about like celebrity wannabes—which is why I've made it crystal clear that I'm not interested in getting back together with her. I want to be with somebody who wants me—and my deeply flawed character."

When she looked at him in confusion, he smiled. "You know, my supreme arrogance and rudeness. It's possible you mentioned a few others."

She felt a blush heat her cheeks. "I—uh—may have been a bit harsh that day."

He grinned. "Really? You mean I'm growing on you?" Stepping close he reached out and tucked her bang behind her ear—she loved it when he did that—and then trailed his fingers over her cheek. "Tess, I want you to move your things into my place."

She looked up, startled by his unexpected suggestion. Startled and worried. His thumb was now tracing her lower lip. It trembled against the calloused pad. "I—I don't think that's a good idea, Ward. It's too soon. I—"

He raised his hands to frame her face. His beautiful eyes were mesmerizing and intent. "Tess, I'm crazy about you. I want to do this."

"Oh, Ward—" she began in an agonized whisper. "I—I care for you too. Really, I do. It's just—" She stopped and closed her eyes. Oh God, life was so messy and complicated. She wanted this so much, but how could she move in with him when she wasn't sure she was ready to be in a real relationship yet? It wasn't only the pain of her ruined marriage that held her back; she'd yet to talk to him about the Bradfords. Her aim in coming to Acacia had been to escape every last tie to them. Then today, their name had been spoken by sweet, kind Carrie, and all the ugliness associated with them had returned. Tess only hoped Ward would understand why she'd taken their money when she did find a way to tell him. She couldn't make the attempt now. She needed more time.

She covered his hands with hers and drew them down to clasp them tight. "Ward," she began, her voice low and pleading. "So much has happened to me during this past year. Terrible, terrible things that I'm still struggling with. And so much has happened since I came to Acacia and Silver Creek. This job as the guest ranch's events planner, I love it. And I love organizing Brian and Carrie's wedding. But it's all a lot of work, and I'm so scared of screwing up. Can't we just keep things as they are for a while longer? Until after the wedding, perhaps? Until after Erica is really gone from your life?"

She breathed a sigh of relief when he gave a short nod and said, "Erica's not in my life, Tess. But I understand what you're saying. So, okay, we'll do it your way. We'll take it slowly and keep things as they are for the time being."

"Thank you," she whispered.

Somehow she would have to find the courage and the words to explain.

Chapter THIRTY

WARD DIDN'T KNOW what alerted him to Tess's absence. Perhaps it was no longer feeling the warmth of her soft curves inches away that roused him from a deep sleep. Perhaps it was some quiet noise she had made as she slipped from the bed. Perhaps it was the subtle shift of light as she drew back the curtain to stand before the window. Or perhaps it was the vague yet persistent notion that had been haunting him for the past two months that one day she would slip away, leaving his life as quickly as she'd entered it.

His eyes searched the dark of the bedroom and found her by the window, her figure bathed in silvered light. She had her back to him and had pulled on his shirt. Its hem grazed the backs of her thighs. It took a second longer for him to realize that she was shaking.

He rolled out of bed and was across the room in three strides. She drew a quick breath and then stilled as she felt him approach. Wordlessly he wrapped his arms about her middle, drawing her close until the silk of her hair and the fine cotton of his shirt pressed against his naked chest. Her shoulders shook as she tried to control her breathing.

"What's wrong, Tess?" He kept his voice soft.

"It's—" She swallowed audibly. "It's just so beautiful." The sadness in her voice was heartbreaking.

His arms tightened about her protectively. She yielded, sinking back against his body. Reassured by her gesture, he rested his chin lightly on top of her head and gazed out the window. It was a view he'd known all his life but had never taken for granted or stopped loving. That Tess, his dyed-in-the-wool city girl, now shared his appreciation made him feel triumphant. He knew she was happy here. He saw it in the enthusiasm with which she approached the new projects and events they'd scheduled for the fall and winter: wine tours of local vineyards, and Tess's own idea, initiated by one of the guests with whom she'd become friendly and whose watercolors of Silver Creek she'd allowed Tess to post on Pinterest. Madlon Glenn, an amateur artist, had mentioned to Tess that Silver Creek would be a wonderful place to hold an artists' weekend. Professional artists—draftsmen, painters, watercolorists, and photographers—could hold workshops for amateurs and professionals alike. Tess had floated the idea at a morning staff meeting. His father and mother, back now from their trip to South Carolina and Spain, had been delighted at the idea.

"I knew having you take over as our events planner was inspired, Tess," Adele had said.

It wasn't only the enthusiasm Tess brought to her work that revealed her attachment to Silver Creek. A week before, Ward had taught her how to lope on Brocco. The grin on her face as she'd mastered the easy roll of the faster gait was a sight to behold.

Later, just before dusk, he'd taken her on a celebratory picnic in the pear orchard. They'd spread an old blanket over a grassy patch under the trees that were heavy and fragrant with blossoms. They'd fed each other bites of chicken pesto, pan-seared shrimp and guacamole, and a selection of Roo's macaroons. He'd slipped a bottle of a new chardonnay, which Reid had discovered, into the picnic basket and made sure the blanket he chose for them was the softest one in his linen closet, because watching her ride that afternoon and seeing how far she'd come in mastering her fears had made him proud and possessive as hell: reason number 259 to get Tess Casari naked. It had been just as much fun sweet-talking her into letting him peel off her clothes layer by layer as the first time they'd made love. He knew to his marrow that he'd never tire of devising new ways to seduce her or of watching her gloriously naked and poised above him, riding once more, now following the thrust and grind of his hips as he moved inside her, rocking faster and harder as their bodies and hearts raced toward their climax.

It was a sensation like no other. He'd watched Tess's face as she came, her body pulsing and quivering around him, her face flushed with passion, her eyes dazzling, filled with the wonder and delight of what they'd shared. Overhead, a breeze had rocked the branches above them to release a gentle shower of pear petals that floated to the ground like celebratory confetti.

She'd thrown back her head, laughing, and accused him of arranging the spectacle just for her. And he would have happily negotiated with Mother Nature to create that special effect just to hear her joy, to see her lips curve in that special, intimate smile. A smile for him alone.

They were doing well. Everyone accepted that he and Tess were an item. His mother was careful not to show how thrilled she was. And even though Tess hadn't moved all her belongings into his house, they were, for all intents and purposes, living together. It had been a subtle campaign on his part to convince her that her sexy shoes and even sexier cowboy boots needed a little more space, and he had closets aplenty, and that he really liked her cosmetics and creams and brushes cluttering his bathroom vanity.

And God, he loved the sound of her laughter filling his house.

So why had he awakened at three A.M. to find her bowed and desolate? It was frustrating that he couldn't get her to open up and reveal the source of her troubles, that even though they'd come so far in their relationship, there was still this deep reserve to her. But he knew better than to push her. Tess had been hurt before. In a sense, she was as skittish as one of Quinn's rescues. He needed to be patient. Soon enough she'd realize that she could trust him with her troubles, with her heart.

He lowered his head, bringing his mouth to the sensitive hollow behind her ear, pressing a kiss there before running his lips down the length of her neck. She arched her neck, offering him greater access, and then hummed in pleasure as he nuzzled her collarbone. Her hands rose to tangle in his hair and he took advantage of her position to slip his hands beneath the tails of the shirt and cup her breasts, letting their lush weight fill his palms.

"Your brother's okay?"

"I guess. My mom says he's sleeping more. But he's not having outbursts so the floor supervisor hasn't threatened to up the dosage of his medication. And Christopher seems to like his new aide so maybe it's just a phase he's going through."

"And is he still hooked on his video game?"

"Oh, yeah." Her voice lightened. "Pokémon's still his fave. We'd all be really worried if he lost his love of Joltik's Super Circuit."

"Anna's fine?" His thumbs traced the pebbled surface of her areolae.

"She and Lucas and another backer signed a lease for a commercial space on Cobble Hill in Brooklyn. Her hope is to get all the paperwork and remodeling done and open the restaurant by next year. She's over the moon."

He could hear in her voice how much she loved and missed her friend and family. But he didn't sense they were the reason behind her sadness.

Fatigue? Stress? He knew it wasn't that time of the month—and yes, call him a chauvinist, but he had noticed that women tended to go off the deep end emotionally at certain times of the month. Quinn, a case in point. He and Reid could tease their little sister for three weeks out of every month. They risked life and limb if they messed with her the couple of days prior to her period. With Tess, all he'd noticed was that she gravitated toward the chocolate in a big way and that her breasts became even more wonderfully sensitive than they normally were. Which was saying something, he thought with a smile, as he lightly pinched her beaded nipples and benefited from her immediate response. Moaning, she pressed the delicious curves of her ass against his erection, rubbing slowly.

"The wedding? Is that what's bothering you?" His voice now held a rough rasp, his arousal battling with his desire to discover the source of Tess's unhappiness. Overseeing the preparations for a wedding was a monumental responsibility and he knew how seriously she took it. But his mother had mentioned just the other day how impeccably organized things seemed to be. There was none of the last-minute craziness they'd experienced with many of the weddings they'd held at Silver Creek. "Everything's set, right? You and Phil have placed all the guests—all the ones that have bothered to reply, that is. And tomorrow's the deadline to RSVP, right?"

She turned in his arms, moving her own so that they looped around his neck. "You have some pretty slick interrogation techniques." She kissed him.

"Do I? 'Cause I feel like I'm coming up short."

"You're not. It's just that I'm not used to feeling like this, Ward. I'm happier than I've ever been. It makes things complicated." Her voice dropped even lower as she added, "It makes me scared that I might lose what I've found with you."

He couldn't resist. He kissed her, tasting the sweetness her words had left. Their lips clung, their tongues tangled and danced. When at last they parted his breath was ragged with desire. "It doesn't have to be complicated. Tess, you know things have changed between us—and they've only gotten better. But I don't want to pressure you into something you're not ready for. We've got time."

"Ward, was it like this for you and Erica?"

Where had that come from? he wondered. Since the weekend when Brian, Carrie, and her stepsister visited, he and Tess had pretty much avoided the subject of Erica, a relief for both of them. He'd also become a master at avoiding talking *to* Erica. He screened calls not to block telemarketers but ex-fiancées. When she did sneak past his guard, he kept the conversation to one and only one topic, Brian and Carrie's wedding, before hanging up. The message, conveyed in the bluntest terms possible, was simple: He had no intention of letting her into his life, let alone his heart.

He was pretty sure he'd convinced Tess of how he felt about his ex-fiancée. But if she needed reassuring in the dark hours before dawn, he'd give it to her. "No, it was nothing like with you, Tess. It's not to say it wasn't good between us. You didn't see Erica at her best, but she's bright and clever and energetic. And I thought she loved me. But then, a couple of months after we'd gotten engaged, Erica and I had our extremely enlightening discussion about her vision for the ranch and our life as a married couple. It was a real kick in the gut to realize I was just a means to an end."

Tess angled her head to gaze up at him. "Oh, Ward, I'm so sorry."

He raised his hand to stroke her hair. "At least I found out what Erica wanted sooner rather than later. But you want to know the worst of it? It was when I realized that what was really wounded was my pride. My pride, not my heart. I was pissed at myself for being so arrogant as to believe that I really knew Erica, that I could trust her to understand what it was I cared for most in the world—my family and this place. I thought she felt the same way. Realizing how stupid you can be about a person is damned humbling—not a great feeling when you're as arrogant as me." He grinned and dropped a kiss on her lips.

"You're not arrogant." Her voice was low. "I was an idiot when I called you that before. I was just embarrassed about my car dying on me. I knew so little about them. I'd never owned one before coming here. I was stupid enough to believe the guy who sold it to me that although the body might look a little the worse for wear, the engine was in fine shape. Unfortunately, it hasn't been the only time I've made a stupid decision—" For the space of several heartbeats she was silent. Then she spoke and her voice dropped even lower, as if buried under a terrible weight. "Ward, I need to tell you—"

At the anxiety in her voice, his earlier frustration with her reticence disappeared.

His soft "Shh" stopped her. He brought his fingers to her chin and tipped it to gaze into her eyes. Despite the darkened room he could see the trouble clouding them.

He hated even the thought of her being unhappy.

"Tess, I know you've got a lot in your past, but whatever it is can wait until you're less worried and stressed from dealing with Brian and Carrie's wedding. Everything's going to be all right, I promise. It will be better than all right, and Brian and Carrie are going to be blissfully happy with their wedding. So much so that I'm willing to wager they end up calling their first child Tess. Let's hope it's a girl."

When she cracked a little smile he kissed her. "Let me love you, Tess," he whispered. "Please."

Triumph shot through him as she rose on her toes and pressed her mouth to his, kissing him feverishly. He had his answer. She was his. He just had to keep proving it to her.

He made love to her, ministering to her with a passion fierce and tender, with an unflagging focus that left her gasping, writhing, and shimmying beneath his hands and mouth. And when he dove into her slick heat, he exulted at the raw cry of pleasure she made. Whispering his name in a desperate incantation, she arched and rocked against him, urging him on.

His hands gripped hers, sure and strong, as he set a rhythm for them both. He rained kisses on her parted lips, on her breasts, quivering and lush, on the enchanting curves of her body. He breathed in the scent of her body, as fragrant as sun-warmed honey, and his passion burned that much hotter, wilder. He feasted with wet lashes of his tongue and tender bites of his teeth. And when he gazed into her eyes and saw that he'd chased away the clouds dimming them, and had replaced them with a bright, rapt light, he knew a piercing joy. Holding her hands tighter, he plunged deeper, fulfilling the promise he'd made: loving her, body and soul.

Chapter THIRTY-ONE

TESS HAD A clipboard in one hand, a pen tucked behind her right ear, and a cup of coffee—number three of the day and it was only eight A.M.—cradled in her other. Her cell, encased in a jewel-encrusted "bling" case that Anna had sent her as a good-luck gag present, was dangling from her wrist by a white strap, at the ready. The most recent call had been from Samantha Nicholls. She was packing up the flowers and would be leaving within the hour.

Tess paused to sip her coffee as she scanned the grounds. Walter the handyman and his crew of groundskeepers were busy carrying tables and chairs and arranging them in clusters for the cocktails and champagne that would begin flowing after the five-o'clock ceremony had ended. Less than nine hours remained until then, but things were going well. So far there hadn't been a single glitch or crisis—minor or major league—to fix.

The morning was beautiful, the ranch awash in the greens of late California spring, their hues enhanced by the pinks, yellows, and violets of flowers that danced in the light breeze.

With a wave to Walter and a call to Pedro, Walter's nephew who'd been lending an extra pair of hands all week, that one of the tables should be moved a little closer to the flower bed, where there was a big clump of peonies and Siberian irises, she continued her inspection, moving toward the dinner tent. Against the vibrant green of the grass, the tent, pristine white and designed with a scalloped roofline, looked spectacular. It made her think of a medieval pageant. She stepped inside. The company had done an excellent job stringing the bistro lights. Tess and Walter had done a test run the night before while the guests were enjoying their barbecue up at the lodge. The effect of the lighting was magical. And it would look even more so once Samantha installed the hanging floral arrangements and the long tables were covered with white linen, the tables set, the small lanterns lit, the sweet bouquets placed in pretty tin vases, and the tent filled with laughter and happiness for the wedded couple.

The wood laminate dance floor was folded in the center of the tent. In the afternoon, when the tables were set, the floor would be carried outside, and torches and more tables would be arranged for the evening's celebration. According to the forecast, the glorious California weather would hold. Carrie and Brian would get their night of dancing beneath a full moon and a star-studded sky.

Then, after Carrie and Brian had mingled with their friends and family and had danced their fill, they would slip back to their cabin that Tess and Anita, the head housekeeper, would have transformed into a romantic bower.

Once again, Tess glanced down at her clipboard. She flipped to the fourth page and made sure she had champagne and chocolate-dipped strawberries marked down. She'd scribbled so many notes to herself that there were moments when she couldn't sort out what she'd written from what she'd intended to write.

Yup, she thought with relief. She hadn't lost her mind yet. The champagne and strawberries were noted and at the ready. Roo had the strawberries waiting on a tray in the refrigerator. She'd even written down that Jeff was making a few special sandwiches for the newlyweds—in case they got hungry after celebrating in private.

She left the tent and walked to where Carrie and Brian would exchange their vows with the minister, Reverend Williams, the three of them standing in front of a large dogwood tree covered in pale creamy pink flowers. White bamboo chairs were already arranged in a semicircle, with a wide aisle down the center where Carrie would walk on the arm of her father to meet her future husband.

Looking at the scene made Tess's stomach flutter with nerves. She wanted everything to go right for them. Not just today, but for all their days together.

Despite her nervousness, Tess was happy as well. The event she'd been planning for months was nearing its most beautiful and important moment, when Brian and Carrie would pledge their love and devotion to each other.

Whatever reservations she'd had back in February about planning a wedding had vanished. Tess realized how lucky she was to have been able to organize such an important and special ceremony for a couple she believed was truly in love and deeply committed to each other. Once it was over she'd have to thank Adele for twisting her arm so gently and masterfully.

There was, she admitted, another reason for her happiness. A clawing fear had been removed from her heart. It had lodged there since the morning of the breakfast meeting she'd had with Carrie and Brian and Phil, when Tess had heard Carrie list the Bradfords as invitees. Very important invitees.

From that moment Tess had waited with mounting

apprehension for when Phil would hand her the guest list with a final updated head count, and she would read Edward and Hope Bradford's names in the "yes" column.

Of course, the possibility of the Bradfords attending hadn't been her only or greatest fear. The thing she'd dreaded most was having to tell Ward of her connection to the Bradfords and why they might be less than pleased to see her (never mind how she felt about them).

There'd been a number of times when she'd summoned the courage to open her heart and share her painful past with him, only to fail. With each attempt, a messy mix of fear and embarrassment and self-loathing had rendered her mute. She'd been too unsure of Ward's reaction or of her ability to explain coherently what she'd experienced during those weeks at Mass General. Would she be able to make him understand why she'd chosen to take the Bradfords' money? Would he end up judging her as harshly as she so often judged herself?

The last instance had occurred the night before all the guests were supposed to RSVP. Half-convinced that the Bradfords would accept at the eleventh hour, she'd been on tenterhooks, unable to sleep.

Not wanting to disturb Ward, she'd slipped from the bed and silently crossed the darkened room to the window, where she'd stared out at the eerily beautiful nightscape and wondered whether the world she'd come to love would be threatened by a simple notecard accepting an invitation.

Lost in her pensive thoughts, she hadn't registered Ward's approach until his arms were about her waist. The strength of his body, the unmistakable concern in his voice as he'd gently probed and questioned to discover the reason behind her wakefulness, had been sweet and so wonderful, more than anything she'd ever experienced with David. Once again, she'd nearly recounted the whole bizarre and unpalatable tale (and would doubtless have followed it up by weeping a torrent of tears, further proof of her sheer piteousness).

But this time it was Ward who stopped her. He'd kissed her and then whispered the words she found impossible to resist: "Let me love you, Tess."

The following morning her unspoken wish had come true.

The specter she'd dreaded never materialized. The Bradfords didn't even bother to RSVP to the wedding. Their absence had not only spared her the ugliness of a confrontation, it had also allowed her to avoid something even more distressing: explaining to Ward her connection to them.

It was an enormous reprieve. A part of her wasn't sure she deserved one. Oh, intellectually she knew she'd done nothing wrong. She'd taken money from an unpleasant rich man and used it to help her severely disadvantaged brother. Some might praise her action.

She couldn't, however. She could only remember the blistering shame she'd felt when she'd seen the contempt and dislike blazing in Mr. Bradford's eyes, an emotion undimmed after the weeks she'd sat by David's bedside, watching the husband she'd never truly known slip away.

It wasn't that she had expected the Bradfords to love her or think she was a hybrid Florence Nightingale and Saint Agnes—Tess had written a report in eighth grade about Agnes of Bohemia's dedication to the poor and sick—but she would have hoped she'd earned their respect and understanding. Yes, the love she'd felt for David when they first married was gone, but her decision to remain at the hospital had been an attempt to honor what she and he had once had, and to offer what support she could to his parents.

Instead of acceptance, they'd shown her their disdain. Poisonous and mean, it had invaded her system.

"Okay, judging from the look on your face you've realized that you forgot to tell Carrie and Brian that they needed a marriage certificate."

Startled, Tess nearly bobbled her coffee. Righting her clipboard, she said, "That is really not funny, Reid. I had Brian mail the certificate two weeks ago, and your dad put it in the ranch's safe for me. Your dad also put Brian and Carrie's wedding rings in there. Carrie's dress is hanging in the room where she'll change, and Brian's suit is pressed and hanging in his closet—"

Reid held up his hand. "Stop. You are scary sometimes, you know? Especially because you don't look like an alien."

"Ha. Your family's paying me to be obsessive-compulsive about every aspect of this wedding." She smiled, glad Reid had interrupted her bleak thoughts; she didn't have time for them now. Besides, it was hard not to smile around Reid, especially if one was a woman. This morning he was as killer handsome as always, dressed in faded jeans and a faded red button-down shirt, its sleeves rolled up to expose tanned, sinewed forearms. A number of single women—Carrie's college friends—were attending the wedding, and they were already following Reid around in droves; Tess was surprised not to see any hovering in the background.

Before she could ask what he'd done with his female fan club, he spoke. "You still haven't answered my question, which is all the more pertinent if you've got every 't' crossed and 'i' dotted, and every petal counted in Carrie's wedding bouquet. Why the tragic expression?"

She smiled that much more brightly. "I have no idea, since I'm feeling anything but tragic. I was just picturing how pretty this will look after Samantha attaches the arrangements to the aisle chairs. Is Ward down at the barns?"

"Yeah, He's inspecting the horses to make sure they're as spiffy as everything else in this place." He glanced at his watch. "About forty of the guests have signed up for a trail ride. Thankfully Erica's not among them, so it should be an uneventful outing for Jim, Pete, Carlos, and Al." They shared a grin.

"Erica does seem to be on her best behavior." Tess could only assume that now that Ward had made his disinterest in any kind of reunion plain, she had moved on in her hunt for Mr. Right—another reason to smile a little more broadly on this fine morning.

"I've got some time before I escort a bunch of the guests to the Red Leaf vineyards. Ward sent me down to see if I could be of any help."

Tess hoped that her expression wasn't turning too misty. "No, thanks. Everything's under control. Just do your best to keep the guests who are touring the vineyard—and I'm assuming most of them are the women who've been trailing after you with rapturous expressions—from getting sloshed."

"Something tells me that you've already told Roo and Jeff to have gallons of coffee on hand to sober them up."

She didn't bother trying to deny it. "They can get drunk after the wedding, not before."

He smiled fondly at her. "You know, I'm going to miss your special brand of crazy when I'm in South Carolina."

Daniel and Adele had asked Reid to go help Lucy and Peter Whittaker with the riding operation at their inn. He was scheduled to leave the following week.

"Just make sure you're back here for the cowgirls' weekend," she told him. "We can't have that event without you."

"Don't worry. Quinn has issued some very graphic threats about what will happen to me if I don't show. Though from the way you're riding Brocco, Ward may have you doing a demo for the ladies."

"Save the jokes for the wedding guests."

It didn't take long for Tess to wish that she could rollerblade across grass. But somehow, even though she seemed to be in constant motion, covering miles as she crisscrossed the grounds of the ranch, overseeing the setting and decorating of tables, making sure that the photographer snapped candid shots of the guests, and checking to see that no crises erupted in the kitchen, Ward nonetheless managed to catch her, stealing a moment with her as she carried a box of miniature ivory rosebuds to the cabin that had been transformed into a salon and boudoir for Carrie and her bridesmaids.

Ordinarily, Samantha would have brought the flowers to Carrie herself, but she was dealing with a mini crisis. At the last minute she'd decided the height of the flowers in the vases that would surround Brian and Carrie and the minister were too low. Blocks of florist foam were being cut to size and inserted into each vase. Then, of course, each arrangement would have to be tweaked to meet Samantha's exacting standards. Not wanting Carrie to grow nervous waiting, Tess had volunteered to take the rosebuds herself.

The box containing the flowers was balanced on her clipboard—she'd dropped off her coffee cup in the kitchen long ago—when Ward snuck up behind her, slipping his arm around her.

"Gotcha. Mmm." She felt his ribs expand as he inhaled deeply. "You smell wonderful." He dropped a kiss on the column of her neck.

She shivered. "It's the roses."

"No, it's you. You look beautiful, too."

She'd been up before dawn, and the pale lavender linen shift she'd chosen to wear was probably a mistake. "I look like a rumpled bag." Luckily she'd allotted fifteen minutes in her schedule to change her outfit.

"Sexiest rumpled bag I've ever seen."

She snorted. "Stop. I have important things to do. I'm on my way to deliver the crowning touch for Carrie's hairdo."

"I'll only let you go if you promise me a dance tonight."

"I may be too busy."

"Tease," he said, laughing, but then added in a more serious tone, "I'm crazy about you, you know."

"Then I guess I'll have to dance with you." She half-turned so she could brush her lips against his. "I've got to go. I don't want Carrie to get nervous. And, by the way, I'm crazy about you, too."

Ward's parting grin was more intoxicating than the champagne Reid had ordered for the wedding. Tess walked, or rather floated, to the cabin reserved for Carrie's special day, her elation tempered only slightly when she encountered Erica.

It was obvious she'd just had her makeup and hair done by Ava. She looked beautiful—quite an admission, but it was only right that Tess check any of her former hostility toward Erica. She'd been nothing but wonderful to Carrie this weekend. Gracious and relaxed. And although she may have smiled a few too many times at Ward, she hadn't made any blatant overtures toward him. Really, Tess could almost like her.

"Oh, hi! Is everything okay? I see that Ava's arranged your hair—it's beautiful. Stunning." The updo, an elegant twisted knot at the base of Erica's neck, did look spectacular. Classic, it suited Erica's bone structure to a T.

"Yes, she did a good job."

"And I just wanted to say how terrific you've been with Carrie and Allie's two little girls. Carrie's so lucky to have you here for her today."

A small smile curved Erica's lips. "I love Carrie. Of course I want her wedding to go well and to make things as easy as possible for the Knowleses. They've been so generous to us all. And somehow I think this is going to be one of the most exciting weddings I've ever been to."

An odd statement. Tess pondered it as she knocked and then, at Ava's cheery call of "Come in, unless you happen to be Brian Nash," pushed open the door. But all thoughts of Erica flew from her mind when she stepped inside and saw Carrie standing in the middle of the room, looking like a vision.

"Oh, Carrie," she said, awed.

Chapter THIRTY-TWO

IT HAD BEGUN.

Tess had sent a radiant Carrie down the aisle on the arm of her proud father as the strains of the string quartet filled the air. Brian and Ward—Tess's heart thudded at the sight of Ward in an impeccably tailored gray suit—were standing beside the Reverend Williams, a wiry, bespectacled man. The smile on Brian's face was warmer than the afternoon sun.

As she watched Carrie walk toward Brian, moving with such grace and joy, Tess had daubed her eyes with a handkerchief. Then, collecting herself, she stole around the back row of the chairs, circling the assembled guests, to stop several rows from where Brian and Ward stood.

She could spare a few minutes before going back to the kitchen and ensuring the appetizers were ready and checking in with the bartenders and servers. The ceremony was too lovely to resist.

Reverend Williams was calling the gathered guests to worship, and they were listening attentively. Tess's gaze swept over the faces of Brian's and Carrie's families, looking proud and happy and already a little misty-eyed, to the rows closer to where she stood. She hadn't met many of Brian's and Carrie's friends, but by now their faces, as well as those of the older family friends, had grown vaguely familiar. Then—her heart seemed to stop in her chest—she saw a face that was all too familiar. She knew that long, thin blade of a nose, with the bump that protruded just below the bridge. She knew the silver hair that was combed back to reveal a high forehead, knew the thin lips that had never smiled at her. How many times had that profile been turned toward her as she sat by David's bedside those long weeks while the hospital's pale yellow walls assumed the dingy gray of a prison and the tubes attached to David's body began to resemble manacles?

Hope Bradford wasn't next to him. It was bizarre that Tess should feel disappointed at her absence, but Mrs. Bradford hadn't despised her quite so openly.

Oh God, she thought. She'd had her chance to tell Ward about her past, and now here was the very worst of it, sitting ten feet away.

Tess realized that she was shaking. A part of her longed to run away. But then a shift in the wind brought Reverend Williams's words to her ears.

"And now Brian and Carrie will exchange their wedding vows."

She heard Brian's surprisingly strong voice. "Carrie, you are my moon and my stars. And though we may change, and things we can't even predict may befall us, my love for you will remain constant and eternal. This I promise."

The words pierced her. This was the kind of enduring and courageous love she wanted to have with Ward. And as her mind conjured up images of their time together, she knew that they could have something just as special. But it involved infinite trust. Tess knew she already trusted Ward on so many levels. With his help she had conquered long-standing fears. Because of him, she not only rode, she loped, her hand free of the saddle horn. But now she had to trust him to believe in her—and in her goodness. That he might not was her greatest fear of all.

Once the ceremony was over she would have to steal a moment alone with Ward. Mentally she ticked off the schedule of events. Perhaps after Liz Reading, the photographer, had taken the bride and groom shots, she could find a way to tell him, at least warn him of the unexpected guest's identity. She hurried away, intent on keeping as much distance from Mr. Bradford as possible. Would it be too much to hope that she could get through the night without a face-to-face encounter with him?

Ward still had a grin on his face from watching Brian kiss Carrie. He had wondered, and was sure that every assembled guest had wondered, too, whether Brian would ever stop kissing his brand-new wife. Luckily he had before Ward had to tug on his sleeve or Erica had to tap Carrie's shoulder, reminding them that they had a pretty big audience. It had been a fine ceremony. He was so happy for Brian and Carrie, his two closest friends. And he was damn proud of how smoothly the wedding had gone. Not a hitch. He planned to get Tess alone as soon as he could—and when he did, he intended to put Brian's kiss to shame.

"Ward." Erica's voice interrupted his reverie.

Collecting himself, he replied with a pleasant, "Erica," as he kept his gaze focused on the newlyweds. Brian and Carrie were walking to a spot at the edge of one of the gardens, where tall cypresses formed a rich greenish black backdrop. The photographer was at the ready.

"It was a beautiful ceremony, wasn't it?"

He smiled. "Indeed it was." No need to be hostile. Erica had obviously gotten the message. She'd been pleasant and gracious. Carrie had mentioned that Erica had been back east on business. Maybe she'd met someone to pique her interest during the trip.

She walked alongside him toward the newlyweds. "I'm glad so many people came here to celebrate Carrie's big day. Christine and Dad's friends, too. There's one old family friend I think you'd really enjoy meeting. After the photographer's finished with the wedding party shots, perhaps?"

"Why not?" Might as well kill time before he could go find Tess.

The photo session took perhaps twenty minutes. Liz Reading had a comfortable style that put everyone at ease. There was a lot of laughter as everyone changed positions at her bidding. Even Brian's mother and father cracked grins.

When it was over, Erica turned to him. "Shall we go, Ward?"

He was surprised by the eagerness of her smile. Frankly, he'd already forgotten about the introduction she wanted to make. But he couldn't see how he could wiggle out of it after agreeing earlier. "So who is this family friend?" he asked as she led him toward the tent, where guests were mingling and already drinking from champagne flutes.

"Edward Bradford."

He'd thought he'd had the list of guests memorized. After all, he'd heard Phil muttering about them every time he and Tess sat down with him for a meeting. "I don't recall his name."

"Oh, he was Dad's boss for years. Such an interesting man. And very wealthy."

Ward gave a mental shrug. Here was Erica, reverting to type. As she led him through the throng of guests, he thought for the umpteenth time that he'd dodged a bullet. Thank God he wasn't engaged to Erica, and that Tess had entered his life. He'd shake the hand of this very wealthy captain of industry and then make his excuses.

"Mr. Bradford," Erica said, laying her hand on the arm of a patrician-looking man in his midsixties. "I'm so glad that you were able to change your itinerary and come." To Ward she said, "I made a special call to Mr. Bradford, knowing how happy it would make Dad to have him here. Mr. Bradford, I'd like to introduce you to Ward Knowles."

Ward extended his hand, wondering about Erica's seeming fixation with this man. Was she hoping to get a job at his company? "How do you do, Mr. Bradford?"

"Ward and his family own this ranch," Erica supplied.

Mr. Bradford inclined his silver head. "Quite an impressive place. I won't be able to stay long—I'm catching a flight to Japan. Are your parents about?" He asked Erica. "I'd like to say hello to them and offer my congratulations to the happy couple as well. It was a lovely wedding."

"They're with Carrie and Brian but should be here shortly." Erica replied. "It *was* a lovely ceremony, wasn't it? Tess Casari is Silver Creek's events planner. She planned the whole thing. So very talented. I'm sure Ward would be happy to introduce you to her—"

Mr. Bradford had reared back in shock at Erica's words. "Tess Casari?"

"Yes," Erica said, smiling blithely as if she didn't notice that the older man's face had drained of color. "Oh, that's right. Your son was married to a woman named Tess Casari, too, wasn't he?" She turned to Ward. "Did Tess ever mention a David Bradford or how tragically he died? It'd be such a small world if this turned out to be the same Tess. I'm sure she's around here somewhere, making sure everything is running smoothly—she's strikingly efficient." She scanned the crowd. "Ah! I see her!" she exclaimed, lifting a slender hand in greeting.

Reeling from the sucker punch Erica had delivered, Ward turned in the direction she was waving. Tess was there, not more than fifteen feet away, her face an ashen hue to match Mr. Bradford's.

Tess felt the blood leave her face. They were together—Ward, Erica, and Mr. Bradford. How had it happened? She had calculated how long the photography session would last and was sure she'd be able to find Ward and talk to him—at least warn him that Mr. Bradford was there and who he was. But Ward hadn't been with the wedding party. Liz had still been snapping away because the light was beautiful and Brian and Carrie were a photogenic couple. It was Allie, Brian's sister, who'd enlightened her to Ward's whereabouts, informing her that he and Erica had left in the direction of the tent. They'd probably worked up a thirst, Allie said with a smile.

But Ward hadn't been near any of the bars, either inside or outside the tent. And then she'd seen him. And them.

How could he have met Edward Bradford so soon when Carrie's mother and stepfather—the logical people to introduce the two men to each other—were still standing and watching the young couple smile into the camera lens? The question was no sooner asked than the answer came to her. There was no need to look at Erica's satisfied face for confirmation.

Cold lead settled in her stomach.

The shock and confusion were plain on his face. As his eyes met hers, she glimpsed the hurt, too. She stood only a few yards away but suddenly the distance between them yawned as wide as the Pacific.

Oh God, what had she done? She'd lost her chance to explain things fully, properly. To give him time to understand. It was impossible now to tug the sleeve of Ward's suit and tell him she needed to speak to him urgently for about thirty minutes to an hour—because that's probably how long it would take to tell him the story of that grim period in her life when her estranged husband hovered at death's threshold.

It was too late. The thought hammered at her. She'd ruined everything by not being open with Ward. Though her heart shrank against the despair filling her, she fought for control. She couldn't let her fear win. This was Ward, the man who loved her with such tenderness, such generosity.

As she reached the group, she said, "Ward, I don't know what David's father has told you—"

Edward Bradford cut her off. "Oh, I can tell him plenty, I assure you, but I'm much more interested in your version. Would you like to tell him how you seduced my son into marrying you?"

Why should she be surprised that his outsized hatred for her hadn't diminished? She was such a fool. "I did no such thing. David was the one who insisted we marry. I thought he loved me." Perhaps one day she'd find consolation in the fact that her voice hadn't broken when she uttered those words. It would be cold comfort.

"I can only think that David was already suffering from the effects of the brain tumor when he met you. It's the only way you could have duped him into marrying you."

"You're wrong and you're insulting. You don't know me and you don't know anything about David and my relationship."

"Please," he scoffed. "You had such a wonderful relationship that it took a million dollars to make you stay by his side while he was dying?" His voice quivered with rage and pain.

Tess's throat constricted, making the words she forced out feel as sharp as broken glass. "Yes, I took your money. I regret that." She met his crystal blue eyes. "I should have followed my instinct and ripped up the check."

Bradford's laugh was short in duration but infinite in cruelty. "I wasn't born yesterday. You kept my money because you were afraid you'd failed to sweet-talk David into making you the beneficiary of his trust fund." His gaze raked her. "You underestimated yourself. The lawyer has been trying to locate your whereabouts—to no avail. David obviously was as bad a judge of lawyers as he was of women."

"What trust fund? What are you talking about? I didn't ask David for anything!"

"I don't believe you. But you know what I do believe? That you saw a chance to squeeze as much money out of my family as you possibly could and you took it. I think you are nothing but a heartless gold digger."

With a cold abruptness to match his speech, he dismissed her. He turned to Ward and Erica. During the course of the exchange, she had inched closer to Ward. "I don't know what your relationship to this woman is, young man, though I can guess," Bradford said, "but I suggest you take care. She can't be trusted and she's brought only misery to the people I love. I'm leaving now. I won't stay another minute in her presence."

"Good. Because I would have been forced to ask you to leave. My family doesn't tolerate people speaking to our employees in this manner."

The spurt of elation and hope she felt at the beginning of Ward's reply was short-lived. It lasted about a second before it was crushed by disappointment and shock. Was she now nothing but an employee to Ward? Had he somehow recognized her in Bradford's description?

With a terse nod of goodbye for Erica and Ward, Bradford left. With his departure, the sounds of the guests enjoying themselves returned, as if someone had turned the knob on the volume. Focused on Edward Bradford, she'd forgotten her surroundings. Luckily, no one seemed to have overheard the nasty conversation unfolding in their midst. No curious glances were being cast their way. There was only laughter and amiable chatter and the clink of glasses as the servers wove their way in and out of the crowd, passing hors d'oeuvres on silver trays. So far the ugliness of her past hadn't marred Brian and Carrie's day.

"Well, that was certainly illuminating." Erica's voice oozed satisfaction.

Tess ignored her. She wasn't going to give her the added pleasure of seeing how much damage she'd wrought. She'd used Edward Bradford to destroy her, setting up the ambush with the ruthlessness of a mafia don.

"Ward, can I talk to you, please?"

He looked at her. Oh God, she thought. The love-killing doubt was there, in his eyes, in the rigid set of his mouth.

"You were married to his son?"

"Yes."

"He paid you a million dollars to stay by his son's side?"

"Yes. But it wasn't like that—please, can we talk?"

A muscle twitched along his lean jaw as if he were biting back more angry questions. "No, not now."

A part of her longed to scream and beg and plead. Shake him for not saying, "Christ, Tess, what kind of messed-up situation did you land in?" But another part was too numb to act. After all, the fault lay with her. She'd kept Ward at bay emotionally, too fearful to put her heart on the line, to put herself on the line. Now, for the first time, he was closing himself off to her. The hurt was unimaginable.

A rustle of commotion swept through the tent as people began to murmur excitedly. Carrie and Brian had entered with their parents; Brian's sister, Allie; his brother-in-law, Paul; and their girls, Hannah and Grace, who were still wearing their flower girl wreaths upon their heads.

It was time to introduce the married couple to the guests. Then the toasts would begin. As members of the wedding, Erica and Ward should be standing with them.

"You both should go," she told them tightly. Then to Ward, "I'm sorry I didn't tell you before about David and his family, but it's not like Edward Bradford described."

"And yet he was so convincing, wasn't he, Ward?" Erica's voice was mild, all reasonableness. With a smile, she tucked her arm inside his. "I suppose she's right. We should go join the others. I can't wait to hear your toast, Ward. Will you make Brian squirm?" Erica's laugh was light.

"Ward, please?" She didn't know what she was asking for. Some kind of sign that it would be all right.

He didn't reply. He didn't acknowledge her plea. He simply turned away.

And she could do nothing. She couldn't call him back. He was Brian's best man and had duties to perform. She had duties as well. This was the most important day of Brian and Carrie's lives. It didn't matter that it had suddenly become, in a horribly frightening way, the most important of Tess's life, too.

She watched as he walked away with Erica, her mind in chaos, her happiness in jeopardy. Thoughts skittered, racing through her head. Would talking to him have even done any good? She tried to remember what she'd said just now. She'd admitted that she'd accepted a million dollars from the Bradfords. But David's father had made it seem as if he'd had to bribe her to stay at the hospital. It hadn't been like that, but would she have been able to make Ward understand the situation from her point of view?

She'd failed again at love. The first time with David, she'd opened her heart completely, leaving herself vulnerable when he used his words like lethal weapons. With Ward, fear and shame had made her veer to the opposite spectrum. She'd guarded her heart too carefully, afraid to share her past with him and let him see the real, imperfect her.

A part of her had hoped she'd find only indignation and outrage in Ward's eyes as Edward Bradford hurled his accusations. Neither emotion had been evident. When she considered how much she'd withheld from him, she realized it was too much to ask.

It was over.

From the beginning she'd sensed that the love she had for Ward ran far deeper than any she'd felt before. With David, she'd believed she'd learned all about the pain that came with failing at love. It turned out that she hadn't even scratched the surface.

Chapter THIRTY-THREE

WARD WAS WORKING on getting drunk. Not sloppy, falling-down, puking-behind-the-rhododendrons drunk. Just sloshed enough to turn his brain to slush and to anesthetize his heart. Ordinarily he was pretty good at accomplishing his goals. Quinn and Reid often ribbed him for being an overachiever. Tonight, however, he was failing big-time. His brain had yet to succumb to the bourbon, and his heart felt like Tess had driven one of her spiked heels through it.

He'd held off on the hard liquor—no way was the job going to get done on champagne—until after he'd given his best man's toast. The toasts were scheduled at the end of dinner, just before Carrie and Brian would cut the first slice of their wedding cake. The interim left far too many minutes—interminable minutes—for him to covertly spy on Tess and track her as she whisked in and out of the tent, tending to the myriad details still on the docket before this hellacious evening was over.

Each time he spotted her, his mind circled back to Bradford's accusations. The picture the man had painted was bizarre and ugly—unfathomable, in that it was radically unlike the Tess Casari whom Ward had fallen hard for. It had been a shock to hear her admit to taking a million dollars from Bradford. But the greater shock had been that she'd never breathed a word of any of this to him. Why had she never told him about it? He'd been open with her, had even shared the story of why Erica decided he wasn't worth marrying. Yet he'd never heard a peep from Tess about an episode that must have been a pretty fucking big deal.

A million-dollar fucking big deal.

There was definitely something screwy about the money. Even were he to consume an entire bottle of bourbon, he wouldn't accept the fact that she had a million dollars lying around; after she bought that car from Mike O'Roarke, he'd be surprised if she had three thousand dollars.

Though the topic of the money and what exactly had happened between Tess and the Bradfords while David Bradford lay critically ill in a hospital was troubling, what bothered Ward most, and poked at a still-raw wound, was the suspicion that the reason Tess hadn't spoken a word to him about any of this business with the Bradfords was that he meant nothing to her. What else could he conclude but that she'd never intended to go the distance with him? That she'd never loved him.

If that was the case, was she any different from Erica? A damned depressing thought, especially after having stood up in front of the ninety-plus assembled guests, raised his glass of champagne, and launched into an account of how Brian had fallen for Carrie Greer, knowing from the first time he laid eyes on her at a football game that she was "the one." Ward had managed to keep his smile firmly in place as he recounted Brian's calling him after his first date with Carrie. Half an hour later Brian had still been talking about her pretty blue eyes.

Ward had gotten the guests to chuckle, while inside, battered and reeling from the blow, he cursed love as the nastiest joke ever played on mankind. He'd gotten through the rest of the speech somehow, and Brian and Carrie, blind with happiness, didn't see that his smile was more a rictus of pain.

He should go find her. Demand some answers from her. He at least deserved to know why the hell she'd hidden so much about herself.

Instead, he took another swallow of his bourbon. Slouched in a chair by the small table he'd claimed as his own, he stared at the dancers on the wooden dance floor. He didn't need to check his watch to know that by now he should have had Tess in his arms, swaying to the slow beat of the band, anticipating the night ahead of them. She'd be tired; he'd take care of her, kissing her slowly, deeply, as he caressed her lazily. It would have been an easy, gentle loving. And when she came with a shuddered cry, he'd have wrapped her in his arms and kissed her damp brow until she drifted off to sleep.

"I've come to claim my dance, Ward." Amazingly—or perhaps not—Erica's voice was light and cheerful.

He didn't straighten, remaining in his indolent pose. "Sorry, after the stunt you pulled, I think not. You set this up. You set Tess up. Edward Bradford hadn't accepted any invitation to come to the wedding."

"He and his wife, Hope, were in Switzerland. They have a home on Lake Geneva. The invitation must not have reached them. Or maybe it did and they simply couldn't bring themselves to respond to a wedding invitation."

"But you figured out that Tess was connected to them."

"She looked like she was going to pass out when Carrie mentioned the Bradfords. I thought that was funny since she couldn't possibly have known them. But then I remembered hearing something about David's sneaking off and marrying some nobody from New York and how furious Mr. Bradford had been when he discovered what David had done. I put two and two together and then called up Mr. Bradford and asked him to come, knowing how much it would mean to Dad."

"And knowing how much it might embarrass Tess."

She sat down on the empty chair beside him as if they were having the nicest of chats. She lifted a bare shoulder that gleamed like gold dust in the lantern's light and gave a careless shrug.

He looked at her, trying to recall what he'd ever seen in her.

"I thought you'd be grateful to have avoided a terrible mistake by falling for Tess's act. What better way to open your eyes to what she was really like than to introduce you to one of the people she'd hurt?"

"So charitable of you."

She gave a light laugh as if he'd just delivered a really good joke. "I simply wanted you to see, Ward. I'm sure you've had some less-than-charitable thoughts about me since I stupidly called off our engagement, but now that you know what Tess is really like, maybe you'll recognize—"

"Actually, the only thing I recognize is your role in this scheme. I assume the point in setting up this nasty encounter during your stepsister's wedding was so that I might see you in a new light. Let me show you how successful you've been. The only reason I'm even willing to give you the time of day is because of Carrie—though I doubt she'd blame me if I refused to do even that. Unlike you, she's got a heart."

She looked at him. "You're not the man I thought you were."

For the first time in more than an hour he managed a genuine smile. "God, I hope not. Goodbye, Erica. I hope you find the man you deserve."

He picked up his highball—it still had two fingers full of dark gold liquid—without bothering to watch her leave; for all he cared, Erica could go to the devil. He had more important things to do. He took a healthy swallow of the liquid fire and waited for numbness to settle like a heavy blanket over him.

The alcohol had almost performed its magic when his mother's voice reached him.

"Whatever are you doing here, Ward, all by yourself? Where's Tess? She and Anita must be done scattering the rose petals on the nuptial bed and setting up the table with nibbles and champagne for Brian and Carrie. I would have thought she'd be with you. The last I saw her—"

"I don't know where she is."

"Oh. So that's why she's looking like that."

"Looking like what?" The words were out before he could stop them, and he couldn't even blame the bourbon. A part of him missed Tess already. It had been hours since he'd caught her on the lawn, wrapped his arm around her, and breathed in her unique scent. He was so angry at her, yet he couldn't stop himself from caring.

"Looking like the loneliest person on earth—oh, she was doing a good job of hiding it. It's just that I've gotten to know her."

He'd thought he had, too. "I don't think you know her quite as well as you believe, Mom, or you probably wouldn't have been so gung-ho to throw us together." Christ, the alcohol had chosen a hell of a time to make him loose-lipped. "Her ex-father-in-law was here."

"Edward Bradford? I thought he and his wife never responded."

He put down his drink. "You knew Tess was connected to them?"

His mother crossed her arms over her pale blue sleeveless dress. "I knew Tess was married to a David Bradford.

I had Neil in security find out who the family was. They're wealthy Bostonians."

He must have looked surprised, for his mother gave an exasperated "hmmph" noise. "You don't honestly think I'd hire Tess as my personal assistant without doing a background check? So her former father-in-law doesn't like her—yes, I knew that, too—does that justify turning away a lovely young woman who might love you?"

The pain in his chest spread. His mother was an eternal optimist, a totally out-of-the-closet romantic; it wouldn't occur to her that Tess might just as easily *not* love him or that they might have been wrong about her character.

His voice was rough when he answered. "I'm afraid Neil missed a couple of minor details in the background check he ran. The father-in-law may have legitimate cause for his dislike. A million dollars' worth."

"Excuse me?"

Briefly he listed the accusations Bradford had cast. "Apparently Tess has also inherited her husband's trust fund, so in Bradford's eyes she's not only a woman willing to turn her back on her dying husband; she's also a hustler."

"And you're sitting here? Why haven't you gone and talked to her about this?" It was infrequent, now that he was no longer a cocky, know-it-all teen, for his mother to sound genuinely annoyed with him, but the snap to her voice was unmistakable.

"I am assessing the situation. She admitted she took the money from Bradford."

"Then she must have had an excellent reason to do so," she replied crisply, unhesitatingly.

Ward looked at her and raised his glass, draining it. Another time he'd have been pleased that his mom was so quick to defend Tess. But no matter how much bourbon he poured down his throat, he couldn't manage to drown his sense of betrayal. It hurt.

From his standpoint, he was the wronged party here, so why wasn't he getting an ounce of sympathy from his mother?

As if she'd read his mind, which she probably had since she was far too perceptive, his mother shook her head. "No one ever said love was easy. What's that line? 'Life is messy. Love is messier.' Go find her, Ward. For both your sakes."

Of course he'd known he'd have to track her down eventually. He'd half-expected to see her step out of the dark night to hover at the edge of the dance floor, where she could monitor Brian and Carrie's blissful state as they danced with their friends. She hadn't. Perhaps something was wrong, some late wedding-related snafu had arisen—a passed-out guest or one who'd succumbed to a food allergy. Here was a wedding-related excuse that had nothing to do with the hurt he'd been dealt, a hurt that had sliced deeper than the wound he received when the gangsta with the switchblade had tried to slice him in two. Ward rose from his chair. To clear his head, he sucked in the night air.

It smelled sweet, like her.

Damn it to hell, he thought. He had to disengage—get some distance—or risk humiliating himself and letting her see his pain, the bloody wound that was his heart.

Chapter THIRTY-FOUR

TESS USED THE garbage bags Ward stowed under his kitchen sink to carry her shoes to her car. So many damned shoes, she thought, hurrying toward the open hatchback, the car's interior light providing a meager illumination. It didn't matter. Her stride was a quick *crunch, crunch* over the gravel. She'd been in this hyper-efficient mode since making her decision. Her inevitable, inescapable decision.

All that remained was a rapid tour of the rooms in the house—something she'd gotten really good at in the past five months—to guarantee no offending trace remained: no forgotten panties or bras under the bed that had been sent flying there as she and Ward tore at each other's clothes in desperation to reach skin, kissable, caressable skin; no hair scrunchies left lying on the bathroom vanity; no lipstick tube nestled next to Ward's car keys on the side table in the entry; no raincoat hanging next to his suede-collared jean jacket in the front closet. There was nothing but the notes she'd left for Adele and Daniel and another for Quinn next to the coffee machine. None for Ward, however, since he was clearly uninterested in any explanation. That much had become clear hours ago.

She had no idea what time it was. Late, after midnight, she supposed, since she could no longer hear the band playing. There'd be a motel someplace east of here where she could crash for a few hours. Not to sleep. She didn't dare let her guard down and allow her unconscious to assault her with more twisted images of Edward Bradford condemning her. The motel shower would have to suffice and revive her enough to get behind the wheel again. She'd make it an ice-cold shower. The question was whether she'd even feel it.

Distress had turned to anger as the minutes had turned to hours and Ward had kept his distance. Did he care so little that he wasn't even curious to know why Edward Bradford had spat such vile slurs at her?

By now, though, her anger had turned to an awful emptiness. She tossed the bag of shoes onto the pile of luggage and clothes she'd gathered from her cabin and then reached up to grip the rear door panel. She slammed it shut and hurried back to the house.

She made a final trip to Ward's bedroom and opened the bifolding closet doors once more, scanning the rows of neatly hanging shirts.

She'd taken everything that belonged to her. There was nothing left here. She reached out to trail her fingers down the soft white cotton sleeves. Unable to resist, she lifted one, raising it to her cheek and inhaling. It smelled of laundry detergent and fabric softener. She summoned the man scent of Ward, of leather and citrus soap and fresh air. Her throat closed, clogging with unshed tears.

"What are you doing?"

Thank God she had her back to him. He couldn't see what she'd felt: her face crumpling in anguish at the sound of his voice.

She swallowed. The shirtsleeve fell from her fingers. "I'm packing, of course. I'm going home."

Steeling herself, she waited for him to come forward, to reach out to her. He was always touching her. She loved that. He didn't move, keeping his distance.

"Why?"

To her ears, his question held only mild curiosity. Okay. There was her answer, she told herself. He didn't care—or whatever emotions he'd felt for her had withered the second Edward Bradford opened his mouth. It was over.

She carefully closed the doors and then turned, keeping her back close to one of the panels. She needed the support.

"I can't stay here. That's obvious, isn't it?" she said. At least her voice trembled only slightly. Unable to look at him, she fixed her gaze on the tan-and-black-patterned bedspread, staring at it until the arabesque lines blurred. They'd made the bed together this morning and then had sat outside on the patio, sipping their first cup of coffee and watching the sun come up. Ward had made a joke about this being the calm before the storm. And she'd laughed. So happy. It seemed so long ago.

Ward spoke. "You could have told me. For Christ's sake, you didn't even tell me David's last name. Then I hear from his father that he had to give you a million dollars to get you to stay at the hospital, and you didn't deny it. We were together for months and you never mentioned any of this. What am I supposed to think now?" He hadn't raised his voice, but the raw betrayal in it carried.

She ducked her head and wrapped her arms about her ribs to keep from shattering into pieces. When she thought she could stand it, she looked at him. "When I got to the hospital in Boston, I hadn't seen David in months, not since he'd left, telling me he no longer wanted to be married to a nagging bitch like me." No point in prettifying the tale since he'd witnessed its ugliness firsthand.

"I'd barely gotten over David's leaving me and maybe a part of me was hoping for something from him when I entered his hospital room. But he had only one word for me: 'Sorry.' That was it. I think it was his goodbye. Then he looked away and shut me out. It couldn't have been more obvious that he didn't want me there. Whatever we'd had was finished. This wasn't going to be a made-for-TV moment where he repented of his terrible treatment and begged me to love him again.

"After he was wheeled away to pre-op I had no reason to stay. He didn't need the wife he'd abandoned. And his parents were there. Though we'd never met, they didn't exactly welcome me with open arms."

"They'd never met you?"

"David wasn't on speaking terms with them. Mr. Bradford's attitude toward me has been remarkably consistent. So you can imagine my surprise when, in spite of his open dislike, he objected to my leaving. He demanded that I stay until David had recovered from the surgery to remove his brain tumor. He was fixated on the idea that because David said 'Sorry' to me, we still had a relationship—which only shows how toxic theirs was.

"I explained I couldn't afford to stay away from my job. His response was to offer me a million dollars. I thought it was a sick joke, and I wouldn't have stayed, but then David went into a coma and everything changed. From the way the doctor described his chances, I knew they were slim at best. David had broken my heart, but I stayed for the memory of what he'd been to me for that short period. And I stayed for his parents.

"Eight weeks later David lost the battle. He hadn't been dead more than thirty minutes before his father shoved an envelope at me and told me to get lost. Pronto. He and his wife, Hope, wouldn't even let me attend the funeral. That would have been the only thing I would ever have asked of them."

There, she'd done it. She knew she should have gathered her courage and done this weeks ago, but why would anyone want to abase oneself by sharing such a tale? She felt so weary. Weary, dirtied, and unloved.

She straightened and made for the door, keeping her gaze fixed ahead. She went into the living room and looked around. No possessions here, either.

He followed her. "You didn't marry David Bradford for his money."

Her gaze swept over him. He looked so handsome. "No, I didn't. But you don't know that for sure, do you? And that's the problem. You aren't certain that I'm not just as mercenary as Mr. Bradford accused me of being. After all, I took that money, didn't I? I didn't tear up the check or mail it back. That I used the money to pay for my brother's care doesn't change the fact that I *did* take it. Christopher's care is expensive. It's drained my parents of every penny they saved. The money I put in my brother's fund will run out eventually. Perhaps sooner than later."

He was silent. She knew him well enough to realize he was digesting this new piece of information. "Why didn't you tell me any of this?"

The anger returned. Blessed anger. "Why didn't I tell you that my husband chose to hide from me that he'd suffered from a brain tumor as a teen and lashed out at me when I naively expressed concerns about his debilitating headaches and his mood swings? That if I'd known about his earlier illness I would have dragged him to a specialist—done everything I could to save him? Why didn't I mention that my ex-in-laws loathed me? But because they clung to this illogical belief that my presence might help their son they chose to tolerate me? Why didn't I tell you that David's body wasn't even cold before they paid me off like the prostitute they considered me to be—or that I, to my eternal humiliation, took their filthy money? Gee, I don't know. It does make for such a fun tale."

She made herself stop and draw a deep breath. "Let me ask you something. Have you ever in your entire life been made to feel unworthy of respect? Have you ever been treated like dirt because you didn't have money or blue blood or a fancy job or a beautiful home?"

When he said nothing, she smiled tightly. "Right. You have no idea. When I came here and saw you, and realized how attracted to you I was, I fought it. I was worried that I was going to fall in love with another rich man who'd always had everything. But I fell in love with you anyway because you were wonderful and strong and generous. A part of me felt you could only love the Tess you knew, who'd driven here in that nearly kaput car. Not the whole me. So I kept my past locked away and tried to guard my heart as best I could—a big mistake since it didn't do any good. So now I'll go."

He dragged a hand through his hair with rough frustration. "So you'll just walk away? What about Carrie and Brian? What about my family?"

"I've left your parents and Quinn a note. I hope they'll understand my reasons. I think Estelle Vargas would make an excellent replacement for me. And Natalie would be great at keeping the Twitter feed going and posting pictures on Pinterest. I already said goodbye to Carrie and Brian. I told them something had come up, so you don't have to worry that they'll ask questions, though I'm sure Erica will fill them in on the real story as soon as she can."

"And what about us, Tess? Why are you turning your back on us and what we had together?"

She looked at him sadly. "Because I'm not sure it was real, any more than what I had with David was real. That love turned to ashes all too quickly. I kept something important about myself from you, and that was stupid, yes. Tonight, when I came up to you and Erica talking to Edward Bradford, I was so scared—terrified that my actions had destroyed all my hopes for you and me and the future we might have. But you know what? A tiny part of me was hoping, just hoping, that you'd believe in me, Ward. That you'd think I'm even better than I am."

"Tess—"

"No, I'm sorry. I can't stay any longer. I've got to go. This hurts too much."

"Tess, you can't go. I want you to stay."

"Don't you see? It won't work, Ward. You'll always wonder whether or not I'm using you just like Erica tried to—" For the first time she glimpsed the naked pain in his eyes. Her heart sank when she realized she'd hit upon the truth. His next question seemed only to confirm it.

"And what about David's trust fund? Did you know about that?"

"No." She refused to say more. She was through trying to defend herself. He was going to think as he chose. Would it be easier for him to believe that she was a gold digger? Would it hurt her any more to know he thought of her as one? She knew the answer to that.

"Tess, you can't leave. It's late. It's dangerous."

"Yes, I can. I have to. Don't worry, I've been through this before."

She brushed past him, avoiding the hand that reached out to catch her. Grabbing her purse from the side table, she ran to her car, her heart shattered and bleeding.

* * *

At first, she was grateful for the darkness as she drove from Silver Creek. It hid from her the ranch's lush green meadows, the sheep and cattle dozing on the other side of the fence line, the contours of the forest-covered mountains beyond. Seeing those would start the tears, and she couldn't start crying. If she did, when would she stop?

At the end of the private road, she turned right. Her fingers were wrapped tightly around the steering wheel, and she stared at the inky blackness ahead. She knew the roads she had to take, knew now how to get to Route 101. Farther on she'd turn onto Route 20, which would take her to Route 80. Three thousand exhausting miles later she would reach New York. Home. Was it still?

The two-lane road was empty, the few houses that were built near it lit by single porch lights or lanterns suspended over front doors. No motels appeared with vacancy signs. The world was dark and asleep.

A wave of fatigue hit her: physical exhaustion combined with the emotional turmoil of what she'd just done . . .

Oh God, had she been a fool to leave? Yes—no—she wasn't sure anymore, only knew that her heart hurt more than she could have ever imagined. She'd lost Ward, and she wasn't sure she'd ever find such happiness again. Her eyes closed against the pain and then abruptly she opened them, terrified at what she'd just done. It was increasingly clear that she was in no condition to drive. She needed a place to rest.

Maybe when she neared Route 20 she would come upon one of the larger chain motels and she'd find refuge, a place to gather herself.

Suddenly, Tess became aware of a car following her. Had it been there long and she'd been too preoccupied to notice? She wasn't sure, but for some reason its presence on the lonely road caused her heart to stutter and then race as the darkness pressed closer. She was now miles from anything she knew.

Maybe the car would turn off into a driveway or onto a crossroad. She alternately cast nervous glances in the rearview mirror as she checked ahead for intersections. Whenever one neared, she looked back, hoping to see the bright orange flicker of a turn signal. None. Her apprehension grew.

Was the car following her? Really following her? Was it getting closer, the driver planning to overtake her? Tired and wrung-out, she could no longer distinguish justified alarm from paranoia.

Fear clawed at her. Her breathing grew heavy as panic edged closer. She jumped at the ring of her cellphone lying on the seat next to her. "Yes?" Her voice was shrill.

"It's me. I'm behind you. There'll be a Super 8 Motel in about eight miles. I'll wait until you're safe in your room." Ward disconnected before she could reply.

Oh God, oh God, what had she done? She pressed her lips tight to stop their trembling, the words ricocheting inside of her, bruising. Even now, after everything, he was still keeping her safe.

She made it to the motel and roused a sleepy night clerk for a key to a room. Stepping outside again, she saw his Jeep idling. But he didn't leave the car. She took that as a sign. Too much had gone wrong—was still wrong—between them.

Her fingers were clumsy as she inserted the key and pushed open the door to a sterile box of a room. It was almost more than she could manage to shut the door and draw the deadbolt, because she knew what she would find when she moved to the window and drew back the drab yellow curtain to peer out at the parking lot. Ward's Jeep was gone.

Exhaustion and misery overtook her. She fell onto the bed and lay curled on it as sleep claimed her, too quickly, too thoroughly, to resist. Her dreams were not, as she'd feared, of Edward Bradford. Worse, they were of Ward, of his smiling face as he held her in his arms.

Chapter THIRTY-FIVE

Astoria, Queens

Dear Tess,

If you're reading this, I'm dead. Who knows how much time has passed. It could be weeks; it could be years. To butcher Faulkner, "Only when the clock stops does time come to life." My clock has stopped and so it's time to give you the answers you deserve. I'm not sure an apology is possible. I've acted selfishly, yet I know myself well enough to recognize I'd fail again if I were lucky enough to meet you in a crowded party and see your smile. The first time I heard your laughter, it reminded me of the Trevi Fountain on a bright summer day, one of my favorite places on earth. I'd have liked to have gone there with you. I would have liked to show you so many of the places I love.

Unfortunately, even then I knew it was not to be.

The first headache struck a week before that party where you were passing appetizers. The headache had been accompanied by vertigo, the dizziness severe enough to empty my stomach before I could reach the bathroom. The sensation was not new. I'd suffered such headaches before, when I was a senior in high school. I knew what they heralded. I already understood that faithless time was slipping away from me.

But when I saw you, I wanted that smile for my own. You were so very lovely. I repeat, I was selfish, I was greedy.

The headaches began to plague me with tiresome, vicious regularity. I managed to keep them from you, even once I'd convinced you to move in. But their frequency told me that I had to act quickly. So I proposed and was given the light shining in your eyes as my reward. In asking you to marry me, was I out of my mind as well as dying? Not at all. I wanted to be able to give you what was mine and the only way I felt confident that my wishes would be respected was to make you my wife.

Would I have asked you had I not been knocking on hell's door? I know you're wondering. Honestly? Probably not. I spared you the unpleasantness of my family, Tess—perhaps my one unselfish act—but let's say my parents' example of matrimony wasn't particularly inspiring.

Anyway, we wed. And then a problem I hadn't anticipated presented itself. I hadn't really thought about how my illness would affect you once the symptoms became obvious. I could handle my love for you. I couldn't cope with yours for me. Tess, my intent in marrying you was never to have you nurse me or grieve for me, but to allow you to spread your wings and fly—that would come after my death. So I had to rectify things.

Here I must tell the ugly truth again. It wasn't that hard to hurt you, Tess. The pain I've been suffering for months now is merciless. It's made me so, too. But, though I did my best to drive you away as quickly as I could, you were stronger than I ever gave you credit for. My only recourse was to leave you and kill any remaining affection you might hold in your heart.

You may no longer want even the memory of my love. My money, however, is now yours, all yours, and I hope it will allow you to achieve your dreams. The lawyer's letter that you'll find included here will outline the basics. When you meet with him, he'll explain everything in full.

I regret much, my darling Tess. Knowing you, never.

David

The letter rustled between Tess's shaking hands. A tear and then two escaped and fell, with more following. She didn't notice. She was already rereading her husband's words.

The letter had been waiting for her on the dresser in her childhood room, propped against an old photograph of her and Christopher when they were children, before Christopher had to be placed in the facility.

After four days of solid driving, she'd reached home late that afternoon, pulling up to the modest brick house. Her mother's rosebushes, planted along the metal fence enclosing their front yard, were in bloom. Her father had mowed the tiny lawn. A few stray clippings were scattered along the walk up to the house. Her mom and dad must have been listening for her, for they were there, pushing open the storm door and stepping onto the stoop before she'd reached the concrete steps.

Exhausted and heartbroken though she was, Tess had been happy to see them after so many months and had smiled tremulously as she and her parents exchanged hugs. Her mother's pretty, careworn face was creased in a smile, and her father, in his short shirtsleeves and pressed trousers, had patted her back as they entered her childhood home.

The house was the same as always: immaculate and

just a little threadbare. The aroma of her mother's marinara sauce reached her, drifting in from the kitchen's open door, past the dining room with its square dining table and cut-glass vase of her mother's roses in its center.

She sniffed. "It smells good, Mom."

"It's almost ready. We'll eat early. I can see how tired you are, Teresa."

"Dead on my feet." And sick at heart.

"Give me your keys," her father had said. "I'll bring in your bags for you."

Dinner had been a quiet affair. Tess had nearly fallen asleep before finishing her pasta. "I'm sorry, Mom. I haven't been sleeping well. I'll be more myself tomorrow, I promise."

"Don't apologize."

"That's a long drive you made, Tess," her father had said. "And in such a small car."

A car that, thanks to Ward, was a lot safer than the one her father had steered her toward. Just the thought of Ward opened a floodgate of pain and regrets. She forced her thoughts to the here and now. This was her real life. "It's small but it runs really well, Dad. I'm afraid that other car wasn't up to a cross-country drive. Can I go with you to visit Christopher tomorrow?"

Her mother smiled. "Your father is going to take the afternoon off. We'll visit Christopher together."

"That'll be nice. Really nice." She'd risen from her chair and made to clear their plates, but her mother put a stop to her effort.

"Leave the dishes, Teresa. I'll tend to them. You go upstairs now. Sleep will do you good."

On leaden legs she'd tripped up the stairs and then made it down the short hallway to her room, which overlooked the backyard—the same postage-stamp size as their front yard. She glanced out the window.

The sun hadn't even set yet. At Silver Creek, Pete, Jim, Carlos, Holly, and Frank would be beginning to water and feed some of the animals. Quinn might be in the garden, weeding or pinching back lettuce, or perhaps she'd be working with Tucker or making sure her goats hadn't gotten into mischief. Up at the main lodge, Roo and Jeff would be ratcheting up the energy level in the kitchen. She could almost hear the music coming out of the iPod's playlist. Jeff would have liked her mother's marinara. The tomatoes tasted so fresh.

And Ward? Where would he be? Would he be training Bilbao, putting the gelding through his high-speed spins or galloping him flat-out across the corral to stop on a dime as if the horse came equipped with antilock breaks? Maybe the gelding was practicing staring down a heifer or a young steer. Or was Ward out riding Rio with a group of guests, leading them down a trail at a lope? Was he thinking of her? Was he staring off in the distance, filled with longing, aching for her with every breath he took? Could he possibly miss her and feel as miserable as she did?

Despair rocking her, she'd swayed and had to put her hands on the window ledge to steady herself. Drawing a ragged breath, she'd turned slowly, and that was when her gaze had landed on the legal-sized envelope on her dresser.

It was the one her mother had told her about so many weeks ago. Her parents hadn't forwarded it. She didn't blame them. She'd told them not to, had stressed how little import it could contain. She decided to open it. Her emotions were so dulled and battered that nothing more could affect them. As she sat down on the edge of her bed, she'd glanced at the return address printed on the envelope.

Yes, "Roberts and Little" sounded like a law firm—a law firm with a nice Park Avenue address, she'd noted as she tore open the back flap. She'd wondered whether Lucas, Anna's boyfriend, knew of the firm. Inside, she was surprised to find two separately folded packets of stationery. Frowning, she unfolded the first and saw her husband's bold, slanted script. Without thought, she dropped the other in her lap. Her heart hammering in her chest, she began reading.

Dear Tess . . .

The tears she'd been unable to shed for so many months fell at last as she read and reread David's words.

She would have to sort out her feelings eventually, but right now her sadness warred with anger and disbelief that David had gone to such lengths to manipulate her. Not only that, he'd willingly crushed her heart and her belief in herself in order to drive her away when his illness could no longer be hidden. That was what he had called love.

How blind he'd been to her character. He'd thought he could excuse the betrayal she'd suffered at his hands by leaving her his money, as if that would erase the damage he'd inflicted. She'd married him for love. He'd married her to foil his parents—wasn't that what it ultimately boiled down to?

A thought struck her. What if this letter had reached her shortly after David's death? What if her parents had forwarded it out of respect for its official, legal appearance?

How would she have reacted? Would the bitterness and anger that was consuming her as she considered the scope of David's machinations have ruined her relationship with Ward?

No. She'd quickly recognized Ward's true character—

his strength and desire to protect those he loved. The answer brought relief tinged with sorrow.

The problem with her and Ward's relationship revolved around trust. She'd been so traumatized and shamed by her dealings with David and the Bradfords that she'd hidden her past from Ward, someone she loved. But she wasn't alone in her inability to trust. Because of the damage Erica inflicted when she rejected him, Ward hadn't been able to put complete faith in Tess. He hadn't been able to banish the doubt that she might ultimately be as mercenary as his ex-fiancée.

She glanced at the now slightly crumpled sheets of paper and realized that there was one crucial reason she wished she'd had this letter in her hands sooner. If she could have seen, written in these inked lines, just how shallow David's love had been, she knew she would have had the courage to tell Ward the whole truth. But she'd instructed her parents not to forward the envelope—another mistake she would have to live with.

Wearily, she picked up the second letter, unfolded it, and read its contents. When she finished her lips were pressed in a grim line. Fine, she'd contact Paul Roberts, Esq., first thing tomorrow. The sooner she handled the matter of her inheritance, the better.

Tess came downstairs the next morning in a severe navy blue dress. It was as no-nonsense a business outfit as she could find in the suitcases she'd hastily packed and lugged to her car. She'd hung the dress in the bathroom while she showered. The steam generated as she tried to scour the cobwebs from her mind and the grit of days in a car had taken care of the creases.

What the shower hadn't cleared of her groggy mind and the gritty sandlot that had piled up behind her eyes, the aroma of her mother's coffee promised to erase. Her parents drank espresso at breakfast. Just breathing its scent did wonders.

Her mom must have heard Tess turn the shower water off because two golden slices of toast were on her plate next to an empty cup and a glass already filled with orange juice.

Tess kissed her mother on her cheek. "That smells good," she said.

"Sit, or your toast will get cold. I thought you'd be down sooner." Her mother too was already dressed. She'd have been to the seven-o'clock Mass.

Tess clasped the handle of the stovetop espresso maker, the kind her parents had used since forever, and poured the thick black brew into her cup. She took a sip and felt her brain settle into order. "Sorry. I had to make a call. Mom, that letter upstairs? It was from David's lawyer. That's who I was calling just now. There are some papers I need to sign. I'm meeting with him at eleven-thirty, but I'm sure to be back by early afternoon. What time do you and Dad plan to visit Christopher?"

"I was thinking three P.M. so that it won't interfere with Christopher's dinner. You know how that upsets him."

Tess nodded. Anything that disturbed Christopher's anticipated routine could cause terrible distress. "But he's doing okay otherwise?"

"He's still sleeping more than he used to and he's kind of subdued, but he doesn't seem unhappy or in pain. He likes the postcards you've sent him. I put them in a stack on his dresser so we can look at them together."

"I'm glad he likes them." She'd picked up a bunch of goofy cards at rest stops along the way to California. "I still have a few left. I'll bring them for him. And maybe I can buy a video game on my way back from the meeting with the lawyer."

Her mother sat down in the chair next to her. "You're a good girl, Teresa."

Tess's heart squeezed painfully. "No, Mom, I'm afraid I'm not. I hurt a man back in California, a man I cared deeply for. A man I loved. I kept things from him because I didn't want to face them again myself or have him think less of me when he heard what I'd done. He found out anyway and so it's over between us."

"I don't believe you could have done something that would truly make this man think less of you. You *are* a good person. Your life hasn't been easy—other people would be tempted to feel sorry for themselves, but not you, Teresa. You're strong. You'll make it right with him somehow, I know."

Tess smiled at her mother's staunch faith. She wished she had the same.

Her mother reached out and laid her hand on Tess's bare arm. Her voice was tentative, as if she were finding her way along a tricky path. "The thing you didn't want to discuss with this man, was it about that money you received from David's family? Your father and I, we were so grateful when you told us about it. You did a wonderful thing for Christopher. But, Teresa, your father and I can manage the expenses on our own—"

"No." The word came out fiercely. "Setting up Christopher's fund is the one good thing I've done. I'm not going to regret that I helped my brother and you and Dad."

Her mother nodded tightly and squeezed her hand, too overcome to speak. For the first time in many days Tess felt better, like maybe she *had* done something right.

Midtown Manhattan, with its weekday noise of squealing car tires and rumbling bus engines, with its press of pedestrians moving down the sidewalk like a wall of flesh and babbling tongues, seemed alien to Tess after her five months at Silver Creek. While waiting for a red light to change, she looked up and saw a strip of sky bounded by concrete, steel, and glass. To think that six months ago she wouldn't have noticed she was missing anything.

It wasn't that she no longer loved the city. New York was still amazing, with an energy and a vibrancy like nowhere else.

It was just that now she appreciated the rustle of the wind through the trees; the scent of a pine forest in early spring; the feel of a powerful horse moving beneath her, responding to the pressure of her legs, the subtle opening of her hands. What in the noisy urban congestion of New York could compare with those newfound pleasures?

Nothing, of course, in the mad glittering city could compare with the slow smile of a Stetson-wearing Californian cowboy. Ward's smile made everything else just a touch dull and commonplace.

She never would have believed it, let alone admitted it, but while crossing Fifty-Fourth Street and narrowly avoiding being flattened by a speeding bike messenger, she recognized another truth: She missed her cowboy boots.

It was only a seven-block walk to the subway station from the lawyer's swank office on Park Avenue, but her feet were killing her. She'd forgotten how brutal New York's sidewalks were on the feet and she was sure she could have dodged the cyclist faster and more nimbly had she been wearing her Luccheses.

Still, at least she'd signed the necessary papers before narrowly becoming an urban statistic. Paul Roberts, the lawyer, was disgruntled, but she was not. Indeed, despite her aching feet, she walked with grim satisfaction to Fifty-Ninth and Lexington and descended into the subway to take the N train back to her parents' house.

* * *

"Mom," she called out as she unlocked the front door and walked inside. "The video game place didn't have a huge selection, but I found Bubblez. Does Chris have that already? If he does, I'll go return it."

She cocked her head. The house wasn't big enough for her voice not to reach to the farthest corner. Her mom was home, and she'd seen her dad's Buick in the carport. They must be in the backyard, she thought. It was a beautiful day, and a breeze made her mother's curtains flutter lightly.

She crossed the dining room and then the kitchen on her way to the back door. On the kitchen counter, her gaze landed on a stack of dishes piled next to the sink, waiting to be washed. Tess frowned. Her mother would never leave a dish unwashed. Her way of handling the chaos in her life was to run a house that would have taught a number of hospitals a thing about sanitary cleanliness. Bacteria from dirty dishes were routinely vanquished.

She pushed open the storm door with a question on her lips. "Mom, Dad, is everything all—" The rest of her sentence fell away. No other thought replaced it. Just a name. "Ward?"

Dressed in a suit and tie, he looked like he should have been having lunch on Madison Avenue rather than sitting in one of the aluminum patio chairs next to her father. Though, of course, he wasn't sitting; he'd risen to his feet as she pushed the storm door open.

His eyes were locked on her. Although his neat dark olive suit enhanced his tanned complexion, there was a shadow to his eyes and his features looked drawn. He looked as if he'd slept just as poorly since the previous Saturday as she had.

As her heart thudded with impossible hope, she scrambled to regain her scattered wits. "Ward, what are you doing here?"

"I came to see you and to meet your parents. I took the plane late last night."

"And your friend Ward arrived just as your father and I were sitting down to lunch. We've been having a nice talk. Of course, if I'd known we'd be having company to lunch, I'd have made something fancier."

"It was delicious, Mrs. Casari."

Was she dreaming? Really, hearing her mother say that Ward's visit was unexpected—well, that was pretty much the essence of her unconscious longings. Her dreams since Saturday had been full of Ward appearing as if by magic. But in none of them did he look as wonderful as he did right now, in her parents' minuscule yard. Had Tess had any inkling that Ward might come to New York, she'd have been hyperventilating from nerves. And to hear Ward speak so calmly after everything that had happened between them and have him say he wanted to meet her parents? It wasn't unexpected; it was unimaginable in broad daylight.

She dug her nails deep into her palms. It stung, so this must be real and not her wildest dream. Her heart leapt.

"Maria, why don't we go inside and make some coffee for Tess and Ward?" her father said.

"Oh! Yes, that's a fine idea. Ward, do you like espresso, or shall I make American coffee?"

"Espresso, please. The stronger, the better."

Tess could hear the smile in her mother's voice as she told her father to come along. She couldn't see it, however—she and Ward were still staring at each other. At the click of the door catching in the latch, she launched herself, flying across the manicured grass.

He caught her, sweeping her into his arms, lifting her off her feet, as his mouth found hers, his kiss desperate.

Hers was just as desperate. She clung to him, crushing

her lips to his, moaning as she opened her mouth wide in invitation. She needed to feel him close, needed the wonder of his arms about her.

They broke off, panting, gazing wide-eyed at each other. He opened his mouth to speak but she cut him off. Cupping his lean cheeks between her hands, she poured her sudden joy into another fierce kiss.

"I love you," she whispered. "I said it too late last time. I love you, and it's the one truth that's been in my heart all along."

His smile was tender. "Tess, I'm sorry I was an idiot. Erica didn't just set you up; she set me up, too. When Edward Bradford showed up and said all that nonsense, I let my lurking fear that you might not love me overshadow what I knew here." He moved their clasped hands to the left side of his chest. Beneath his summer suit she felt the solid thump of his heart, a beat steady and true.

"I let you go the night of the wedding because I knew I had to stop being a drunken jackass—I'd been attempting to drown my sorrows steadily all night. Your leaving sobered me up faster than a gallon of Roo's coffee, so I was able to follow you to the motel, but I still needed to think things through. One thing didn't need sorting out. It's this: I love you, Tess. I'm sorry I let you down when Bradford started in on you. I should have kicked him off the premises."

"Ward, about what Edward Bradford said—"

"Tess, once I could think straight, I realized how it must have been at the hospital. Bradford made it pretty obvious that he never treated you with the respect you deserved. He's the type of rich man who uses money as a weapon. I bet he was secretly pleased that you took the million."

She nodded. "I think so, too. It confirmed his opinion of me. Ward, it turns out that David did leave me all his money. He wrote me a letter telling me that I'd receive his inheritance after his death."

He looked surprised. "He wrote you a letter?"

"Yes, I'll show it to you." She drew a breath. "The letter, it's not very flattering to him or me. He used me, Ward. He never truly loved me. He even admitted he wouldn't have married me if he hadn't realized he was dying."

"Jesus, what a crappy thing to say. The guy was a fool, Tess."

She managed a smile. "Actually, I'm glad he said it. At least he was being honest. Our marriage soured so quickly and I couldn't figure out why. In the letter he justified his behavior, his pushing me away emotionally, as a way of protecting me. I think it would hurt more if I still believed he'd really loved me. The money, too, was just another power play, another manipulation. He claimed his idea in leaving his trust fund to me was so I would be free to pursue my dreams, but I think he also really wanted to anger his parents. Ward, I didn't marry David for his money. I never expected to inherit his millions. And I refuse to be the pawn in the war he's waging from the grave. I told the lawyer that I wouldn't take a cent of the inheritance. I don't know what will happen to it. I imagine the money will go back to his parents. I kind of hope they choke on it."

"So you renounced your claim, huh? Oh, well, there goes my secret ambition to marry a wealthy woman."

Distracted by the warm light of laughter in his blue-green eyes, Tess didn't immediately recognize the significance of his comment. "You want to marry me?"

His slow, reverent, and endlessly sweet kiss was his first answer. His husky voice gave her the second, no less thrilling one. "Tess, remember our first night together? I woke up the next morning happy. It was a deep-down happy, one I'd never felt before. While I was making coffee for us, I stared out the window. It was a beautiful dawn. You know how Silver Creek looks on a morning like that. I remember thinking that when Erica broke up with me, my heart had felt good and bruised and my pride battered, but that I'd been basically okay. I still had what really mattered: Silver Creek and all it represents for my family and me." His expression solemn, he raised his hand and stroked the side of her face. "I didn't need five days with you gone from my life to know that if I were really to lose you, I would never be the same."

She caught her breath at his words. Like a balm, they healed the wounds to her heart.

Ward reached into his pocket, drew out a small velvet box, and opened it. The diamond sparkled in the June sun. "This is yours, Tess, just as I am."

"Oh, Ward, it's lovely," she whispered.

"It belonged to my grandmother. Mom and Dad thought you'd like it." Holding her hand, he sank onto bended knee. "Marry me, Tess. I love you, and I will love you in sickness and health for all our days to come."

"Yes, yes, and yes again," she whispered. "I love you so."

Slowly he lifted the ring from the satin-lined box and slipped it onto her finger.

Her mother's happy gasp was audible. Tess turned toward her parents. The storm door ajar, they stood on the top step, with wide smiles stamped on their faces. Tess thought that she'd never seen them so happy.

Ward rose to his feet. He kept her hand clasped in his. "Your daughter has agreed to marry me, Mr. and Mrs. Casari."

"Well, we told you we thought she would," her father replied, his happiness and approval as thick as his New York accent.

Tess grinned. She'd told Ward enough about her family for him to understand that they were old-fashioned.

So Ward had done it properly, going to her father and mother and asking for her hand before he presented her with a ring. She squeezed his fingers in silent thanks for giving them this.

"Tess and I haven't ironed out the details, Mrs. Casari, but I can guess that she would like to be married here in New York with you and your friends present, as well as the one person who means so much to you. We'll do whatever is needed to arrange a ceremony that would allow Christopher to attend."

Her mother bobbed her head, too overcome to answer, so Tess replied for her.

She turned to Ward and said with a joy she knew to be profound, "This is why I will love you forever."

He smiled. "That's all I want."

ACKNOWLEDGMENTS

Writing is a lonely occupation. I count myself lucky that with each book I write, the number of people to whom I am indebted grows longer. I owe thanks to John and Julia Hoskins, owners of the Old Bridge Hotel in Huntingdon, UK, for letting me tour their wonderful inn and for answering all my questions about the art of hotel keeping; to Denise Chakoian-Olney and David Olney, for the wonderful stories they've shared with me; to my critique partners, Marilyn Brant and Karen Dale Harris, whose suggestions and comments improved this story immeasurably; to my friends and editors at Random House—Linda Marrow, Kate Collins, Gina Wachtel, and Junessa Viloria—I would not know what to do without you; to my agent, Elaine Markson, who is unfailingly wise; to my family, for their ceaseless encouragement. And to Charles, as ever.